Under the blazing sun, the trees and hillsides were turning brown. The TV news had announced that: *"It is unusually hot in Merlin City, and scientists are concerned! They think this heat wave is probably due to climate change. The emergency services are asking everyone to be especially careful! In these extremely dry conditions it is dangerous to light fires in woodland areas..."*

Tom was out enjoying the countryside. How nice and peaceful it was! Then, suddenly, the sound of a siren broke the silence. PAM-POM! PAM-POM! A fire engine went rushing by: whoom! Then another one: whoom! And a third one. Oh no! Look over there! A tall column of smoke was rising high into the sky. A forest fire must have started, right outside Merlin City! What a disaster! Tom suddenly felt very anxious.

He thought of his friend Lila the fox. He hoped with all his heart that she hadn't been trapped by the flames. He hurried off in the direction of the fire. The firemen looked like warriors in armour, fighting an orange monster! Their long hoses were spraying tons of water onto the blaze and there was thick black smoke everywhere. It was getting into Tom's throat and making him choke, so he covered his mouth with his T-shirt.

One of the firemen shouted:

"The fire's too big! We won't have enough water in the fire engines!"

The Chief Fireman turned and looked towards the river. There was a very solemn expression on his face.

"With all this dry weather, there's not enough water in the river either" he said. "This is serious!"

Tom glanced quickly all around him. "Lila! Where are you?" he yelled. "Lila! LILAAAA!"

At that very moment, Lila the fox came running up to him and brushed against his legs.

"Oh, Lila! I'm so glad you're safe!" said Tom.

But Lila still looked terrified. She kept nuzzling Tom's legs and turning round and round in circles. Then she grabbed the trouser leg of one of the firemen, whose name was Max. He knelt down beside her.

"What is it, my pet?" he asked. "What are you trying to tell us?"

Lila made little whimpering noises. She seemed to be saying: "Come with me! Follow me!" Then off she dashed, quick as an arrow, towards the blazing fire. She disappeared down a narrow path among the trees, and a curtain of flames closed behind her. Max followed, taking great strides to keep up with her. Breaking through the curtain of fire he too disappeared from sight. All Tom could hear was the roaring and crackling of the flames.

"LILA!" he shouted: "BE CAREFUL!!"

The Chief Fireman came over to where Tom was standing.

"Don't worry" he said: "Max is the best fireman in the whole country! Lila is in good hands! Still... we need water, and quickly!"

Tom had an idea.

"I know where there's a secret spring!" he said. It's in that cave over there!"

"Are you sure?" asked the Chief Fireman.

"Yes, I am!" shouted Tom.

The Chief Fireman grinned.

"Right!" he said: "We'll take the hose over there. Lead me to the spring, my lad! By the way, what's your name?"

"Tom", said Tom, and the two of them set off running towards the cave.

"Why is the weather so hot just now?" asked Tom, as they ran. "On TV they said…"

"Yes, I heard that too" said the Chief. "You see, Tom, the problem is that the world is getting warmer. The climate is changing, so we're getting heat waves like this one. And storms, and floods, and all sorts of other natural disasters! The ice at the north and south poles is melting, and so are the glaciers on high mountains like the Alps. The melted water runs off into the rivers and down to the sea, so the sea level is rising. Some islands and coasts are likely to disappear under the water!
At the same time, if the climate goes on getting hotter, some countries will become deserts!"

"But why is all this happening?" asked Tom.

The Chief Fireman was getting out of breath running and talking at the same time, but he tried to explain anyway.

"Well, Tom, you know that cars and planes and factories and all sorts of things like that give off exhaust fumes and gases?"

"Yes, I know about that" said Tom.

"Well, some of those gases we call 'greenhouse gases'. They go up into the atmosphere, which forms a sort of transparent bubble all around the earth. Up there in the atmosphere, the greenhouse gases trap the heat from the sun – just like a greenhouse traps heat and thus helps plants to grow faster. But we are producing too many greenhouse gases, and it's getting warmer and warmer on earth. You see?"

"Yes" said Tom. "I see. So there really is something wrong with the weather".

By now they had reached the cave. "Hurray! Here we are!" shouted Tom: "Let me help you with the hose!"

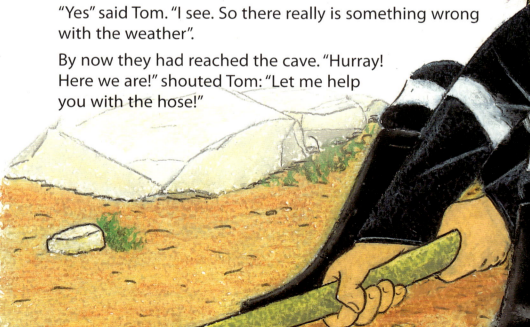

Tom took the end of the hose and went forward into the cave. A few moments later, his voice rang out, echoing in the darkness:

"REA-DY-y-y-y!! WA-TER-ter-ter-er!!"

The Chief Fireman understood. He called out to his men:

"START PUMPING!!"

The hose began swelling as it filled with water from the spring.

"Well done, Tom!" shouted the Chief Fireman. "There's enough water here to put out the fire! Hurray!"

Tom came back out of the cave, his face muddy but happy. He came over and sat down near the Chief Fireman. Looking into his eyes, Tom asked:

"So, human beings are responsible for climate change?"

The Chief Fireman was silent for a moment. Then he said:

"Yes, Tom, the greenhouse gases come from our cars, our planes, our factories, even our fire-engines; so we all have to take our share of the responsibility".

"Oh" said Tom, who was thinking hard. "Right. So… What can I do to stop these gases getting into the atmosphere and warming up the earth?"

"What *you* can do, Tom, is ask your Mum or Dad not to use the car so often. Instead of going to work or school by car every day you could walk, or take public transport, or go by bike".

"Yes, I could cycle to school!" said Tom.

"Right" said the Chief Fireman. "Then you could make sure you keep your bedroom window shut when the central heating is on. Because central heating boilers produce greenhouse gases too, and because we need to save energy!"

"Yes, of course" said Tom.

"You'd be surprised" went on the Chief Fireman "how much of the heat in our homes gets wasted. Draughts come in under the door, and through windows that don't close properly. And that means we have to turn the heating up! And more heating means more greenhouse gases!"

"I never thought of that" said Tom. "That's really interesting! So, what *else* can I do?"

"Well," said the Chief Fireman, "make sure you switch off all the lights you don't need because electricity is made in power stations, and they too produce greenhouse gases! So before you leave for school in the morning, check that your bedroom lights are all switched off".

"I will!" said Tom. "And what else?"

"You could ask your parents to buy electricity that's produced by the wind or by the sun... That's what we call 'renewable' energy, because the wind keeps blowing and the sun keeps shining, so the energy doesn't run out. And the wind and sun don't produce greenhouse gases!"

Suddenly, a loud shout interrupted their conversation.
"WE'RE BACK!"

It was Max the fireman, and he had Lila with him! They had come back safe and sound from the burning forest! Tom and the Chief Fireman were delighted to see them – and also to see that the firemen were managing to put out the fire at last, with all the water from the secret spring.

Max, his face exhausted and blackened with soot, had tears in his eyes. He said, in a hoarse voice:

"Look what Lila wanted me to save" – and he showed them what he was carrying in his arms: four little fox cubs!

Lila nuzzled her head against Tom.

"So that's what you were trying to tell us, Lila!" he said to her, gently.

The Chief Fireman patted Tom on the head.

"Yes, Tom, she wanted us to save her children! And thanks to you and her..."

A sudden flash of light interrupted his words.

It was a photographer, and just behind him came the Mayor of Merlin City. The Mayor stepped up to the Chief Fireman and shook his hand. FLASH! Another photo.

"Hot, isn't it!" said the Mayor. FLASH! He bent down and picked up Tom. FLASH! The Mayor wiped his sweaty forehead with a handkerchief. FLASH!

"Well done" said the Mayor. "Thanks to you, to your courage and hard work, the forest fire at Merlin City has been extinguished! I wish to express to you my deepest gratitude and to present you with these medals..."

FLASH!

Lila, Tom and Max – carrying the four fox cubs – stepped forward to greet the Mayor. Tom said:

"Mr Mayor, please take a look at these poor little fox cubs. They nearly died today... And it's all because of climate change! I think you should give these medals to people who are trying to save the earth!"

FLASH! Another photo.

"Really?" said the Mayor, rather taken aback. "But I thought... I mean, I just wanted..."

Then the Chief Fireman spoke up.

"Mr Mayor, we're fireman. We were just doing our job. But we see that the earth is warming up. Today's forest fire was not a coincidence. We humans were probably responsible. The climate *is* changing!"

And so saying, the Chief Fireman took Lila's cubs and gave them a gentle hug. They looked so sweet! FLASH! Yet another photo.

"I tell you what" said Tom: "Why not give medals to everyone who rides their bike every day, and everyone who uses energy from the wind and the sun, and everyone who leaves their car at home and takes the bus instead... Give medals to everyone who tries to stop producing greenhouse gases! Those people are the *real* heroes!"

The Mayor smiled at Tom.

"That is a great idea!" he said. "I will do something about it straight away!"

The fire was out. In the morning, the photos were in all the Merlin City newspapers. There was the Mayor with the Chief Fireman. There was Max smiling, standing next to his fire engine. There was Tom, looking tired.
But everyone's favourite picture was of Lila feeding her four little cubs. They were all alive and safe. But it had been a close thing...

EXPLORING LOYALTY

Veröffentlichungen des Collegium Carolinum

Band 136

Herausgegeben vom
Vorstand des Collegium Carolinum
Forschungsinstitut für die Geschichte Tschechiens
und der Slowakei

Exploring Loyalty

Edited by
Jana Osterkamp and Martin Schulze Wessel

Vandenhoeck & Ruprecht

Cover picture: The Empress Marie Therese of Austria during her visit to Hungary receives the oath of loyalty from the Hungarian nobles in 1741. Watercolours by Eduard Schaller around 1840 (© Austrian National Library Vienna, classification number: Pk 3050, 12).

This publication is based on a cooperation with CAS LMU – Center for Advanced Studies at Ludwig-Maximilians-Universität Munich and was supported by funds of the Emmy Noether Junior Research Group "Vielfalt ordnen. Föderalismusmodelle in der Habsburgermonarchie und ihren Nachfolgestaaten" (OS 377/1-1) at the Collegium Carolinum and the Graduate School (GSC 1046) for East and Southeast European Studies in Munich and Regensburg (both Deutsche Forschungsgemeinschaft).

Bibliografische Information der Deutschen Nationalbibliothek

Die Deutsche Nationalbibliothek verzeichnet diese Publikation in der Deutschen Nationalbibliografie; detaillierte bibliografische Daten sind im Internet über <http://dnb.ddb.de> abrufbar.

Bibliographic information published by the Deutsche Nationalbibliothek

The Deutsche Nationalbibliothek lists this publication in the Deutsche Nationalbibliografie; detailed bibliographic data available online: <http://dnb.ddb.de>.

ISBN 978-3-525-37317-0

© 2017 Collegium Carolinum, 81669 München
(www.collegium-carolinum.de)

Verlag: Vandenhoeck & Ruprecht GmbH & Co. KG, Göttingen/
Vandenhoeck & Ruprecht LLC, Bristol, CT, U.S.A.
(www.v-r.de)

Das Werk einschließlich aller Abbildungen ist urheberrechtlich geschützt. Jede Verwertung außerhalb der Grenzen des Urheberrechtsgesetzes ist ohne Zustimmung des Collegium Carolinum unzulässig und strafbar. Das gilt insbesondere für Vervielfältigungen, Übersetzungen, Mikroverfilmungen und die Einspeicherung und Bearbeitung in elektronischen Systemen.

All rights reserved. No part of this book may be reproduced or translated in any form, by print, photoprint, microfilm or any other means without written permission from the Collegium Carolinum. Violations of the above may result in criminal prosecution or civil damage awards.

Für Form und Inhalt trägt der/die jeweilige Verfasser/in die Verantwortung.

Redaktion: Collegium Carolinum, München

Satz: Collegium Carolinum, München

Layout des Einbands: SchwabScantechnik, Göttingen (www.schwabscantechnik.de)

Druck und Einband: Druckerei Menacher, Augsburg (www.druckerei-menacher.de)

Gedruckt auf säurefreiem, alterungsbeständigem und chlorfrei gebleichtem Papier.

CONTENTS

Jana Osterkamp/Martin Schulze Wessel: Exploring Loyalty 1

Mikhail Dolbilov: Loyalty and Emotion in Nineteenth-Century
  Russian Imperial Politics 17

Tatiana Khripachenko: Two Concepts of Loyalty in the Debates on
  the "Polish Question" in Late Imperial Russia 45

Alexei Il'ich Miller: National Identities and the Forging of Political
  Loyalties: Little Russians versus Ukrainians during the
  Nineteenth and Twentieth Centuries 61

Franziska Davies: Generating Loyalty: The Crimean Tatars and
  Military Reform in Late Imperial Russia 73

Mark Cornwall: Loyalty and Treason in Late Habsburg Croatia:
  A Violent Political Discourse before the First World War 97

Viorica Angela Crăciun: The Democratic Party of Bukovina and Its
  National and Imperial Loyalties (1902–1918) 121

Peter Bugge: Loyal in Word and Deed: The Czech National
  Movement and the Habsburg Monarchy in the Long Nineteenth
  Century 137

Martina Niedhammer: Loyalty as a Tool of Analysis for the Self-
  Image of Minorities: Prague's Jewish Upper Middle Class in the
  First Half of the Nineteenth Century 157

Doris Danzer: Communist Intellectuals in the German Democratic
  Republic Experiencing Conflicts of Loyalty 167

Heléna Tóth: From Content to Ritual: Name-Giving Practices and
  Political Loyalty in Hungary (1880–1989) 179

Todd H. Weir: Spurious Loyalty in the Soviet Bloc: Four Perspectives ... 203

Jens Boysen: In the Service of "the People" and of the "Socialist Community:" The Loyalties of Military Elites in the Polish People's Republic and the German Democratic Republic (1970–1990) 215

List of Abbreviations 235

Contributors 239

Jana Osterkamp/Martin Schulze Wessel

EXPLORING LOYALTY

On the frontispiece of this volume, the image of the loyalty oath of Hungarian nobles before Empress Maria Theresa in 1741 shows the young Queen standing under the royal baldaquin as she receives her coronation sword stroke from the Hungarian nobles. By swearing the oath *Vitam et sanguinem pro rege nostro*, the Hungarian elite was assuring Maria Theresa of their military support against the background of the War of the Austrian Succession. In literary depictions, the coronation was presented as a covenant sealed through tears—that is to say, as one secured through the symbolic use of genuine emotions. "We all wept with the Queen [...] The Queen had appealed to the gallant spirit of a warlike nation, and its heroic spirit burned brightly."[1]

The picture alludes to a number of important elements in the concept of loyalty: to emotion as a personal internal symbol of political affinity, to the promise of political and military allegiance, and not least to the various competing references tied to the concept of loyalty. The watercolour was produced by Vienna historical painter Eduard Schaller during the *Vormärz* period.[2] It forms part of a long tradition in the sculptural, artistic and historical stylisation of Maria Theresa in the nineteenth and twentieth centuries.[3] But the image does more than simply portray the bond that obtained between all those present. Acts of homage as a form of political communication were designed to mediate the terms and conditions of rulership and the mutual expectations of loyalty.[4] The reception of the scenes of homage of 1741 in the world of politics and art points to the multi-layered nature of the loyalty promised and expected by the parties involved. The oath of fidelity "For King [sic] Maria Theresa we will die!" implied a promise not just to be true to the actual royal person, but also to remain loyal to their rulership of the land.

---

[1] Waltraud Heindl, "Prinz Eugen von Savoyen. Heros et Philosophicus. Gedanken zu einem männlichen Schulbuchhelden," *L'Homme* 7, no. 1 (1996): 56–74, here 65.

[2] G. K. Nagler, *Neues allgemeines Künstlerlexikon oder Nachrichten von dem Leben und den Werken der Maler, Bildhauer, Baumeister, Kupferstecher, Formschneider, Lithographen, Zeichner, Medailleure, Elfenbeinarbeiter, etc.*, vol. 15 (Munich: Fleischmann, 1845), 142.

[3] Cf. Werner Telesko, *Maria Theresia: Ein europäischer Mythos* (Vienna: Böhlau, 2012), 160–163.

[4] Cf. Matthias Schwengelbeck, *Die Politik des Zeremoniells: Huldigungsfeiern im langen 19. Jahrhundert* (Frankfurt: campus, 2007).

However, in this context there was some controversy between Hungarian nobles and the Empress—as well as her successor Emperors—as to precisely what rulership the oath and acts of homage actually referred. The act of homage at the Pressburg Landtag was interpreted by later observers variously as a symbol of the bond between the Hungarian nobility and the Habsburg dynasty, of the bond of loyalty between the Hungarians and the *Gesamtstaat* of the Habsburg Empire or as a testimony to the special position of Hungary as a *nation*. The last of these interpretations was to become the one through which Maria Theresa was to emerge as a national figure for Hungarians, mainly during the late nineteenth century.[5] Thus, depending on one's interpretation, the oath of loyalty of 1741 might be taken as an expression of loyalty to a person (Maria Theresa), to a territorial unit (the entire monarchy) or to a community (the Hungarian nobility and, later, the Hungarian people). This ambiguity was to be lost after the Austro-Hungarian Compromise of 1867: at the great act of homage in Vienna in 1908 honouring the sixtieth jubilee of Kaiser Franz Joseph I's accession to the throne, Hungarian representatives were ostentatiously absent.[6]

The Concept of Loyalty as an Analytical Category

The concept of loyalty in historiographical analysis relates to the history of emotions, to the history of agency and political communication and also to the multi-layered relationships that loyalties create. The latest research has focused on loyalty in terms of its historical semantics (Martin Schulze Wessel), on the relationship between the nation state and national minorities (Martin Schulze Wessel, Peter Haslinger, Joachim von Puttkamer, Václav Petrbok), on state socialism (Volker Zimmermann, Peter Haslinger, Tomáš Nigrin) as well as in terms of its relation to the military and war (Nikolaus Buschmann, Karl Borromäus Murr).[7] Moreover, there is hardly a historical

---

[5] Telesko, *Maria Theresia*. Such a national figuration of the monarch was not an isolated phenomenon in Europe, cf. Schwengelbeck, *Politik des Zeremoniells*, 354.

[6] Cf. *Daniel Unowsky*, "Dynastic Symbolism and Popular Patriotism in Late Imperial Austria," in *Comparing Empires: Encounters and Transfers in the Long Nineteenth Century*, ed. Jörn Leonhard and Ulrike von Hirschhausen (Göttingen: Vandenhoeck & Ruprecht, 2011), 256; cf. Emil Niederhauser, "Maria Theresia in der ungarischen Geschichtsschreibung," in *Ungarn und Österreich unter Maria Theresia und Joseph II.*, ed. Anna Drabek, Richard Plaschka and Adam Wandruszka (Vienna: Verlag der österreichischen Akademie der Wissenschaften 1982), 29–41.

[7] Martin Schulze Wessel, "'Loyalität' als geschichtlicher Grundbegriff und Forschungskonzept: Zur Einleitung," in *Loyalitäten in der Tschechoslowakischen Republik 1918–1938: Politische, nationale und kulturelle Zugehörigkeiten*, ed. Martin Schulze Wessel (Munich: Oldenbourg, 2004), 1–22; Peter Haslinger and Joachim von Puttkamer (eds.), *Staat, Loyalität und Minderheiten in Ostmittel- und Südosteuropa: 1918–1941* (Munich: Oldenbourg, 2007); Volker Zimmermann, Peter Haslinger and Tomáš Nigrin (eds.),

work on empires that does not take on the topic of loyalty, at least as a side issue, as an indicator of inclusion and exclusion within imperial states.

Loyalty is the internal—and at the same time social—disposition to stand up for one another. A number of important analytical conceptual elements of loyalty have developed within historical research: duration, mutuality, sequentiality and communication.[8] By means of these categories, loyalty is protected from the danger of becoming lost in a fog of conceptual imprecision. The temporal component underlines, firstly, that the willingness to give loyalty is based on a particular horizon of experiences and expectations. The analysis of loyalty tends to be concerned with previous histories that have developed over long periods of time, and with past expectations of loyalty from those previous times. Secondly, loyalty is a category of relationships, which presupposes the existence of a personal or institutional counterpart. Thus, there is always a certain mutuality between the recipient and the giver of loyalty. Thirdly, understanding loyalty as a category of historical processes clarifies that loyalties must be created, can erode and may be reoriented. Fourthly, linked to this is the meaning of loyalty as a form of social communication: Loyalties are conditioned by spoken and unspoken communication and only become visible when they are expected, provided or drawn upon.

Loyalty in the History of Emotions

The negotiation of loyalty and belonging marks both historical sources and current political debates with an emotional loading. The epistemologies of nationalism and patriotism in particular have used and still use emotionally charged concepts of loyalty that bind the identity of the individual to the fulfilment of duties of loyalty and equate their refusal with self-betrayal and self-abandonment. A case in point would be the moral and theoretical debate on nationalism and patriotism currently taking place in the USA: Is a partisan ethics of patriotic loyalty legitimate? Communitarian approaches to such questions understand social relations as being a pre-condition for individuality: "the ethic of loyalty takes relationships as logically prior to the individu-

---

Loyalitäten im Staatssozialismus: DDR, Tschechoslowakei, Polen (Marburg: Verlag Herder-Institut, 2010); see also: Nikolaus Buschmann and Karl Borromäus Murr, "'Treue' als Forschungskonzept? Begriffliche und methodische Sondierungen," in *Treue: Politische Loyalität und militärische Gefolgschaft in der Moderne*, ed. idem (Göttingen: Vandenhoeck & Ruprecht, 2008), 11–35; Václav Petrbok (ed.), Neviditelná loajalita? Rakušané, Němci, Češi v české kultuře 19. století. Sborník příspěvků z 35. ročníku sympozia k problematice 19. století. Plzeň, 26.–28. února 2015 (Prague: Academia, 2016); Alfred Eisfeld and Konrad Maier (eds.), *Loyalität, Legitimität, Legalität: Zerfalls-, Separations- und Souveränisierungsprozesse in Ostmittel- und Osteuropa 1914–1921* (Wiesbaden: Harrassowitz, 2014).

8 Cf. Jana Osterkamp and Martin Schulze Wessel, "Texturen von Loyalität. Überlegungen zu einem analytischen Begriff," *Geschichte und Gesellschaft* 42, no. 4 (2016): 553–573.

al," according to George P. Fletcher, the most important theoretician in this area aside from Josiah Royce.[9] Thus Fletcher fully recognises the contradiction that his conception of loyalty poses for universal morals and the potential xenophobic effects of a necessarily particularistic, nationalist or patriotic bond of loyalty.[10]

In historical analysis, loyalty thus contributes to the *emotional turn* in history.[11] In addition to such terms as fidelity, trust or solidarity,[12] loyalty indicates both an emotional relationship and a category of agency and negotiation. In relation to these terms, loyalty shows a number of conceptual overlaps and differences. One distinctive feature of loyalty is its accentuation of the political.

Loyalty has a great semantic proximity and similarity in content to the concept of fidelity. Fidelity indicates primarily a personal bond. But fidelity seems to lack the analytical multi-layeredness of loyalty.[13] While one may speak unproblematically of loyalties, the term 'fidelity' grammatically resists any use of it in plural, thus also rejecting any pluralisation of the social bonds it implies. This observation incidentally also applies to studies on patriotism, which merely illuminate one aspect among many of the concept of loyalty.[14]

The concept of 'trust' addresses the emotional disposition in a mutual relationship and provides a *leitbegriff* in the new research field of "history of emotions" (Ute Frevert). Like the relationship between the giver and recipient of loyalty, a bond of mutual trust can be defined through a personal or institutional relationship (*social trust*). It can be of a symbolic nature or it can be determined by agency.[15] Trust also includes expectations in terms of beha-

---

[9] George P. Fletcher, *Loyalty: An Essay on the Morality of Relationships* (New York: Oxford University Press, 1993), 15; see also: Richard Rorty, "Justice as a Larger Loyalty," *Ethical Perspectives* 4:3 (1997), 139–151.
[10] For criticism, see: Simon Keller, *The Limits of Loyalty* (Cambridge: Cambridge University Press, 2007).
[11] Cf. another account Alain Blum, "Emotions, Trust, and Loyalty. The Fabric and Expression of Immaterial Relationships in History," *Kritika. Explorations in Russian and Eurasian History* 15, no. 2 (2014): 853–872.
[12] See also references to the concept in the anthology by Ute Frevert, Christian Bailey and Pascal Eitler (eds.), *Emotional Lexicons: Continuity and Change in the Vocabulary of Feeling 1700–2000* (New York: Oxford University Press, 2014), 25 and 223.
[13] For an interesting operationalisation of fidelity, compare in particular the anthology by Nikolaus Buschmann and Karl Borromäus Murr (eds.), *Treue: Politische Loyalität und militärische Gefolgschaft in der Moderne* (Göttingen: Vandenhoeck & Ruprecht, 2008).
[14] On the controversy over patriotism as a virtue of loyalty between universalist and communitarian morality, see Alaisdair MacIntyre, "Ist Patriotismus eine Tugend?," in *Kommunitarismus: Eine Debatte über die moralischen Grundlagen moderner Gesellschaften*, ed. Axel Honneth (Frankfurt am Main: campus, 1995), 84–102.
[15] See Ute Frevert, *Vertrauensfragen: Eine Obsession der Moderne* (München: C.H. Beck, 2013); Geoffrey Hosking, *Trust: A History* (Oxford: Oxford University Press, 2014); each with further support references.

viour and explains "mentalities of mistrust" or "forced trust"—as expressed, for example, in state socialist societies.[16] In contrast to loyalty, the historical analysis of trust seldom involves the examination of actual behaviour.

Solidarity, like loyalty, also indicates a willingness to stand up for one another. However, the private component, which is important for both the concepts of loyalty and of trust, is largely absent here. Since the beginning of the nineteenth century, a symmetrical conception of solidarity has asserted itself —as the duty of all to show solidarity to all. In historiography and in political theory, however, solidarity is closely associated with the history of social reform, workers' movements and the related ideological background.[17] In the light of everyday language usage there is much to be said at first sight in favour of treating the horizontal level of loyalty simply as solidarity. However, it seems more convincing to analyse loyalty both in its vertical and horizontal dimensions in combination with its mutual conditionalities.

A particularly revealing exercise is to juxtapose loyalty with identity. Most importantly, the concept of identity is not a relational category. In recent research, identities are no longer regarded as essentialist and static, but as fluid, complex and subject to transformation. They are loaded with national, religious, social, economic and cultural charges.[18] Loyalties are often founded on a similar basis. Compared to the over-complex concept of identity, loyalty has the advantage that it restricts itself to the analysis of specific relationships. As an analytical category, loyalty describes the multi-layered and relationship-rich fabric of loyalties to a state, a society or a community.

Words and Deeds: Loyalty as a Behavioural Category

The analytical value of loyalty largely results from the fact that loyalty is a category of social behaviour and agency. This is clearly demonstrated through the institutional economic perspective that sees loyalty as "a person's identification with the goals of a society" in which "feelings and perceptions play a role."[19] However, the concept of loyalty in the institutional economy becomes clear only when it is conceived as a behavioural option compared against its alternatives. In Albert O. Hirschman's influential study *Exit, Voice, and Loy-*

---

[16] Cf. Geoffrey Hosking, "Trust and Distrust in the USSR," *Slavonic and East European Review* 91, no. 1 (2013): 1–25; Alena Ledeneva, "The Genealogy of *Krugovaia Poruka*. Forced Trust as a Feature of Russian Political Culture," in *Trust and Democratic Transition in Post-Communist Europe*, ed. Ivana Marková (Oxford: Oxford University Press, 2004), 85–108.

[17] On this topic, cf. Kurt Bayertz (ed.), *Solidarität: Begriff und Problem* (Frankfurt: Suhrkamp, 1998).

[18] Rogers Brubaker and Frederick Cooper, "Beyond Identity," *Theory and Society* 29, no. 1 (2000): 1–47.

[19] Rudolf Richter and Eirik Furubotn, *Neue Institutionenökonomik: Eine Einführung und kritische Würdigung* (Tübingen: Mohr Siebeck, 1996), 176.

alty[20] the acts of leaving and of protest figure among such alternative strategies that actors in businesses, organisations or states have at their disposal.

In contrast to mere obedience, loyalty implies an internal disposition towards certain behaviours. Loyalty is, in principle, affirmative by nature because it is based, at least to a certain extent, on (staged) free volition. Whether alternative behaviours are rejected out of loyalty (such an attitude being expressed, for example in the expression "My country right or wrong") or accepted will in the end depend on the individual's will. However, given the implied long-term commitments, which do not bind the actor unconditionally from the point of view of theory of agency, loyalty occupies an intermediate position. In this sense, it differs on the one hand from the models used in making rational choices, which emphasise the interests and the agency of the actors involved. Although loyalty may involve a sort of calculation, it should nevertheless be distinguished from the concept of 'opportunity,' which is *exclusively* guided by one's interests and oriented towards the most advantageous course of action. On the other hand, loyalty should be distinguished from models that minimise the options for action of the relevant actors through concepts such as 'identity' and 'memory,' because loyalty can always be revoked—in spite of all its long-term orientation.

The exploration of loyalties becomes especially revealing in crisis situations in which the existing order is under political and ideological challenge. In times of crisis-generated change, the state or some other institution will regularly produce new offerings in order to inspire loyalty. Such top-down strategies are aimed at socially anchoring a new order through ideologies or myths of legitimation.

Communicating and Performing Loyalty

An exceptional communicative situation arises in cases where loyalties are explicitly called upon. The requirement for and the granting of loyalty is not tied up via language alone, but also through performance. Individuals and groups will maintain several loyalties at once, some of which may conflict with one another. Religious or political authorities may demand loyalty in order to establish a level of consistency and to replace a plurality of loyalties with a *single* one. The communicative conditionality of loyalty becomes especially clear in the times of social and political crises in which various possible alternatives are visible: whether an act is considered to constitute a refusal to give loyalty or an act of disloyalty or even betrayal will depend on the interpretation of a variety of actors, each with a different set of perspectives.

---

[20] Albert O. Hirschman, *Exit, Voice, and Loyalty: Responses to Decline in Firms, Organisations, and States* (Cambridge, MA: Harvard University Press, 1969).

The analysis of this reciprocal dynamics of loyalty becomes revealing wherever loyalty cannot be presupposed, but needs to be demanded and delivered by means of some performative act. It becomes essential to look at the reciprocal nature of loyalty when studying, for example, the relationship between national states and the national minorities on their territory, or when looking into the loyalties of actors in the religious or national spheres, along with "their" institutions beyond the boundaries of the state. In both cases, the performance of expectations and concessions of loyalty takes centre stage. Nation states, which tend to distrust the loyalty of national minorities and to demand explicit avowals of such loyalty, will often force the performance of loyalty or a refusal to do so on such minorities. States which intervene across borders in favour of their minorities in another state claim to be loyal to that group and at the same time manage to create the appearance of disloyalty on the part of "their" minority in the other state. In both cases one can speak of a "loyalisation" in these relationships.[21] This loyalisation can usually only be reversed through another long-term process of re-building trust. The history of empires can reveal comparable processes in the "complex frontiers" of European and Eurasian empires.[22]

The Multi-Layeredness and Multi-Polarity of Loyalty

One of the most important benefits of working with the concept of loyalty is its capacity to bring together under the same heading the very different levels of social relationship that exist within one political order. Employing the concept elucidates horizontal processes of community formation between different national, denominational or social groups. It also illustrates the vertical levels of loyalty between a monarch and his subjects that existed in the nineteenth century, or between the party apparatus and the people under state socialism. However, exploring loyalties in multi-level imperial orders involves different questions to the ones posed by explorations of loyalty as it relates to nation states or to state socialism.

In historical research on loyalties in the *nation state*, crises, conflicts and competing interests have long been at the centre of focus. This set of priorities arose from the tension between expectations of loyalty and actual relationships of loyalty. Thus, special attention was dedicated to loyalties towards nationalities and denominations in nation states that contained large minor-

---

[21] Martin Schulze Wessel, "Identitäten und Loyalitäten im Zeitalter (neo-)imperialer Politik. Die Tschechoslowakei 1938 und die Ukraine heute im Vergleich," in *Dekonstruieren und doch erzählen: Polnische und andere Geschichten*, ed. Yvonne Kleinmann et al. (Göttingen: Wallstein, 2015), 39–45.

[22] Cf. Alfred Rieber, "The Comparative Ecology of *Complex Frontiers*," in *Imperial Rule*, ed. Alfred Rieber and Alexei Miller (Budapest: CEU Press, 2004), 177–208.

ity populations.²³ German Research into the history of post-war refugees began early to deal with the contradictions between citizenship and loyalty—in relation to Czechoslovakia in the interwar period, for example.²⁴ Works in Jewish history focus on the subject differently, interpreting the reports of voluntary war service in the First World War on the one hand as a proof of loyalty and on the other as a tool in the Jewish struggle to achieve political recognition, acceptance and naturalisation.²⁵

This addresses another subject of loyalty research in the nation state: the institutions which are tasked with ensuring loyalty to the nation state, such as schools or the army.²⁶ Such institutions can be characterised as agencies of loyalisation, designed as they are to inculcate a strong sense of loyalty to the nation. This inculcation of loyalty to the nation has its own retroactive effect on the instrument of citizenship. To a liberal understanding, the concept of citizenship replaces pre-modern bonds of personal fidelity with a loyalty that can be seen as the inner expression of a legal relationship.²⁷ By that understanding, loyalty may be seen as the result of a modern process of rationalisation.

The analysis of loyalties in *empires* only differs in nuances. The potential harboured by the concept of loyalty lies in the analysis of negotiation processes between imperial authorities, groups and individuals, with their various affiliations and interests. The concept of loyalty can be used to show how political and administrative practice, particularly at the margins of empires, affected the integration and disintegration of the various groups and individuals. Empires too possessed agencies for the inculcation of loyalties, including

---

[23] Schulze Wessel, ed., *Loyalitäten in der Tschechoslowakischen Republik*; Peter Haslinger and Joachim von Puttkamer, *Staat, Loyalität und Minderheiten*.

[24] Cf. Otto Luchterhandt, *Nationale Minderheiten und Loyalität* (Köln: Verl. Wiss. und Politik 1997; Kurt Rabl, *Staatsbürgerliche Loyalität im Nationalitätenstaat: Dargestellt an den Verhältnissen in den böhmischen Ländern zwischen 1914 und 1938* (Munich: Lerche, 1959).

[25] Their expectation of eventual naturalisation was, however, to be regularly disappointed. On this, see Sarah Panter, *Jüdische Erfahrungen und Loyalitätskonflikte im Ersten Weltkrieg* (Göttingen: Vandenhoeck & Ruprecht, 2014); see also Hannelore Burger, *Heimatrecht und Staatsbürgerschaft österreichischer Juden: Vom Ende des 18. Jahrhunderts bis in die Gegenwart* (Vienna: Böhlau, 2014), 131.

[26] Studies that deal with the concept of loyalty include Ingo Eser, *'Volk, Staat, Gott': Die deutsche Minderheit in Polen und ihr Schulwesen 1918-1939* (Wiesbaden: Harrassowitz, 2010); Pascal Trees, "Zweifelhafte Loyalitäten. Deutsche in der polnischen Armee nach dem Ersten Weltkrieg," in *Aufbruch und Krise: Das östliche Europa und die Deutschen nach dem Ersten Weltkrieg*, ed. Beate Störtkuhl, Jens Stüben and Tobias Weger (Munich: Oldenbourg, 2010), 379-402.

[27] Ulrich K. Preuß, *Politische Verantwortung und Bürgerloyalität: Von den Grenzen der Verfassung und des Gehorsams in der Demokratie* (Frankfurt am Main: Fischer, 1984).

schools[28] and armies.[29] Yet in such imperial contexts, loyalty is always thought of in the plural and leaving space open for other social references.

In empires, the element of personal fidelity—to the dynasty and especially the person of the ruler—remained an important factor even into the modern era. The integrative function of personal loyalty was particularly relevant to the Habsburg Monarchy, since the unity of its crown lands was conceptualised as a bond of fidelity to the Emperor.[30] Imperial jubilees and dynastic celebrations provided both the regional and the urban elite of the Empire with the opportunity to demonstrate their loyalty. This served the unity of the Empire as much as it consolidated the social position and the agendas of its loyalists.[31]

Thus a conceptual understanding of multiple and layered loyalties is an essential consideration in research on loyalties in empires. The special attention that empires placed on the establishment of loyalties in border regions can be interpreted as part of imperial strategy: It was intended to compliment the establishment of territorial and military "buffer zones" on the margins—a typical pattern of policy[32] in empires—by making efforts to develop effective personal loyalties. It is therefore no coincidence that studies on loyalty structures in empires primarily direct their interest at imperial peripheries.

---

[28] Joachim von Puttkamer, "Schooling, Religion and the Integration of Empire. Education in the Habsburg Monarchy and in Tsarist Russia," in *Comparing Empires*, 359–371; Erich Bruckmüller, "Patriotic and National Myths. National Consciousness and Elementary Education in Imperial Austria," in: *The Limits of Loyalty: Imperial Symbolism, Popular Allegiances, and State Patriotism in the Late Habsburg Monarchy*, ed. Laurence Cole and David L. Unowsky (New York: Berghahn, 2007), 11–35.

[29] Cf. Laurence Cole, "Militärische Loyalität in der späten Habsburgermonarchie," in *Treue: Politische Loyalität und militärische Gefolgschaft in der Moderne*; Martin Zückert, "Imperial War in the Age of Nationalism. The Habsburg Monarchy and the First World War," in *Comparing Empires*, 500–517; Yohanan Petrovsky-Shtern, *Jews in the Russian Army, 1827–1917: Drafted into Modernity* (Cambridge: Cambridge University Press, 2009); Werner Benecke, *Militär, Reform und Gesellschaft im Zarenreich: Die Wehrpflicht in Rußland 1874–1914* (Paderborn: Schöningh, 2006).

[30] Matthias Stickler, "Die Herrschaftsauffassung Kaiser Franz Josephs in den frühen Jahren seiner Regierung. Überlegungen zu Selbstverständnis und struktureller Bedeutung der Dynastie für die Habsburgermonarchie," in *Der österreichische Neoabsolutismus als Verfassungs- und Verwaltungsproblem: Diskussionen über einen strittigen Epochenbegriff*, ed. Harm-Hinrich Brandt (Vienna: Böhlau, 2014), 35–60.

[31] Daniel L. Unowsky, *The Pomp and Politics of Patriotism: Imperial Celebrations in Habsburg Austria, 1848–1918* (West Lafayette: Purdue University Press, 2005).

[32] On this topic, cf. Jürgen Osterhammel, *Die Verwandlung der Welt. Eine Geschichte des 19. Jahrhunderts* (Munich: C.H.Beck, 2010), 616; Hans-Christian Maner, *Grenzregionen der Habsburgermonarchie im 18. und 19. Jahrhundert: Ihre Bedeutung und Funktion aus der Perspektive Wiens* (Münster: Lit, 2005).

Contributions to this Volume

The contributions to this anthology demonstrate once again the historical diversity that accompanies any attempt at "exploring loyalty." For the first time, this volume summarises questions of loyalty by both comparing between empires and making a diachronic comparison to test the accuracy of the concept of loyalty under various political orders and in various epochs. Typical elements of loyalty, including emotion, agency and communication, play a role, as does the phenomenon of competing loyalties and the interplay between accusations of disloyalty and the performance of loyalty.

Political tears appear in Mikhail Dolbilov's essay as part of an emotional performance to demonstrate political belonging within the Russian Empire. During his coronation in 1856, the young Russian Tsar Alexander II touched the emotions of his subjects and retinue as he revealed himself with tears in his eyes under the new burden of his crown. The nineteenth-century historical recollection of the act of homage to Maria Theresa made much use of similar imagery and for this reason has recently been critically interpreted as having emphasised feminine helplessness.[33] Dolbilov, in contrast, tackles the issue of how interest in forms of emotional loyalty relates to the recently emerged history of emotions. According to his account, loyalty as "assessment, negotiation, and performance of political allegiance" was so essential for the Russian Empire precisely because reliable, legally determined rules on affiliation such as citizenship were absent from the autocratic state. Imperial politics suffered from "under-institutionalisation" in other ways too. Belonging, therefore, had to be reaffirmed through the "sentimentalist celebration of sincerity and emotionality" that permeated the political language of the regime, the understanding of the Russian nation, and religious practice in the Empire. Dolbilov shows that such forms of emotional loyalty ultimately addressed the Tsar less than it appealed to a particular idea of Russia.

Authors Tatiana Khripachenko, Alexei Il'ich Miller and Franziska Davies recount complementary stories from the margins of the Russian Empire. Given the link between "under-institutionalisation" and the loyalty practices discussed by Dolbilov, it is not surprising that the process of constitutionalisation of Russia and the introduction of the concept of imperial citizenship at the instigation of the Duma would lead to a contentious renegotiation of loyalties. As Khripachenko shows in relation to the Poles and Finns of Russia, the reform among the liberals was linked to the idea of making active and affirmative citizens of a reformed Russia out of passive, obedient subjects of the Tsar, as "a civic loyalty would serve to supplement and bolster the traditional loyalty to the Tsar." Khripachenko's contribution shows that the language of emotional loyalty, as described by Dolbilov, found hardly any echo

---

[33] Heindl, "Prinz Eugen von Savoyen. Heros et Philosophicus. Gedanken zu einem männlichen Schulbuchhelden," 65.

in the western provinces, and any sense of affiliation to the Tsar in the west did not go beyond mere obedience to the law. The liberal project of a centralised, citizenship-based idea of loyalty directed towards the entire Empire failed not simply due to the nationalist political resistance of its Polish and Finnish inhabitants, but also because of the conservative majority of the Third Duma, which trumped the "national egoism" of the Empire's nationalities with its own Russian "national egoism."

Miller too addresses the interplay of ideas of community and political loyalties at the margins of the Russian Empire. Communities such as the Ukrainians, the Little Russians and the White Russians were claimed throughout the long nineteenth century by the Tsarist regime to constitute the "various branches that form the autochthonous Russian nation," with each group being distinguished solely by its own separate colloquial language. According to Miller's account, this insight is where the regime's "most radical project for creating a nation out of the Empire" can be located. Against that vision was a competing idea of community that emphasised national autonomy, and thus other political loyalties too. While for the so-called Little Russians the idea of autonomy did not contradict the concept of the Empire, the so-called Ukrainophiles wanted to secede from it. Increasing nationalism and the sharpening of such affiliations was to accelerate the policies of repressive violence pursued by the empires during the First World War. Some groups were interned as potentially disloyal by the one empire, and at the same time backed as a separatist movement by the other belligerent powers.

The history of the Crimean Tatars provides a further example of the contradictory imperial policy of inclusion and exclusion, of loyalty building and accusations of disloyalty. Davies reconstructs a period of increased imperial effort during the late nineteenth century to include the Muslim Crimean Tatars; an effort complicated by the fact that St. Petersburg had for a long time tolerated and even encouraged the migration of the Tatars to the Ottoman Empire. Through discussion of the implementation of the general military reform of 1874 in the region, the author shows how the Empire made numerous concessions to the Crimean Tartar population, especially in relation to the rules on religious practice in the army. In contrast to the cases discussed by Dolbilov, the accompanying expectation of loyalty was not directed towards any emotional performance. What came centre stage were questions of general affiliation on the basis of citizenship and of the corresponding general duties with regard to a military loyalty. The imperial policy towards the Crimean Tatars cannot be understood without considering it as a part of the competition between two empires. For the Russian and the Ottoman Empires were pursuing opposing strategies in their attempts to win the loyalty of the Muslims of Crimea. It was precisely against this backdrop that the Tsarist Empire tended to doubt the loyalty of the Muslims and therefore to force them to position themselves explicitly, an approach that was to undermine the loyalties of the Crimean Tatars towards the Tsarist Empire in the long run.

Similarly to the Crimea, the Croatia of the Habsburg Monarchy was both a region of great military sensitivity on the frontier with the Ottoman Empire and a territory whose inhabitants were very diverse in terms of nationality, ethnicity, religion and social structure. The analysis of Croatia in the years between 1908 and 1910 by Mark Cornwall provides a clear parallel with the allegations of disloyalty in the Russian Empire against minority nationalities and denominations. Vienna and Budapest made great efforts to foster the political loyalty of the population—in the area of economic development, for instance. Contemporary caricatures portraying the new Croatian *banus* as a tamer of wild Croatian wolves subtly imply that behind such acts of loyalty building lay the fear of local imperial violence. In the course of the annexation of Bosnia and Herzegovina and the subsequent war with Serbia, the climate of mutual distrust in Croatia was to reach a climax, culminating in the trials for high treason against a number of leading Serbian politicians, as Cornwall puts it: "'treason' as the precise antithesis of 'trust' became the watchword of the regime." News of the trials, which may well be compared with those of the Dreyfus Affair, were to reach the whole of Europe. The trials were directed not just against a unified national movement of southern Slavs, but also against the Serbian Orthodox religion. Both domestically and abroad, they were regarded as a stage upon which expectations of loyalty were asserted, and were meant, as one contemporary put it "to pass judgment over what is dynastic and what is anti-dynastic." The result of the trial debilitated loyalty to the Empire in the region in favour of ideas of national community.

Viorica Angela Crăciun's contribution provides us with a view of another multi-ethnic and multi-confessional frontier region of the Habsburg Monarchy, one which served militarily as an imperial buffer zone between Austria-Hungary and the Russian Empire: the province of Bukovina. In her piece, Crăciun addresses the juxtaposition of and the competition between imperial, regional and national senses of affiliation. Her study on the Democratic Party of Bukovina portrays its founding figure, Aurel Onciul, in his attempt to overcome the national cleavages between the various population groups of the land and to create a sense of belonging based on the common good of the entire province. The Austrian monarchy was praised in party magazines as the best possible world for the economic, social and cultural development of the land, claiming that "Bukovinian Romanians are Austrian and dynastic to the backbone." Loyalty to Austria remained Onciul's preferred option (he was an ethnic Romanian) over any loyalty to the Kingdom of Romania until the end of the war in 1918—a choice that had geopolitical grounds too, as he feared that a Greater Romania would not be militarily strong enough to withstand its neighbour and enemy, Russia.

Nor was loyalty to the monarch necessarily seen as incompatible with loyalties towards individual nations in the other provinces of Austria-Hungary.

In the Bohemian Lands it took a decade longer than in the Croatian case, for example, before the political elite began to exhibit a similar contrast in terms of political affiliation. This contradiction was fuelled by a popular wave of mutual distrust at the outbreak of war in 1914, and by a number of trials for high treason against high-ranking politicians. Yet, through letters expressing loyalty to the Kaiser, Peter Bugge emphasises that a commitment to the Emperor and simultaneously to the Czech national project was still widespread at the time. Bugge refers in particular to the wide range of loyalties to the sovereign in Vienna, who could be addressed as Emperor of Austria, King of Bohemia or Margrave of Moravia, thus allowing him to be appropriated on a national or regional level. Thus, according to Bugge's account, patterns of "national mobilisation without the factor of nationalism" so typical of eastern central Europe can be seen in the Bohemian Crownlands. Conceptually, Bugge points to the implications for the history of nationalism. For one thing, according to his account, studies in nationalism will need to open up in analytical terms to the presence of strong non-national loyalties. For another, it would be wrong to downplay or underestimate the integrative value and rationale of such loyalty directed towards a particular ruler or towards an entire state within a multi-national empire.

Martina Niedhammer extends Bugge's perspective through her contribution to the many-faceted connecting factors involved in the concept of loyalty available within the political space occupied by one particular marginalised, yet an economically, culturally and religiously highly influential group. In the Jewish population of the upper-middle-class of Prague, loyalty not simply ranged between monarchs, the state and a particular national or linguistic group, but was also essentially related to religion. This is shown not least by the fact that many Jews in this group, despite all the disadvantages associated with their faith in the world of politics and in society, refused either to convert or to adopt "an aggressive religious indifference." Niedhammer uncovers various levels of loyalty by concentrating on the momentum provided by the voluntary nature and multi-polarity of loyalty, thus distancing the term conceptually from "situational ethnicity." Official letters expressing loyalty and gratitude to the Kaiser—for having abolished the *Judensteuer*, for example—can be read here too as an ostentatious response to accusations of disloyalty which the Jewish population of Bohemia constantly faced.

Finally, this anthology also takes on the issues of loyalty as they arose under state socialism. While the case studies on the German Democratic Republic (GDR), Hungary, Poland and the Soviet Union should not lead one to make any modification of the concept of loyalty, it should be noted that these studies exhibit significant differences to the contributions on the history of empire. This can be seen, for example, in the repeated interplay between ostentatious expressions of loyalty and accusations of political, military or national disloyalty. If mistrust and disloyalty in the nineteenth century were a phenomenon that mostly took place across particular rifts and boundaries between groups, the practice became radicalised in the twentieth century in such a way that it now began to emerge even among like-minded peers. In her case study on the GDR, Doris Danzer tells of the writers who were expelled from the Socialist party, and how their exclusion from the public political space was at the same time also aimed at their private sphere. Friendship, an intimate and private form of loyalty, was generally subordinated to the logic of the public space and to loyalty to the state party.

It was only in the later, more consumption-oriented, stage of state socialism that the categorical "whoever is not with us is against us" transformed into the more resigned "whoever is not against us is with us." In her contribution, Heléna Tóth concerns herself with changes in rites of passage in Hungary. Even before the Second World War, name giving, and particularly name changing—changing German names into Hungarian, for example, or Jewish names to Christian ones—was already interpreted as a manifestation of a specific loyalty. Then, from 1959 on, new rituals were introduced into spheres that were genuinely private, including rites of baptism and burial. These new forms, or so the leadership of the Hungarian party intended, were to displace the role of the Church in the private sphere, creating instead a secular, state socialist community. In effect, loyalty to the state and the party could and should now be ritually demonstrated in the private sphere. At the same time, numerous cases demonstrate that the new rituals by no means rendered tradition irrelevant. Tóth takes one double funeral at the time as an example: "the dead in the family were buried with a socialist funerary orator but the priest came to bless the graveside in the evening." With very strong grounds for doing so, Tóth deconstructs the outward signals of loyalty as no more than opportunism.

Todd Weir interprets transparencies, slogans and other affirmations of loyalty to the Soviet Union that adorned the walls of factory buildings or streets in the GDR and elsewhere as a "Potemkin-like" façade and as "spurious loyalty." He reveals the peculiar character of loyalty under state socialism using three parallel approaches to the subject. The first approach he takes is directed at the inherited burden of "divided loyalties" carried by the socialist states' military alliance, the Warsaw Pact. This imposed on the Soviet Union in particular the duty of keeping the lid on all those historical conflicts of loyalty that had festered on the Soviet territory, and among the various so-called "brother states," as exemplified in the contributions on the history of empires from Miller, Khripachenko and Davies. In his second approach to the topic, Weir emphasises the role of loyalty as a substitute for the weak democratic legitimation of socialist statehood: "statements of loyalty stood in for actual consent." His third approach looks at loyalty as an important ritual component of the political culture, which, as shown in the annals of Stalinism, had been internalised by the population. This emotional loyalty devolved into a functional and purely superficial loyalty during late socialism, which "served the self-organisation and self-representation of the communist system."

Soldiers personally stood prepared to guarantee this cohesion, which was merely superficially adverted to in state socialist societies. With this in mind, Jens Boysen concludes the anthology with a discussion of the various forms of military loyalty under state socialism. Speaking of the national armies of the GDR and Poland, he explains how the Warsaw Pact's military alliance affected the relationships between the national armies taking part in it. Boysen occupies himself with the peculiarities of military loyalty as it existed under state socialism. While soldiers in the Western democracies are also bound into a special relationship of loyalty with the state, the issue of loyalty was magnified and complicated by the close intertwining of military and political leadership within the Warsaw Pact and by an opaque interlacing of domestic and foreign policy, along with the issues of internationalism under state socialism. In his assessment of these realities, Boysen contends that the military elite within state socialism constituted "an epistemic community (a community containing a shared educational and technical orientation)."

Summary

Loyalty studies thus offer new inspirations for investigating the ways in which complex ruling structures are stabilised and how they erode. This central issue affects all political orders alike, whether they be empires, nation states or countries under state socialist rule. It is not just state power and political institutions that play a role in the integration or disintegration of ruling systems: the multi-layered network of affiliations within society also has a part to play. Looking at it from the point of view of integration, the concept of loyalty highlights the personal internal side of affiliations, the performance of such loyalty and its fulfilment by means of positive action. Looking at it from the other side of the coin—disintegration—the emphasis is on the precariousness and fragility of loyalties, their dependence on the personal will of the individual and their mutability when challenged by competing affiliations or by a political culture of distrust.

Our volume equips the reader to recognise the various different logics of loyalty. The examples it provides from the history of empire illustrate the wider range of politically relevant loyalties that were in play within the great empires. Imperial loyalties were tied up not just with social, confessional and national affiliations, but also betrayed a significant personal element in their embodiment as loyalties to Tsar, Kaiser or King. In the transition to modern statehood, as it emerged into the national state of the short twentieth century, one can identify a tendency towards a certain rationalisation and unification of loyalties. The element of a personal affiliation to a ruler steps back in favour of a universal and egalitarian idea of institutional affiliation based on citizenship. Multi-layered networks of affiliations are becoming increasingly unified into the assertion of citizenship-based and national affiliations. Loyalties adapt themselves within this process into a force binding societies together in a long-term process that is rich in contradictions. However, the study of loyalties reveals that their power to bind together communities unfurls over longer periods of time than the establishment or dissolution of imperial or national orders. Loyalties thus represent the shadow of an older time within a new order. An example to illustrate this point is provided by the emotionally charged loyalties that some presidents, such as Tomáš G. Masaryk and Paul von Hindenburg, a bit like *ersatz* monarchs, attached to certain sections of "their people." Above all, though, the process of replacing the multi-layered loyalties typical of empires with the comparatively unambiguous relationships of loyalty in the democratic nation state is not an irreversible process.

Translated by Jaime Hyland.

Mikhail Dolbilov

LOYALTY AND EMOTION IN NINETEENTH-CENTURY RUSSIAN IMPERIAL POLITICS

For the study of modern history, loyalty is one of the most frequently used but least clearly defined categories of historical analysis. For earlier periods, loyalty is often associated with highly ritualized structures of power or visible and unequivocal gestures of sovereignty and subjugation. Yet, for the modern period it remains an elusive phenomenon that seems to be located everywhere and nowhere. Historians may refer to loyalty as something taken for granted when discussing a sweeping range of issues—power, empire, geopolitics, war, conquest, justice, social class, landownership, ideology, religion, nationalism, assimilation, etc.

The case of the Russian Empire is all the more challenging to historians in this regard, because throughout almost the entire imperial era, membership in the state (as distinct from modern citizenship), as argued recently by Eric Lohr,[1] was never formulated as a unified legal status. Hence, reliability was often understood in negative terms, as entailing the opposite (or the absence) of the gravest crimes and transgressions, such as *lèse-majesté*,[2] violation of the military oath, espionage, or political subversion. Most tellingly, any consistent laws or rulings concerning who should swear the oath of allegiance to the emperor and when were not implemented for most of the imperial era. In this setting, political loyalty defies simple historical conceptualization.

During the last decade or so, the issue of political loyalty in historical scholarship has been connected most visibly with the "imperial turn" in the Russian/Eurasian field—that is, with studies of the formation and reshaping of ethno-national identities in a multiethnic empire.[3] From this point of view, assimilation or at least acculturation into a Russian nationhood constituted a prerequisite for political loyalty as demanded by state authorities. However, a number of recent contributions to the history of empires in Eurasian stud-

---

[1] Eric Lohr, *Russian Citizenship: From Empire to Soviet Union* (Cambridge, MA: Harvard University Press, 2012), 3–5, 15–7.
[2] See for example: Angela Rustemeyer, *Dissens und Ehre: Majestätsverbrechen in Russland, 1600–1800* (Wiesbaden: Harrassowitz, 2006).
[3] For insightful criticisms of the studies of identity in this framework see: Stephen Kotkin, "Mongol Commonwealth? Exchange and Governance across the Post-Mongol Space," *Kritika: Explorations in Russian and Eurasian History* 8, no. 3 (2007): 487–531.

ies have demonstrated that loyalties to imperial establishments may well have been maintained and practiced at the intersection of competing identities—ethnic and national as well as linguistic, cultural, religious, and local. Thus, Robert D. Crews's study shows the importance of religion to the loyalty of the Russian Empire's diverse Muslim populations to tsarist authorities.[4] Darius Staliūnas's monograph reconstructs an impressive variety of imperial policies toward specific groups and minorities in the western region.[5] Larry Wolff's analysis of modern politics of "non-national" dynastic loyalty and regional identities in Habsburg Galicia presents a remarkable case of the manufactured "national indifference" that can be compared with less successful similar undertakings in the Russian Empire's adjacent regions.[6]

Moreover, as several recent works on imperial Russia have shown,[7] political loyalties were not absolute, unconditional, or indivisible even in an autocratic monarchy. The state of being loyal, for a member of the highest as well as lower estates (*sosloviia*), did not necessarily exclude ambivalence in one's attitudes toward the throne, nor did it preclude the possibility of boldly touting one's loyalty for a higher reward. That said, one could argue that loyalty had to do less with well-articulated ideas and unidirectional indoctrination than with a changeable mixture of "practical sense" and spiritual experiences.

In the recent historiography of late imperial Russia, political loyalty is perhaps most fruitfully addressed for the era of World War I. Using the evocative metaphor of "tragic eroticism," Boris Ivanovich Kolonitskii has inquired into the strenuous but eventually failed effort by the members of the Romanov dynasty to reshape their public image and consolidate the traditional affection for the monarch with a sense of nationhood heightened by the war.[8] For the Habsburg Empire in the same period of time, Alon Rachamimov has shown the particular bureaucratic techniques of assessing political loyalty in the case of Austria-Hungary's subjects—namely, prisoners of war held in

---

[4] Robert D. Crews, *For Prophet and Tsar: Islam and Empire in Russia and Central Asia* (Cambridge, MA: Harvard University Press, 2006).

[5] Darius Staliūnas, *Making Russians: Meaning and Practice of Russification in Lithuania and Belarus after 1863* (Amsterdam: Rodopi, 2007).

[6] Larry Wolff, *The Idea of Galicia: History and Fantasy in Habsburg Political Culture* (Stanford, CA: Stanford University Press, 2010). For an extremely important point about the constructed "non-national" see also: Larry Wolff, "'Kennst du das Land?' The Uncertainty of Galicia in the Age of Metternich and Fredro," *Slavic Review* 67, no. 2 (2008): 277–300, here 278, 280.

[7] Most notably, Serhii Plokhy's latest study of persistent Ukrainian-Cossack identities in the Russian Empire: Serhii Plokhy, *The Cossack Myth: History and Nationhood in the Age of Empires* (Cambridge: Cambridge University Press, 2012). On multiple loyalties see also: Michael Khodarkovsky, *Bitter Choices: Loyalty and Betrayal in the Russian Conquest of the North Caucasus* (Ithaca: Cornell University Press, 2011).

[8] Boris Ivanovich Kolonitskii, "*Tragicheskaia erotika*": *Obrazy imperatorskoi sem'i v gody Pervoi mirovoi voiny* (Moscow: Novoe literaturnoe obozrenie, 2010).

Russian camps.⁹ This focus on the Great War seems to have to do with an assumption that the *fin de siècle* and World War I era, with its burgeoning mass politics and increasing governmental interventionism, would make dilemmas and controversies over loyalty more visible and more accessible to historians. I would suggest looking further back to identify the emergence of modern complexities of loyalty in Russia.

The project of which this essay is an early anticipatory glimpse approaches loyalty as one of the organizing tenets of imperial politics and conceptualizes it as a dynamic structure for which three undercurrents are analytically significant: 1) a certain mode of self-consciousness and self-understanding related to the person's or the group's political subjecthood and their subordination to the authorities; 2) the authorities' capability—both real and perceived—of instilling a sense of belonging, conformity, reliability, and responsiveness in their subjects of various social strata, ethnicities, faiths, etc.; 3) practices of manifesting and accepting (or questioning and rejecting) allegiance that arose from a clash or convergence of expectations emanating "from above" and those generated at the grass roots level.

The emotional perspective on loyalty in this project elaborates the theme of assessment, negotiation, and performance of political allegiance. A well-established direction of historical inquiry that has begun to expand into the field of Russian studies only relatively recently,[10] the history of emotions offers a methodological and heuristic arsenal. Thus far I have drawn less on highly theoretical works[11] than on those interpretive and evidence-laden case

---

[9] Alon Rachamimov, *POWs and the Great War: Captivity on the Eastern Front* (Oxford: Berg, 2002), 133–59. An interesting comparative perspective, as well as theoretical reflections on the history of loyalty, can be found in: Martin Schulze Wessel, ed., *Loyalitäten in der Tschechoslowakischen Republik 1918–1938: Politische, nationale und kulturelle Zugehörigkeiten* (Munich: Oldenbourg, 2004).

[10] Mark D. Steinberg and Valeria Sobol, eds., *Interpreting Emotions in Russia and Eastern Europe* (DeKalb: Northern Illinois University Press, 2011); Jan Plamper, "Emotional Turn? Feelings in Russian History and Culture," *Slavic Review* 68, no. 2 (2009): 229–37; and Jan Plamper, Schamma Schahadat and Marc Elie, eds., *Rossiiskaia imperiia chuvstv: Podkhody k kul'turnoi istorii emotsii* (Moscow: Novoe literaturnoe obozrenie, 2010).

[11] Inasmuch as I have, my thinking on theoretical aspects of the history of emotions has been mostly informed by attempts at applying Pierre Bourdieu's practice theory to historicizing emotions, a good example of which is the recent essay: Monique Scheer, "Are Emotions a Kind of Practice (and Is That What Makes Them Have a History)? A Bourdieuian Approach to Understanding Emotion," *History and Theory* 51, no. 2 (2012): 193–220. Elaborating the point that people *do* rather than just *have* emotions, Scheer's model emphasizes the role of "bodily knowledge" (ingrained but socially and culturally regulated bodily habits, arousals, performances, etc.) in experiencing emotions and seeks to solve a number of the often taken-for-granted dichotomies, including the one between "inner feeling" and its "outer expression." In Scheer's words, "emotions not only *follow* from things people do, but *are* themselves a form of practice, because they are an action of a mindful body" and, moreover, "this feeling subject is not prior to but emerges in the doing of emotion," which is why, "[r]ather than seeking to reconstruct

studies—Ruth Harris's penetrating reexamination of the Dreyfus affair being for me a most inspiring example[12]—that explicate the centrality of the irrational and the "visceral" to historical phenomena that have traditionally been approached from the Cartesian perspective of the logical and the "cerebral." In the case of the Russian Empire, emotions provide a valuable window onto the functioning of an autocratic regime that was very demanding about the quantity of loyalty it desired but not so predictable and articulate with regard to its criteria and precise content. This state of affairs evokes a parallel with the prevalence of myth and symbolic representation over political ideology in the Russian monarchy's legitimizing structures, as argued by Richard S. Wortman in *Scenarios of Power: Myth and Ceremony in Russian Monarchy*[13]. Also, the examination of emotions can enable us to re-approach the debatable issue of the prolonged coexistence and confusion between personal (to the monarch) and institutional (to the state) loyalties in late imperial Russia.

What particularly invites a student of Russian imperial politics of loyalty to "go emotional"[14] is a specific pattern and style of political loyalty, made explicit by Ernest A. Zitser's analysis of a distinctly violent yet otherwise prototypical scene dating back to the Petrine era, namely, the Russian Emperor Peter I's conflict with Tsarevich Aleksei of Russia. Zitser has demonstrated that Peter tied his demand for allegiance to the newly introduced idea of justification by faith (as opposed to that by works, that is, genuine belief as opposed to hypocrisy, sanctimony, and the lack of spirituality). Quoting from one of the most politically charged sermons by Feofan Prokopovich, Peter's ideologue and bishop, the historian explains Peter's logic in the following way: "[S]ince man had a conscience, 'which itself is also the seed of God' [...] that obedience could not be coerced; in other words, political loyalty, like religious belief, had to come straight from the heart."[15] Thus, Peter chastised Aleksei not so much for inaction and poor "works" as for "hypocrisy" and the lack of (quasi-)religious zeal: "[...] Aleksei's real problem was his lack of faith in the tsar's divine gift of grace. [...] That kind of faith was a matter of con-

---

emotional 'truth,' the question becomes how and why historical actors mobilized their bodies in certain ways, cultivated specific skilled performances, and debated emotional practices among themselves." Ibid., 220, 215. See also footnote 57 in this paper.

[12] Ruth Harris, *Dreyfus, Politics, Emotion, and the Scandal of the Century* (New York: Metropolitan Books, 2010).

[13] Richard S. Wortman, *Scenarios of Power: Myth and Ceremony in Russian Monarchy*, 2 vols. (Princeton: Princeton University Press, 1995–2000).

[14] This vector of research has also been pointed to in a recent review essay by Alain Blum, incidentally, with a title mirroring that of the present article: Alain Blum, "Emotions, Trust, and Loyalty: The Fabric and Expression of Immaterial Relationships in History," *Kritika: Explorations in Russian and Eurasian History* 15, no. 4 (2014): 853–72. Our sharing the two key words notwithstanding, I disagree with what seems to me Blum's overemphasis on the *immaterial* nature of emotions related to loyalty.

[15] Ernest A. Zitser, *The Transfigured Kingdom: Sacred Parody and Charismatic Authority at the Court of Peter the Great* (Ithaca: Cornell University Press, 2004), 143.

science, a spiritual 'inclination' that could come only from within."[16] Several years later, the so-called *Ecclesiastical Regulation* (Dukhovnyi reglament), issued by Peter the Great to reform the administration of the Orthodox Church, solemnly stated what was bound to become one of the most famous definitions of the Russian autocracy's nature: "The All-Russian emperor is an autocratic and absolute monarch. God himself commands to obey His supreme power not only out of fear, but in good conscience (povinovat'sia ne tochno za strakh, no i za sovest')."[17] Reverberations of this maxim can be easily found in later foundational pronouncements of the Russian autocracy, crucial for its relationship to the noble elite. For example, Peter III of Russia's "emancipation" manifesto of 18 February 1762 honed the Petrine notion "in good conscience" in such a florid way: "We hope that all the well-born Russian Nobility [...] will remain in their most submissive loyalty and devotion to Us, and not seek to escape from service, but rather enter it willingly and zealously [...]."[18]

These ambivalences of loyalty are further highlighted from the perspective of modern philosophical reflection, ranging from David Hume's Tory-inspired argument in *On the Original Contract* (1748) that allegiance to the government is premised on a pragmatic sense of the "apparent interests and necessities of human society,"[19] rather than on people's tacit acquiescence or moral obligation, to Josiah Royce's idealist treatise, *The Philosophy of Loyalty* (1908), to, most recently, John Kleinig's *On Loyalty and Loyalties: The Contours of a Problematic Virtue* (2014). This latter study makes a strong case for controversies over the particularistic and divisive (hence the expanding use of the word in plural), as well as anti-individualistic, properties of loyalty and its nevertheless continuous appeal as a virtue and a model of behavior:

> Whereas it is the conformist quality of conduct that constitutes it as loyal for some, for others it is a passionate attachment and/or devotedness. And whereas the unquestioning attachment of a dog is paradigmatic of loyalty for some, for others loyalty is a quality of character for which dogs are ineligible.[20]

Likewise, Kleinig addresses a complex relationship between loyalty and emotion: "[...] Loyalties are generally associated with strong feelings, because our primary loyalties are to objects with which we often strongly associate or identify ourselves—our friends, families, country, and so forth. Such identifi-

---

[16] Zitser, *The Transfigured Kingdom*, 146, 152.
[17] *Polnoe sobranie zakonov Rossiiskoi imperii, Sobranie 1-e*, vol. 6 (St. Petersburg, 1830), no. 3718.
[18] Quoted in translation from: James Cracraft, *Major Problems in the History of Imperial Russia* (Boston: Houghton Mifflin College Div., 1994), 153.
[19] David Hume, "On the Original Contract," in *Three Essays, Moral and Political: Never before Published* (London: A. Millar, 1748), 48–51.
[20] John Kleinig, *On Loyalty and Loyalties: The Contours of a Problematic Virtue* (Oxford: Oxford University Press, 2014), 1–17, 128–44, 245–66; the quote comes from p. 15.

cations can be expected to have an affective component."[21] And though "the affectivity of loyalty is not its central or determinative constituent"—after all, one can have strong feelings of loyalty and fail to be loyal at a challenging moment—the phenomenon of "affectless loyalty" suggests some deficiency:

[...] Consider [...] the loyalty of a lawyer to his client or a public servant to her minister. The lawyer and public servant may have only feelings of contempt for those they serve. Does this make it inappropriate to speak of their loyalty? Maybe, though one might argue in such cases that the affective loyalty has been transposed to abstractions—that is, to the ideals of zealous advocacy [...] or civil service.[22]

This insight invites the historian of imperial Russia to take a closer look at the role of emotions in how shifts between different modalities of political loyalty occurred or how the person of the monarch was being supplanted with a notion of the state as the principal object of loyalty.

In this light, concurring with Zitser that Peter I equated a presumed lack of the relentlessly demanded spiritual faith in the ruler's charisma with high treason, I would argue that, for all the difference in civility between Peter I's and his remote successors' regimes,[23] this secularized and vulgarized counterpart of the doctrine of justification by faith persisted well into later eras. By the same token, bureaucrats and courtiers closest to the monarch remained enmeshed in an intricate code of communication, behavior and performance that behooved them to present their loyalty as a blessed "light burden," as something far more than mere tepid conformity, and to reinforce the ruler's sense of legitimacy through a compelling display of profound, apostle-like support.

---

[21] Ibid., 16.

[22] Ibid., 17.

[23] For the purposes of this article, I approach the case of Peter's inner circle as a paradigmatic example rather than a chronological point of departure, which, I hope, somehow excuses the paper's failure to discuss the politics of loyalty under Peter's eighteenth-century successors, a truly tantalizing subject. Yet another reason for the lack of such discussion is that I seek to focus on a specific relation of the later politics of loyalty to the post-Enlightenment idiom of sentimentalism that gained circulation no earlier than the end of the eighteenth century. However, a couple of surmises about how exactly the Petrine notion of apostle-like, affective loyalty was conveyed into later eras is due here. For one, among the institutions and practices that may have maintained, evocatively, the synonymy of political allegiance and religious faith, one can suggest the Order of St. Andrew the First Called, with its proverbial motto, *For Faith and Faithfulness*. By way of implication, this link might also have been reinforced by so long-functioning an institution as the anathematization of Ivan Stepanovych Mazepa that had become part of the Orthodox liturgy after 1709. See for an excellent analysis: Nadieszda Kizenko, "The Battle of Poltava in Imperial Liturgy," *Harvard Ukrainian Studies* 31, no. 1/4 (2009–10): 227–69, here 227–44. The intensity of the apostate's demonization implied the inestimable value of the loyalty of the faithful. I am grateful to Ernest Zitser for helping me think in this direction.

On a brief historical-linguistic note, it is worth observing here that the multifarious phenomenon—or, to quote Kleinig, the "problematic virtue"—described by the English word loyalty/loyalties could not be referred to in nineteenth-century Russia by a single equally pithy Russian word (let alone the possibility of using an abstract noun of this type in plural). The Russian calque *лояльный* (*loial'nyi* often spelled earlier as *лойальный*) was not widely used until at least the late nineteenth century. For the modern English word's connotation of conformity, the nineteenth-century Russian vocabulary would have as a close approximation *верноподданный*, *верноподданство* (*vernopoddannyi*, *vernopoddanstvo*); and this particular meaning of loyal is predominant in the modern lexeme *лояльный*, today quite common (but increasingly used also in a curious, peculiarly Russian deviant meaning "tolerant, lenient"). As for the "hotter" connotation of devotedness and attachment, less pronounced in the Russian *лояльный*, it is perhaps best captured by the Russian words *верный*, *верность*; *преданный*, *преданность* (*vernyi*, *vernost'*; *predannyi*, *predannost'*), commonly used both in the nineteenth century and nowadays.[24] Noticeably, "dog-like loyalty" finds its Russian counterpart in the equally well-coined *собачья преданность* (*sobach'ia predannost'*). In a sense, this essay's subject can be defined as a persistent tension between *верноподданство* (conformity), and *преданность* (devotedness), approached historically.

Loyalty and Sentimentalism

My hypothesis is that this Petrine pattern of allegiance had long-lasting repercussions for the cultural and emotional frameworks of political loyalty in imperial Russia. Highly ambivalent and manipulative binaries of sincerity and hypocrisy, spirituality and ritualism, inner faith and outward observance, warmth and tepidness, ardent soul and cold mind, conscience and fear, and so on, continued to inform discourses and practices of loyalty—both from above and from below—long after the tragic denouement of the Tsarevich Aleksei affair. Elasticity of meanings of what was valued about loyalty provided some grounds for political contest under a stubbornly authoritarian regime, partially compensating for the lack of more institutionalized forms of politics (and at the same time hindering such institutionalization).

More particularly, I would argue, the nineteenth century witnessed a deflection of this quest for warm loyalty and sincere devotion through the prism of sentimentalism. As suggested by William M. Reddy in his often-cited book,

> in the context of the absolutist state [...] sentimentalism delivered a clear, liberatory political message. [...] The sentimentalist ideal of simple sincerity and egalitarian empathy offered

---

24 For a perceptive remark on the contemporary use of the Russian word *loial'nost'* see: Irina Borisovna Levontina, *Russkii so slovarem* (Moscow: Azbukovnik, 2010), 134–36.

one of the most important standards by which the monarchy was judged and found wanting in the years before the Revolution.[25]

It could be surmised that the Russian autocracy, for various reasons, far more successfully met the challenge of sentimentalism and appropriated respective emotional styles. While in France, according to Reddy, the sentimentalist cult of sincerity and "naturalness," as well as belief in the natural origin of good feeling, proved to be destructive during the Revolution, in Russia there were no preconditions for a similarly rapid disappointment about sentimentalism. Moreover, it came to be gradually instrumentalized by political actors. Thus, adoption of sentimentalism, as Viktor Markovich Zhivov has shown in one of his most imaginative essays, facilitated—in a very peculiar way, through such otherwise dissimilar figures as Nikolay Mikhailovich Karamzin and Fyodor Vasilyevich Rostopchin, count,—the crystallization of nationalist sentiment across a spectrum of milieus, including the imperial elite.[26]

In my view, in the realm of political loyalty a sentimentalist celebration of sincerity tended to merge with earlier patterns of allegiance and devotion that originated in the tenacious Russian Orthodox tradition of opposing grace (spirituality, authenticity, etc.) to law (ritualism, falsity, etc.). A strong case for far-reaching cultural implications of the Russian dichotomy between the glorified New Testament's grace and the wryly tolerated Old Testament's law—not reducible to religion only—has been made for the nineteenth century in two studies by Mikhail Vaiskopf, and if my argument could offer some insight, it is owed, to no small extent, to these books.[27] A more immediate factor behind the persistence of sentimentalism as related to politics may have been its importance for the education and upbringing of members of the Romanov dynasty themselves. In this respect, there were continuities over consecutive reigns, and Mikhail Nikitich Murav'ev—whose own emotional use of the sentimentalist canon has been shrewdly analyzed by Andrei Zorin[28]—for Alexander I of Russia and Vasilii Andreevich Zhukovskii[29] for Alexander II of Russia were the most prominent court teachers of sentimen-

---

[25] William M. Reddy, *The Navigation of Feeling: A Framework for the History of Emotions* (Cambridge: Cambridge University Press, 2001), 325–6.

[26] Viktor M. Zhivov, "Chuvstvitel'nyi natsionalizm: Karamzin, Rostopchin, natsional'nyi suverenitet i poiski natsional'noi identichnosti," *Novoe literaturnoe obozrenie* 91 (2008): 114–40.

[27] Mikhail Vaiskopf, *Pokryvalo Moiseia: Evreiskaia tema v epokhu romantizma* (Moscow: Mosty kul'tury, 2008); Vaiskopf, *Vliublennyi demiurg: Metafizika i erotika russkogo romantizma* (Moscow: Novoe literaturnoe obozrenie, 2012).

[28] Andrei Zorin, "Leaving Your Family in 1797: Two Identities of Mikhail Murav'ev," in *Interpreting Emotions*, ed. Steinberg and Sobol, 44–61.

[29] On Zhukovskii's major contribution (in his capacity as tutor to the Grand Duchess Aleksandra Fedorovna, the wife of the future Nicholas I), to the dynasty's culture of emotion, see: Ilya Vinitsky, *Vasily Zhukovsky's Romanticism and the Emotional History of Russia* (Evanston, IL: Northwestern University Press, 2015), esp. 179–236.

talist values but not the only ones. Private correspondence of some of the Romanovs persisted in sentimentalist rhetoric, to the point of sounding quite *passé*, as late as the second half of the nineteenth century.

The search for sincerity and emotionality permeated the practices of encounter and negotiation between the emperor and his adviser(s). Invocations of lofty feelings, heartfelt experiences and instincts of soul overwhelmed bureaucratic "advice literature" for monarchs—proposals and memoranda seeking to discuss (insofar as it was permitted by autocratic rules) the major principles of policy making. Take, for a brief example, Faddei Venediktovich Bulgarin, the well-known journalist, novelist and, at the same time, analyst (not to say, a "nose") in the service of the notorious Third Section (*Tret'e Otdelenie*) under Nicholas I of Russia. In numerous dispatches and reports to the Third Section, he never shied away from giving counsel to top bureaucrats and, by implication, Nicholas I on how to maintain and enhance the loyalty of various groups of imperial subjects. In 1828, he suggested a kind of emotional *rapprochement* between Nicholas I and the increasingly discontented Polish aristocracy:

> Any just person, loyal to the Sovereign, would say that the good of the millions [...] and the benefits of Russia demand that decisive measures be undertaken so as to calm minds in Poland [...] and so the Poles feel the Sovereign's concern about their fate [and] attach themselves to Him in their hearts. [...] It would suffice to steer their enthusiasm to make most faithful and dedicated subjects out of them.[30]

Loyalty is presented here as a matter of gratitude for the emperor's sincerity and candor to be displayed in a series of bold public gestures.

In a sense, nineteenth-century political culture continued to demand warm emotionality from rulers themselves. Emperors and their heirs were particularly exposed to intense expectations—in a range of milieus—of showing sublime sensibilities. Evidence is abundant. Reminiscing in the late 1850s about Nicholas I's 1826 coronation, Mikhail Alexandrovich Dmitriev, the poet and retired official, found much hope for the newly enthroned son of Nicholas, Alexander II, in the perceived stark contrast between what one would call the affective dispositions of the father and the son (made evident as early as 1826, precisely at the former's coronation, when the latter was a child):

> Nicholas Pavlovich recited the credo loudly and pluckily [*molodetski*]. To tell the truth, during all this most august ceremony I failed to observe in his face not only any warm feeling but even the merest veneration. He did everything somewhat bravely, briskly [...] as though not in a cathedral but on a parade ground! The little heir apparent, the presently ruling Emperor Alexander II, eight years old at that time, stood next to the Grand Duchess

---

[30] [Faddei Venediktovich Bulgarin], *Vidok Figliarin: Pis'ma i zapiski F.V. Bulgarina v III Otdelenie*, ed. A.I. Reitblat (Moscow: Novoe literaturnoe obozrenie, 1998), 353.

Elena Pavlovna, softly sobbing the whole time: obviously, this ritual, majestic and sacred, moved his tender adolescent heart.[31]

To Dmitriev, this contrast found its extension in the realm of loyalty—if Nicholas insisted on subservience and obsequiousness, Alexander was believed to have a "simple soul" associated with true loyalty and obedience "in good conscience," as the above-quoted *Ecclesiastical Regulation* would demand: "I wish [...] one thing—that the damned flattery that enveloped his father like a cloud of incense would cease lest it taint his simple soul with its stink!"[32]

The glimpse in Dmitriev's recollections of the weeping young Tsesarevich is anything but occasional. The theme of the "most august" tears is a recurrent motif in the discourse on royal emotions throughout the nineteenth century. At his own coronation in 1856, Alexander II projected the image of a deeply feeling, impressionable, almost self-sacrificing—and weeping—ruler:

> The Sovereign was walking [from the Assumption Cathedral] quite slowly, tears seemed to be welling in his eyes, a sadness and spiritual confusion were expressed in his whole face [...] I noticed tears in the eyes of all those around. He stirred in all of them a feeling of pity and heartfelt grief, looking just as if he were buckling under the weight of his crown, just as if he were the innocent victim of an insuperable destiny.[33]

Thus, at that juncture the impression of the sovereign's frailty, accentuated by imagined or real tears in his eyes, may have provoked even deeper loyalty, and the Christological allusions in the above-quoted description were quite meaningful, signaling the necessity of a revitalized sense of faithfulness.

Moreover, as it seems, feelings of compassion for the ruling monarch or his heir apparent, even if appearing sometimes gratuitous and conveyed in a trite, conventional parlance, were regarded in the framework of what Richard S. Wortman has called the "dynastic scenario"[34] as an implicit attribute of a truly "warm," singularly experienced loyalty as opposed to mere conformity, *vernopoddanstvo*. In 1837 Iosif Viel'gorskii, the young count, Tsesarevich Alexander's companion and would-be adviser (had he not died next year), exclaimed at the sight of exuberant mobs that welcomed Alexander in Kostroma—a form of popular acclaim that had not been much encouraged by Russian monarchs previously: "When one comes to think about the Grand Duke's destiny, about what is in store for him, and takes a look at him, young,

---

[31] Mikhail Alexandrovich Dmitriev, *Glavy iz vospominanii moei zhizni* (Moscow: Novoe literaturnoe obozrenie, 1998), 247.
[32] Ibid., 248.
[33] Obolensky's diary of 13 September 1856 (a few weeks after the coronation: *Zapiski kniazia Dmitriia Aleksandrovicha Obolenskogo* (St. Petersburg: Nestor-Istoriia, 2005), 140.
[34] Wortman, *Scenarios of Power*, vol. 1, part 4.

blossoming in his beauty, happy, with no experience of grief, one can't help but be moved to tears."[35] (In hindsight, this sounds prophetic.)

The Rulers' Emotional Tutors

In a characteristic way, the emotionality-loyalty nexus was embodied in persons who could be called "emotional mentors"—or, perhaps more accurately, "affective tutor-guides"—of the actual or future ruler. Not necessarily all informal advisers sought to cultivate a certain emotional regime in their relationship to their august advice-receiver.[36] But those who strove to procure direct and informal access to the ear of an emperor or tsesarevich and claimed to be thinking and feeling in unison with him, presenting their loyalty, in an unmistakably sentimentalist way, as unique and undivided, the only exception to, and refuge from, the "dry," "cold", and "soulless" ways of the "court" or *camarilla* (of which some of them were in fact members). Emotional influence on the ruler by the most successful of them would interfere with decision-making mechanics and specific policies and measures; to no less an extent, it could have set up a tone in broader politics of imperial loyalty.

One such imperial "affective tutor-guide" was Iakov Ivanovich Rostovtsev, general in the second cohort of the military elite under Nicholas I,[37] but later,

---

[35] Quoted in: Ekaterina Liamina and Natal'ia Samover, *"Bednyi Zhozef": Zhizn' i smert' Iosifa Viel'gorskogo; opyt biografii cheloveka 1830-kh godov* (Moscow: Jazyki russkoi kul'tury, 1999), 163.

[36] For the early nineteenth century, Richard S. Wortman has examined particular cases of the intelligent officials and courtiers (first of all, Ivan Ivanovich Dmitriev and Nikolai M. Karamzin), whom the sentimentalist ethos of the time and their own literary imaginations helped to forge a personal bond of friendship with the monarch, their pessimism about the government's workings notwithstanding. Richard S. Wortman, *The Development of a Russian Legal Consciousness* (Chicago: University of Chicago Press, 1976), 125–31. The emotional tutors that appear on these pages shared in a specific culture of sentimentalism but were more optimistic as regards the emperor's capability to improve institutions.

[37] The story of Rostovtsev's famous first encounter with Nicholas on 12 December 1825, when the young officer alerted the then grand duke and future emperor to the threat of a rebellion in the army, and, in doing so, presumably did not betray any of his friends, involved in the current Decembrist conspiracy, has recently received a measure of attention from Russian historians. See Tat'iana Vasil'evna Andreeva, *Tainye obshchestva v Rossii v pervoi treti XIX veka: Pravitel'stvennaia politika i obshchestvennoe mnenie* (St. Petersburg: Liki Rossii, 2009), 603–6. Although Rostovtsev's motives remain not fully disclosed (and some historians have even identified him as an agent of a court faction seeking to intimidate Nicholas and thus preclude his enthronement), this case seems to me representative of the larger issue of the Decembrists' ambiguous loyalties, a situation in which taking part in a secret society might not undermine at all one's allegiance to the monarch, the secrecy itself being considered a shield against the persecution by the

mostly from 1858 to 1860, Alexander II's confidant and, despite a lack of special expertise, the leading figure in the legislative process of the emancipation of serfs. Elsewhere, I have tried to describe Rostovtsev's role as the tsar's reformist *alter ego* who taught and coaxed Alexander into the elevated image of a "reformer-liberator," transcending a plethora of partisan interests and selflessly bent on reconciling deadly antagonisms between two social classes. This symbolic representation found its way into the very fabric of the 19 February legislation.[38]

Regarding this essay's subject, it would make sense to point to Rostovtsev's language of emotional loyalty. As early as seven years before Alexander's enthronement, in a notice hastily written at the moment of a grave illness, Rostovtsev formulated his credo as a man born to serve Alexander:

> With all the power of my soul I love and esteem the kind, dear, honest, cautious, tactful, warm, and thoughtful Grand Duke Alexander Nikolaevich. He fully understands the conditions of this age. I am praying to God that both of my sons will die for Him, as honest people ought to die in His Reign; it will be grave.[39]

One of the key words here is the epithet "warm" associated in this sentimentalist idiom—as well as in the vocabulary of religious feelings—with sincerity, authenticity, and permanence ("warm faith," *teplaia vera*). In a later *profession de foi*, also written as a diary entry, Rostovtsev, by that time a top figure at Emperor Alexander's side, described himself as a devoted soldier of the monarch, embattled by the *camarilla*: "The envy of a vile camarilla rises against me. [...] The camarilla cares about neither the interest of the Fatherland, nor love for the Sovereign, nor respect for laws." The notice abruptly stops short, saying: "You poor, poor autocratic monarchs"—an exclamation that referred to the motif of the autocrat's tragic loneliness and the uniqueness of genuine loyalty.[40]

Rostovtsev died in 1860, even before the emancipation legislation for which he had been struggling (though not always quite as nobly as he imag-

---

monarch's nominally high-positioned yet in fact unworthy servitors. This of course is more likely to be true for the earlier (proto-)Decembrist groups than for the less conciliatory and more conspiratorial "northern" and especially "southern" societies. As for the competing interpretations of Rostovtsev's action on 12 December, I side with the one that seeks to explain it from the perspective of the man's persistent political self-perception and emotive predispositions: Fedor Sevast'ianov, "'Postupok' Ia. I. Rostovtseva 12 dekabria 1825 g.: Popytka rekonstruktsii politicheskikh vzgliadov istoricheskogo deiatelia," in: *Dekabristy: Aktual'nye problemy i novye podkhody*, ed., Oksana I. Kiianskaia, (Moscow: Rossiiskii gosudarstvennyi gumanitarnyi universitet, 2008), 343–66.

[38] Mikhail Dolbilov, "Rozhdenie imperatorskikh reshenii: Monarkh, sovetnik i 'vysochaishaia volia' v Rossii XIX veka," *Istoricheskie zapiski* 9 (2006): 5–48.

[39] A brief private note on a separate sheet of paper, June 23, 1848: ll. 12–12v, 12v–10, d. 286, op. 1, f. 1155, Gosudarstvennyi Arkhiv Rossiiskoi Federatsii [State Archives of the Russian Federation] (hereafter GARF).

[40] An undated note, not earlier than November 1848: ll. 2–3v, d. 14, op. 1, f. 1155, GARF.

ined) was promulgated. However, Alexander appropriated his model of emotional guidance and even many years later continued to look for an outside moral authority to confirm and validate what he did or ought to feel about politics. In 1876, in the midst of the Balkan crisis and on the eve of a war with Turkey, faced with the disturbing rise of political Panslavism,[41] he confided to his mistress, Princess Ekaterina Mikhailovna Dolgorukova, that he was happy to read two recent articles by Mikhail Nikiforovich Katkov, the editor of *Moskovskie vedomosti* (Moscow News) and one of the leading shapers of public opinion,

> car personne ne sait me comprendre mieux que lui et éprouver tout ce que j'éprouve dans des moments pareils comme celui de hier en présence de l'enthousiasme général qui s'est emparé de tout le monde à la suite de mon discours [a speech delivered earlier in Moscow, cautiously responding to the rise of Panslavist sentiment, M. D.].

> (because nobody can understand me better than he can and feel all that I feel at the moments like that of yesterday, in the presence of the general enthusiasm that has seized all the people, following my speech.)[42]

The words "nobody can understand me better than he can and feel all that I feel" present Katkov as if felicitously divining Alexander's feelings, though in reality he shared with the emperor a certain "emotional community" and therefore was able to not just voice but also partly shape the ruler's affective dispositions. On a similar occasion in January 1878, when the Russian army, after several months of fighting and besieging, at last managed to roll the Ottomans back and was advancing in the direction of Constantinople, Alexander (who had returned from the theater of war only a month before) wrote to Dolgorukova, complaining about the British diplomatic intervention:

> Mais il faut avouer que la conduite des Anglais à notre égard est infâme et notre honneur ne nous permet plus de le supporter plus longtemps [...] Oh! que je fus heureux de voir que tu comprenais si bien tout ce qui se passait en moi en apprenant cette nouvelle infamie anglaise. Au reste cela ne peut pas être autrement quand on ne forme qu'un seul être au moral, comme au physique.

> (One has to admit that the conduct of the English toward us is vile, and our honor does not allow us to tolerate it any longer [...] Oh! I was so happy to see how well you understood all that passed in me when I learnt about this new English infamy. But it cannot be otherwise as we form a single being morally, as well as physically.)[43]

---

[41] On Alexander's gradually growing exposure to the influence of Panslavist agitation, as well as decision-making that led up to the declaration of war in April 1877, see: A.V. Mamonov, "Samoderzhavie i 'slavianskoe dvizhenie' v Rossii v 1875–1877 godakh," *Otechestvennaia istoriia* 3 (2004): 60–77.

[42] Emperor Alexander II to Princess Ekaterina Mikhailovna Dolgorukova, 30 October/ 11 November 1876, l. 9v, d. 108, op. 2, f. 678, GARF.

[43] Emperor Alexander II to Princess Ekaterina Mikhailovna Dolgorukova, 28 January/ 9 February, 1878, ll. 33–33v, d. 119, op. 2, f. 678, GARF.

The very wording (it is not about mere like-mindedness, but understanding "tout ce qui se passait en moi"—all that passed in me) is indicative of the emperor's cultivated need for an empathizing addressee of his politically charged emotions.

Alexander II's son and (from 1865) heir apparent, Grand Duke Alexander Aleksandrovich, too, had persons at his side who claimed the mantle of the future ruler's "emotionality tutor." Perhaps the most aspirant of them was Vladimir Petrovich Meshcherskii, prince and in the 1860s a not particularly prominent civil official (who boasted, however, an aristocratic pedigree and connections at the imperial court) but later notorious right-wing nationalistic journalist. Along with a number of the tsesarevich's teachers and advisers, Meshcherskii actively participated in what Richard S. Wortman has termed "the fashioning of a Russian tsar"—making the future Alexander III

appear Russian by stressing particular features that distinguished him from the Westernized court and that they defined as national. [...] They made uncouthness and unsociability signs of the authenticity and candor of the Russian man, untouched by the duplicity of Western culture. [...] His taciturnity and difficulties with verbal expression became signs of inner certainty, the intimidating silence of the epic hero.[44]

This discursive reversal, however, was not Meshcherskii's initial plan. As is clear from his extensive private correspondence with Alexander, during the second half of the 1860s he had been seeking to affect the tsesarevich's "uncouth" personality far more straightforwardly, in order to make him more sociable and responsive to nationally (or even nationalistically) minded Russians—that is, ultimately, to make him more emotional. What ran through Meshcherskii's letters over several years is the sentimentalist trope of friendship—friendship as the young heir's almost sole escape from all kinds of falsity surrounding and haunting him at court. A grandson of N.M. Karamzin, Meshcherskii often resorted to the rhetoric of a once happy yet now unrequited love: "Those people could not touch Your soul, but I experienced the charm of this touch, of this exchange of thoughts and feelings, in whose midst glimmered sweet moments of hope for a bright future!"[45]

In 1869, at the critical moment when he thought he was about to lose Alexander's favor and "touch" to his soul forever, Meshcherskii forcefully developed the theme of Karamzin as the founder of a long-lasting familial tradition of personal devotion to the dynasty. His maddeningly lengthy letter to Alexander of 12 August 1869 interspersed with the open expressions of jealousy toward other intimate acquaintances of the tsesarevich and mixing confession with sermonizing, gives us a glimpse into how affective loyalty could be thought of as a kind of hereditary privilege, a spiritual gift that separated

---

[44] Wortman, *Scenarios of Power*, vol. 2, 178.
[45] Vladimir Petrovich Meshcherskii, *Pis'ma k velikomu kniaziu Aleksandru Aleksandrovichu, 1863–1868*, ed. N. V. Chernikova (Moscow: Novoe literaturnoe obozrenie, 2011), 205.

the elect from, as he put it, "people, this crowd [*liudi, etot sonm*] referred to in French by 'on'" (a linguistically inventive reincarnation of Rostovtsev's *camarilla*) and incapable to understand "[my] certain warmed and luminous feeling of attachment to you." Meshcherskii strove to argue that his friendship with Alexander must be the fulfillment of a double testament—if to him it had come from the grandfather, Alexander was to have inherited it from his elder brother, Nicholas, who had prematurely died in 1865 and to whom Meshcherskii had sought to be a confidant as well:

> My mother, Karamzin's daughter, inherited all the noble fervor and glow of his soul, love for the Sovereign and lofty love for the State. With her vivid reminiscences of the friendship between Emperor Alexander I and Karamzin, and especially [that of Karamzin and] the young Nicholas [I] in the first year of his reign [...] she was able to keep all this world at the level of something sacred, [...] so I as early as 15, 16 years old started to live by a certain striving, incomprehensible to me, to achieve the happiness of befriending the One who seemed to me the future ideal [...] I yearned to be his [the young Grand Duke Nicholas Aleksandrovich's, M. D.] Karamzin.[46]

In this setting, loyalty emerged as a sincere, exceptional devotion of the few truly "warm": "If God grants him [the Grand Duke Alexander Aleksandrovich, M. D.] two or three honest, warm and Russian [sic] people to help him in his current maturation, many bright hopes can be placed in him!"[47] Chastising Alexander—in an ostentatiously candid, "truth-delivering" tone—for aloofness and the indiscriminately ungracious treatment of people, Meshcherskii further elaborated the binary of tepid compliance and warm loyalty:

> Not limiting the reform of your court to getting more hirelings, you will clean up this world profoundly and bring into it truth, a loyalty that is not feigned and not timorous; joy, not tension; trust, not fear; kindheartedness and service instead of servility; and true light instead of false luster.[48]

Can this be read as a paraphrase of Peter the Great's *Ecclesiastical Regulation*—"God Himself commands to obey His [the emperor's, M. D.] supreme power not only out of fear, but in good conscience"[49]—couched in the grandiloquent parlance of nineteenth-century sensibilities?

The Notion of the "Russian in Soul"

The phenomenon of a political loyalty that was divided and redistributed between the person of the ruler and a certain impersonalized notion of the state

---

[46] Vladimir Petrovich Meshcherskii, *Pis'ma k velikomu kniaziu Aleksandru Aleksandrovichu, 1869–1878*, ed. N. V. Chernikova (Moscow: Novoe literaturnoe obozrenie, 2014), 191, 195.
[47] Meshcherskii, *Pis'ma k velikomu kniaziu 1863–1868*, 143.
[48] Ibid., 179.
[49] *Polnoe sobranie zakonov Rossiiskoi imperii, Sobranie 1-e*, vol. 6 (St. Petersburg, 1830), no. 3718.

or a patriotic concept of Russia, detectable as early as the eighteenth century, expanded with the rise of nationalist sentiment in the nineteenth century.[50] Telling, for example, is the case of a number of Decembrists who cultivated a pronounced patriotism while condemning (along with N.M. Karamzin) Alexander I for his cosmopolitanism, dynastic legitimism, and pro-Polish sympathies. Emotionality and manipulations with it proved to be crucial for this mode of loyalty as well.

Below I will address the functioning of one of the most emotionally charged idioms that from the early nineteenth century on served to invoke and celebrate a certain regime of feeling about Russia, marked as particularly warm and sincere. This is the notion of *russkii v dushe* (Russian in soul)—a kind of fixture in the political (and broader) lexicon of the day, though with a meaning that may not be self-evident nowadays. Moreover, the emotions implied by this label would come to interplay with imperial loyalties in a remarkably complex way.

As I have argued elsewhere,[51] the expression *russkii v dushe* entered the politically oriented vocabulary at the beginning of the nineteenth century. Very probably, it originated from the French expressions *français dans l'âme* and *français au fond du cœur* that had been widely used in the eighteenth century. After the war of 1812, the term assumed the function of meaningful patriotic cliché. For example, Alexander Sergeyevich Pushkin in a short sketch known under the title *An Imagined Conversation with Alexander I* compared Ivan Nikitich Inzov, general and his superior in Chișinău, with Mikhail Semënovich Vorontsov, count and governor general of Novorossia, whom he detested: "[...] General Inzov is a brave and honest old man, he is Russian in soul; he does not favor the first English rascal he meets over his own compatriots, known and unknown."[52] Most frequently, this label was used to denote not so much a hidden (as seems to be implied by "v dushe") but a spontaneous, unfeigned, "lived" sense of Russianness, as distinct from an official and dry compliance with certain Russian ways.

---

[50] In an insightful essay, Claudio Ingerflom argues that the idea of the impersonal state under Peter the Great was still fairly vague: Claudio Sergio Nun Ingerflom, "'Loyalty to the State' under Peter the Great? Return to the Sources and the Historicity of Concepts," in *Loyalties, Solidarities, and Identities in Russian Society, History, and Culture*, ed. Philip Ross Bullock, Andy Byford, Claudio Nun Ingerflom, Isabelle Ohayon, Maria Rubins, and Anna Winestein (London: School of Slavonic and East European Studies, University College London, 2013), 3–19.

[51] Mikhail Dolbilov, "'Poliak' v imperskom politicheskom leksikone," in *'Poniatiia o Rossii': K istoricheskoi semantike imperskogo perioda*, vol. 2., ed. Aleksei I. Miller, Denis A. Sdvizhkov, and Ingrid Schierle (Moscow: Novoe literaturnoe obozrenie, 2012), 292–339.

[52] Alexander Sergeyevich Pushkin, *Polnoe sobranie sochinenii*, vol. 11, Kritika i publitsistika, 1819–1843 (Moscow: Izdatel'stvo Akademii nauk SSSR, 1949), 23–4. A thorough analysis of *An Imagined Conversation with Alexander I* in the context of Pushkin's monarchical loyalties (and the lack thereof), see: Mark Al'tshuller, *Mezhdu dvukh tsarei: Pushkin, 1824–1836* (St. Petersburg: Akademicheskii proekt, 2003), 20–27.

Most pertinent to our present subject are attempts made by imperial policy-makers to translate the metaphorical notion of the "Russian in soul" into specific criteria and practices of loyalty. One of them, closely related to the Romanovs' idiosyncratic understanding of personal loyalty, was undertaken by Nicholas I in 1838 when negotiating with the young Maximilian de Beauharnais, Duke of Leuchtenberg, on the issue of the latter's match with Nicholas's daughter, Grand Duchess Maria Nikolaievna. The projected marriage was not a simple matter at all. Maximilian was coming from a European aristocratic milieu too alien, both culturally and politically, to the Romanov dynasty—he was the son of Eugène de Beauharnais, Napoleon I of France's stepson, and a Roman Catholic, a close relation on his maternal side to the ruling Bavarian dynasty; besides, in the hierarchy of European royalty he was inferior to a daughter of the Russian emperor.

Stooping to the future couple's feelings, Nicholas set several conditions for what to him smacked of a *mésalliance*. Some of them, being formal, were stipulated in a special oath of allegiance to Nicholas that Maximilian swore and signed; thus, he pledged to settle and live with Maria in Russia and to have all their children baptized into Orthodoxy. Other expectations were less formal and legible, suggesting more of a spiritual and emotional initiation. "I have announced him that I demand that he from now on consider himself a member of *our family* and therefore Russian in soul and body,"[53] wrote Nicholas to his son and heir, Grand Duke Alexander Nikolaevich, who was at the time traveling abroad. The expression "Russian in soul and body" sounded so compelling that Alexander immediately reciprocated it to his father, writing from Venice that he thanked God that "I bear *the name of Russian* and that it is to *Russia* that I belong in soul and body."[54]

Being "Russian in soul and body," however, demanded less of the Duke of Leuchtenberg than of the tsesarevich. Nicholas did not insist on Maximilian's conversion to Orthodoxy; nor, as it seems, was he concerned with the lack in his prospective son-in-law of eagerness to learn Russian. Instead, Maximilian was subjected by Nicholas to a series of more or less surreptitious tests involving a broadly defined respect for Russian tradition, as well as guards-style camaraderie and bravado. It ranged from shooting crows (the Russian character of this amusement was accentuated by Nicholas's comment that the outing did not go so well, as "our crows, upon hearing a foreign language, do not get too close"[55] to traveling for forty-seven hours, in a carriage on the ice-crusted road, from St. Petersburg to Moscow, culminating in Maximilian's introduction to the Muscovite public at a service in the Assumption Cathedral (Uspenskii Sobor): "Upon entering the cathedral our Max kissed the

---

[53] Larisa G. Zakharova and Sergei V. Mironenko, eds., *Perepiska tsesarevicha Aleksandra Nikolaevicha s imperatorom Nikolaem I, 1838–1839* (Moscow: ROSSPEN, 2008), 158.
[54] Ibid., 165.
[55] Ibid., 171.

cross [...] and even kissed the bishop's hand the way we do [...], and word of this immediately spread across the city and everyone liked it."[56]

Yet, even after passing these tests successfully, Maximilian's humble request that his Bavarian relatives be invited to attend his wedding with Maria was turned down: "It is necessary for Max to be here alone at this moment and appear as Russian before the Russians! (Later we will be glad to welcome all of them here) but let our Max first *get Russified*, and sincerely [prezhde nash Maks *obrusei*, i iskrenno)!"[57]

"Let our Max first *get Russified*, and sincerely!" was of course a very far cry from Peter the Great's intimidating ultimatum to Tsarevich Aleksei, "to see if *without hypocrisy* you convert [pozhdat', ashche *nelitsemerno* obratish'sia]," but "sincerity" was here, too, the key criterion for one's loyalty in the making, defined again in an arbitrary and manipulative fashion.

By the mid-nineteenth century, the idiom of "Russian in soul" assumed new, nationalistic overtones. Some of its proponents strove to endow it with clearer and more binding meanings, adding also to its emotional components. A noticeable case of the initial success and eventual failure of this effort is that of Petr Alekseevich Bessonov, a Slavophilic folklorist and journalist who for a short period of time in the mid-1860s, after the 1863 January Uprising in the Kingdom of Poland and the Western provinces, happened to serve in an educational position in Vil'na/Vilnius (the so-called Northwestern *krai*), crucial for the governmental policy of enhancing loyalties and reshaping ethno-national identities of local populations. Bessonov sought to promote a balanced vision of state-driven Russification that would reconcile the homogenizing spread of Russian language and culture (and, to a lesser degree, Orthodox faith), on the one hand, and a cautious fostering of the non-Russian groups' cultural and religious distinctiveness, on the other. In particular, he experimented with the acculturation of the Jews by means of Russian-language school instruction and translation of Judaic scripture and

---

[56] Ibid., 193.

[57] Ibid., 332–3. Nicholas's interest in testing Maximilian's presumed Russianness both morally *and physically*, as well as, more generally, the weighty bodily implications of the "Russian in soul/heart" notion (weeping, laughter, bows, postures, kisses, blushing, handshakes, hugs, drinking toasts, etc.), in my view, fit neatly with Monique Scheer's methodological suggestions on how to detect "emotional practices" in the primary sources traditionally used by historians: "How do we know when a source is talking about an emotion? The use of language that links the body with the mind (metaphors that vary culturally and change over time) can serve as a signpost such as when actors speak of their 'blood boiling,' when they 'feel' and 'sense' their thoughts, or describe a physical space or movement in their immaterial, 'inner' parts. In these cases, the experience of emotions is very often described as a merging of body and mind [recall also Alexander II's phrase in the above-quoted 1878 letter about "[us constituting] a single being morally, as well as physically," M. D.], as a physical involvement in thought. Shifts in this language will likely be accompanied by shifts in bodily practices, as they support one another." Scheer, "Are Emotions a Kind of Practice," 218.

prayers into Russian while not encroaching on most forms of traditional Jewish religiosity.[58]

This program—integration without homogenizing excesses—suggested the idea of various levels—or perhaps circles—of interiorized loyalty, formulated by Bessonov in one of his official memoranda. He distinguished between the two principal notions—"loyal Russian subject" and "Russian in heart" (actually, the equivalent of the French *au fond du cœur* and a paraphrase of the "Russian in soul"): "Any inorodets [a widely used designation of several categories of non-Russians, mostly in the Empire's eastern parts and/or deemed to be less civilized than the Russians, M. D.] [...] who strictly adheres to the oath of loyalty and, furthermore, does not detach himself from Russian societal development recognized by the authorities can be a loyal Russian subject," whereas "only a genuine Russian, that is, Russian by ethnicity, language and nation [...] by Orthodox faith" could claim to be "Russian in heart."[59] Even if the former obviously did not boil down to mere docility and compliance, requiring also participation in "Russian societal development recognized by the authorities," the latter implied a far more intimate and emotional embrace of Russian identity and was, in the final account, to draw a sharp line between ethnic Russians and even Russianized non-Russians (avoiding the extremes of forcible assimilation or segregation).

Bessonov's reflection on loyalty, however, led up to his own trustworthiness being called into question by his fellow Russifiers. His close informal contacts with reform-minded Jews (*maskilim*) in Vil'na incurred suspicions of some hidden motives. "He is positively Orthodox, Russian, though for some reason is inclined toward the Jews," wrote one of his superiors to St. Petersburg, as if denying him the right to be "Russian in heart" according to his own formula.[60] Even more important, Bessonov failed to fit with an "emotional community" in the midst of fellow officials of the Ministry of Public Education (Ministerstvo narodnogo prosveshcheniia) who had come to this Polish-influenced borderland (officially labeled as a "Russian country from time immemorial") mostly from St. Petersburg or Moscow and were combating the sense of Polish cultural preeminence by clinging to a set of ostentatiously Russian (or so they were supposed to look) forms of in-group conviviality and public conduct. In Bessonov's sarcastic depiction of "performances" staged by this "pedagogical circle," the notion of "Russian in

---

[58] See more in Mikhail Dolbilov, *Russkii krai, chuzhaia vera: Etnokonfessional'naia politika imperii v Litve i Belorussii pri Aleksandre II* (Moscow: Novoe literaturnoe obozrenie, 2010), chapter 9.

[59] L. 15, b. 1204, ap. 6, f. 567, Lietuvos valstybės istorijos archyvas [Lithuanian State Historical Archives] (hereafter LVIA), Vilnius.

[60] Ivan P. Kornilov, *Russkoe delo v Severo-Zapadnom krae: Materialy dlia istorii Vilenskogo uchebnogo okruga preimushchestvenno v murav'evskuiu epokhu*, 2nd ed. (St. Petersburg, 1908), 214.

soul" is shown to have worked as a yardstick for one's affective conformity, and it is worth quoting at length:

> The subordinates were receiving official notifications from the circle, written on letterhead: "On a certain day, Mr. so-and-so has his name day or birthday; we need to get together and prepare a surprise" [...]. On the arranged day, they should get together in a certain garden or wood near the dacha, then suddenly appear, some singing an improvised service for the health [...], some with small bottles of vodka, lanterns, illumination for the night. The waves of the Vilia [the river Neris, M. D.] at nighttime would carry the rumble of celebration far. Having gotten drunk, the guest ought to show himself a truly Russian man, to prove that his is a "Russian soul indeed" [...] which meant chairing [throwing up in the air, M. D.] the hero of the occasion, going from the dacha up to the Antokol' hills [...] singing "Vniz po matushke po Volge" [Downstream Little Mother Volga] etc. Not only was a renegade threatened on the spot, not only did people burst into his office or home with threats, but also he was denounced to St. Petersburg that, say, "the pedagogical circle had a celebration in the name of Russian unity, and Mr. so-and-so did not take part or aroused suspicion; so would you be so kind, Your Excellency, as to rid the united Russian family of him [...] for the good of the province. Most of all, the offender was blamed for his *mind* [...] "Mind we don't need, in this province the mind is not required," scoundrels were hugged and kissed, with words like this: "Well, chap, whatever they say about you, you are a Russian soul, you have a Russian heart!" [...] A man who was suspected of possessing a full mental faculty was dishonored by the circle's agitators. It is horrid to remember this fateful month of July [1866, M. D.] [...]⁶¹

The way of demanding and asserting political loyalty described above is essentially emotional, centered on public gesture and bodily practices (hugging, kissing, cheering, and chairing) no less than on ideology and value systems, a kind of in-group conviviality notably reminiscent of the meaningful rites of Peter I's "All-Drunken Council (Vsep'ianeishii Sobor)."⁶² Invocation of the "Russian soul/heart" extends to the point of opposing it to "mind,"—a constitutive binary indicative of the showily populist and plebeian slant of emerging Russian nationalism.⁶³ Interestingly, even a folk song sung when sitting on the top of a hill by a river may have reflected the emotionally loaded antinomy of anguish and hope. As observed by Mikhail Vaiskopf, the trope of singing by a foreign river, alluding to the lines "By the rivers of Babylon we sat and wept when we remembered Zion" from Psalm 137 (in the Russian Orthodox Bible numbered 136), had been long appropriated by the "musical-patriotic metaphysics of Russian romanticism."⁶⁴ From this perspective, a

---

61 L. 90, 87, d. 384, f. 56, Otdel pis'mennykh istochnikov Gosudarstvennogo Istoricheskogo Muzeiia (hereafter OPI GIM), Moscow.
62 Here I refer mostly to Ernest Zitser's interpretation, in his *The Transfigured Kingdom*, of the "All-Drunken Council" as a loyalty-building project. Zitser, *The Transfigured Kingdom*, passim.
63 On how the soul-mind binary was a decade later exploited in the so-called popular literature with a special goal of rekindling feelings of loyalty to the monarch among the lower classes, see: Il'ia Vinitskii, "O diade Gordee i zhide Leibe (Pouchitel'nyi sluchai iz istorii russkoi 'literatury dlia naroda')," *Novoe literaturnoe obozrenie* 93 (2008): 129–154.
64 Vaiskopf, *Vliublennyi demiurg*, 530–1.

famous song about the Volga resounding over the waters of quite another river, the Vilia, was both an assertion of the land's declared Russianness and an indirect expression of the singers' nagging sense of being so far from their true homeland—an unsettling mixture of nationalist feelings indeed. Bessonov, so keen on rationalizing the processes of Russification, failed this emotionality test.

Attesting once more to the manipulative nature of the "Russian in soul" idiom, this story also points to some evolution in thinking about the addressee of feelings of loyalty. Those performers of *Vniz po matushke po Volge*, though officials in imperial service, hardly associated themselves with the person of the ruler more than with a possibly vague yet still evocative image of Russia (or a nation?). However, in that era various combinations of affective attachment to the dynasty and emotional commitment to the state/nation were still viable. For example, another middle-ranking official in Vil'na, in a private letter, condemned the newly appointed governor general, Eduard Baranov—a man of Lutheran faith and Baltic German descent and a courtier very close to Alexander II—for his lack of energy on behalf of the "Russian cause," but profusely praised him for his love for the tsar, waxing even sentimental: "I am unable to name it–a personal, private love for the Sovereign, a very subtle and tender feeling [...] which I very much like in him."[65]

Loyalty, Emotion and Religion

At certain critical moments of crisis, challenge, or endeavor, a similar search for sincerity[66] and demand for spiritualized loyalty could extend beyond the circle of court politics or nationalist-minded elites to lower strata and groups of the population. One such juncture was the realm of imperial religious policies. As is well-known, while celebrating and uplifting Orthodoxy as the "ruling and predominant faith," the imperial rulers condescended—more or less readily—to tolerate a number of other religions, Christian and non-Christian, in their status as "recognized by the state." Moreover, their existence and their believers' commitment to the "fathers' faith" was often presented as crucial for the state's stability and domestic order. Thus, the religious sphere was subject to a kind of dialectics of tolerance and intolerance, the former associated with the regularizing—*Polizeistaat* or Josephinist—approach to religion, the latter, with the largely laudable Orthodox zeal, piety, and "warmth." By the mid-nineteenth century, a set of administrative practices was developed to assess or forecast the measure of loyalty through the supposed collective

---

[65] M.F. De Pule to P.A. Bessonov, April 12, 1867, ll. 123–123v, d. 515, f. 56, OPI GIM.
[66] On usages of the trope of sincerity in different sites (including politics of religion) across eras and cultures, see: Ernst van Alphen, Mieke Bal, and Carel Smith, eds., *The Rhetoric of Sincerity* (Stanford, CA: Stanford University Press, 2009).

political and cultural qualities of a certain religion and through the character and depth of particular persons' religiosity *per se*. Imperial evaluative optics were shaped by a number of basic categories: confessional discipline, the extent of insulation from religious "fanaticism," proper hierarchical organization of the relationship between clergy and laity, the proportion of spirituality versus ritualism, and ability to experience "true" religious feelings.[67]

However, the application of these categories varied whimsically from religion to religion, and was contingent on specific circumstances of region and time. Evangelical and pietistic aspirations, widespread among the imperial elite in the early nineteenth century and institutionally renounced with Nicholas I's enthronement, continued to reverberate throughout the century in the highly manipulative and politicized discourse of "inner" or "warm" faith, opposed to what could be described as an "untrue" religiosity—"false," "fanatical," "sanctimonious," "external," too ritualistic or too individualistic beliefs. In turn, this polarizing discourse exerted a strong influence on various strata's perceptions of loyalty to earthly authorities. An important variable in the implicit formulae of political loyalty, emotion played a major role in how the rulers and the ruled saw and thought about one another's religiosity.

Thus, particular assessments of this or that religious group's or milieu's loyalty did not necessarily follow the formulaic official premises of confessional policy or pieces of conventional bureaucratic wisdom. The common notions of the relative trustworthiness of various faiths with regard to their believers' real or imagined involvement in subversive political activities did not apply always and not everywhere. Thus, Roman Catholicism, especially after the 1830 uprising in Russian-ruled Poland, was intimately associated with Polish nationalism and often contrasted with Lutheranism, associated, in turn, mostly with the Baltic Germans and reputed to be a moderate and reliable faith. Yet, here and there, Catholicism and individual Catholics continued to retain an irresistible appeal in the eyes of the imperial authorities, owing to "Latinism's" time-honored hierarchy and order, the Polish Catholic nobility's persisting influence, and, not least, the aesthetic and emotional allure it held as an "aristocratic" religion. In another example, as shown recently by Robert D. Crews, Islam at the grass roots level in the Russian Empire, especially in the Volga-Ural region and Central Asia, for decades demonstrated an almost uncanny capability to interact with central and local bureaucracies in the everyday matters of religious life.[68] This, however, did not hinder many members of the same bureaucracies from nurturing and disseminating Islamophobic clichés and feelings of disgust at various aspects of Muslim religiosity. This visceral aversion to their own practices of gover-

---

[67] See especially: Paul W. Werth, *The Tsar's Foreign Faiths: Toleration and the Fate of Religious Freedom in Imperial Russia* (Oxford: Oxford University Press, 2014). My contribution to studying this subject is to be found in Dolbilov, *Russkii krai, chuzhaia vera*.
[68] Crews, *For Prophet and Tsar*.

nance, however well-established, came to affect both the imperial *imaginaire* and the formulation of broader policies toward Islam at the turn of the twentieth century.[69]

No less related to emotionality than such managerial inconsistencies was—since the 1840s—the noticeable drift in imperial religious policy toward defining "popular" religiosity in more individualistic terms. In this vein, the conformity and docility of large communities of believers were increasingly cited by officials as signs of the "people's" "simple yet firm" religiosity; likewise, an outward observance of Orthodox rituals by newly or relatively recently converted people—the former Greek Catholics in Belarus, "reunited" with the Synodal Church in 1839, or former Muslim Tatar-speaking peasants in Kazan province—came to be questioned by a number of missionaries and officials as a supposed marker of their voluntary acceptance and deep appropriation of Orthodoxy. There appeared new decrees that emphasized the task on the part of secular officials and Orthodox priests to ensure that in each particular instance conversion take place after the convert's "sincere" embrace and "clear understanding" of Orthodox teaching and dogma.[70] (At the same time, the issue of whether the very text of the oath of allegiance was intelligible to non-Russians began to be raised.) This emphasis on individual rather than collective forms of religious experience pointed to a new (and certainly different from the earlier state-sponsored pietism and evangelism under Alexander I) shift from "external" ritualism to "internal" spirituality in the bureaucracy's thinking about religion.

This shift was bound to produce conflicting results, though. That was so not only because there remained in place many secular and clerical proponents of a "simpler" and more pragmatic—and not rarely, more cynical—understanding of religiosity and motives behind conversion. What was even more important was precisely the contradiction, ingrained in the very fabric of confessional policies, between the "tepid" and the "hot," between the *Polizeistaat* regular management of properly ranked and copositioned diverse faiths and the far less "regular" and presumably charismatic (Peter the Great style) quest for spirituality in the realm of loyalty. This contradiction implied open challenges to, and crackdowns on, non-Orthodox faiths (and sometimes to the Orthodox Church itself, insofar as the secular government perceived Church leaders and institutions as rivals, labeling them in such cases as "power-seeking," "ignorant," "conniving at superstitions").

For example, the government-prescribed procedures for ensuring that conversion to Orthodoxy be undertaken in "sincere" conviction may well

---

[69] See for example: Michael A. Reynolds, *Shattering Empires: The Clash and Collapse of the Ottoman and Russian Empires, 1908–1918* (Cambridge: Cambridge University Press, 2011).

[70] This trend is reflected in contemporaneous literary writings as well—for example, in Nikolai S. Leskov's *Vladychnyi sud* and *Na kraiu sveta*.

have provoked bureaucratic arbitrariness,[71] not dissimilar to the emblematic prototype of such inquiry I have already invoked in this essay—Peter I's demand that his son Aleksei "without hypocrisy convert" to the belief, religious-cum-political, in Peter's imperial mission. At the same time, in a curious twist of this search for sincere conversion, there were cases in which secular officials, instead of overformalizing the inspection procedure, ostentatiously rejected even the basic requirements of modest tsarist legality. By doing so, they sought to create an impression of spontaneity and free will—a mass of people rushing to Orthodoxy. In such a fashion, in the aftermath of the 1863 Polish uprising, a group of middle- and lower-ranking officials in the "Northwest region" (Severo-Zapadnyi krai, roughly, present-day territories of Belarus and Lithuania)—an area most fervently contested by Russian and Polish nationalisms—arranged and instigated a campaign of converting almost eighty thousand Catholic peasants (mostly Belarusian) to Orthodoxy. Not only did these "engineers" of conversion brag of their undisguised contempt for Catholicism, but they also indiscreetly sidelined members of the *Orthodox* clergy from their quasi-missionary work and claimed a special bond to the souls of people to be converted. In their encounters with Catholic peasants, they consistently called Orthodoxy the "tsar's faith," implying that conversion to it would be the best expression of peasants' spiritual and lofty gratitude to the monarch for their recent emancipation from serfdom. (However, many Catholics had their own notion of a truly spiritual choice.) In one such case that involved a bitter dispute with Catholics over a miracle-working icon, a petty official assumed the tone of a romantic nation-builder:

> This movement has not been initiated by the Orthodox clergy and the police [...] but has grown up in the popular memory and ripened in its [the people's, M. D.] consciousness at the present propitious moment, as a grain sown in the soil grows and ripens at the propitious time [...] The faith in the original possession of the icon by the [Orthodox] church and its venerability are so deeply imprinted in the hearts of Orthodox Belarusians that neither hoary time nor historical and political vagaries could muffle this sacred feeling in them.[72]

The populist emphasis in this piece of bureaucratic prose is striking—the "popular memory" and "faith in the original possession of the icon" were op-

---

[71] Paul W. Werth, *At the Margins of Orthodoxy: Mission, Governance, and Confessional Politics in Russia's Volga-Kama Region, 1827–1905* (Ithaca: Cornell University Press, 2002), 79–95; Werth, "Changing Conceptions of Difference, Assimilation, and Faith in the Volga-Kama Region, 1740–1870," in *Russian Empire: Space, People, Power, 1700–1930*, ed. Jane Burbank, Mark von Hagen, and Anatolyi Viktorovich Remnev (Bloomington, IN: Indiana University Press, 2007), 169–95, here 181–88; and Nicholas B. Breyfogle, *Heretics and Colonizers: Religious Dissent and Russian Colonization of Transcaucasia, 1830–1890* (Philadelphia, PA: Ph.D. dissertation, University of Pennsylvania, 1998), 298–303.

[72] A petition from a group of Roman Catholics, as quoted in Dolbilov, *Russkii krai, chuzhaia vera*, 643.

posed to the formal documentary proofs that the Catholics were able to present, as "inner faith" to mere external observance.

Manipulations of the idea of "true faith" also took place in the case of those experiments with Roman Catholicism that were somewhat subtler than forced conversions to Orthodoxy. A telling example is the 1870s campaign of introduction of the Russian language (instead of Polish) into the so-called supplementary Roman Catholic church service, a policy at the intersection of nationalism, religion, and language that targeted not so much the Polish nobles (deemed mostly "incorrigible") as the Belarusian-speaking lower classes (historically deemed Russian, but not fully so in practice). In fact, it was for the first time that, in the spirit of both the anti-Polish repressions and the Great Reforms civic-mindedness, the authorities turned to the issue of the content of major Catholic prayers, read in Latin and Polish, their compatibility with the demand of political loyalty, and their comprehensibility to believers. Simply speaking, previously the government had stayed relatively uninterested in *what* exactly Catholics uttered when praying.

The prayer in Latin for the emperor and the ruling house was the focus of attention, but an assortment of highly popular hymns and chants was also affected.[73] In their effort to make the transition of believers to the newly translated religious verse as seamless as possible, the campaign's architects sought to hew closely to the song's original melody and the lyrics' rhyme and meter. In their implicit understanding, the simple-minded believers regarded melody, meter, and rhyme as sacred attributes of the faith as such, whereas a change of language (accompanied by inevitable aberrations in the meaning of religious poetry) had to do for most of them with external ritual only. At a deeper level, the loyalty of these Catholics was expected to manifest itself not so much in a grateful acceptance of prayers and songs translated into their supposedly native language as in their trust in the officials' declarations that the introduction of a Russian-language service would in no way entail a new wave of forced conversion to Orthodoxy (which certainly sounded dubious after the confessional upheavals of the previous decade in the same region). In a word, a cordial and spontaneous trust in the monarch's solemn promise of religious toleration was invited as a major emotional testimony of loyalty.

Most interestingly, a number of Catholics who were more or less brusquely encouraged to petition for a Russian-language service proved capable of appropriating the idiom of "true faith" to their own end. Also in the spirit of the Great Reforms, they invoked the newly circulated personalized idea of a sincere and therefore trustworthy faith. In their petitions to the higher au-

---

[73] Curiously, in Habsburg Galicia, the Josephinist adaptation of the politically suggestive Catholic prayers chanted by Polish-speaking believers had taken place as early as the 1790s. For example, the phrase referring to the Holy Virgin, "Queen of Poland pray for us," had been replaced by "Queen of Galicia and Lodomeria pray for us". Wolff, *The Idea of Galicia*, 53.

thorities, complaining about pressure and intimidation from lower officials, they implied that sincerely believing Catholics were more reliable subjects than those who readily accepted Orthodoxy or any major change in Catholic ritual. They meant that not conversion but precisely a continued commitment to their traditional religion, be it even a rival to Orthodoxy, would prove their firm and sincere faith and, therefore, their allegiance to the throne. In one such case, the petitioners went as far as to allude to the Russian Old Believers as an example of the compatibility of firm loyalty and sectarian dissent:

[Permit us] to pray, not changing our church service, as our fathers prayed, and if the need arises, we will prove that one can be both a good [Roman] Catholic and [at the same time] truly Russian and prove by deed that, praying according to *the old rite*, we are willing to spill the last drop of our blood for the Liberator, our Father Monarch![74]

In Lieu of a Conclusion

The most general rubric under which I could try to extract a meaningful conclusion from the above-presented loosely connected analyses is the point about the underinstitutionalization of Russian imperial politics. Indeterminate and vague (which is not synonymous with being low) standards of political loyalty were a function of, and a factor in, the poorly regularized authoritarian system of power. A range of modes of demanding and expressing one's loyalty reflected a succession of concentric circles of the broader political elite and a kind of cultural mechanics that facilitated moving through them toward the center of the whole system. What I dub—overusing, admittedly, thermic metaphors—a "hot," spiritualized, apostle-like loyalty was at once a duty and a privilege of those within the innermost circle around the ruler. This quest for "sincerity," couched throughout much of the nineteenth century in sentimentalist rhetoric, lent the stubbornly autocratic regime a degree of added legitimacy and dynamics, at the same time providing a space for cultural and ideological manipulation of authority. In this realm, important decisions or actions came to be framed by sentiments of friendship, confidence, hope, compassion, mutual understanding, etc.—as well as by their opposites. In a sense, changing modes of emotionality surrounding the encounters between the monarch and those seeking to influence her or him were at the root of a fairly flexible system of interaction and interdependence between the ruler and the elite.

Disagreeing with a discernible trend in the studies of modern East and Central European monarchies—exemplified in the German term *Kaisertreue* (fidelity to the emperor), often cited and used as an analytical category by

---

[74] In the quote, emphasis added. I analyze these encounters in more detail in Dobilov, *Russkii krai, chuzhaia vera*, 602–708.

historians,[75]—I would argue that notions and visions of monarchical loyalty were not so much predominantly about one's allegiance to the *person* of the ruler. As early as the turn of the nineteenth century, in the discourses—and practices—of loyalty a certain idea of "Russia" began to be almost inextricably meshed with a sense and lived experience of faithful service to the monarch personally. Highly typical of this symbiosis is the recurrent motif in the 1830s and 1840s correspondence of Nicholas I with his son and heir apparent Alexander, the future Alexander II, conveyed through the following phrases by the latter:

> I am inspired by a single feeling, [the desire] to please You and be worthy of You, my dearest Papa, and of our little mother Russia. [...] We can take pride in belonging to our little mother Russia, calling her our Motherland and You, dearest Papa, our Sovereign and Father.[76]

With the rise of Russian nationalism in the educated society by the mid-nineteenth century, a subtle yet essential choice between various modes of incorporation of the monarch's figure into (or its very cautious exclusion from) the patriotic sentiment partially compensated for a narrow legal space in which competition between civic nation-building projects was possible.

Lastly, from the perspective of emotion, imperial structures of political loyalty emerge to be seen as highly manipulable, and not solely by royal actors. In this essay, I avoid discussing the issue of distinguishing between the "true" experiencing, representation, and imitation of emotions. Yet, I would argue that, regardless of such distinctions, there was a set of situations and junctures at which claims "from below" to be "hotly loyal" had to be taken quite seriously by the imperial authorities. The idiom of "inner faith," ingrained in the imperial politics of loyalty since at least Peter I's reign, could be used by ordinary subjects, caught up in state-sponsored or state-arbitrated confessional tensions and conflicts, for proving their religious-cum-political trustworthiness. Somewhat paradoxically, a quest for sincerity both contributed to the maintenance of an overly authoritarian regime and helped alleviate at least some of its excesses.

---

[75] See for example: Laurence Cole and Daniel L. Unowsky, eds., *The Limits of Loyalty: Imperial Symbolism, Popular Allegiances, and State Patriotism in the Late Habsburg Monarchy* (Oxford: Berghahn Books, 2007).

[76] Larisa G. Zakharova, ed., *Venchanie s Rossiei: Perepiska velikogo kniazia Aleksandra Nikolaevicha s imperatorom Nikolaem I, 1837–1838* (Moscow: Izdatel'stvo MGU, 1999), 40, 49.

Tatiana Khripachenko

TWO CONCEPTS OF LOYALTY IN THE DEBATES ON THE "POLISH QUESTION" IN LATE IMPERIAL RUSSIA

During their time within the Russian Empire, Poles were never seen as loyal subjects. They were rather perceived as a source of instability or—even more often—as historical enemies of Russia, who sought to undermine the foundations of the Russian state.[1] Earlier hopes of "re-educating" the Poles to transform them into faithful servants of the Russian Tsar were seen as having been proved to be in vain after the January Uprising of 1863. Aside from the Polish nobility who took part in the rebellion, the uprising's leaders had also managed to mobilize other layers of the Polish population.[2] The subsequent history of Russian-Polish interaction clearly demonstrates mutual mistrust that existed between the two sides after the uprising. Even the attempts by Russian liberals at the beginning of the twentieth century to propose an agreed arrangement with the Polish parties on mutually beneficial terms failed to yield any positive results.[3]

If one considers this situation from the perspective of today, the separation of Poland from the Empire would seem to have been inevitable. This judgement, however, can only be the product of teleological hindsight. According to such a teleology, everything that actually happened is seen as if it inevitably had to happen. But in fact the option of staying within the Russian Empire under certain conditions was available to Poland for a period. As it turned out this option was not realized in reality. The prospect had been proposed by Russian liberals who envisioned a Russia transformed into a constitutional state based on the idea of citizenship on the French model (i.e. on a civic model as opposed to its German alternative, which was based on ethnic origin).[4] According to Russian liberals, as soon as nationality-based re-

---

[1] Mikhail D. Dolbilov, "Poliak v imperskom politicheskom leksikone," in *Poniatiia o Rossii: K istoricheskoi semantike imperskogo perioda*, ed. Alexei I. Miller, vol. 2 (Moscow: Novoe Literaturnoe Obozrenie, 2012), 292–339.

[2] Mikhail D. Dolbilov and Alexei I. Miller, eds., *Zapadnye okrainy Rossiiskoi imperii* (Moscow: Novoe Literaturnoe Obozrenie, 2006), 180–203.

[3] Pavel N. Miliukov, *Natsional'nyi vopros: Proiskhozhdenie natsional'nosti i natsional'nye voprosy v Rossii* (Moscow: Gosudarstvennaia publichnaia istoricheskaia biblioteka Rossii, 2005), 140–1.

[4] Rogers Brubaker, *Citizenship and Nationhood in France and Germany* (Cambridge, MA: Harvard University Press, 1992), 1–17.

strictions on their freedoms had been abolished, the Poles would be willing, if not to simply accept the Russian statehood as their own, then would at least be motivated to stay within Russia in pursuit of their own economic interests. Thus, separation from the Empire on the basis of their separate ethnicity was not the only possibility available to Poles.

So then, if Russian liberals were considering such a possibility, were there any advocates of such an approach among the Poles? In this paper I will consider how Polish political activists understood the loyalty of the portion of Poland within the Russian Empire towards that empire, as well as explore what kind of loyalty was expected from the Poles by the Russian authorities and by the various political groups at the Imperial center.

Loyalty versus Obligation

Recent theoretical accounts on loyalty tend to distinguish between the term loyalty itself, interpreted as a sort of emotional attachment to a political body, and the concept of obligation, which, in contrast, is based on rational motives and calculations.[5] In the Polish case, the distinction between these two varieties of affinity was very clear. On the one hand, ever since the incorporation of the Kingdom of Poland into the Empire, the Poles, irrespective of their own wishes, had simply become Russian subjects. The Polish population regarded their incorporation in this manner as an occupation. However, deprived of any opportunity to resist by means of an open uprising, the Poles had no option but to become subjects of Russia and to express their loyalty to it, even if that loyalty necessarily be passive, in the form of pragmatic obedience to the Imperial institutions. In other words, Poles were forced by circumstance to recognize the power of Russian bureaucracy in Poland as legitimate, however unwished this imposition might have been. They complied with Russian laws and the policies of Russian officials, but had no interest in matters relating to the entire state as a whole, except insofar as they affected Poland.[6] On the other hand, Poles continued to express a strong sense of loyalty to their own nation. The most influential Polish view at the time held the nation to be the highest form of social life and that loyalty to the nation should take a priority over all other forms of group solidarity.[7]

---

[5] Judith N. Shklar, "Obligation, Loyalty, Exile," *Political Theory* 21, no. 2 (1993): 181–97, 183–4; Ilan Z. Baron, "The Problem of Dual Loyalty," *Canadian Journal of Political Science* 42, no. 4 (2009): 1024–44, here 1027–28.

[6] Theodore R. Weeks, *Nation and State in Late Imperial Russia: Nationalism and Russification on the Western Frontier, 1863-1914* (DeKalb, IL: Northern Illinois University Press, 1996), 112–21.

[7] Brian A. Porter, *When Nationalism Began to Hate: Imagining Modern Politics in Nineteenth Century Poland* (Oxford: Oxford University Press, 2000), 189–219; Zygmunt Balicki, "Egoism narodowy wobec etiki," in *Parlamentaryzm: Wybór pism*, ed. Zygmunt

In the wake of the revolutionary events of 1905, Russia embarked on the path of constitutional transformation, a process, which opened out a way for Poles within the Empire to regard themselves not simply as subjects, but also as citizens of the Empire. The population of the former Kingdom of Poland was granted the right to take part in the elections to the State Duma, which, at least in theory, should have provided a feeling of having an active involvement in the state matters. Within this new framework the Russian authorities sought to instil among the population an alternative or supplementary concept of civic loyalty, one which would serve to supplement and bolster the traditional loyalty to the Tsar.[8] It was supposed that, under the control of the Tsar, the state's Empire-wide institutions would be able to cement Russia together as civic nation and to inspire among the populations of the borderlands an interest in the state matters of common concern instead of just involving themselves in local issues.[9]

In the Polish case, this approach faced an impediment from the most influential circles within the Polish National Democratic Party. The ideology of the party rejected the idea of Empire-wide citizenship for Poles living in the Empire. However, faced with the need to defend the interests of the Poles in statewide Russian institutions, party representatives' views underwent a certain evolution as time went on. And the more Poles became involved in the Russian politics, the more they became prepared to look upon themselves as Russian citizens. However, the problem they faced was that at the very time the Poles were finally recognizing their common interests with Russia and beginning to express a readiness to acknowledge their Russian citizenship, they came up against a chauvinist Russian majority in the Duma strongly opposed to including Poles as full members of the community of Russian citizens.

Thus considered, the Polish case differed considerably from the situation of the Finns. Representatives of Finland tended to frame their country as a separate political entity linked to the Empire via the person of the monarch. Legal interpretations of this connection differed among various influential Finns. Finnish senator Leo Mechelin saw the union of Russia and Finland as a personal union,[10] while Finnish theoreticians Robert Hermanson and Richard Danielson understood it in accordance with the ideas of Georg Jellinek on

---

Balicki and Piotr Koryś (Cracow: Ośrodek Myśli Politycznej, 2008), 335–84, here 346–63.

[8] *Polnoe sobranie zakonov Rossiiskoi imperii. Sobranie III.*, vol. 25 (St. Petersburg, 1908), 132–3, 687–89; "Manifest ob usovershenstvovanii gosudarstvennogo poriadka 1905 g. 17 oktiabria," in *Rossiiskoe zakonodatel'stvo X–XX vekov*, vol. 9, ed. Oleg I. Chistiakov (Moscow: Iuridicheskaia literatura, 1994), 41.

[9] *Polnoe sobranie zakonov Rossiiskoi imperii*, 637–8.

[10] Leo Mechelin, *Précis du droit public du grand-duché Finlande* (Helsingfors: J.C. Frenckell, 1886).

non-sovereign states.[11] Yet, whatever about the theory, in practice Finnish representatives refused to participate in the elections to the State Duma. For them, Finland already enjoyed its own representative institutions and did not need any representation in the Russian parliament.[12] They regarded the Russian State Duma as a legislative authority for the Russian Empire *excluding* Finland. Even after attacks by Russian right-wing parties on what the Finns called the "constitutional rights" of Finland, the latter continued to refuse to send deputies to the Russian parliament. In other words, they behaved as if they were the citizens of a separate Finnish state, one from which Russia was reciprocally also entirely separate.[13]

A comparison between the Finnish and the Polish cases provides an important analogy. The political rhetoric of the Finns tended to avoid employing the new and to them entirely unacceptable concept of Russian citizenship. Instead, Finnish political activists sought to enforce the archaic notion of subjecthood, interpreting it simply as loyalty to the person of the Emperor. At the same time, the Emperor was understood as the legitimate constitutional monarch of Finland.[14] Such an interpretation allowed them to avoid accepting any idea that Finnish citizens[15] were at the same time the citizens of Russia, a state in which the Russian nation played the dominant role. It did not matter how that Russian domination was understood—and it was not necessarily seen as the domination of ethnic Great Russians—Finnish politicians

---

[11] A German theoretician of law, Georg Jellinek introduced the term "non-sovereign state" to describe the legal status of units of the German federative state. According to the German thinker, in the process of unification German lands preserved their state organization, yet ceded their sovereignty to the central authority, which represented the entire union. Finnish legal thinkers Robert Hermanson and Richard Danielson applied this framework to specify the connection of Finland and the Russian Empire. Thus, they sought to prove that Finland was a distinct state, yet a non-sovereign one. For more details see: Robert Germanson, *Gosudarstvenno-pravovoe polozhenie Finliandii* (St. Petersburg: Gosudarstvennaia tipografiia, 1892); Robert Germanson, "Stat'ia 2 rossiiskikh osnovnykh zakonov i finliandskaia konstitutsiia," *Pravo* 16 (1908): 898–911; Richard Danielson, *Soedinenie Finliandii s Rossiiskoi derzhavoiu. Po povodu sochineniia K. Ordina "Pokorenie Finliandii"* (St. Petersburg: Tipografiia I.K. Frenkelia i syna, 1890); Georg Jellinek, *Allgemeine Staatslehre* (Berlin: Häring, 1905).

[12] Osmo Jussila, *Velikoe Kniazhestvo Finliandskoe, 1809–1917* (Helsinki: Ruslania, 2004), 714–17.

[13] Rabbe Vrede, "Budushchee Russkoe narodnoe predstavitel'stvo i Finliandiia," *Pravo* 22, no. 6 (1905): 1790–91.

[14] Germanson, *Gosudarstvenno-pravovoe polozhenie*, 10–23.

[15] In the Finnish political thought, native Finnish and Swedish population were recognized as citizens of what they called the Finnish constitutional state, within which they enjoyed full citizens' rights. In their discourse the notion of "citizen" implied belonging to the Finnish nation as opposed to the idea of all-Russian citizenship. Max Engman, Finliandtsy v Peterburge (St. Petersburg: Evropeiskii Dom, 2008), 33–37. Henrik Stenius, "The Finnish Citizen. How a Translation Emasculated the Concept," *Redescriptions: Yearbook of Political Thought and Conceptual History* 8 (2004): 172–86.

rejected the idea of any such dominance entirely. They simply considered themselves to be citizens of Finland, rather than of Russia.[16] For the Finns, loyalty to Russia meant no more than their status as the subjects of their monarch, who at the same time just happened to be also the Russian Emperor.

At the beginning of the twentieth century, Polish politicians had attempted to develop a similar rhetoric. However, the former Kingdom of Poland was in a very different political situation to that of the Grand Duchy of Finland. Historically, two uprisings had occurred in Poland, both directed at a complete separation from Russia.[17] Nothing similar happened in the case of Finland. For that reason, the Finns were to meet with success in their efforts to appeal to their loyalty as subjects, while the Poles found themselves unable to give a convincing performance in this role. The strategy of defending such a traditional idea of loyalty, as opposed to any new understanding based on the concept of Russian citizenship, could only be perceived as complete hypocrisy on the part of the Poles. Moreover, in contrast to the Finnish case, the Poles faced the added problem of the presence of a Polish minority in the *kresy wschodnie* (eastern borderlands)—historical territories of the former Rzeczpospolita that had been incorporated into Russia as the result of partitions of the eighteenth century.[18] Within these territories, the Poles were a minority, albeit a culturally and socially influential one. The Polish parties, who themselves claimed to represent the interests of the whole Polish people in the State Duma, therefore had to consider not just the interests of Poles living in the Kingdom of Poland, but also of the Poles who inhabited the western provinces.[19] Thus, no complete separation of the Russian Poland from the rest of the Russian Empire similar to the approach taken in the Grand Duchy of Finland was possible. It was clear to the Poles that without the support of the parties from the former Kingdom of Poland, the interests of the Polish minority of the western provinces could not be effectively defended by the direct representatives of that minority on their own.[20]

The Dilemmas of the Revolution

Deprived of any political autonomy as a result of the January Uprising, Poles had few options available on how to interpret their relationship with the Rus-

---

[16] Vrede, "Budushchee Russkoe narodnoe predstavitel'stvo," 1790–91.
[17] Stefan Kieniewicz, Andrzej Zachorski, and Władysław Zajewski, *Trzy Powstania Narodowe: kościuszkowskie, listopadowe, styczniowe* (Warsaw: Książka i Wiedza, 2000).
[18] Weeks, *Nation and State*, 110–31.
[19] Glenn Alfred Janus, *The Polish Koło, the Russian Duma and the Question of Autonomy* (Columbus, OH: Ohio State University, 1971), 72–4.
[20] Jan Stecki, *W sprawie autonomii Królestwa Polskiego* (Cracow: G. Gebethner, 1907), 34–5.

sian state. However, the revolutionary events of 1905 confronted the Polish political forces with a dilemma: whether to take advantage of the weakened state of the Russian monarchy in order to reassert independence, or to come to an arrangement with the Russian government in order to suppress the revolution. The Polish socialist camp opted for the first variant without hesitation.[21] But, in contrast, representatives of the National-Democratic Party, particularly those with links to the large and middle-scale entrepreneurs in the Polish bourgeoisie, regarded the Polish revolutionaries as no less of a threat to their interests than the Tsarist regime and considered a compromise with the Imperial authorities to be the better option.[22] Although even the bourgeois element within the Polish national movement still continued to pursue the goal of full independence, in the revolutionary conditions of the time they lacked forces of their own to suppress "disorders" threatening their property and were thus forced to recognize the need for the state to protect their interests. This implied supporting the Imperial forces of "order," in spite of the fact that they still very much regarded them as foreign.[23]

There was, however, a third approach available, an option that presupposed establishing contacts with the Russian liberal opposition. This possibility opened out a "middle way" between joining the revolution and supporting the government, a chance of acquiring a level of autonomy for the Kingdom of Poland within a Russian state reconstituted in accordance with constitutional principles. And indeed in this connection representatives of Polish parties and members of the Union of Liberation[24] actually managed to conclude an agreement in April 1905.[25] However, the National Democrats were not entirely united on perspectives for cooperation with the Russian liberals. Some of the leaders of the National Democrats were anxious that after a constitutional order was established in Russia, chauvinist Russian parties would take a majority of the seats in the Russian parliament, with the result that re-

---

[21] Józef Piłsudski, leader of the Polish socialists, and Konni Zilliacus, a member of the Finnish active resistance movement, had been receiving the money from the Japanese government to organize armed uprisings in the Russian borderlands. Janus, *The Polish Koło*, 36–8; William R. Copeland, *The Uneasy Alliance: Collaboration between the Finnish Opposition and the Russian Underground, 1899–1904* (Helsinki: Suomalainen Tiedeakatemia, 1973), 141–47.

[22] Stanisław Kozicki, *Historia Ligi Narodowej, okres 1887–1907* (London: Myśl Polska, 1964), 209–18.

[23] Edward Freeman, *The National Democratic Movement in the Kingdom of Poland, 1886–1903* (Ann Arbor, MI: University of Colorado, 1974), 420–25.

[24] Soiuz Osvobozhdeniia is the organization, which preceded the creation of the Konstitutsionno-demokraticheskaia partia.

[25] Russian-Polish Meeting in Moscow, April 1905, 1–23, item. 39, op. 1, f. 279, Rossiiskii gosudarstvennyi arkhiv sotsial'no-politicheskoi istorii [Russian State Archive of Social and Political History] (hereafter RGASPI).

pression against the Poles would actually increase.[26] For the National Democrats, even if Poles were elected to the parliament, they would inevitably form no more than a minority there. Finally, representatives of the Polish political groups realized that supporters of a constitutional arrangement in Russia, even those among them who sympathized with Polish interests, would never agree to grant Poland complete independence, because the majority of the Russian society was opposed to the disintegration of the Russian Empire.[27]

Interaction between the two parties was further complicated by the fact that they could not reach an agreement on what the concept of autonomy should actually mean in practice. Russian constitutionalists recognized Polish autonomy as the right of the Polish nation to self-government and to organize its life on its territory, which had historically enjoyed a separate constitutional jurisdiction, though this status had been abolished in 1830 as the result of the November Uprising. On the other hand, Russian liberals also sought to preserve the political unity of the Russian Empire, which, according to their programmatic aims, was to become a modern unified constitutional state.[28] In this sense, Polish autonomy was understood as a means of establishing such a unity on the basis of common economic and political interests, in a process that would inevitably draw the Russian and the Polish nations closer together, despite the historical tensions between the two. Abolishing oppression on the basis of nationality would, in the opinion of the liberals, turn the Polish patriots into loyal citizens, actively contributing to strengthening the political authority of a shared Russian state.[29]

The Polish National Democrats led by Roman Dmowski considered the concept of autonomy entirely differently. The initial program of the National Democrats (published in 1903) declared that the party aimed to "accomplish an independent Polish state."[30] It specified that any belonging to another state, even one that relied on the principle of autonomy, would inevitably impede the development of the Polish people, as it would compel Poles to take

---

[26] St. B., "Dążenie do autonomii Królestwa, ego źródla i podstawy ogólne," *Przegląd Wszechpolski* 5 (1905): 288–90.

[27] Informator "Pis'ma o sovremennoi Pol'she," *Osvobozhdenie* 20–21 (1903); "Pis'ma o sovremennoi Pol'she," *Osvobozhdenie* 24 (1903): 444–45.

[28] A whole range of polemics among the Russian constitutionalists regarding the possible status of Poland: *Liberal'noe dvizhenie v Rossii, 1902–1905* (Moscow: ROSSPEN, 2001), 160; Peter B. Struve, "Demokraticheskaia partiia i eë programma," *Osvobozhdenie* 67 (1905): 279–280; Nikolai Kareev, "K voprosu o russko-pol'skikh otnosheniiakh," *Pravo* 10 (1905): 721–24; Nikolai Kareev, "Novaia pol'skaia partiia" *Pravo* 15 (1905): 1175–82; and Alexander R. Lednicki, "Pol'skii vopros," *Russkaia mysl'* 7 (1905): 130.

[29] Fedor Fedorovich Kokoshkin, *Oblastnaia avtonomiia i edinstvo Rossii* (Moscow: Tipografiia O. L. Somovoi, 1905), 2–13; Vladimir M. Gessen, *Avtonomiia, federatsiia i natsional'nyi vopros* (St. Petersburg: Narod i svoboda, 1906), 1–45; and Nikolai I. Lazarevskii, *Avtonomiia* (St. Petersburg, 1906), 3–24.

[30] "Program stronnictwa Demokratyczno-Narodowego w zaborze rosyjskim," *Przegląd Wszechpolski* 10 (1903): 724.

into account the essential interests and needs of a foreign state.³¹ Later, as new revolutionary events occurred, the National Democrats sought to reconsider their initial attitude towards autonomy. However, their project of autonomy continued to presuppose the maximum possible degree of separation of the Kingdom of Poland from the Empire. It included a claim that compulsory military service for Poles should be served on the territory of the Kingdom of Poland, and that Poland should have complete financial independence, with the proviso that the Kingdom would make certain payments to the central treasury to meet the cost of the shared needs of the state. At the same time, the program suggested establishing a separate parliament and stipulated a principle according to which all state positions in Poland should be reserved exclusively to native Poles.³² Thus, what the National Democrats called "autonomy," gave Poland the status of semi-independent state, following the Finnish model.³³ In certain areas the status claimed for Poland went even beyond the liberties allowed to Finland.

The political behavior of the Poles during this period was characterized by the absence of any loyalty in the sense of faithfulness to any force in Russia. Far from choosing their allies on the basis of ideological similarity or long-term relations of trust, the National Democrats did so on the basis of what they calculated to be in their short-term interests. Such tactics was an expression of the main tenets of their theory of "national egoism." Despite their best efforts, this theory proved ineffective in reaching trusting relations with any of Russia's political forces.

The tactics of the National Democrats were, at least by their own lights, quite logical. They assumed that no matter what political force were to take power in Russia, the regime would be equally hostile towards the Poles.³⁴ Having rejected the idea of independence as unrealistic for the time being, but unable to predict how the situation in Russia would develop, the National Democrats assumed a position aimed at giving them a "free hand," promising support to whatever power was willing to offer them the most favorable conditions.³⁵ Sustaining limited contacts with each of the conflicting parties, the National Democrats sought to negotiate possible future concessions in return for their support in the present. The government did not consider any concessions to the Kingdom of Poland, yet in the eyes of the Poles, it still had real power and could at least represent a reliable ally against Polish socialists.³⁶ The Russian constitutionalists, although ready to offer the Poles limited au-

---

[31] Ibid., 727.
[32] St. B., "Dążenie do autonomii Królestwa," 288–90; "Stanowisko stronnictwa Demokratyczno-Narodowego w chwili obecnej," *Przegląd Wszechpolski* 11 (1905): 767.
[33] Jan Popławski, "Stosunek prawno-polityczny Królestwa Polskiego do Rosyi," *Przegląd Wszechpolski* 7 (1905): 361–86.
[34] St. B., "Dążenie do autonomii Królestwa," 286–90.
[35] Kozicki, *Historia Ligi Narodowej*, 233–41.
[36] Ibid., 260–76.

tonomy, could not provide any guarantees that their promises could be fulfilled.[37] Although they were an influential force among the Russian parties in the early revolutionary period, their ability to convert their political influence into an instrument capable of implementing real reforms remained limited.

In the event, the Poles' strategy of seeking to bargain with two conflicting groups simultaneously was to severely damage their reputation as a reliable ally. In his memoirs, Sergei Witte, a former minister of finance, expressed doubts about his negotiations with Roman Dmowski, leader of the National Democrats. Witte was at one stage almost ready to begin considering the question of the status of the Kingdom of Poland. However, several days later he was "unpleasantly surprised" to discover that Dmowski and other Polish activists had taken part in the meeting with Russian constitutionalists in which they had condemned the policies of the government on the Kingdom of Poland.[38] Russian constitutionalists were likewise wary of their Polish partners and demanded a guarantee that the Poles would ask the Duma, rather than the government, to be the body to recognize their autonomy.[39]

Finally, on the eve of the elections to the State Duma, the National Democrats lost the trust both of the majority of the Russian opposition groups and of the forces supporting the government. While the former regarded the Poles' behavior as shortsighted and inspired by wounded national feelings, the latter interpreted the tactics of the National Democrats as proof of the notion that the Poles could never in principle share common goals with the Russian state and would always inevitably seek to weaken Russia.[40] The Kadets, as party members of the Constitutional Democratic Party were called, still harbored the hope that they would be able to "re-educate" the Poles in the Duma and convince them to accept a more realistic position.[41] However, the efforts of the Kadets faced criticism from the right-wing parties. They complained that the Kadets, by insisting on maintaining contacts with the Polish parties, were contributing to Russia's disintegration.[42]

---

[37] "Rosyjska izba ogólnopanstwowa a zadania polityki polskiej," *Przegląd Wszechpolski* 8–10 (1905): 576.
[38] Sergei Iul'evich Witte, *Vospominaniia*, vol. 2 (Berlin: Slovo, 1922), 143.
[39] "Zjazd ziemcow w Moskwie wobec spraw Polskich," *Przegląd Wszechpolski* 11 (1905): 848.
[40] See, for example, a series of articles authored by "P. K." under the title "Russko-pol'skie otnosheniia," *Okrainy Rossii* 4, 6, 7, 21 (1906).
[41] "Pol'skaia deklaratsiia," *Rech'* 63 (1906); Pavel Nikolaevich Miliukov, "K.-d. i pol'skie partii" In: *God bor'by: publitsisticheskaia khronika, 1905–1906*, ed. Pavel Nikolaevich Miliukov (Moscow: Kniga po trebovaniiu, 2013), 264–66.
[42] *Napadki na partiiu narodnoi svobody i vozrazheniia protiv nikh* (Moscow: Tipografiia G. Lissnera, 1906), 50; Anton Budilovich, "Vopros ob okrainakh Rossii v sviazi s teoriei samoopredeleniia narodnostei i trebovaniiami gosudarstvennogo edinstva," *Okrainy Rossii* 22 (1906): 382–84.

Unwanted Integration into Russian Politics

When the National Democrats finally agreed to take part in the elections to the State Duma, their decision was not meant to imply that they were ready to become part of a single Russian civic nation, as the Russian constitutionalists and at least for a time the Russian government appeared to envision. Having won a majority of the Polish seats in the Duma, the National Democrats came to the Russian parliament holding a notion of themselves as a sort of "Polish embassy" to a foreign state.[43] The goal of this embassy was to acquire maximum gains for its people by means of negotiating with either one political force or the other. At the same time, following the example of the Finns, the National Democrats refused to take part in any discussions on questions that did not concern the interests of the Polish people. They also decisively renounced any prospect of forming a coalition with any of the other parties in the Duma.[44]

These tactics were to yield quite upsetting results for the Poles. Their first attempt to articulate Polish claims in the Duma did not meet with any response from their audience.[45] In their declaration, Polish deputies appealed to the principles of international law and the acts of the Congress of Vienna to demand the restoration of the previous status of the Kingdom of Poland.[46] These demands effectively implied the creation of a separate Polish state. Moreover, according to the claims of the Polish deputies, international law rather than the will of the Russian authorities would provide the source through which this claim to statehood was to be justified. Clearly no Russian political party could support this declaration expressed in such a form. Even the Kadets, who controlled the majority of seats in the first and second Dumas, were careful to distance themselves from the Polish position.[47]

The failure of these opening tactics forced the Poles to reformulate their goals in the Russian parliament as time went on. After the dissolution of the first Duma, the National Democrats did not abandon their efforts to achieve Polish autonomy, a topic they were determined to raise for the discussion in the new Duma. This time, Jan Stecki, one of the "old" members of the National Democrats, took on the lead role in developing this project. Stecki suggested limiting the ambition of Polish claims and accepting the idea of a provincial form of autonomy as opposed to the sort of autonomy enjoyed by the Finns.[48] The author hoped that this concession would open out the prospect of a *rapprochement* with the Kadets and attract wider support among the

---

[43] "Rosyjska izba ogólnopanstwowa," 576–77.
[44] Ibid.
[45] "Sozyv 1: Sessiia 1," in *Gosudarstvennaia Duma: Stenograficheskie otchety* (St. Petersburg: Gosudarstvennaia tipografiia, 1906–1907), 51.
[46] Ibid.
[47] "Pol'skaia deklaratsiia," Rech' 63 (1906).
[48] Stecki, *W sprawie autonomii,* 17–20.

Russian parties.⁴⁹ His proposal signified a gradual change in the tactics of the National Democrats as it increasingly began to give due consideration to the attitudes held by Russian public opinion. The change of tack did not, however, imply any change in the ultimate strategic aims of the Polish *koło* (circle). The new project for Polish autonomy continued to be part of their ultimate goal of complete independence and the greatest possible level of separation from Russia.⁵⁰

The Kadets took on an approach of delay and silence in relation to the Poles, tactics that could not help but irritate representatives of the Polish *koło*.⁵¹ Partially as a result of this irritation, the Polish deputies adopted a new strategy of maneuvering between the left and the right-wing parties, by analogy with the practice of the Irish party in the British parliament.⁵² They offered their support for the position of either the left-wing or right-wing parties in the parliament in relation to all-Russian issues in exchange for support for Polish claims to autonomy. The use of such tactics by Polish deputies, inspired by the ideas of "national egoism," was to cost them the loss of a significant number of seats in the Duma as a result of the constitutional coup of June 1907.⁵³ Referring to the political behavior of the Poles, Petr Arkad'evich Stolypin's manifesto openly declared, that *inorodtsy* (foreigners) should not be allowed to interfere in discussions on purely Russian matters.⁵⁴

Examining the political behavior of the National Democrats during the period, one cannot but notice a transformation in the Poles' civic engagement with the Russian state, from a pattern of self-alienation during the term of the first Duma to active involvement in the second one. Still pursuing their "egoistic" interests, the Poles found themselves becoming more involved in the Russian politics and were forced by this involvement to take the opinion of the Russian parties and of Russian society into account in their decision making. In conditions of parliamentary conflict, the Poles used debates on purely Russian issues as the occasion to promote their own national goals. Thus, even if their intention was nothing of the sort, this approach forced the Poles to some extent to accept the rules of the game and to become in a sense an active participant of the Russian civic nation, thus opening up a space for dialogue with the Russian constitutionalists. However, this new behavior did not make loyal citizens of the Poles in the eyes of the Russian parties of the right. The latter regarded citizenship as a synonym of subjecthood. They consid-

---

49 Ibid., 38.
50 Ibid., 18.
51 Edward Vincent Chmielewski, *The Polish Question in the Russian State Duma* (Knoxville: University of Tennessee Press, 1970), 33–43.
52 Janus, *The Polish Koło*, 199.
53 Chmielewski, *The Polish Question*, 40–2.
54 *Polnoe sobranie zakonov Rossiiskoi imperii. Sobranie III.*, vol. 27 (St. Petersburg, 1910), 320.

ered Poles an alien people that did not have any right to interfere in discussion of matters that intrinsically only affected the Russian nation.[55]

A paradox of the situation was that the National Democrats adhered to an essentially right-wing form of Polish nationalism. They disapproved of revolution from below and sought to negotiate on the issues most important to them with political groups that held essentially similar ideological outlooks. Despite this fact, their counterparts on the Russian side, i.e. Russian politicians of the right, were unwilling to deal with the Poles. They essentially took the passive obedience of the Poles as granted and assumed that such conformity would not become the subject of bargaining. Meanwhile, Russian liberals were ready to make certain concessions, expressing a willingness to conclude a mutually beneficial agreement with the Poles. However, the liberals' vision of the future of the state was based on a different ideological grounding. Roughly speaking, the Poles were realists. They started from an idea that held interaction between the nations to be fundamentally a zero-sum game. In contrast, the liberals were essential idealists who assumed it would be possible to arrive at a position that was beneficial to both sides. The Poles simply did not believe in the idea that there could be common interests between two nations and consequently opted to plough on with an independent strategy. Yet it was these "realist" values that were ultimately to prove to be a trap for the Poles.

The Trap Closes

In the new situation the National Democrats saw the need to develop new tactics. One of their attempts to set the new course was expressed by Roman Dmowski's speech in the third Duma on 16th November 1907. Dmowski began his speech with reverential appeals to Russian right-wing groups. He depicted the first two Dumas as "time of slogans, ambitious claims, demands that could not be fulfilled immediately, along with ones that could not be fulfilled in principle."[56] The orator further remarked that "now, everything has settled down"[57] and that it was now time to reflect calmly on the reasons for the recent revolutionary events and to consider what might be done to prevent a repetition. In Dmowski's view, excessive centralization was one of the factors behind the revolutionary situation. The state, he argued, should put more reliance on positive forces available locally.

Dmowski proposed that the government provide more independence to the borderlands, arguing that the border areas would willingly assist the government in its struggle against the revolution. He addressed the centrist and

---

[55] See, for example, Mikhail Menshikov, "Ch'e gosudarstvo Rossia?" in *Pis'ma k russkoi natsii* (Moscow: Moskva, 2005), 73–78.
[56] "Sozyv 3. Sessia 1," in *Gosudarstvennaia Duma: Stenograficheskie otchety*, 341.
[57] Ibid.

right-wing majority with an appeal "to call the social forces to work [...] to delegate the weight of the decisions from the center [...] to local institutions, because only they can make decisions in a manner useful to the population."[58] However, he also complained about the reduction in the number of the Polish deputies in the Duma. He inferred from the reduced representation that the Russian authorities regarded the population of the Kingdom of Poland as *vtorostepennye grazhdane* (second-class citizens). According to the records of the session, at this point in his speech a voice from the right shouted: "Certainly!" Outraged, Dmowski proclaimed, that "the Polish people will never accept the status of second-class citizens in the state and will never be able to reconcile themselves with a state in which they are assigned second-class status."[59]

In response to Dmowski's criticism, prime minister Stolypin claimed in his concluding speech that he was not opposed to relying on local forces. He declared, however, that "the force of self-government, on which the central government will rely must always be a national force."[60] Stolypin also declared that those, "who had just referred to themselves as second-class citizens"[61] had only themselves to blame. They did not enjoy the benefits of normal educational institutions, for example, because "they did not want to use the Russian language in high school."[62] He further appealed to them to "take our point of view, accept that the highest good is to become a Russian citizen, and to carry this status as proudly as Roman citizens once did, and then you can call yourself first-class citizens and acquire all your rights."[63] It should be understood, however, that this call to "become Russians" did not imply any acceptance of any particular ethnic characteristics. At the same time, Stolypin made it clear that all dreams of decentralization and equality based on nationality would be useless until the Poles accepted the idea of belonging to the Russian state.

So the circle had finally closed. The National Democrats had started with a wary isolationism based on what they called "national egoism." In a similar way to the Finns, they sought to accept an idea of a passively obedient subject to the monarch. Then, in their efforts in the Russian parliament to pursue their goal of Polish autonomy, the Poles were driven into Russian politics. In the end, they were to come face-to-face with the "national egoism" of Russian nationalist forces, who had come to dominate in the third Duma.

It is plain that the central government's attempt to turn passively obedient Polish subjects into active citizens of the Russian constitutional state failed

[58] Ibid.
[59] Ibid.
[60] Ibid., 352.
[61] Ibid.
[62] Ibid.
[63] Ibid.

utterly. The reason for this failure was not only that the combination of right-wing and Russian nationalist parties ended up holding a majority in the State Duma as the result of the ultimate failure of the 1905 revolution, but also that the National Democrats had failed to find a common language with the Russian constitutionalists during the period when liberals and left-wing parties had been in the majority. Their understanding that they might have a commonality of interests with Russian forces simply came too late. Besides, the attempts made by the National Democrats to find common ground with right-wing parties did not do anything helping to promote mutual understanding between Poles and Russian liberals. Another reason for the way events turned out was also that, while the National Democrats started from the idea of a struggle between nations for existence, the Russian liberals put their emphasis on the rights of the individual, disregarding the importance of collective rights. Thus, the idea of developing among Poles of that held loyalty to be constituted by an active involvement in civic activity was ultimately to fail due to mutual misunderstanding in addition to the fundamental differences in the strategic aims of the two sides.

So could Poles ultimately have become loyal citizens of a new Russian constitutional state? Or was this prospect no more than a figment produced by the mindset of idealist Kadets? To what extent were those who believed that the Poles could only, and therefore had to be, kept in line by force right?

The history of gradually increasing involvement by the Polish parliamentary delegation in the Russian politics demonstrates that even the staunchest supporters of "national egoism" among the Polish representatives were eventually to realize the need to partake in politics and to acquire "civil rights" in Russia. However, those parties on the Russian side who were the closest counterparts to the National Democrats in relation to social and political issues were unwilling to grant such rights. Therefore, even if the Poles had consciously opted to convert themselves into loyal members of the Russian "civic nation," they would still have had to cooperate with left-wing and liberal parties—forces entirely incompatible with the National Democrats in terms of ideology. This paradox required time to resolve itself and, as it turned out, the required time was not available.

Thus, the alternative strategy that was mentioned at the outset of this article was never realized in reality. Yet despite this, and in the course of changes in the situation, an independent Poland happened to emerge. The fact that it did so can be seen as the inevitable result of the policies and attitudes of the Russian right-wing parties. Holding onto someone by force is only possible when the dominating power is in possession of such force. No attempt to create a unitary state by force can be successful if there exists a well-developed national movement within that state. Although it might seem paradoxical, the alternative strategy attempted by the Kadets—namely, to convince the Poles to give their loyalty to the state on grounds of the interests shared with it—represented the only possible route to the goal of Polish autonomy within the

Empire. The failure of this alternative strategy to produce results should be attributed to the actions of the Russian authorities and pro-government parties. However, one should not absolve the Poles themselves entirely of the blame for the failure of the tactical agreement between Poles and the Kadets. Certainly, this agreement seemed meaningless to the political forces, who strove towards independence. Yet, in the particular historical circumstances of revolutionary upheaval in Russia, the Poles' strategy could only promote the success of Russian right-wing groups.

Alexei Il'ich Miller

NATIONAL IDENTITIES AND THE FORGING OF POLITICAL LOYALTIES
Little Russians versus Ukrainians during the Nineteenth and Twentieth Centuries

Beginning in the nineteenth century, when the process of formation of national identities in the lands now making up Ukraine first began to gain momentum, the region's nation builders used two clear-cut mutually opposing strategies. While this dualism has changed in its forms and content in the course of time, it has maintained a significant impact on the political loyalties of the region's population right up to the present day.

By the middle of the seventeenth century, as a consequence of the 1648 Cossack insurrection led by Bohdan Khmelnytsky and the ensuing war between the Muscovite Tsardom and the Polish-Lithuanian Commonwealth, the lands on the left bank of the Dnieper River came under the control of Moscow as the autonomous Cossack Hetmanate. The Hetmanate's autonomy was increasingly cut back in subsequent decades, until it was ultimately abolished in 1775. By the end of the eighteenth century, following the partitions of the Polish Commonwealth, most lands inhabited by Orthodox or Uniate populations had fallen under the sway of the Russian Empire.[1]

Memories of the Hetmanate and regional patriotism among the Little Russian nobility slowly faded during the eighteenth and early nineteenth centuries. An American scholar with Ukrainian roots, the historian Zenon E. Kohut, writes about two types of opinion that prevailed in the minds of Ukrainian nobility. One of them Kohut calls "assimilationist," oriented at incorporation into the Russian nobility, while the second he defines as "traditionalist," who strove to preserve and restore the rights and privileges they had before Little Russia fell under the rule of the Romanovs.[2] This comment is an accurate account of the actual situation at the time, with one reserva-

---

[1] For a general survey on the Russian Empire's politics in its western borderlands, see Mikhail Dmitrievich Dolbilov and Alexei Il'ich Miller, eds., *Zapadnye okrainy Rossiiskoj imperii* (Moscow: Novoe Literaturnoe Obozrenie, 2006).

[2] Zenon E. Kohut, "The Ukrainian Elite in the Eighteenth Century and Its Integration into the Russian Nobility," in *The Nobility in Russia and Eastern Europe*, ed. Ivo Banac and Paul Bushkovitch (New Haven: Yale Concilium on International and Area Studies, 1983), 65–98, here 78, 83.

tion—there was in effect no such thing as a *Ukrainian* nobility. The local elite, who had oftentimes been ennobled only relatively recently, emanated from the Cossack *starshina* (leadership), a people who by no means thought of themselves as belonging to a Ukrainian nation.

Eastern European nationalism saw its first major surge during the Napoleonic Wars. *Russkaia Pravda* (Russian Truth) emerged as one of the most vociferous and radical writings of the time, reflecting on questions of identity and loyalty in a very new way. It arguably constitutes the most thorough programmatic document of the Decembrist movement. Its main author was Pavel Ivanovich Pestel', and it was endorsed as a general programme by the conference of the Decembrists' Southern Society held in Kiev in 1823.

The following is what Pestel' had to say on the subject of Slavic nations:

[...] the Slavonic tribe that forms the autochthonous Russian nation, possesses five hues: (1) the so-called Russians themselves, dwelling in the great Russian governorates; (2) the Little Russians, dwelling in the governorates of Chernigov and Poltava; (3) the Ukrainians, dwelling in the governorates of Kharkov and Kursk; (4) the inhabitants of the governorates of Kiev, Podolia and Volhynia, who call themselves Russnaks and (5) the Belorussians, dwelling in the governorates of Vitebsk and Mogilev.[3]

Pestel' went on:

While this difference will soon cease to exist, in matters of state no such distinction can be allowed to exist at all, since (1) the language is the selfsame everywhere: only the vernaculars are different, and these are not the same even within the Great Russian governorates, and there is no great language which does not have different vernaculars; (2) the faith is everywhere the same, it is Orthodox in all the governorates just as in the Great Russian ones and, although the Uniate faith is still professed at some places, that is nothing else than the weak relict of a seduction that was hatched by the Florentine council, brought into the country by foreign forces in those unlucky times, but is now being rooted out ever more. [...] (3) The civic conditions in these governorates are exactly the same as they are in the Great Russian governorates since one finds everywhere the same estates possessing the same rights.[4]

From this Pestel' concluded,

[...] there is no essential difference between the various branches that form the autochthonous Russian nation, and what may be noted as minor variants should poured into a single common mould. And for these reasons it should be decreed that all inhabitants dwelling in the governorates of Vitebsk, Mogilev, Chernigov, Poltava, Kursk, Kharkov, Kiev, Podolia and Volhynia should be considered true Russians and not to be distinguished from the latter by their various names.[5]

Thus, the most radical project for creating a nation out of the Empire formulated during course of the nineteenth century in Russia declared its top priority to be the amalgamation of Great Russians, Little Russians and Belarusians into a single nation.

---

[3] Aleksandr A. Pokrovskii, ed., *Vosstanie dekabristov: Dokumenty*, vol. 7: *"Russkaia Pravda" P.I. Pestelia i sochineniia ei predshestvuiushchie* (Moscow: Gospolitizdat, 1958), 138.
[4] Ibid., 139.
[5] Ibid.

The Polish Insurrection of 1830–31 finally convinced the Tsarist government that using the principle of royal legitimism would not succeed in putting the nationalist genie back into its bottle. It was in response to that very uprising that, under the patronage of Sergei Semenovich Uvarov, minister of education, the concept of a triune Russian nation first began to take shape, embracing Great Russians, Little Russians and Belarusians, as historian Nikolai Gerasimovich Ustrialov most explicitly expressed the idea.[6]

Thus, the concept emerged of an all-Russian nation encompassed all eastern Slavs. The various differences between Great Russians, Belarusians and Little Russians were considered insignificant when compared against their close kindredship. A frequent explanation for such differences was found in the detrimental influence of the Poles, who had separated Belarusians and Little Russians from their brethren in faith and their national community by forcing them to live in the *Rzeczpospolita*. Certain of the traits of the Little Russians (sometimes also referred to as Iuzhnorusy—the Southern Russians) were considered extremely interesting or sometimes inspiring, but only as yet another of the many different variants of Russian culture. For this school of thought, the Little Russian identity was merely a regional trait, and as such could coexist quite pacifically with an all-Russian identity.

In the 1840s, members of the Brotherhood of Saints Cyril and Methodius developed the first project to define the Ukrainian identity as a separate national identity, thereby rejecting the rival all-Russian view. They regarded Ukraine as an autonomous body politic that was capable of separate existence within a wider Slavic federation. Emperor Nicholas I of Russia did not hesitate to link the foundation of the Brotherhood to ideas that Polish emigrants were infiltrating into Russia after the defeat of the insurrection of 1830–31: "This is quite obviously the work of common propaganda from Paris; for a long time, We have not been able to bring Ourselves to believe that this work is being done in Ukraine; there can now no longer be any doubt."[7]

After several prominent members of the Brotherhood were arrested and exiled to Great Russian governorates (guberniia) in 1847, this controversy marked the frontline in the struggle for identity which was to be waged between the Empire and the Ukrainian nationalists—usually referred to as Ukrainophiles[8], right up until the very demise of the old regime. Within these new politics of identity, one powerful strategic weapon was to define Russian as a "foreign" language, and to emancipate the Ukrainian tongue as the universal medium of communication of a "resurging nation." The censorship

---

6   Alexei Il'ich Miller, *The Romanov Empire and Nationalism: Essays in the Methodology of Historical Research* (Budapest: Central European University Press, 2008), 139–60.
7   Quoted after: Petr A. Zaionchkovskii, *Kirillo-Mefodievskoe obshchestvo, 1846–1847* (Moscow: Izdatelstvo Moskovskogo Universiteta, 1959), 118.
8   On the evolution of the notion of "Ukrainophilia" see Alexei Il'ich Miller, "Ukrainophilia," *Russian Studies in History* 44, no. 2 (2005): 30–43.

instructions of 1863 and their even more stringent 1876 version set narrow limits to the public use of the Ukrainian language, which was officially regarded as a no more than vernacular of the common people. The government's policy was to preserve the exclusive status to the language of Russian literature as sole vehicle for the education and cultural life of the all-Russian nation.⁹

During the 1850s and 1860s, when the members of the Brotherhood of Saints Cyril and Methodius had returned from their period of exile, they were at last able to voice their opinions in public—at a time when their opponents were also busy outlining their own positions. Thus began the confrontation within Ukraine between the Little Russian (or all-Russian) identity on the one hand and the Ukrainian version on the other. In October 1858, Panteleimon Oleksandrovych Kulish, who had been a member of the Brotherhood of Saints Cyril and Methodius, wrote to Slavophile Sergei Timofeevich Aksakov:

> Not alone is the government pitted against us, but also public opinion as voiced by you. Even our half-witted compatriots are against us. Those few of us who still believe in our future, which, as we are deeply convinced, cannot coincide with the future of the Great Russian nation.¹⁰

As a matter of fact, both of the opposing ideologies contained a variety of different undercurrents. Among the Ukrainophiles during the nineteenth century, however, there were only a few who advocated immediate separation from the Russian Empire. On the contrary, some, including such figures as Mykhailo Petrovych Drahomanov, were sincere and convinced federalists.

Amongst the followers of Little Russianism, who remained loyal to the Empire and the concept of an all-Russian nation, there were some who supported that ideology less out of conviction that out of fear of the "Polish threat," which they regarded as the greater evil. Over the course of time, however, unqualified supporters of pan-Russianism came to dominate that camp. In December 1859, Silvestr Silvestrovich Gogotskii, a professor of education at Kiev University and advocate of Little Russianism, wrote to Vasilii

---

⁹ For printed versions of the *Valuevskii tsirkuliar* (the Valuev Circular) of 1863 and the *Emskii ukaz* (the Ems Ukaz) of 1876 and a detailed analysis, see Alexei Il'ich Miller, *The Ukrainian Question: The Russian Empire and Nationalism in the Nineteenth Century*, trans. Olga Poato (Budapest: Central European Press, 2003). On the choice between the Cyrillic and Latin alphabets see Alexei Il'ich Miller and Oxana Ostapczuk, "The Latin and Cyrillic Alphabets in Ukrainian National Discourse and in the Language Policy of Empires," in *A Laboratory of Transnational History: Ukraine and Recent Ukrainian Historiography*, ed. Philipp Ther and Georgiy Kasianov (Budapest: Central University Press, 2008), 167–210.

¹⁰ Panteleimon Oleksandrovych Kulish to Sergei Timofeevich Aksakov, October 1858, l. 1–2, ed. chr. 1762, op. 1, Sekretnyi arkhiv [Secret Archive], f. 109, Gosudarstvennyi Arkhiv Rossiiskoi Federatsii [State Archive of the Russian Federation] (hereafter GARF).

Vasil'evich Grechulevich, a priest based in St. Petersburg, who had authored one of the many Ukrainian primers that were being published at the time:

> We must preserve the unity of the three Russian tribes at all costs, otherwise [...] the Latin-Liakh faction [i.e. the Roman Catholic Poles, A.M.] will either crush [the Little Russian nation], or will straightforwardly suppress and assimilate it. The Liakhs understand that perfectly, and that is why, under the pretense of being most sympathetic to our cause, they do not cease to suggest to us that Little Russia can become independent. We, the western Little Russians, are not susceptible to this deception; but the eastern Little Russians, I am well aware, are easily deceived and have indeed already been deceived. They are totally unaware that the Liakhs and Jesuits have to do but little in order to (1) kindle the resentment of Little Russians against the Great Russians; (2) instil the idea of separatism in them, and (3) cause them to denounce the use of the language of Russian literature. The Liakhs know perfectly well that no sooner than Little Russia separates herself from Great Russia will they be able to subdue her, and especially her western regions, and will then be in a position to strangle her as a cat strangles a mouse.[11]

This division between the two types of advocate of Little Russianism was never to diminish; while one group was fond of the specificities of Little Russia and wished to preserve them, the other side saw such peculiarities as hallmarks of parochialism and advocated full assimilation with the Great Russians. However, what both ideological camps shared was an enmity towards the idea of a Ukrainian nation, which they jointly derided as *ukrainstvo* (Ukrainophilia), unflatteringly referring to supporters of a Ukrainian national project as *mazepintsy*.[12] Kiev opponents of Ukrainophilia continuously played an important role—at times a decisive one—in initiating and implementing the repressive measures taken by the Imperial centre against the Ukrainian national movement.[13]

---

[11] Silvestr Silvestrovich Gogotskii to Vasilii Vasil'evich Grechulevich, December 1859, l. 1–3, ed. chr. 1762, op. 1, Sekretnyi arkhiv, f. 109, GARF.

[12] By the mid-1870s, Gogotskii had given a different accent to his anti-Ukrainophile polemic: "Who indeed authorised the Ukrainophiles to take the time-honoured name of Russians from us and all that comes with it, among other things our common, civilised Russian language, which was created in a protracted and laborious historical process, and replace it all with something Ukrainian, which came into being much later, which belongs to the private sphere only and is limited to local usage [...] What a risible and pathetic predilection to maintain that all things Ukrainian could be nobler and more important than Russian!" Silvestr Silvestrovich Gogotskii, *Russkii vestnik* 17 (1875), 414–15. As is often the case, the name of "Ukrainophiles," originally meant as a sobriquet by their opponents, came to be adopted by the activists of the Ukrainian national movement; that is why their opponents adopted the new nickname of *mazepintsy* for them, which was deliberately derisive. [Translator's note: derived from Ivan Stepanovych Mazepa (1639–1709), Hetman of the Ukrainian Cossacks and traitor to the Russian cause in the view of Russian nationalists].

[13] For a more detailed survey of relations between the imperial government and Ukrainian as well as Russian nationalism in the nineteenth century see Miller, *The Ukrainian Question*.

Meanwhile, among the Ruthenian population of Habsburg Galicia a lot of infighting was also going on between followers of a variety of different conceptions of self-identification. As early as in the 1850s, the power of a Ruthenian-Polish identity, which had earlier been particularly attractive to sections of the Ruthenian elite, and which had found formulation in the motto *gente ruteni, natione poloni* (Ruthenian by birth but Polish by nation), was already losing its foothold.[14] The principal struggle was now being waged by "Russophiles"—supporters of pan-Russianism—against *narodovtsy* (populists), who defended a conception centred around a Ukrainian identity. Thus, under the very different conditions of Galician society and politics, a conflict along more or less the same lines was being waged as the one going on within the Russian Empire.

Towards the end of the nineteenth century the *narodovtsy* were gaining the upper hand, though the Russophiles continued to exert considerable influence right up until early in the twentieth century. This political state of affairs was in part due to the fact that the *narodovtsy* of Galicia were favoured by the Habsburg government while, starting in the 1880s, the Russophile side came under severe persecution. The Imperial repressions of the Russophiles were pre-emptive in nature insofar as the vast majority of the target population up to that time had in fact remained loyal to the Habsburgs. Seen from Vienna though, they were considered to be either latent or potential agents of St. Petersburg—an attitude that was actively nurtured by Galician Poles. The stronger the tensions between Vienna and St. Petersburg grew, the more unrelenting the Habsburg government became in its attitude towards the Russophiles.[15] Furthermore, the Russophile camp was also dwindling through emigration to Russia. In contrast, the Ukrainian side in Austria-Hungary was bolstering up its forces through the arrival of people and financial resources from Ukrainophile groups within the Russian Empire.[16] The best known example of such immigration was personified by historian Mykhailo Serhiio-

---

[14] During that period another more typical occurrence, and one that happened not only in Galicia but in Russian Ukraine as well, was that of switching a Polish identity for a Ukrainian one. Historian Volodymyr Bonifatiiovych Antonovych, Metropolitan Andrei (Roman Mariia Oleksandr Sheptytskyi) and conservative political theoretician V'iacheslav Kazymyrovych Lypynskyi, who played an important role in Ukraine, all provide typical examples of this phenomenon. People who made this switch tended to adopt a pro-Polish orientation after their switch in identity.

[15] Anna Veronika Wendland, *Die Russophilen in Galizien: Ukrainische Konservative zwischen Österreich und Rußland, 1848–1915* (Vienna: Österreichische Akademie der Wissenschaften, 2001).

[16] John-Paul Himka, "The Construction of Nationality in Galician Rus': Icarian Flights in Almost All Directions," in *Intellectuals and the Articulation of the Nation*, ed. Michael D. Kennedy and Ronald Grigor Suny (Ann Arbor: University of Michigan Press, 1999), 109–64.

vych Hrushevs'kyi, who was destined to play a most significant role in the Ukrainian movement in Galicia.

Conflicts between the Galician *narodovtsy* and the Ukrainophiles of the Dnieper region were neverending. Linguistic and other cultural differences were much emphasised by both sides. Addressing activists of the Ukrainian movement in 1906, Hrushevs'kyi saw fit to explicitly point to the case of Serbs and Croats in order to warn against the danger of forming two different nations among a people who shared a common ethnicity.[17]

Up to the First World War, national identity was a subject for discussion only among social elites and a few urban commentators. The overwhelming mass of the population were still peasants, among whom literacy and national ideas were only just beginning to gain a foothold in the early twentieth century. It was not a dualism between Western and Eastern Ukrainian identities that came to the fore in such controversies—though differences between western and eastern parts of Ukraine were indeed numerous and had the potential to generate serious conflict. Yet, at the beginning of the twentieth century, as before, the main line of demarcation between Galicia and the Russian parts of Ukraine continued to be drawn by pan-Russian as against Ukrainian national identities and loyalties.

After the 1905 Russian Revolution, which hugely broadened the range of political opportunities available, the two camps became pitted against each other in an ever more inimical way, and both sides began to acquire more public forms of organisation. It was at this time that a Ukrainian press came into being, albeit still at a fledgling stage. One example of these new media is provided by the daily newspaper, *Rada* (Council). Alongside the already existing underground *hromady* (communities), the Ukrainian camp set up the *Tovarystvo ukrainskykh postupovtsiv* (Society of Ukrainian Progressives, TUP), which possessed many of the features of a fully-fledged political party. Opponents of Ukrainophilia had newspapers of their own, such as *Kiev* and *Kievlianin* ("the Kievian"), and their own organisation, the *Kievskii klub russkikh natsionalistov* (the Kiev Club of Russian Nationalists, KKRN), headed by Kiev-born Dmitrii Ivanovich Pikhno and Anatolii Ivanovich Savenko. Kiev increasingly became the arena in which Little Russians and Ukrainians staged their conflicts, in which the former played the role as ever more determined supporters of the Empire and of Russian nationalism, while the latter presented their Ukrainian nationalism as unfalteringly opposed to the project of creation of a pan-Russian nation and presented itself, with momentum that was to increase over time, as opposed to the Empire itself.[18]

---

[17] Mikhailo Hrushevs'kyi, "Ukraina i Galychyna," *Literaturno-naukovyi visnyk* 36 (1906).
[18] On the notion of "Little Russian" and the terminology of the struggle between followers of Little Russianism and Ukrainophilia see Anton Leonidovich Kotenko, Olga Vladimirovna Martyniuk, and Alexei Il'ich Miller, "Maloross," in *"Poniatiia o Rossii:" K istori-*

How this struggle between the all-Russian and Ukrainian factions could have developed in conditions of relative stability in the Empire will forever remain unanswered. Among the Ukrainian national activists at least, there seems to have been no expectation of success for their cause in the near future. A simple analogy like the kettle on fire, in which water is gradually becoming hotter and hotter, before it inevitably reaches its boiling point, does not apply to the development of national identities. The formation of national identities tends to move in leaps and starts under specific conditions, encompassing large sections of the population. But in times when no abrupt outbreaks of social unrest are occurring, the vast majority of the population are likely to pay little attention to matters of national identity. During a crisis, in contrast, questions of identity and loyalty will quickly take on the importance of matters of life and death, both for social groups and for individuals. And this was precisely the state of affairs after the outbreak of the First World War.

During the war many factors, which in various ways mobilize ethnicity, were at work. Behind the frontlines, the great powers were careful to relentlessly subdue any potential allies of their enemies. At the same time, they began to take advantage of the support of irredentists with a shared national identity, abandoning the limitations they had imposed upon themselves in earlier, more peaceful epochs, when solidarity among empires in the suppression of national movements had seemed a wiser course.[19] During the Russian occupation of Galicia in 1914–15, Ukrainian activists were hunted down, while the Austrian authorities went so far as to set up concentration camps for Ruthenians suspected of Russophile inclinations.[20] Merely having the "wrong" ethnicity or national identity could now provide the justification for arrest, deportation, expropriation or even execution, while, on the contrary, simply being the "right" nationality one could sometimes be rewarded with unexpected privileges.

The German authorities, later imitated by the Austrians, established special camps for Ukrainian prisoners of war (POW), who more often than not had to be informed of their happy condition as Ukrainians. The task of doing this was assigned to propagandists from Galicia, but as soon as it became

---

cheskoi semantike imperskogo perioda, vol. 2, ed. Alexei Il'ich Miller, Denis Sdvizhkov, and Ingrid Schierle (Moscow: Novoe literaturnoe obozrenie, 2012), 392–443.

[19] Mark von Hagen, "The Great War and the Mobilization of Ethnicity in the Russian Empire," in *Post-Soviet Political Order: Conflict and State Building,* ed. Barnett R. Rubin and Jack Snyder (London: Routledge, 1998), 34–57; Alexei Il'ich Miller, "The Value and the Limits of a Comparative Approach in the History of Contiguous Empires on the European Periphery," in *Imperiology: From Empirical Knowledge to Discussing the Russian Empire,* ed. Kimitaka Matsuzato (Sapporo: Slavic Research Center, Hokkaido University, 2007), 19–32.

[20] Aleksandra Iu. Bakhturina, *Politika Rossiiskoi Imperii v Vostochnoi Galitsii v gody Pervoi mirovoi voiny* (Moscow: AIRO-XX, 2000).

clear how far the estrangement between "Russian" Ukraine and the Galicians had gone, new propagandists originally from the Dnieper region had to be brought in. An analogous propaganda campaign was also being conducted among POWs in Russian camps,[21] the difference being that here it was Czech and Slovak prisoners, who already had a highly developed national self-awareness, in whom Russian propagandists were trying to imbue pro-Russian loyalty, while in the camps for Ukrainians, any Ukrainian national identity and associated political loyalty had to be created from scratch. In Ukrainian lands occupied by the Central Powers, the occupiers were also working towards achieving a thorough-going change in the identity and loyalty of the local population.[22]

After a string of German victories and Russian defeats in 1915, the idea of creating an independent Ukraine outside the Russian Empire but under German tutelage began to appear far less chimerical than it had ever been previously. Responding to the new situation, Emperor Nicholas II of Russia finally used the term "Ukrainians," for the first time publicly and with positive connotation in 1915, thanking them for their loyalty to the Empire.[23] By this time, it was dawning on the Tsarist regime that Russia would need to win over the Ukrainians to their side as their army was suffering setbacks against a Germany that had joined the list of Russia's traditional opponents in Ukrainian question—the Poles, Vienna and the Holy See. Petrograd now began playing the Ukrainian nationalist card, trying to convince Ukrainians that only a Russian victory could ensure the unification of all the lands claimed by their national movement.

The belligerent imperial governments now directed unprecedented resources towards supporting separatist movements within their respective enemy states.[24] The Great War had convinced them that a person or group's national identification was one of the most essential, if not *the* most important indicator of one's political loyalty or lack of it. For this reason, policies of repression and deportation were directed against ever larger numbers of the population on the basis of their national identities, and all the great powers at war entered the fight after having constructed and firmly established specific national identities and the associated political loyalties in their own interests.

---

[21] Miller, *Romanov Empire*, 181–210.
[22] Vejas Gabriel Liulevicius, *War Land on the Eastern Front: Culture, National Identity, and German Occupation in World War I* (Cambridge: Cambridge University Press, 2000); Frank M. Grelka, *Die ukrainische Nationalbewegung unter deutscher Besatzungsherrschaft 1918 und 1941/42* (Wiesbaden: Harrassowitz, 2005).
[23] Telegram by Vladimir Borisovich Frederiks, count and the minister of court, 24August 1915, l. 12, el. hr. 27, op. 474, f. 135, Arkhiv Vneshnei Politiki Rossiiskoi Imperii [Archive of Foreign Policy of the Russian Empire] (hereafter AVPRI).
[24] Wolfram Dornik, *Die Ukraine zwischen Selbstbestimmung und Fremdherrschaft 1917–1922* (Graz: Leykam, 2011).

After the February Revolution of 1917, Lavr Georgievich Kornilov, general and then Commander-in-Chief of the Russian Army, ordered the Ukrainization and Belarusification of army units. He was hoping in this way to inoculate them against Bolshevik influence, and at the same time respond effectively to German policies in relation to the Ukrainian and Belarusian questions. Pavlo Petrovych Skoropads'kyi, a Hetman of Ukraine in 1918 and a loyal general of the Russian Empire in 1917, who was tasked by Kornilov to ukrainize his army corps, remembered two years later:

> I answered Kornilov that I had just been in Kiev, where I had met with Ukrainian activists, who had left me with the rather unpleasant impression, that as a result [of Ukrainization] the corps could easily become a factor pushing the Ukrainian movement in a direction undesirable for Russia, etc. Kornilov's nonchalant approach to the question proved to me that he was completely ignorant and uncomprehending of the situation.[25]

In the event, the Russian Provisional Government's effort to mobilize new forces by bolstering Ukrainian national identity proved an utter failure.

The Bolshevik revolution effectively destroyed any legitimate Petrograd government to which the national movements in the peripheries of the Empire could have addressed themselves in order to negotiate either the federalisation of the entire country or their own autonomy. The revolution even led many to seriously ponder the possibilities of full independence for the first time. Moreover, even pro-Russian activists began to see in Ukrainian nationalism a force that might have potential in containing Bolshevik expansion into the south.

It would be impossible to give a full account of events in the years 1917 to 1920 in Ukraine within the confines of this article. It must suffice to mention that during that period power in Kiev changed no fewer than fourteen times. The Tsentral'na Rada (Central Rada) was followed by Skoropads'kyi's hetmanship, then by Symon Vasyl'ovych Petliura's Directorate. In the east, a Ukrainian Soviet Republic (Ukrains'ka Radians'ka Respublika) was established with Kharkiv as its centre, while in Galicia an ephemeral West Ukrainian People's Republic (Zakhidnoukrains'ka Narodna Respublika) briefly came into being. Having suffered defeat, Petliura went over to the Poles. Equally, after having lost the battle for L'viv to the Poles in March 1919, Galician Ukrainian units attached themselves to Anton Ivanovich Denikin's White Russian forces. The Red Army, in combination with Nestor Ivanovych Makhno's anarchist army, which was overwhelmingly made up of local peasants, defeated White Army General Petr Nikolaevich Vrangel'. Thus, in the 1919–20 period various Ukrainian military formations were siding with the Poles, the White Russians or the Bolsheviks in a perfect illustration of how bizarrely interwoven the antagonisms and alliances of the Ukrainian lands

---

[25] Pavlo P. Skoropads'kyi, *Spohady: Kinec' 1917 – hruden' 1918* (Philadelphia: Skhidnoievropeis'kyi Doslidnyi Instytut Im. V. Lypyns'koho, 1995), 64.

were, with the various national and social orientations giving rise to an inextricably complex pattern of political alliances and animosities.

Within a timespan of not quite seven years from the outbreak of the First World War up to the end of the Polish-Soviet War, the population of Ukraine had been addressed under the name of "Ukrainian" by propagandists from Ukrainian, German, Austrian, Polish, French, Russian and Bolshevik forces. The population was promised land, order and protection from Bolshevism in an independent Ukraine and, on the contrary, a shining communist future within a Soviet Ukraine, among many other breathless pledges. Soldiers from Ukrainian territories served in a wide variety of Ukrainian units and were interned in separate camps set up especially for Ukrainian POWs. When historians talk of a "long nineteenth century" ending in 1914, one of their implications is that from that year on nationalism began to spread at a hugely accelerated speed, together with the nationalist patterns of identification and of loyalty building that went with it.

Today's opposition between "Western Ukrainian" and "Eastern Ukrainian" identities came into being during the twentieth century, and especially following the experiences of the interwar period, when the Bolsheviks relentlessly removed all indicators of any Little Russian identity from the public sphere. Supporters of Little Russianism and all-Russianism were forced into exile, and their political loyalty was addressed to a Russia and to a Russian nation that would emerge free of Bolshevism in some unpredictably distant future. A much more influential dichotomy of two different Ukrainian identities developed in Poland and the Ukrainian Soviet Republic of the interwar years.

In the Eastern variant of Ukrainian identity, which developed in Soviet Ukraine, Russia and the Russians were never cast in the role of the "defining other." Antisemitism was not a constitutive part of this identification. Also, the history of the Great Patriotic War, as it was told over and over again by Soviet propaganda, left the Eastern Ukrainians in the belief that they alone among Ukrainians had done the fighting in the righteous cause alongside the Russians. As a consequence, the dividing lines between Russianness and Ukrainianness were permeable—they could be crossed easily through mixed marriages and within the individual biographies of the people of the region. For example, Leonid Il'ich Brezhnev, as he was embarking on his party career on a local level in Dnipropetrovsk, was officially registered as Ukrainian. But as soon as his career began to soar up to the higher echelons of the Union, his personal documents listed him as Russian.

The Western Ukrainian identity, as it was shaped in the interwar Poland, saw Russians and Jews as the enemies. This identity was based on a historic narrative, in which the Ukrainian Insurgent Army, which cooperated with Nazi Germany and fought the Soviets during and after the war, played the role of the main national heroes.

Mutual relations between these two Ukrainian identities in some elements resembled those that had existed between Ukrainians and Little Russians up until the First World War. From the Ukrainian point of view, the Little Russians needed some national education and had to be subjected to social engineering, as their problem was that they had lost their way and had been turned into bad Ukrainians through the influence of Russian assimilation. Western Ukrainians have come to view Eastern Ukrainians in a very similar way. If the Little Russian refused to let go of his identity, and more especially if he went so far as to insist that his Little Russianism should become the dominant identity of the territory, this turned him into an "enemy compatriot" for the Ukrainian, a mere appendage of the Muscovites. And it is in just such a light that the Western Ukrainian of today sees the Eastern Ukrainian who insists on defending his position. Likewise, Little Russians thought of the Ukrainophiles as being under the damaging foreign influence of the Poles, the Austrians or the Germans, and accused them of propagating a damaging and aggressive form of nationalism. Similarly, for today's Eastern Ukrainians, Western Ukrainians are essentially radical nationalists subservient to the interests of Poles and Americans. Both sides purport to better represent democratic values and modernisation than their opponents.

In 2014 the long history of conflicts over national identities and loyalties in Ukraine once again took a tragic turn. As in the past, powerful foreign players are taking an active part in fomenting the confrontation.

Translated by Andreas R. Hofmann.

Franziska Davies

GENERATING LOYALTY
The Crimean Tatars and Military Reform in Late Imperial Russia

One of the most systematically oppressed groups in Russian occupied Crimea at present are its Tatar inhabitants, who have constantly been targeted by the authorities since the annexation of the Ukrainian peninsula by the Russian Federation in 2014. Activists in particular have become victims of arbitrary detentions and violence while Tatar institutions, most visibly the Crimean Tatar television channel, have been closed down.[1] The Russian government regards this ethnic group as being a particular threat to their claim to Crimea as a Russian territory. Indeed Crimean Tatars were at the forefront of those among the peninsula's population who rejected the takeover of their homeland and expressed loyalty to the Ukrainian state.

The annexation of 2014 is not the first Crimean Tatar encounter with Russian rule. It was back in the late eighteenth century, during the reign of Empress Catherine II, that the Crimea was annexed by Russia for the first time. Discussing questions of loyalty can serve as a vantage point to conceptualize the history of the Crimean Tatars within the Russian Empire, because such questions constantly shaped imperial policies in the region. The most brutal episode of Russian-Tatar history of the twentieth century, i.e. the 1944 deportation of the Crimean Tatars from their homeland based on (false) allegations of collective collaboration with Nazi Germany, sometimes obscures the fact that imperial policies in the nineteenth century were not founded solely on repression, even if repressive measures played an important role in the region.[2] In fact, the Tsarist Empire employed a variety of different strategies to try to secure the Crimean Tatars' loyalty, particularly in view of the clear presence of the Ottoman Empire as an alternative homeland. By the 1860s, many in the Russian administration no longer deemed the emigration of the Crimean Tatars to the Ottoman Empire desirable and thus strategies of keeping them in the Russian imperial realm began to gain relevance.[3]

---

[1] See for example: Uwe Halbach, "Repression nach der Annexion. Russlands Umgang mit den Krimtataren," *Osteuropa* 9–10 (2014): 179–90.
[2] Mara Kozelsky, "Casualties of Conflict: Crimean Tatars during the Crimean War," *Slavic Review* 67, no. 4 (2008): 866–91.
[3] James H. Meyer, "Immigration, Return, and the Politics of Citizenship: Russian Muslims in the Ottoman Empire, 1860–1914," *International Journal of Middle East Studies* 39, no. 1 (2007): 15–32.

This article analyzes the process of forging loyalties within an imperial order by examining the history of military service among the Crimean Tatars between the 1870s and the 1890s. It will approach these questions from two perspectives in order to reconstruct both the practices and the semantics of loyalty in this particular case. After a brief outline of the history of the Crimean Tatars in the Russian Empire it will concentrate firstly on the policies employed by the state with regard to the implementation of the 1874 military reform among the Crimean Tatar population. The decree of 1874, the last of Tsar Alexander II's so-called Great Reforms, was an attempt to introduce universal liability to military service to an autocratic and ethnically and religiously heterogeneous empire. As the example of the Crimean Tatars shows, the challenge faced by the reformers in this context forced them to maneuver between what were potentially contradictory principles. On the one hand, the very idea of universal liability to military service encompassed the notion that it was *every* male subject's duty to serve the tsar as a soldier and thus express his loyalty to the fatherland. On the other hand, the empire's non-Russian subjects were bound to St. Petersburg through specific historical experiences, which in turn determined the nature of the policies directed toward them. In case of the Crimean Tatars the recent experience of migration to the Ottoman Empire was a decisive factor and, as I demonstrate below, induced the authorities to do more than simply draft Crimean Tatars into the army in the regular manner, as such an approach might have encouraged them to flee Russia again. Instead the military offered them certain concessions in return for their loyalty. In this context, the war ministry paid particular attention to the implications that recruitment as soldiers would have on their religious life. At the same time, military service was itself regarded as an instrument with the capacity to generate loyalty and thereby promote the Russification of the Tatars. The second part of the article looks at the semantics of loyalty as expressed in historical narratives produced in the late imperial period on the military service provided by Crimean Tatars. I argue that these narratives constructed a shared Russian-Tatar history in which the Tatars' role in the army, and in particular their participation in the war against Napoleon, was interpreted as a symbol of their allegiance to Russia and to the tsar, and as a token of the Tatars' successful integration into the empire.

The Crimean Tatars in the Russian Empire

The Crimean Khanate was annexed by Empress Catherine II in 1783. As a result of this annexation, the political, social, religious and ethnic landscape of the peninsula was to change profoundly over the course of the nineteenth century. Back in the fifteenth and sixteenth centuries the Crimean Khanate had been an important political player in Eastern Europe and up until the sixteenth century it had competed with Muscovy in the effort to succeed the Golden Horde. During the period of rivalry between Muscovy and the Polish-

Lithuanian Commonwealth it occasionally allied with the latter, yet at the same time the khanate served as a "buffer zone" separating the Ottoman Empire from both the Muscovite state and the Polish-Lithuanian Commonwealth. The dynamics of power between Russia and the Crimean Khanate began to change with the reign of Tsar Peter I, who managed to transform the Muscovite state into a powerful empire. From that time on there were numerous efforts of Russian rulers to subdue the khanate to Russian power until it finally lost its independence during the reign of Catherine II as a result of increasing Russian intervention in Crimean affairs in order to repel Ottoman influence in the region.[4]

The newly acquired territory was then fairly swiftly incorporated into the administrative structure of the state within the newly created Taurida Governorate. Initially Catherine II attempted to co-opt the aristocratic elite of the Crimean Tatars into the Russian system of estates. While her efforts may be read as a policy of integration, the process of incorporation actually dragged on for many decades and the numbers granted noble status were continually reduced.[5] The Russian annexation of the Crimea thus led to the gradual disempowerment and marginalization of local elites. On a symbolic level, too, the peninsula was re-imagined as Russian, but also as an imperial space in which Greek, Russian, Tatar and Byzantine heritage could co-exist.[6] A turning point in the history of the encounter between the Crimean Tatars and the Russian state was the Crimean War from 1853 to 1856, during which both local authorities and central government in St. Petersburg grew increasingly suspicious of the loyalty of the Crimean Tatars. Harassment and arbitrary detentions followed. Deteriorating relations with the state, combined with the economic misery brought about by the war, eventually led to a mass exodus of the Tatar population to the Ottoman Empire, a process at first welcomed by some in the imperial administration, including the tsar. The exodus of the Crimean Tatars was followed by a strengthening of Crimea's Christian infrastructure at the expense of Islam through the increased influx of Russian settlers and the creation of a new diocese on the peninsula.[7]

However, in spite of these experiences, historians have also pointed to different political strategies employed by the Russian Empire toward the Crimean Tatars. For instance, Alan W. Fisher, whose assessment of Russian policies in Crimea is fairly negative overall, identified the annexation of

---

[4] Alan Washburn Fisher, *The Crimean Tatars* (Stanford, CA: Hoover Institution Press, 1978), 47–80.
[5] Kelly O'Neill, "Rethinking Elite Integration: The Crimean Murzas and the Evolution of Russian Nobility," *Cahiers du Monde Russe* 51, no. 2–3 (2010): 397–417.
[6] Kelly O'Neill, "Constructing Imperial Identities in the Borderland: Architecture, Islam, and the Transformation of the Crimean Landscape," *Ab Imperio*, no. 2 (2006): 163–92.
[7] Kozelsky, "Casualties of Conflict," and Kozelsky, *Christianizing Crimea: Shaping Sacred Space in the Russian Empire and Beyond* (DeKalb: Northern Illinois University Press, 2010), esp. 150–74.

Crimea in 1783 as a turning point for the formulation of a more tolerant approach to Islam under Catherine II.[8] In 1788 the Orenburg Muslim Spiritual Assembly (*Orenburgskoe magometanskoe dukhovnoe sobranie*) was founded for the Volga-Ural region and the Taurida Muslim Spiritual Administration (*Tavricheskoe magometanskoe dukhovnoe pravlenie*) in Crimea followed in 1794. Both institutions were headed by a state-appointed mufti, who was to serve as a contact person for the Muslim communities of European Russia. This institutionalization of Islam took place within the wider context of a new religious policy under Catherine II, which foresaw the exercise of government control over non-Russians through the use of religious intermediaries. The partitions of Poland, the Bashkir uprisings and the annexation of the Crimea all pointed to the need to arrive at an arrangement with the non-Russian subjects of the empire. By Catherine's logic religion had the potential to serve not only as a tool for disciplining the new subjects, but also for generating loyalty toward the Russian Empire.[9]

The Russian Empire found itself in a situation in which it was competing for the loyalty of its new Muslim subjects against the Ottoman Empire. The Crimean Tatars were spared the fate of the Volga-Ural Muslims in the sixteenth century after the conquest of the khanates of Kazan and Astrakhan under Ivan IV: in Crimea, there was to be no destruction of mosques or coercive campaigns of conversion. Instead Prince Grigorii Aleksandrovich Potemkin instructed Baron Osip Andreevich Igel'strom, who commanded the Russian troops in the Crimea, to ensure that culture and religion of the local Tatars were respected by the new rulers.[10] Igel'strom's experiences in the Crimea were to prove vital for the implementation of the new policy on Islam in the Volga-Ural region, where he attempted to impose a church-like structure onto Muslim communities.[11] While the degree to which Muslims were integrated into the Russian imperial realm still remained limited, this new approach nonetheless entailed a form of state recognition of Muslims living in European Russia who had been subjected to violence only a few decades earlier.[12]

---

[8] Alan W. Fisher, "Enlightened Despotism and Islam Under Catherine II," *Slavic Review* 27, no. 4 (1968): 542–53.

[9] Catherine laid the foundations for this approach, which was to develop further in the first half of the nineteenth century. For a thorough analysis of this process with regard to all of the Tsar's "foreign faiths," see Paul W. Werth, *The Tsar's Foreign Faiths: Toleration and the Fate of Religious Freedom in Imperial Russia* (Oxford: Oxford University Press, 2014), esp. 46–73.

[10] Fisher, *Crimean Tatars*, 72.

[11] Robert D. Crews, *For Prophet and Tsar: Islam and Empire in Russia and Central Asia* (Cambridge, MA: Harvard University Press, 2006), 52–56.

[12] Werth, *The Tsar's Foreign Faiths*, 73. Most recently Mustafa Tuna has pointed out that, in spite of the institutionalization of Islam in the late eighteenth century and the attempt to turn state-recognized Muslim religious elites into agents of the state, the level of day-to-day interaction between state and Muslim communities in the Volga-Ural re-

In spite of this relatively tolerant approach to Islam in the late eighteenth century in the Crimea and in the Volga-Ural region, over the course of the nineteenth century Russian perceptions of Islam changed for the worse. By the second half of the century, a "Muslim question" had emerged.[13] Central to the administrative elites' apprehension of the Muslim population in various regions was their isolation from Russian state and society, accompanied by their allegedly questionable loyalties. Several factors contributed to this intensified fear of Islam, including experience of Muslim resistance to Russian conquests in the Northern Caucasus, the penetration of Central Asia and the repeated waves of apostasy from Orthodoxy to Islam in the Volga-Ural region.[14] Another important factor was the Crimean War and the suspected disloyalty of the Crimean Tatars. The emergence of the "Muslim question" was also connected to broader reform debates in the Russian Empire. Russia's humiliating defeat in the Crimean War triggered the reforms of Tsar Alexander II's reign from 1855 to 1881.[15] The war had exposed the Russian Empire's military, social and economic backwardness as compared to Britain and France. The tsar's reforms aimed at modernizing the country and hereby preserving Russia's standing as one of Europe's great powers. The liberation of the serfs in 1861 marked the beginning of ambitious plans for transformation and indeed profound changes were to follow in the empire's judicial, administrative and educational systems, culminating in 1874, when a universal liability to military service was introduced. In relation to the non-Russian population, the transformation of the state also posed challenges to tested strategies of imperial rule. One example of the intersection of reform debates with practices of imperial rule are the deliberations surrounding the introduction of military service among Crimean Tatars living in the Taurida Governorate, which were among the regions in which Alexander's reform were to be im-

---

gion in fact remained quite limited until at least the 1860s, when this model of "mediated distance" began to come under critical scrutiny, see: Mustafa Özgür Tuna, *Imperial Russia's Muslims: Islam, Empire, and European Modernity, 1788–1914* (Cambridge: Cambridge University Press, 2015), esp. 37–56. In this respect Tuna has convincingly challenged Robert Crews' interpretation of imperial Russia as a "confessional state," see: Robert D. Crews, "Empire and the Confessional State: Islam and Religious Politics in Nineteenth-Century Russia," *The American Historical Review* 108, no. 1 (2003): 50–83.

[13] For a comprehensive analysis for the discourse on the "Muslim question" within the Russian administration, see: Elena I. Campbell, *The Muslim Question and Russian Imperial Governance* (Bloomington, IN: Indiana University Press, 2015).
[14] Ibid., 21.
[15] For a critical discussion of Alexander's reforms, see for example: Larissa Zakhorova, "The Reign of Alexander II: A Watershed?," in *The Cambridge History of Russia*, ed. Maureen Perrie, Dominic Lieven, and Ronald Gregor Suny, vol. 2, *Imperial Russia, 1689–1917*, ed. Dominic Lieven (Cambridge: Cambridge University Press, 2006), 593–616.

plemented.¹⁶ This process also illustrates how certain logics of imperial rule brought about by the rivalry between the Ottoman and Russian Empires over the loyalties of the Crimean Tatars remained in play, in spite of the serious deterioration in relations between Muslims and the Russian state in the second half of the 19th century.

Generating Loyalty: Universal Liability to Military Service and the Crimean Tatars

The central aims of the military reform of 1874 were to organize the armed forces more cost-efficiently, to considerably reduce the length of military service, to organize a reserve system and to improve educational standards in the army. All this had to be achieved without placing an excessive burden on civilian life.¹⁷ However, the introduction of universal liability to military service had another dimension in the multiethnic and multireligious Russian Empire: it was intended to serve as an instrument for the cultural integration of non-Russian recruits by means of exposing them to Russian language and culture.¹⁸ This was not a new idea, but had been one of the motives for subjecting the Jews of the Russian Empire to service in the army in 1827.¹⁹ The army was thus looked upon as an institution which could level Russia's cultural heterogeneity, which bureaucratic elites increasingly regarded as a potential threat. In this context, recruiting non-Russians into the army also bore potential problems. Who could be trusted as soldiers and how could their loyalty be ensured? On an ideological level at least, the reform of 1874 articulated a heightened expectation of loyalty toward the Tsar's subjects. In the decree itself, the defense of the "fatherland" was religiously elevated to the status of a "holy endeavor" (*sviatoe delo*) for the entire population.²⁰ The use

---

[16] Campbell, *The Muslim Question*, 28. Alexander's reforms reached other regions, such as the Caucasus, later and often in a modified form. For the link between the "Great Reforms" and the efforts at Russification in the Muslim Volga-Ural region in education, see: Tuna, *Imperial Russia's Muslims*, 57–78.

[17] See: Werner Benecke, *Militär, Reform und Gesellschaft im Zarenreich: Die Wehrpflicht in Russland, 1874–1914* (Paderborn: Schöningh, 2006), esp. 38–41; idem, "Die Allgemeine Wehrpflicht in Russland: Zwischen militärischem Anspruch und zivilen Interessen," *Journal of Modern European History* 5, no. 2 (2007): 244–63.

[18] For a systematic analysis of the imperial dimension in the reform debates, see: Robert F. Baumann, *The Debates over Universal Military Service in Russia, 1870–1874* (Ann Arbor, MI: University Microfilms International, 1982), 158–207.

[19] Yohanan Petrovsky-Shtern, *Jews in the Russian Army, 1827–1917: Drafted into Modernity* (Cambridge: Cambridge University Press, 2009), esp. 24–60.

[20] Ia. Livin, G. Ranskii, and A. D. Protopopov, eds., *Ustav o voinskoi povinnosti (1874 g.) so vsemi izmeneniiami i dopolneniiami, vnesennymi zakonom 23 iiunia 1912 g. cb izmenenii Ustava o voinskoi povinnosti i drugimi zakonopolozheniiami, izdannymi po 20 marta 1913 g., s ocherkom osnovnykh polozhenii novago zakona, raz"iasneniiami, izvlechenny-*

of such words indicate a shift that had taken place between the late eighteenth to the nineteenth centuries: while in the eighteenth century exemption from military service had been regarded as a privilege which would often be granted to new subjects in return for loyalty or for conversion to Christianity, by 1874 it had come to be regarded as the ultimate manifestation of loyalty.[21]

In this context, the reputation of Crimean Tatars was not very reassuring. As outlined above, their loyalty to the Russian Empire had been doubted by many in the administration, including the tsar himself, who had gone so far as to applaud their emigration to the Ottoman Empire. As rumors began to spread about the impending military reform in 1873, this pattern seemed to repeat itself, as the local administration recorded that an increasing number of men were leaving the peninsula and that disturbances were occurring in some districts.[22] The willingness to serve in the Russian army was obviously quite low. However, migration to the Ottoman Empire was no longer welcomed by local and central authorities. By the 1870s, attitudes of the Russian administrators to the emigration of Crimean Tatars had changed considerably, largely for pragmatic reasons. As James Meyer has pointed out, a change of strategy occurred in the aftermath of the Crimean War, partially because of the obvious economic damage caused to the region by Tatar emigration, but also because modern notions of citizenship had become more influential in official thinking.[23] As a consequence, it had become increasingly difficult to renounce Russian citizenship and at the same time the Ottoman Empire had facilitated the process of granting citizenship to Muslim immigrants.[24] Thus, the desire to retain Crimean Tatars within the Russian realm shaped discussions of how best to implement liability to military service among them.

The governor-general of the military district of Odessa, Pavel E. Kotsebu, who reported to St. Petersburg on the disturbances in Crimea, was nonetheless convinced that it was not the prospect of military service itself that the Tatars feared but rather the implications compulsory soldiering would have for their religious life. Finding themselves dispersed across different parts of the empire would make it difficult for them to continue to observe the obligations of Islam. Hence, the governor-general argued, the government would be

---

mi iz opredelenii Pr. Senata, tsirkuliarov ministerstv, instruktsii i t. d., i s alfavitnym predmetnym ukazatelem (Saint Petersburg: Pravo, 1913), 30.

[21] This ideological shift did not, however, prevent Russian administrators from guaranteeing the exemption from military service to the inhabitants of newly conquered regions such as Central Asia. See: Sergei N. Abashin, *Tsentral'naia Aziia v sostave Rossiiskoi* (Moskva: Novoe Literaturnoe Obozrenie, 2008), 88.

[22] Brian Glyn Williams, *The Crimean Tatars: The Diaspora Experience and the Forging of a Nation* (Leiden: Brill, 2001), 185–87.

[23] Meyer, "Immigration, Return, and the Politics of Citizenship," esp. 16–17. For a systematic analysis for the development of "citizenship" in the Russian Empire, see: Eric Lohr, *Russian Citizenship: From Empire to Soviet Union* (Cambridge, MA: Harvard University Press, 2012).

[24] Meyer, "Immigration, Return, and the Politics of Citizenship."

best advised to organize the Tatars' service in the army in such a way that it remained "consistent with the Tatars' own wishes" (*sovpadatlo s sobstvennym zhelaniem tatar*).²⁵ The unrest among the Crimean Tatar population in 1873 induced the government to send Prince Semën Vorontsov to the Crimea to investigate and to try to ease tensions. Vorontsov's father, Mikhail Vorontsov, was still held in high regard among Crimean Tatar peasants for his defense of their landholding rights during his tenure as governor-general of the province of New Russia between 1828 and 1854.²⁶ Following his father's footsteps Prince Vorontsov also distinguished himself as an advocate of the Crimean Tatars. He put the population's reaction down to the fact that the reform bill had been published in Russian and then badly explained by the local administration. Vorontsov advised the government to take great care with regard to the implementation of military service among the Crimean Tatars and declared that "the more humanitarian and the more in correspondence with their customs these measures will be, the stronger and more quickly will a love for military service develop among the Tatars."²⁷ He also championed the idea that the government had to make concessions toward the Crimean Tatars. He demanded that the Tatars inhabiting the steppe region should be granted land, while the living conditions of those living in the remote mountain areas should be improved through investments in infrastructure. Roads should be constructed to connect the towns of Alushta, Feodosia, Karasubazar with the region around Sudak. The named regions were abundant in vineyards, and improved transport routes would therefore be beneficial for the production of wine, as well as bringing the mountain Tatars into closer contact "with other more civilized peoples."²⁸ Vorontsov also advised a fair hearing of all complaints about the expropriation of houses and land that the Crimean Tatars had suffered at the hands of the treasury in the southern coastal areas in 1838. An equally unresolved issue was the status of the *vaqf*, the religious endowments through which mosques were maintained and the Muslim "clergy" (*dukhovenstvo*) was paid.²⁹ At a more general level, Vorontsov proposed issuing passports to all of the Crimean Tatars in accordance with the laws generally in force throughout the empire, thus putting the Tatars on an equal footing with other subjects in this respect. This measure would facilitate their pilgrimage to Mecca.³⁰ In sum, Vorontsov's proposals foresaw the amelioration of the Tatars' economic conditions, a thorough review of their grievances against Russian imperial policies and an

---

[25] Fond 400, opis' 2, delo 2420, ll. 1–2, Rossiiskii Gosudarstvennyi Voenno-Istoricheskii Arkhiv (hereafter RGVIA).
[26] Williams, *The Crimean Tatars*, 84–86, 187. The governor-generalship of New Russia and Bessarabia was in existence until 1874 and included the Taurida Governorate.
[27] F. 400, op. 2, d. 2420, l. 43, RGVIA.
[28] Ibid., l. 44ob.
[29] Ibid., ll. 45ob–46.
[30] Ibid., l. 45ob.

improvement in their legal status, enabling them to fulfill their religious duty of pilgrimage to the holy city of Islam. The plan to implement liability to military service among the Crimean Tatar thus turned into a vantage point from which to consider their rights within Russia's imperial order. These rights remained extremely restricted, but Vorontsov's deliberations indicate that even in nineteenth century autocratic Russia, a certain reciprocity between duties and rights was ingrained in discussions on military service.

Alexander II accepted the recommendations insofar as he decided to have them reviewed by the Ministry of State Property.[31] There was however one suggestion which the Tsar turned down: According to Vorontsov rumors were still circulating that Tatars would gather on Easter to "slit Christians" (*rezat' khristian*).[32] These rumors had proved difficult to dissipate so perhaps the Tsar could assure the Tatars himself that he was aware of their "devotion" (*predannost'*) and their "honorable convictions and customs" (*chestnyia ubezhdeniia i pravila*) and would not for a minute consider such rumors trustworthy.[33] Next to this paragraph the emperor simply wrote "*net*".

Nonetheless, discussions on military reform and the Crimean Tatars were shaped along the lines of the basic idea that Prince Vorontsov had expressed: The government needed to implement the changes with great care, to give due consideration to the traditions and the religion of the Tatars and to offer them something in return for their service. The main staff in St. Petersburg set up a commission in 1874 whose task was to work out how this could be achieved at a practical level.

Their recommendations were forwarded to the military district of Odessa in the same year.[34] The most fundamental of the measures was the decision to allow the Crimean Tatars serve within their own squadron, which was to be stationed in their homeland, and to reduce their length of active service to just two instead of six years.[35] The formation of a Crimean Tatar irregular unit was not a new invention as such a squadron had existed until 1864.[36] However, the decision for its reinstatement in 1874 was clearly a compromise, since the fundamental principle guiding the military reform had been—at least rhetorically—to make every male subject of the tsar, regardless of his social standing or ethnic and religious origin, liable to military service. The reformers seem to have been aware of their own lack of consistency, but ar-

---

[31] See the tsar's handwritten remarks in the cited document.
[32] Ibid., ll. 45ob–46.
[33] Ibid., l. 46ob.
[34] F. 400, op. 2, d. 2765, l. 75, RGVIA.
[35] F. 400, op. 2, d. 5263, l. 2, RGVIA. In 1875 the squadron (*eskadron*) was restructured into a division (*divizion*). During the war against Napoleon regiments (*polki*) had been formed among the Crimean Tatars. In the following I will use the terms "squadron," "division" or "regiment" in accordance with the terms employed in the sources discussed in a given section.
[36] Fisher, *Crimean Tatars*, 8.

gued that this was merely a first step toward the goal of integrating Crimean Tatars into the regular ranks of the army completely. In addition, unlike its predecessor, the new squadron would not be commanded by a Crimean Tatar, but by Russian officers and through a Russian cadre, which meant that rank-and-file soldiers would be trained in a Russian environment.[37] Thus, the squadron's formation was seen as a temporary step which would first weaken the Tatars' resistance to military service, then accustom them to Russian culture and eventually turn them into loyal soldiers who could be recruited into the army on a par with the rest of the Russian population. The Russifying function ascribed to the squadron was expressed explicitly in the commission's recommendations: From the first day of recruitment, Russian officers and noncommissioned officers were to ensure that Crimean Tatar soldiers, who could generally be expected to have no knowledge of Russian, became familiarized with the language.[38] The commission also made clear that absolutely no compromises were to be made in relation to enforcing discipline.[39]

At the same time, however, the military was instructed to pay special attention to the religious traditions of the Crimean Tatars. The commission devoted considerable attention to the question of how Muslim religious life was to be organized within the squadron. This was presumably a response to what both Kotsebu and Vorontsov had already pointed out: that it was fear for their religion that had induced Crimean Tatars to regard military service as a threat. The squadron was to be stationed in the midst of the Crimean Tatar population and it was therefore imperative that their religious traditions were met "with respect"[40]. In practice, this meant that military training would have to be halted half an hour before the five daily prayers so that soldiers could ritually wash their bodies as their religion required. By the same token Muslims were to be freed from service on Fridays and for the high Muslim holidays of *Kurban bairam* (the festival of the sacrifice) and *Uraza bairam* (the end of Ramadan).[41] During Ramadan itself, a period in which the devout Muslim was to fast until sunset and dedicate himself to the study of the Koran, military training would need to be less rigorous. In this context, the commission explicitly instructed the squadron's commanders to ensure that the Russian cadre desisted from making fun of Tatar traditions or employing the term "Tatar" in any derogatory fashion.[42] In its conclusion, the commission even advised the soldiers of the Russian cadre to abstain from hanging Orthodox icons in the military barracks in which they would be living together with the Tatars in order to minimize the likelihood of causing

---

[37] F. 400, op. 2, d. 2420, l. 54ob, RGVIA.
[38] F. 400, op. 2, d. 2765, ll. 41–42ob, RGVIA.
[39] Ibid., ll. 10–12.
[40] F. 400, op. 2, d. 2765, l. 14., RGVIA.
[41] Ibid., l. 14ob.
[42] Ibid., ll. 15–15ob.

offense to the religious convictions of either Christians or Muslims.[43] In effect, the commission was advising the Christian-Orthodox cadre to keep a low profile in religious matters in order to ease potential problems in the multifaith squadron.

The squadron was also to have two Muslim military chaplains, a mullah and a muezzin, who were to be paid from the state's payroll and who were obliged to inform commanders of times of prayer and religious holidays.[44] The official institutionalization of Muslim chaplains by the military in 1874 in just one squadron provides yet another example of the state's concessions toward the Crimean Tatars in return for their loyalty. A comparison with the policy toward the Volga-Ural Muslims illustrates this point: administrators were less worried about the loyalty of the Volga-Ural Muslims as soldiers and there were no reports of their emigration to the Ottoman Empire in 1874. Service in the regular army by Volga-Ural Muslims dated back to the eighteenth century and consequently nobody in the administration questioned that they would serve on a par with Russians in the reformed army.[45] They were dispersed over the whole of the Russian Empire and any cases where Muslim chaplains were appointed were the result of ad hoc decisions by local commanders and not of any systematic policy of the main staff.[46] Indeed, a survey into the status of non-Orthodox chaplains in the armed forces in 1895 revealed that the number and assignments of Muslim military chaplains in the regular army in no way corresponded with the number of Muslim soldiers in any given military district. The war ministry's response was to simply dismiss all of the Muslim chaplains, since the number of Muslim soldiers was not deemed large enough to justify their employment by the state.[47] In this case the war ministry simply did not think it necessary to consider any kind of special treatment due to religious affiliation, because it was simply not

---

[43] Ibid., ll. 50–50ob.
[44] Ibid., l. 15.
[45] For the discussions on the Volga-Ural Muslims in the reformed army, see: Delo po voinskoi povinnosti, *Doklad 2-go otdela ob otpravlenii voennoi povinnosti magometanami Evropeiskoi Rossi i Sibiri (zasedanie 31 marta 1872 g.)* The deliberations do, however, point to a bias against the Volga-Ural Muslims as potential draft dodgers, see esp. 2–4.
[46] I have analyzed this policy in detail in the second chapter of my dissertation on *Muslims in the Russian Army, 1874–1917* defended at the Ludwig Maximilian University of Munich in January 2016 which I am currently revising for publication. For Muslim chaplains in the Russian army, see also: Kh. M. Abdullin, "Musul'manskoe dukhovenstvo i voennoe vedomstvo Rossiiskoi Imperii (konets XVII–nachalo XX vv.)," (dissertation, Tatarskii gosudarstvennyi gumanitarno-pedagogicheskii universitet, 2007); Franziska Davies, "Confessional Policies toward Jews and Muslims in the Russian Empire and the Case of the Army," in *Jews and Muslims in the Russian Empire and the Soviet Union*, ed. Michael Brenner, Franziska Davies, and Martin Schulze Wessel (Göttingen: Vandenhoeck and Ruprecht, 2015), 47–64; and Il'dus K. Zagidullin, *Musul'manskoe bogosluzhdenie v uchrezhdeniiakh Rossiiskoi Imperii: Evropeiskaia chast' Rossii i Sibir'* (Kazan: Institut im. Sh. Mardzhani, 2006), 31–44.
[47] F. 400, op. 2, d. 5627, ll. 182–88, RGVIA.

deemed necessary. This fact points to the utilitarian nature of the Russian Empire's policies toward the Crimean Tatars: the relatively tolerant approach to their religion was not born out of any particular appreciation of Islam, but resulted rather from the specific state of relations between the state and the Crimean Tatars in the 1870s and the ultimate goal of Russian administrators during the period—namely to reduce emigration to the Ottoman Empire and to gradually turn the Crimean Tatars into obedient and thus useful subjects of the tsar.

This long-term strategy of the Russian Empire was to become clear in the ensuing years. After the Crimean Tatar squadron had been successfully established in 1874, both the Odessa military district and the governor of the Taurida province voiced their dissatisfaction with the state of affairs in the late 1880s and early 1890s. In his annual report to St. Petersburg in 1887, the governor of the Taurida province pointed to the fact that the existing arrangement actually favored the Tatar population in comparison to the non-Tatar population, because of the relatively low number recruited into the Crimean Tatar division. Between 1884 and 1887 roughly fifteen percent of the Tatar population had been recruited, while the corresponding figure for non-Tatars was just under thirty percent.[48] The governor emphasized that the military service of the Crimean Tatars was intended to serve two functions: to strengthen the Russian army and to promote the Russification of the Tatars.[49] In practice, however, it had resulted in discrimination against the non-Tatar population. These sentiments were echoed by the local military administration, which also expressed concerns about the effectiveness of the division from a military point of view. In the early 1890s, the Odessa military district pointed to the unit's deficiencies: the reduced terms of service did not give enough time to improve the Russian language skills of Tatar soldiers. Communication between soldiers and Russian officers was often only possible via a translator. The situation also rendered a proper military education impossible. Just like the civilian administration, the military pointed to the principle of fairness imbedded in the reform of 1874. At present, the Crimean Tatars were serving in privileged conditions as compared to their peers in the Orenburg and Kazan regions.[50] They suggested measures that foresaw a gradual increase in the term of active service and a considerable reduction in the number of Crimean Tatars allowed to serve in the Crimean division. Ultimately, only the numbers required for the upkeep of the division would be allowed to serve in it, and all remaining Crimean Tatar recruits were to be

---

[48] F. 400, op. 2, d. 5263, ll. 2–3, RGVIA.
[49] Ibid., l. 3. The term "Russification" remained ill-defined and contested in the bureaucratic and intellectual discourse of late imperial Russia, but did not imply a subject's total assimilation into Russian culture, see: Darius Staliūnas, *Making Russians. Meaning and Practice of Russification in Lithuania and Belarus after 1863* (Amsterdam, New York: Rodopi, 2007), 57–70.
[50] F. 400, op. 5, d. 1167, ll. 2, 43ob, 58ob–59, RGVIA.

allocated in a range of divisions outside of the Crimea.⁵¹ In 1894 the Russian-Tatar newspaper "The Interpreter" (*Perevodchik/Terzhüman*) reported that these men were to be sent to the Fourteenth and the Thirty-Fourth Infantry Divisions in the governorates of Kherson and Bessarabia.⁵² The privileged position of the Crimean Tatars in the army had thus been substantially curtailed.

A number of factors account for this change of policy. Firstly, the concessions of 1874 had always been regarded as a temporary solution. The long-term goal of making the Crimean Tatars liable to military service on the basis of the same principles as the rest of the population was not lost to the civil and military administrations. Secondly, both the military value of the Crimean Tatar division and its effectiveness as an instrument of Russification was modest at best. Thirdly, the drive to universalize military service had also reached other parts of the Russian Empire's periphery. In 1886 military reform had been implemented in the Caucasus, rendering the special treatment enjoyed by a segment of the population in the Taurida Governorate even more anachronistic.⁵³ Fourthly, the governor of the Odessa province also claimed that the 1874 concessions had successfully reduced the number of Crimean Tatars emigrating to the Ottoman Empire to a trickle. In that year 108 Tatars had left, yet in the following year the number had risen to 121. After that, however, numbers leaving Russia had continuously declined so that by 1887 only three men had abandoned their homeland.⁵⁴ In this sense, the military's strategy of accommodating the Crimean Tatars with the realities of military service in order to foster their loyalty to Russia and at the same time weaken the appeal of the Ottoman Empire had been a success. Against this, even when the authorities noted a serious increase in emigration following the curtailment of the Tatars' privileges in 1893, the information did not lead them to reverse their decision.⁵⁵

For the priorities of the military had changed between the 1870s and early 1890s. While in 1874 a compromise between the principle of universal liability to military service and the specific situation of the Crimean Tatars was deemed acceptable as a temporary solution, by the 1890s the priority of universalizing military service had gained the upper hand. This also became clear in the military's dealing with the Bashkir division, which had also been born out of the necessity of reconciling the edict of 1874 with the realities of im-

---

51   Ibid., l. 13, ll. 59–59ob. This measure also involved the disbandment of the rifle battalion which had been formed from the recruits for the Crimean Tatar division.
52   "Dva bairama," *Perevodchik/Terzhüman*, 24 March 1894, 1.
53   F. 400, op. 5, d. 1167, l. 61ob, RGVIA. The main staff explicitly referred to reform in the Caucasus during the discussion about the Crimean Tatars, but omitted the fact that only the Christians had been made liable to service in the army.
54   F. 400, op. 2, d. 5263, l. 2ob, RGVIA.
55   F. 400, op. 5, d. 1167, l. 60ob, RGVIA.

perial rule. This division was suspended in 1882.⁵⁶ However, the Crimean Tatar regiment was not completely suspended and would remain in existence until the fall of the tsarist regime in 1917, showing that, in this case at least, the military did not radically abandon its practice of weighing up the various interests of the state, the Russian army and the Crimean Tatars. The regiment was an expression of the attempt to reconcile the fundamental tensions which governed Russian policies in the late imperial period. Firstly, the precarious position of the Crimean Tatars, poised between the Russia and the Ottoman Empire, prompted Russian administrators to search for ways to accommodate them and turn them into loyal subjects, while still pushing toward their gradual Russification. Connected to this was a second consideration: the attempt to turn a particularistic empire into a modern state, functioning according to universal principles.⁵⁷ The very particularity which had necessitated the compromise of 1874 was at the same time a situation that reformers were seeking to overcome. The guiding principle was that administrative and political practices were not to be guided by regional particularities, but by universally acknowledged rules and laws. The example of the Crimean Tatars points to the limits imposed on the effort to fully implement such a radical approach.

Historical Narratives of Military Service and the Crimean Tatars

As demonstrated above, both military and civilian authorities drew upon military service as an instrument for integrating and disciplining the empire's subjects. In the context of non-Russian peoples it was also ascribed a Russifying function, at least as rank-and-file soldiers were affected. At the same time, the army had played an important role in the century-old process of empire-building before the aim of Russifying non-Russians had become a priority among imperial officials: it had offered career opportunities to the elites in newly conquered regions and hereby served as an institution in which non-Russians could be co-opted into the imperial system.⁵⁸ The most prominent example of this process were the Baltic German nobles, who played an important role in the higher ranks of the army. But there was another dimen-

---

56 Robert F. Baumann, "Subject Nationalities in the Military Service of Imperial Russia: The Case of the Bashkirs," *Slavic Review* 46, no. 3–4 (1987): 489–502, here 501.
57 Paul Werth has pointed to this "fundamental tension between universality and particularity" which marked the late imperial period, see: Paul W. Werth, "In the State's Embrace? Civil Acts in an Imperial Order," *Kritika: Explorations in Russian and Eurasian History* 7, no. 3 (2006): 433–58, here 435.
58 Mark von Hagen, "The Limits of Reform: The Multiethnic Imperial Army Confronts Nationalism, 1874–1917," in *Reforming the Tsar's Army: Military Innovation in Imperial Russia from Peter the Great to the Revolution*, ed. Bruce W. Menning and David Schimmelpenninck van der Oye (Cambridge: Cambridge University Press, 2004), 34–55, esp. 35–37.

sion to military service of non-Russians than merely practical considerations. It was seen and staged as a sign of the non-Russian subjects' devotion to the Russian tsar. As Richard S. Wortman has argued, such symbolic demonstrations of loyalty to the dynastic state were an integral part of the imperial repertoire.[59] This symbolic dimension of military service entered historical narratives of the Russian Empire, especially if a particular group was considered to have distinguished itself in time of war. In case of the Crimean Tatars these narratives of military service helped construct a glorious shared history between Russians and non-Russians and often differed from the largely utilitarian function which administrative elites ascribed to it.

The first comprehensive historical study of Tatar military service was published in 1899 in Simferopol. Its author, Izmail Murza Muftiizade, was born into a noble *murza* family in 1841 and had himself served in the Crimean Tatar division as a colonel. He was a figure of some prominence and influence among both the Tatar and the Russian nobility in the Crimea, and was actively involved in the local administration of the *zemstvo*. He would later be elected to the Third Duma, where he associated with the Octobrist party.[60] Muftiizade wrote articles for the *Bulletins of the Taurida Scientific Archival Commission* (*Izvestiia Tavricheskoi Uchenoi Arkhivnoi Kommissii*), a journal which was dedicated to the study of the history and culture of the Taurida Governorate. Several historical documents bearing witness to this aspect of Tatar-Russo relations in the Crimea were published in the journal.[61]

But it was Muftiizade who covered the matter in most detail. At the end of the nineteenth century he published an intriguing article in which he outlined his reasons for telling the story of the Tatars' military service. There was a time, he explained, in which the stories of the heroic deeds of forefathers who had proudly served the emperor and their fatherland had been passed down from generation to generation. In those past times, these deeds had been captured in poems and tales and disseminated to the population. Now things were different though, and the memory of "glorious service for the

---

[59] Richard S. Wortman, *Scenarios of Power: Myth and Ceremony in Russian Monarchy from Peter the Great to the Abdication of Nicholas II* (Princeton: Princeton University Press, 2006), 3.

[60] Hakan Kırımlı, *National Movements and National Identity among the Crimean Tatars, 1905–1916* (Leiden: Brill, 1996), 110–12.

[61] Izmail Muftiizade, *Ocherk stoletnei voennoi sluzhby krymskikh tatar s 1784–1904 g.: Po arkhivnym materialam* (Simferopol, 1905); G. Gabaev, "Zakonodatel'nye akty i drugie dokumenty o voennoi sluzhbe Krymskikh tatar v riadakh voiskovykh chastei, predkov nynechniago Krymskao koennago Eiia Velichestva Gosudaryni Imperatritsy Aleksandry Feodorovny polka," *Izvestiia tavricheskoi uchenoj arkhivnoi kommissii* 51 (1913): 135–52; Gabaev, "Krymskie Tatary pod Russkimi znamenami: Kratkaia istoricheskaia spravka," *Zhurnal Imperatorskago russkogo voenno-istoricheskago obshchestva* 58, no. 3 (1913): 131–37.

land [*krai*] and the Fatherland" was slowly fading away.[62] Soon, the youth would know nothing of the glorious past. This was why, Muftiizade declared, he felt the obligation to pass on this knowledge as one of the last of those old Tatars who had served. But cherishing their memory was not the only reason for his efforts. Knowledge of this aspect of the history of the Crimean Tatars in the Russian Empire would make the Tatar youth appreciate the merits of service and would encourage them to follow the example given by it, should the necessity ever arrive.[63] Muftiizade portrayed military service to the Russian tsar as an integral part of the Crimean Tatars' history, the memory of which should be preserved primarily for the Tatars' own sake: to boost the sense of duty among the younger generations.

In his most extensive publication on the subject, Muftiizade laid out in great detail how the Crimean Tatars had served in the Russian army since 1784 and how they were still doing so at the time of his writing.[64] The structure of his work interlinked both national and imperial historical narratives. One central episode of this history was the Tatars' participation in Russia's wars against Napoleon. Even when war first broke out in 1806, the "Muslim population of the Crimea" had expressed its wish to contribute to the "defense of the fatherland" by forming cavalry units and Tsar Alexander I allegedly "graciously" accepted the offer.[65] The truly remarkable episode of the Crimean Tatar regiment's history began in 1812 when the Crimean regiments took part in "this famous 'Patriotic war'".[66] Muftiizade described the military decorations that the officers of the regiments received, listed the killed and the wounded and the places where the regiments had fought. He also refered to the fact that not only officers, but also twelve rank-and-file soldiers had received military decorations of the fourth class.[67] In Muftiizade's interpretation, the experience of war had transformed the men. When they returned to the Crimea they were different people:

> they had faithfully fulfilled the duty of their oath, had served the fatherland [*otechestvo*] well and with glory, to which their wounds, the decorations they received bore witness and also the testimony of their command with the signatures of Platov, Bagration, Tormasov and others.[68]

Muftiizade awarded the Crimean Tatars a place in the history of the Russia's glorious "Patriotic War", appealing to some of the Russian army's most famous generals to serve as his witnesses. He concluded his description with a number of documents which demonstrated how the Crimean Tatars had dis-

---

[62] Izmail Muftiizade, "Ocherk voennoi sluzhby krymskikh tatar s 1783 po 1889 god," *Izvestiia tavricheskoi uchenoi arkhivnoi kommissii* 30 (1899): 1–24.
[63] Ibid., 1–2.
[64] Muftiizade, "Ocherk stoletnei voennoi sluzhby krymskikh tatar," 5.
[65] Ibid., 9.
[66] Ibid., 17.
[67] Ibid., 18.
[68] Ibid., 20.

tinguished themselves and implicitly suggested the close proximity of the decorated officers with the elite of the Russian army and even the emperor himself: Sadyk aga Kuntuganskii, officer of the Evpatoriiskii regiment received the third-class Order of St. Anna by order of General Peter Wittgenstein, the officer Il'ias of the Simferopol regiment by order of General Michael Andreas Barclay de Tolly, who had served as war minister between 1810 and 1813. The document attesting that officer Dzhaminskii, who also served in the Evpatoriiskii cavalry regiment, had received the Order of St. Anna, fourth-class, had been signed by Tsar Alexander himself.[69]

Another intriguing aspect of Muftiizade's study is his understanding of the formation of the Crimean Tatar squadron in 1874. As mentioned above, from the point of view of the reformers in the war ministry, its creation had been a compromise between the principle of universal liability to military service and the specific conditions in the Crimea. To the military, the arrangement was a temporary solution in order to appease the Tatar population and only a first step towards their gradual integration into the regular ranks of the army, which would serve Russia's interests best. Muftiizade offered a very different interpretation. To his mind, the regiment's creation in 1874 stood in the tradition of a long history of military service to the emperor. The Crimean Tatars had been "honored with the kind attention" (*udostoilis' milostvago vnimaniia*) of the monarch, as he allowed them once more to form a regiment exclusively from among their midst.[70] It was a privilege granted to the Crimean Tatars that stemmed from the special relationship they enjoyed with the tsar. From now on, the regiment would be commanded by Russian officers. Muftiizade praised the first commanding officer of the regiment, Vladimir Alekseevich Poltoratskii, as a man of education and humanity. In general, the regiment's formation was told as a success story from the word go. Within a few months the young recruits were unrecognizable. Allegedly O. B. Rikhter, lieutenant general, was amazed at the Tatars' performance during an inspection visit, especially with their language skills. After all, only a few months earlier, the majority of them had not known a word of Russian.[71]

This emphatically positive description stands in sharp contrast both to the Tatar population's own reaction in 1874 and to the dissatisfaction the local administration voiced with its progress in Russification in the 1880s and 1890s. After all there had been a noticeable increase in emigration numbers when news of the imminent reform had reached the Crimea. Fear of the army manifested itself in a Crimean Tatar *destan* (a folk song), according to which the prospect of military service was seen as the first step towards a loss of the Tatars' religious identity. The new law was understood in rather apocalyptic terms as a calamity that had befallen the Crimea.[72] Muftiizade did not com-

---

[69] Ibid., 20–21.
[70] Ibid., 40.
[71] Ibid., 41.
[72] Williams, *The Crimean Tatars*, 185–87.

pletely ignore the events of 1874, but he again emphasized how it had all gone well in the end. In May 1874 Prince Mikhail Semënovich Vorontsov had been sent to the Crimea on the orders of Tsar Alexander II to assure the Tatar population of the benevolence the tsar felt towards them and explained the reasonable conditions under which they were expected to fulfill their duty as soldiers, emphasizing that their religious freedoms would be respected. The population responded with joy and the wave of emigration stopped "once and for all".[73] While this account was no doubt extremely optimistic, Russian authorities indeed recorded a decline in migration numbers after the establishment of the irregular Crimean Tatar regiment.[74]

The Russian commanding officers seemed to have put some effort into persuading the Tatar soldiers that service in the regiment was a cause for celebration. One of them, B. B. Bertel' composed a regimental song, which—according to Muftiizade—the soldiers greeted with delight and which could be heard in every district. In the song, the rumors that the Tatars were unwilling to serve Russia, that they preferred to live "with the Turks" and were prepared to abandon the Crimea were dismissed as unfounded. Instead, their service in the squadron was interpreted as proof of their love for the tsar. Vladimir Alekseevich Poltoratskii was described as "our father", under whose command the soldiers would go into the battle "with pleasure".[75] While the song tells us nothing about how the rank-and-file soldiers actually perceived their recruitment into the regiment,[76] it does show how the prospect of military service was inflated with emotions by the commanding officers. It was not simply a sense of duty which made the Tatars serve in the regiment: it was love. And their Russian officer was not merely a military superior, he was actually depicted as a fatherly figure. In this respect, Muftiizade's account echoed the notion articulated by the Russian military reformers in the War Ministry who had also advised in 1874 that he Crimean Tatar regiment's rank-and-file soldiers should look upon their Russian officers as a member of their family.[77]

Muftiizade's depiction of the history of Tatar service was certainly unduly optimistic. Written in Russian, it was directed not least to a Russian-speaking public, presumably to remind Russians of the loyalty that the Tatars had displayed over the course of the nineteenth century and thereby presenting them as obedient and trustworthy subjects. But it was not just the Tatar's conduct which he lauded. The Russian monarchs were also presented in a very favorable light. Throughout the history of military service, Muftiizade portrayed a

---

[73] Muftiizade, "Ocherk stoletnei voennoi sluzhby krymskikh tatar," 41.
[74] F. 400, op. 2, d. 5263, l. 2; RGVIA, f. 400, op. 5, d. 1167, 1, 2ob, RGVIA.
[75] Muftiizade, "Ocherk stoletnei voennoi sluzhby krymskikh tatar," 42.
[76] In a Crimean Tatar song, recruitment into the regiment was lamented as a great misfortune: Aleksei Opesnitskii, ed., *Pesni krymskikh turok: Tekst, perevod i muzyka* (Moskva, 1910), 31–14, 106–10.
[77] F. 400, op. 2, d. 2765, l. 60, RGVIA.

reciprocal relationship between the Tatar's loyalty and the rewards the tsar offered them in return, while at the same time emphasizing that this served as the basis of a history of successful integration by the Crimean Tatars into the Russian Empire.

The author's overt praise of Russo-Tatar relations in this particular sphere, did not stop him from harshly criticizing government policy in other contexts. In spite of his conservative outlook, he reproached the government on several occasions for its treatment of its Muslim subjects after he had been elected to the Third Duma in 1907.[78] In a speech to the duma in 1909 he complained that, in spite of the fact that the Muslims of the empire had died alongside the Russians in many wars, the government discriminated against them.[79]

As a member of the Crimean Tatar elite who had served in the Crimean Tatar regiment himself and as a political figure who lobbied the government on behalf of the Muslim population, it is perhaps not surprising that Muftiizade would emphasize what his people had achieved as officers and soldiers. But he was not the only one to uphold the memory of the Tatars' service. On the occasion of the centenary of Russia's struggle against Napoleon, historian Arsenii Ivanovich Markevich published a study of the history of the Crimean Peninsula during the Napoleonic wars. Markevich was born in 1855 in Brest-Litovsk into a clergy family and went on to study at the University of Warsaw. In 1883 he became a teacher at the boys' *gimnaziia* in Sevastopol. But Markevich devoted much of his professional life to the study of the Crimea's historical heritage. From 1895 until 1896 he was chairman of the Taurida Scientific Archival Commission (*Tavricheskaia uchenaia arkhivnaia komissiia*), which investigated the local history of the Taurida Governorate and in whose journal many of Markevich's articles were published.[80]

In his account of the events between 1806 and 1814, Markevich emphasized—much like Muftiizade—the enormous significance of this historical episode for Russia. The meaning of this war was not confined to who won and lost, but had consequences for Russia's national development. It had triggered an "upsurge of the national soul" (*pod"em natsional'nago dukha*) as "the entire Russian people" (*ves' russkii narod*) had rallied against the common foe.[81] That was the reason why it had rightly become known as the "*Pat-*

---

[78] Kırımlı, *National Movements and National Identity*, 111–12.
[79] Ibid., 112.
[80] Vladimir N. Sukhorukov, *Biograficheskii slovar' Kryma* (Simferopol: Biznes-Inform, 2011), 112–13; Sergej Filimonov, ed., *Khraniteli istoricheskoi pamiati Kryma. O nasledii Tavricheskoi Uchenoi Arkhivnoi Komissii i Tavricheskogo Obshchestva Istorii, Arkheologii i Etnografii, 1887–1931 gg* (Simferopol: Dom Chernomor PRESS, 2004), 61–72, for an overview of Markevich's publications.
[81] Arsenii Markevich, "K stoletiiu otechestvennoi voiny: Tavricheskaia guberniia v sviazi s epokhoi 1806–1814 godov. Istoricheskii ocherk (po arkhivnym materialam)," *Izvestiia tavricheskoi uchenoi arckhivnoi kommissii* 49 (1913): 1–100, here 1.

riotic war" (*Otechestvennoi voiny*); Russia had shown the world her "national dignity" (*natsional'noe dostoinstvo*).[82] To Markevich's mind, the adjuration of Russia's national potency by no means implied that the patriotic fervor had been felt only by ethnic Russians. The aim of his study was to illuminate how the Russia's victory against Napoleon had not been brought about solely by the population immediately affected by the hostilities, but that the people in the peripheries of the empire had sacrificed just as much. Within the Taurida Governorate not only Russian subjects had displayed their "devotion" (*predannost'*) to Russia, but also the non-Russian people, and most of all, the Tatars.[83] Markevich viewed this fact as especially remarkable as the Ottoman Empire had been among Russia's enemies between 1806 and 1812, placing the Crimea in a unique and unenviable situation. These circumstances would be something of a test bed which would reveal the degree of Tatar devotion to Russia. And to his mind they passed the test with distinction: they remained loyal to Russia in spite of the mistrust the government had displayed towards them.[84]

In Markevich's depiction, the most striking sign of the Tatar's devotion was their wish to contribute manpower to Russia's war effort. He devoted much of his study of the Taurida Governorate during the wars against Napoleon to the history of the formation of four cavalry regiments from among the Tatar population. In his narrative these regiments, whose creation had been initiated by members of the Tatar elites, figured as a token of the loyalty of the entire Tatar population. Their deeds stood symbolically for the behavior of "our Crimeans".[85]

In December of 1806, members of Tatar religious leadership and nobility drew up a petition to the governor of the Taurida Governorate, Dimitrii Borisovich Mertvago, asking for permission to form a cavalry unit from among the Tatar population—an act which Markevich characterized as a "patriotic cause" (*patrioticheskoe delo*).[86] Governor Mertvago was all for the idea. The reasons he gave are illuminating: for one thing he thought the Tatars "brave" and in possession of good horses. Aside from this, the Tatars' participation in the war offered them an opportunity to prove their loyalty to the government and to win its "trust". This would put an end to the anxiety which still existed towards this new population on the part of the Russian government. They would be part of Russia's "glory" (*slava*) and they would earn the opportunity to "join hearts with the true sons of the fatherland".[87] On the other hand, it was in Russia's security interests to clear the Crimea of a potentially dangerous military element in case war was to break out with

---

[82] Ibid.
[83] Ibid., 2.
[84] Ibid., 2–3.
[85] Ibid., 58.
[86] Ibid., 9.
[87] Ibid., 10.

the Ottoman Empire once more. Lastly, the Tatars, and especially the noble *murzas* would figure as an *amanat* (a hostage), for their brethren.[88] Here one finds an interesting mixture of motives for endorsing the Tatars' petition. On one level he put forward mere practical considerations and ascribed attributes to the Tatars that would serve them well as soldiers. On another, he was obviously still unsure about the Tatar's loyalty and saw it in the state's security interest to dispatch them to the theatre of war with the French in order to increase their distance from the Ottoman Empire. On a third level, military service would generate something in them that they were possibly still lacking: sufficient political loyalty to Russia and the recognition of that loyalty on the part of the authorities. The formation of the regiments had the potential to create a bond of mutual trust between the empire and its relatively new subjects. After some misgivings in the imperial capital had been overcome, the Tatars' request to form the cavalry regiments finally met with approval.[89]

Over the course of the following years, recruitment to and maintenance of the four regiments was clearly not without its setbacks. Markevich told of problems in conscripting new rank-and-file soldiers, and even of mutinies. Nonetheless, he viewed the overall performance of the regiments in positive terms, dismissing such incidents as isolated events. This euphemistic interpretation of the Crimea's wartime experience was also reflected in his explanation of the resettlement policies towards the Tatars in after the outbreak of hostilities with the Ottoman Empire. He even claimed that the entire process unfolded harmoniously and was actually in accordance with the Tatars' own wishes.[90]

The climax of the Crimean Tatars' military achievements came with the year 1812: Notwithstanding

all their sacrifices [...] our *krymtsy*, in the shape of the Tatar cavalry regiments, actually took part in the struggle with the enemy. The Crimea and its Tatar population must always be proud, that three Crimean regiments took part in the Patriotic War and distinguished themselves in many battles, especially in the great battle of Borodino and pursued the enemy to Paris.[91]

Markevich enumerated the various battles in which the regiments had participated. Due to the peninsula's unique position in the empire, he thought their commitment especially laudable: the population had not long been part of the Russian Empire and was marked by great diversity, and the region had been afflicted with floods and the epidemics during the period of the wars against France, yet nonetheless "Taurida fulfilled its civic duty with honor and selflessness and did not spare any efforts to save the dignity, the freedom

---

[88] Ibid.
[89] Ibid., 10–13.
[90] Ibid., 19–26.
[91] Ibid., 58–59.

and the safety of the state."⁹² The Crimean Tatar officers and soldiers were the embodiment of this astonishing sacrifice:

> Poorly clothed and armed, not used to military service, without knowledge of Russian, in alien circumstances, the Crimean Tatars fulfilled their duty, and for their faithful service their descendants, together with members of the Taurida nobility and the *zemstva*, represented Taurida on the field of Borodino on the 26 August 1912 in the face of the sovereign and of the whole of Russia.⁹³

Nor was the Crimean Tatars' place in the official memory of Russia's past confined to the wars against Napoleon. In July 1891 *Perevodchik/Terzhüman* reported that the Crimean Tatar division had taken part in a memorial service for their "brothers in arms" who had perished during the defense of Sevastopol.⁹⁴ The memory and symbolic representation of the Crimean Tatars' participation in the war was thus upheld not only by historians, but members of the Crimean Tatar elite and of the regiment took part in the empire's public remembrance of two military events which had become central myths in the Russian nationalist discourse: the Battle of Borodino and the Siege of Sevastopol.⁹⁵

In the studies by Markevich and Muftiizade, the Tatars' loyalty in times of war was the focal point for the construction of a shared imperial past. Markevich emphasized what the war against Napoleon had done for Russia's national development, but also pointed to the implications it had had for its relationship with its new Muslim subjects. Muftiizade was also concerned with the meaning that service for the Russian tsar had for the Crimean Tatars' own historical memory and identity. In Markevich's narrative, the Crimean Tatars regiment stood for the conduct of the entire Tatar population. The successful struggle against Napoleon was in some ways a very suitable topic for use in integrating non-Russians in the narrative that the entire population had rallied behind the emperor. This is an example of how closely imperial and national discourses became interwoven in the case of Russia.⁹⁶ Writing about the war of 1812 was not just an exercise in historical enquiry, but also a project in constructing a glorious imperial past. Internal conflicts were downplayed in order to celebrate Russia's heroic achievements as well as the ability of its many and various peoples to stand united in face of the common foe.

Matters were very different, though, in wars in which the empire had been defeated. A few years before his study on the Crimea in the era of the "Patriotic War" was published, Markevich had written an extensive piece on the

---

⁹² Ibid., 99.
⁹³ Ibid., 100.
⁹⁴ "Bakhchisaray," *Perevodchik/Terzhüman*, 30 July 1891, 1.
⁹⁵ For the myth of Sevastopol, see: Serhii Plokhy, "The City of Glory: Sevastopol in Russian Historical Mythology," *Journal of Contemporary History* 35, no. 3 (2000): 369–83.
⁹⁶ For a discussion of the question of "nation" and "empire" in Russian national discourse, see: Aleksei I. Miller, *The Romanov Empire and Nationalism: Essays in the Methodology of Historical Research* (Budapest: Central European University Press, 2008), 161–180.

Taurida Governorate during the Crimean War of 1853–56, in which Russia had been humiliatingly defeated.[97] His evaluation of the Crimean Tatars' behavior in this time was very different. He listed numerous examples of disloyalty, of Tatars spying for the enemy, giving false information to Russian forces and pointed to the generally hostile attitude of the Tatars towards Russia.[98] But Markevich also noted that there were other examples. Many Tatars had made donations towards the war effort. At the beginning of the war, Tatar villages had given Russian troops a warm welcome, and others looked after soldiers who had been wounded in the war.[99] Nor did Markevich fail to mention that some of the soldiers of the imperial army mistreated the Tatars.[100] In conclusion he explained the Tatars' alleged disloyalty by pointing to the influence of Turkish agents and declined to interpret any apparent failure in loyalty as a conscious political act of subversion.[101] This description of the events in the Crimea was more ambiguous than a simple story of Tatar treason and Russian heroism. That is not to say that such negative narratives did not exist after Russia's defeat in the Crimean War.[102] But the discourse on Crimea's history in the Russian Empire was pluralistic in the late imperial period. The studies by Markevich and Muftiizade were not the only ones in which the Crimean Tatars were lauded for their military achievements.[103] In this context, military service of Crimean Tatars served as one important element in the construction of a success story of Russia as an empire that had managed to secure the loyalties of an extremely diverse population.

Conclusion

The Russian Empire's policies toward the Crimean Tatars with regard to military reform in the late imperial period, together with the narratives produced on their military history, point to the many dimensions of loyalties in an imperial order. In the realm of political practices, the empire attempted to ensure its subjects' loyalties in a number of ways: by easing the terms of compulsory military service, by embracing a proactive policy on Islam and by nonetheless pressing ahead with the gradual universalization of military service, which was itself regarded as an instrument for forging loyalty. In general, such practices derived from relatively pragmatic considerations as to

---

[97] Arsenii Markevich, "Tavricheskaia Guberniia vo vremia Krymskoi Voiny: Po arkhivnym materialam," *Izvestiia tavricheskoi uchenoi arkhivnoi kommissii* 37 (1905): 1–260.
[98] Ibid., 11–16, 20, 25, 27–30.
[99] Ibid., 6–10, 30–31, 112–13.
[100] Ibid., 245.
[101] Ibid., 232, 259.
[102] Kerstin S. Jobst, *Die Perle des Imperiums. Der russische Krim-Diskurs im Zarenreich* (Konstanz: UVK, 2007), 248.
[103] Ibid., 250–52 gives a good overview of studies either dedicated to the Crimean Tatars in the Russian army or which mention of their role in the wars against Napoleon.

how Russia could best achieve what her administrators were ultimately attempting to achieve: obedient, disciplined and Russified soldiers whose loyalty belonged to the tsar and not the Ottoman sultan. On a semantic level—especially in the historical accounts produced by Markevich and Muftiizade, but also on the pages of the reformist Russo-Tatar newspaper *Perevodchik/Terzhüman*—military service of the Crimean Tatars was elevated to a symbol of a purported special relationship between the Crimean Tatars and the Russian Empire, founded on a common patriotic past.

Mark Cornwall

LOYALTY AND TREASON IN LATE HABSBURG CROATIA
A Violent Political Discourse before the First World War

In her famous work *The Meaning of Treason*, the novelist and journalist Rebecca West suggests that the concepts of loyalty and treachery are polar opposites in human society:

> There is always loyalty, for men love life and cling together under the threats of the uncaring universe. So there is always treachery, since there is the instinct to die as well as the instinct to live; and as loyalty changes to meet the changing threats of the environment, so treachery changes also.[1]

This chapter analyses these shifting concepts of loyalty and treason (the politicizing of treachery) through a case study from Croatia in the early twentieth century. Late Habsburg Croatia, with its narrow political franchise—less than 2 % of the population—which existed alongside a burgeoning civil society, might rightly be imagined as a territory containing multiple and conflicting loyalties. There was Croatia's complex ethnic and religious mixture (Croat and Serb, following Catholic, Orthodox and even Jewish faiths) and its sensitive geographical location on the Habsburg frontiers, where a military border against the Ottoman Empire had only been abolished in 1881. And not least, there existed historic ties which bound Croatia to both halves of the Habsburg monarchy despite the dualist system that had existed since 1867. In 1868, Croatia, having been joined to Hungary for over seven hundred years, was uniquely given a degree of home rule, with its own government and parliament (the *Sabor*) in Zagreb. Yet despite this "subdualist" solution and the reaffirmation of the territory's firm ties to Hungary, Croatia's politicians usually remembered and displayed a separate allegiance to the Habsburg monarch in Vienna and to his closest ministers there who supervised war and foreign policy for the whole empire. After all, in 1848 Count Josip Jelačić, the viceroy or *ban* of Croatia, had loyally supported the Habsburg cause and led an army against revolutionary Hungary. A daily reminder of this for the Zagreb population was a statue of Jelačić erected on the main square in 1866 by the Habsburg authorities. Demonstrably, the statue's sword was pointing northwards towards the enemy in Budapest.

---

[1] Rebecca West, *The Meaning of Treason: With a New Introduction by the Author* (London: Virago Press, 1982), 165.

The following discussion explores some of the major patterns of political allegiance in the region, how they interacted and overlapped, and what all this can tell us about the power relationships and tensions in Austria-Hungary on the eve of the First World War. During this pre-war era, loyalties were regularly evoked and publicly expressed, often to counter claims of disloyalty, or even treason, at times of political crisis.[2] But to be credible, such expressions always required a mutual dynamic between subject and object that had some basis in reality. In effect, such claims had to be capable of being reliably tested in the minds of observers by comparing them with the actions of the relevant parties. Both for individuals expressing allegiance and others claiming to reciprocate that allegiance, mere promises were insufficient and could easily be interpreted as empty pieties divorced from reality. The period chosen here—from 1908 to 1910—overlaps with the controversial rule of Baron Pavao Rauch as *ban* of Croatia. This was a time when there was real public controversy over who counted as truly loyal to Croatia and/or the Habsburg monarchy, and over what that loyalty actually meant. As we shall see, out of that context a discourse also developed right across Croatian society around the opposite concept of "treason"—an argument that carried with it sinister overtones.[3]

Before delving into our case study, it is useful in our task of conceptualizing loyalty to make a further differentiation between two major strands of the phenomenon, that is to assess it on a vertical and on a horizontal plane.[4] For our purposes, vertical allegiances run in a hierarchical direction between a subject or citizen and a person or institution in authority. In Croatia before 1914, the ruling elite felt quite insecure in its position as it was usually ruling unconstitutionally without calling the *Sabor*. It periodically tried to inspire vertical loyalty from the various strands of the population or tried to give the impression, via formulaic rituals, that such loyalty was alive and well—public

---

[2] For recent comparative research on the concept of loyalty in Habsburg and post-Habsburg Europe, see the essays in Laurence Cole and Daniel L. Unowsky, eds., *The Limits of Loyalty: Imperial Symbolism, Popular Allegiances, and State Patriotism in the Late Habsburg Monarchy* (New York: Berghahn Books, 2007); Martin Schulze Wessel, ed., *Loyalitäten in der Tschechoslowakischen Republik 1918–1938: Politische, nationale und kulturelle Zugehörigkeiten* (Munich: Oldenbourg, 2004).

[3] The few studies that have tried to conceptualize treason remain unsatisfactory, but one of the most interesting is by the sociologist Nachman Ben-Yehuda, who interprets treason as a subset of "betrayal." Nachman Ben-Yehuda, *Betrayals and Treason: Violations of Trust and Loyalty* (Boulder, CO: Westview Press, 2001). See also an ideologically-focused and older study by Margret Boveri, *Der Verrat im 20. Jahrhundert* (Reinbek bei Hamburg: Rowohlt, 1976). We might usefully compare the Zagreb cases of "Serb treason" to the Anglo-Irish treason case against Roger Casement in 1916, in which secession from the state was also the underlying accusation.

[4] See Martin Schulze Wessel, "Loyalität als geschichtlicher Grundbegriff und Forschungskonzept: Zur Einleitung," in *Loyalitäten in der Tschechoslowakischen Republik*, ed. Martin Schulze Wessel, 1–22, 3.

expressions of loyalty from below were supposed by the ruling classes to provide evidence of the regime's legitimacy. On the other hand, horizontal loyalties also exerted an effect. Loyalties built across modernizing communities like Croatia through the increasingly fast communications network of the time bound individuals together through shared nationality, religious affiliation, profession or class. In prewar Croatia, this horizontal loyalty was evoked particularly by using the vocabulary of nation, since all the main political forces of the period claimed to embody and represent best the interests of the national community. There was, however, a wide gap between such rhetorical claims and the actual patterns of national bonding and allegiance at a grassroots level: horizontal ties remained diffuse and fragmentary amidst a largely rural and disenfranchised population.

The relationships between these various vertical and horizontal loyalties—the ways in which they meshed together or competed in the late Habsburg monarchy—adds an extra element of complexity to our discussion. But these relationships can help elucidate why Croatian loyalties became increasingly fluid and harder to predict during the period. The state authorities usually focused their energies on privileging a simple hierarchical relationship, and were aided in 1908–10 by the restrictions imposed on popular representation as well as the extremely narrow electoral franchise in parliamentary elections. Yet they could not ignore the educated sections of Croatian public opinion which were becoming increasingly vocal in expressing their conditional loyalty to the authorities. We might therefore ask of the pre-1914 period: did the legitimacy of the vertical Habsburg axis in Croatia slowly begin to erode as the horizontal national axis strengthened and invaded the public discourse?

* * *

On 12 January 1908, an alarming cartoon appeared in one Hungarian satirical magazine in Budapest (Fig. 1). It portrayed the situation in Croatia that the newly appointed *ban*, Pavao Rauch, was about to encounter. In the cartoon, Croatia is drawn as a pack of vicious hungry wolves entrapped in a cage. Rauch is shown as the "new animal tamer," with a whip in one hand and slab of meat in the other, being ushered into the cage by Sándor Wekerle, the Hungarian prime minister (who had just appointed him): "Just step boldly in among them," whispers a smiling Wekerle, "otherwise you will come unstuck, just like your predecessor!" The reference is to Aleksandar Rakodczay, who had been made *ban* only six months earlier: he is depicted limping away from the cage with his head wrapped in a bandage. Viewers of this image might well deduce that no real dialog was possible between Rauch and his new Croatian subjects. Indeed, they might recall the words of Gyula Andrássy, who had asserted that Croatia needed to be ruled with a whip and oats.[5] The *ban*, or his Hungarian masters, continued to feel that Croatia needed firm rule, but were equally clear that the Croatian wolves could never be house trained. The best one might achieve was to pacify them by means of a judicious or juicy "concession" (the slogan written on Rauch's slab of meat).

Fig. 1: "Az új állatszelidítő" (The New Animal Tamer), *Bolond istók*, 12 January 1908, 3.

Indeed, when Rauch duly arrived in Zagreb three days later to take up his post, the ghastly prediction of the cartoon seemed to be coming true. A huge "mob," encouraged by an opposition press campaign, gathered at the railway station to give him an extremely hostile reception. His carriage was pelted with stones and eggs, with the police seemingly unable or unwilling to keep order (one army officer was seriously wounded in the mêlée), and intelligence

---

[5] These words were circulating in the press (e.g. *Neue Freie Presse*, 11 January 1908) and found visual expression too. In the satirical magazine *Koprive* (Nettles) Rauch, portrayed as a balloon held by Wekerle, grasps a whip in one hand and a bag of oats in the other. "Program bana Raucha," *Koprive* no. 2, January 1908, 1.

sources even suggested that an attack was planned on the house of his octogenarian mother.[6] These events led the new *ban* to draw an immediate conclusion: the mob assault on himself, as the representative of the Crown in Croatia, amounted to what he termed an "anti-dynastic" outrage, which made it an attack on the monarchy itself.[7]

This turbulent episode not only marked the start of Rauch's ultimately unsuccessful two-year struggle to master events in Croatia. It also inaugurated an intense public and political discussion within the Kingdom about the nature of "loyalty," a discourse whose multiple facets made it very complex. At stake were key questions about how Croatia ought to be governed and what national framework should be used to frame Croatia's future within the Austro-Hungarian Empire. This situation conjured up a range of interpretations about what loyalty to Croatia actually meant—interpretations which by 1908 had developed significant historical precedents, since each of them had been tested at some stage or other in Zagreb's political arena over the previous fifty years.

Within this discourse, three political directions stood out most prominently. One privileged values of vertical allegiance in particular, while the other two spoke more to horizontal loyalties, seeking to strengthen Croatian autonomy and/or to restore constitutional rule in the region. The first approach was the unionist or "Magyarone" argument pressed by the Rauch regime itself, which expressed itself largely in terms of vertical loyalty.[8] For this grouping, real loyalty to Croatia meant remaining true to its historic union with Hungary and the home rule arrangements of 1868, in Croatian a settlement known as the *Nagodba*. Rauch did not waver in his defense of this approach, even if he did privately complain that he always lacked sufficient reciprocal support from Budapest for his regime.[9]

The second approach to the concept of Croatian loyalty was the one defended by the *pravaši* or "state-right" enthusiasts, most closely associated with Josip Frank and his party, who pushed a Greater Croatian chauvinist

---

6   Rauch to Géza Daruváry, Kabinettskanzlei in Vienna [Cabinet office], 18 January 1908, Kabinettsarchiv, Haus-, Hof- und Staatsarchiv [Cabinet archive, Haus-, Hof- und Staatsarchiv] (hereafter HHStA), Vienna, Karton 26, Geheimakten [Secret files]. Daruváry was a long-time friend of Rauch and, as head of the Imperial Cabinet Office, provided direct access to Emperor Franz Joseph.

7   Veridicus [Pavao Rauch], *Kroatien im Jahre 1907–1908* (Budapest: Haladás Könyvnyomda, 1909), 14–15.

8   For a recent thorough study of Rauch and his background, see Iskra Iveljić, *Anatomija jedne velikaške porodice Rauchovi* (Zagreb: FF Press, 2014).

9   See Rauch's report to the monarch: "Bericht des Banus Baron Rauch über seine Amtstätigkeit in 1908" [January 1909], Kabinettsarchiv, HHStA, Karton 26, Geheimakten; also reproduced in Iveljić, *Anatomija*, 246–52.

agenda within the Habsburg monarchy.[10] They demanded government by Croats alone, deprecating Serb participation and even denying their very existence as a national entity in Croatia. Based on the principle of "Croatian state right", they also aspired to achieve broader national unity, reflecting Croatia's historic ties to Dalmatia and Bosnia. They pushed especially for union to Dalmatia, which was then divided from Croatia and in the Austrian half of the monarchy, but also envisaged unity to Bosnia which the Habsburgs had occupied in 1878 and run as a separate administration since then.

The third approach was that of the *Hrvatsko-srpska koalicija* (the Croat-Serb Coalition, HSK), which had actually attained power in Zagreb in 1906-7 but now formed the main opposition to the Rauch regime.[11] The Coalition forces promoted Croat-Serb national unity—defending a largely civic concept of the nation—as a basis for true Croatian patriotism and for its program of constitutional reform. They rejected the dominance of Hungary, whose nationalist stance was now interpreted as a betrayal of promises made to the Coalition in 1905. But the theory they defended of a single Croat-Serb nation (i.e. of Yugoslav unity) could naturally be interpreted in a way that made their own loyalties seem highly ambiguous. For over the years they had been developing ties not only with Croats and Serbs in coastal Dalmatia but also, more controversially, with the Serbian regime in Belgrade. Particularly suspect to the Rauch regime was the key Serb political party within the Coalition, the *Srpska samostalna stranka* (Serb Independent Party, SSS) led by Svetozar Pribićević. In contrast, the small *Srpska narodna radikalna stranka* (Serbian National Radical Party, SNRS) which had left the Coalition in 1907, was deemed less threatening. The latter based its claims for Serb equality on historic rights, the privileges granted to them by the Habsburgs in the late seventeenth century and it aimed to sustain this Serb autonomy through its key base within the Orthodox church network rather than through *Sabor* politics.[12]

We should note that each of these three major political interpretations of Croatian loyalty usually contained a basic assumption of (vertical) allegiance to the Habsburg dynasty and monarchy, a loyalty that was often expressed verbally or via ritual. However, during the violent discourse of 1908-9, the allegiances of the protagonists were consistently challenged through accusa-

---

[10] The classic *pravaši* history is by Mirjana Gross, *Povijest pravaške ideologije* (Zagreb: Institut za hrvatsku povijest, 1973). But see also the extensive research of Stjepan Matković, for example: *Izabrani portreti pravaši: prilozi hrvatskoj političkoj povijesti* (Zagreb: Hrvatski institut za povijest, 2011).

[11] On the Coalition's history, see Rene Lovrenčić, *Geneza politike 'novog kursa'* (Zagreb: Institut za hrvatsku povijest, 1972); Mirjana Gross, *Vladavina Hrvatsko-srpske koalicije 1906-1907* (Belgrade: Institut društvenih nauka, 1960).

[12] For a detailed analysis of the Serbs' position, see Nicholas Miller, *Between Nation and State: Serbian Politics in Croatia before the First World War* (Pittsburgh, PA: University of Pittsburgh Press, 1997).

tions of disloyalty, not just to Croatia but also to the monarchy. This soon took a dangerous direction when, on all sides of the political divide, disloyalty quickly became equated with the inflammatory word "treason" as a means of discrediting opponents. The opposition Coalition in particular would accuse Rauch's regime of playing irresponsibly with these notions of loyalty and treason, twisting or relativizing the words for simple political advantage. The two terms, they said, had both become "commodities in the marketplace", with the effect that "today's loyalists are tomorrow's traitors".[13] In fact, as we will see, there was ample scope—not least in Imperial law—for problematizing both the concepts of loyalty and treason, and the Coalition forces were no more innocent of the urge to carry out such rhetorical aggressions than Rauch himself.

Indeed, in the power struggle of 1908–10, it seemed at first that the opposition Coalition of Croats and Serbs was the most provocative, leading the charge by boldly challenging the credentials of the Rauch regime, characterizing it as alien and "un-Croatian". By 1909, however, the reverse was the case. In an effort to destroy the Coalition forces and assert order, the regime proceeded to target the most suspect element within it, the Serb Independent Party, and to question the loyalty, both vertical and horizontal, of those who dared even to call themselves "Serb" in Croatia.[14] Eventually, fifty-three Serbs were prosecuted for treason in a show trial and, in October 1909, thirty-one were found guilty. Alongside the Dreyfus affair in France, this was the most notorious European treason trial of the pre-1914 era, and had major repercussions in terms of alienation from the regime in the southern Slav lands. Yet it has received only minimal attention from historians in the past century.[15] Taken together with the vicious public debates that raged in 1908, it provides an ideal framework within which to analyze how diverse sets of loyalties could fluctuate in importance and how the authorities tried to impose their own preferred prescriptive allegiances in order to eliminate rival politi-

---

[13] See an article in the Croat Progressive newspaper *Pokret*: "Veleizdajnici!," *Pokret*, 11 August 1908, 1.

[14] According to the census, 25 % of the population was Orthodox.

[15] The best account remains that of R.W. Seton-Watson, *The Southern Slav Question and the Habsburg Monarchy* (London: Constable, 1911). There is no good study in Croatian. The work of Mirjana Gross supplies excellent context but is tinged with a certain Marxist determinism. See especially Mirjana Gross, "Hrvatska uoči aneksije Bosne i Hercegovine," *Istorija XX veka: Zbornik radova III* 3 (1962): 153–269; idem, *Povijest pravaške ideologije*, 347–74. See also the useful Austrian doctoral thesis by Waltraud Schuster, "Der Agramer Hochverratsprozeß" (Vienna, 1979); and Arnold Suppan, "Masaryk and the Trials for High Treason Against South Slavs in 1909," in *T.G. Masaryk (1850–1937): Volume 1: Thinker and Politician*, ed. Stanley B. Winters (New York: St Martin's Press, 1990), 210–24. The echoes of the Dreyfus affair in Croatia are analysed in Ljiljana Dobrovšak, "Odjeci Dreyfusove afere u Hrvatskoj javnosti od 1894 do 1906," *Historijski Zbornik*, no. 60 (2007): 129–59.

cal forces. For behind the basic question of what loyalty to the nation actually meant, there always lingered other dilemmas over Croatia's precise vertical relationship to the two parts of the monarchy: in other words, over what Croatians might expect from Budapest or Vienna in return for paying due homage in either of the two Imperial capitals.

By early 1909, moreover, with Austria-Hungary on a war footing with Serbia in the wake of the former's annexation of Bosnia-Herzegovina in October 1908, another factor now dominated the Zagreb hubbub. The discourse had shifted towards scrutinizing citizens who had any type of allegiance outside the monarchy with a view to deciding whether to label them traitors. The Rauch regime played a central role in bringing this state of affairs about. It deliberately tightened up the public interpretation of the concept of loyalty, dangerously casting as "traitors" many who did not live up to the new, extremely exacting definition. In turn though, this campaign of demonization was not the one-way street it is so often portrayed as in Croatian historiography. It was shaped by self-assured antagonists all across the Croat-Serb political spectrum, who were all trying to massage and adjust notions of Imperial allegiance to suit their own radical agendas.

* * *

Let us first examine the discourse of 1908 on the subject of loyalty in more depth. We have rich sources available to us on the evolution of the regime's arguments since, aside from the government's own newspapers—*Ustavnost* (Constitution) and *Narodne Novine* (National News)—Rauch himself published his own justification for the status quo anonymously after one year in office, as well as leaving a number of semi-autobiographical memoirs.[16] Since Rauch had long coveted the office of *ban*, and since his father was the main architect of the 1868 *Nagodba*, his conception of Croatian loyalty was widely known long before his appointment in December 1907. Zagreb's chief satirical magazine, *Koprive* (Nettles), set out this view vividly.[17] In cartoons at the end of the year it portrayed Rauch firstly in a nativity scene, as the holy but illegitimate child of Hungary (Fig. 2). He might well be Croatia's "Christ child" or savior, but in the role of Mary was Sándor Wekerle and his father Joseph looked suspiciously like the wily ambitious *pravaši* politician Josip Frank.

---

[16] Veridicus, *Kroatien im Jahre 1907–1908*; Branka Molnar and Iskra Iveljić, eds., *Memoari bana Pavla Raucha* (Zagreb: Zagrebačko archivističko društvo, 2009).

[17] *Koprive* had been started by a group of young members of the *Hrvatska pučka napredna stranka* (the Croatian People's Progressive Party, HPNS) in June 1906 after the election victory of the Coalition; it was a deliberate generational reaction against the years of censorship before 1903: Josip Horvat, *Povijest novinstva Hrvatske 1771–1939* (Zagreb: Tehnička knjiga, 2003), 304–7.

Fig. 2: "Hrvatski Božić" [Croatian Christmas], *Koprive* no. 18, 1907, 1.

In a second cartoon, Rauch was caricatured as a disciplinarian landowner, determined (as Andrássy had been decades before) to whip the dirty Croatian "pigs" into order.[18] After the publication of these cartoons it became a standard tactic to associate Rauch with pigs and turn the simile against him.[19]

Rauch's government program immediately set out a vision of progressive economic reforms, sections of which he would eventually succeed in imple-

---

[18] "Sretna nova godina!," *Koprive* no. 1, 1908, 1.
[19] See "Politička situacija," *Koprive* no. 15, 15 October 1908, 1; "Božič 1909," *Koprive*, no. 22–23, 24 December 1908, 16. In the latter Rauch and Czernkovich are flying over Zagreb in a giant pig-Zeppelin.

menting.[20] But the first edition of his own newspaper—forcefully titled *Ustavnost* [Constitution]—emphasized the only realistic prospect for Croatia's future. The country simply had to resurrect a true unionist policy with "the fraternal Magyar nation," a union that had served Croatia so well for eight hundred years and whose legal legitimacy was firmly founded on the 1868 agreement. From the outset too, Rauch made it clear that Coalition forces—now engaged in a demagogic onslaught against him through their press—had led the nation astray, hypocritically cultivating a relationship with Budapest for their own ends, only to turn against Hungary as soon as the unionist link seemed no longer to suit their purposes. This immoral stance had left the nation sick and in need of a long period of convalescence or, as Rauch's deputy Nikola Czernkovich imaginatively put it, "suffering from a range of visions and hallucinations."[21]

The new regime therefore would place its trust in fresh elections, relying on what it termed those Croats who possessed a "fervent patriotism" to resurrect the unionist ideal. Indeed, under ideal conditions, some cobbled together coalition of unionists and Frankists might perhaps secure a majority in the *Sabor*. Yet this course was quickly to become abortive. As Rauch himself noted, "The election prospects are not at all rosy, for the terror of the masses is really unbelievable." Not even the votes of civil servants could be counted on.[22] In other words, true patriotism as defined by Rauch had already been so severely corrupted by the Coalition scoundrels during their period of office that normal methods might no longer suffice to purge the body politic of falsehood and disorder. Indeed, Czernkovich, as minister of the interior, actually hoped for an electoral disaster so that the regime could dissolve the chamber and rule as an autocracy.[23]

The opposition certainly appeared strident and confident. As we have seen, Rauch had already labelled the Coalition "anti-dynastic" on the basis of the reception that greeted His Majesty's representative in January 1908.[24] Taking up the gauntlet thrown before them by Rauch's accusations, the Coalition press in Zagreb whipped up the public mood—like a veritable "Witches' Sabbath" in Rauch's words—and immediately interpreted the "an-

---

[20] Mira Kolar, "The Activities of Vice-Roy Pavao Rauch in Croatia," *Review of Croatian History* 1, no. 1 (2005): 133–57. This attempt to rehabilitate Rauch on the basis of his program of socioeconomic reforms is marred by some dubious (and anti-Serb) claims, not least the idea that his administration "rarely breached the law." Ibid., 135.

[21] "Nakon prvog dana," *Ustavnost*, 28 February1908, 1: this was an interview with Czernkovich. See also for the regime's outlook: "Što hoćemo!" *Ustavnost*, 1 February 1908, 1.

[22] Rauch to Daruváry, 31 January 1908, Kabinettsarchiv, HHStA, Karton 26, Geheimakten; also in Iveljić, *Anatomija*, 236–7.

[23] Iso Kršnjavi, *Zapisci: Iza kulisa Hrvatske politike*, vol. 2 (Zagreb: Mladost, 1986), 506.

[24] Cf. Mirjana Gross's interpretation that Rauch entered office with a pre-set agenda of seeking out traitors: Gross, "Hrvatska uoči aneksije," 170–1.

ti-dynastic" label as an accusation of "treason".[25] The accusation was to become a red thread running through the entire public discourse, with both sides competing to dominate the argument on loyalty and to paint their opponents as traitors. This pattern of argument ultimately suited the regime, for in the February elections to the *Sabor* the unionists failed to win a single seat while the Coalition won a two-thirds majority. Therefore, in order to maintain any authority at all, the regime felt itself obliged to fall back either on sheer force or on arguments defending its dynastic credibility as the legitimately appointed executive power. In other words, it was forced to assert vertical loyalty above all other considerations, casting itself in the role of the overriding legitimate authority.

When the *Sabor* met, the King's speech on the government's program was duly read out (by a representative of Franz Joseph). The president of the *Sabor* Erazmo Barčić then provocatively replied with a speech of his own, calling for the expulsion of all "foreigners" from Croatia—mentioning both Hungary and Rauch's government. This gave Rauch the excuse to dissolve the chamber and disregard any constitutional niceties. For he interpreted Barčić's speech as having overstepped the bounds of legality—indeed as tantamount to treason. Not only had it effectively called for revolt; it had been openly abusive to the King's representative and therefore the dynasty itself. Later Rauch would justify his abrupt action by asserting his own superior understanding of loyalty (according to his perception of Croatia's best interests): "It would have been almost a betrayal of the dynasty, state and the Croatian people, if he [Rauch] had not remained calm and unshaken by the wild thunder of emotions."[26]

In the late spring following the dissolution of the *Sabor*, Rauch repeatedly asserted his own credibility by posing as the mediator of true patriotism on behalf of the nation. This involved asserting the trust supposedly placed in him by both the King in Vienna and the Hungarian government in Budapest. As one expert commentator noted, Croatian loyalty was always caught in this vice: "For Croatian politicians, maneuvering between Scylla and Charybdis is a damned necessity as long as this absurd dualism exists"[27]. Rauch sought regular assurance of support for his actions from both capitals, but tended to tilt more towards Vienna in view of public Croatian hostility towards Hungary as well as his own private gripe that the Wekerle government was insensitive to his difficult position.[28] He therefore especially trumpeted the confidence that the monarch had shown in him (by granting him audiences at

---

[25] Veridicus, *Kroatien im Jahre 1907–1908*, 16.
[26] Ibid., 20; "Otvorenje sabora," *Ustavnost*, 13 March 1908, 1.
[27] Kršnjavi, *Zapisci*, vol. 2, 554.
[28] Rauch was particularly irritated when Wekerle boldly told the Hungarian parliament on 11 March 1908 that the *ban*'s role was to implement Hungarian policy in Croatia: Gross, "Hrvatska uoči aneksije," 185.

Schönbrunn on 27 April and 6 June 1908), and claimed to be secure in his position in the face of constant predictions in the press of his imminent demise.[29]

In June 1908, Rauch's team in Zagreb made much of his appointment as a "privy counsellor" to the King. At the official ceremony at the *ban*'s palace granting him this honor, Nikola Czernkovich addressed Rauch, praising his love of Croatia and his loyalty towards Franz Joseph: "The good genius of the Croatian people [...] will protect it from the burdensome mistakes that lead into the deep abyss and to perpetual disaster. You believe in that genius". Rauch replied that he had done everything he had sworn to his monarch that he would do, and concluded by wishing "Živio!" ("long life!") to the Habsburg Emperor-King.[30]

However, this simple public affirmation of the existence of an interdependent network tied together by mutual trust was not quite what it seemed. Firstly, the Habsburg monarch's favor—essential for Rauch's own political survival—would always be conditional on his performance as *ban* and could easily be withdrawn at any time. As Franz Joseph had stressed on appointing Rauch, he wished Croatia to be led on a "conservative" course which promised stability.[31] Secondly, there was the added irony that behind the scenes Czernkovich's own loyalty to Rauch was suspect: he had in fact aimed to overshadow the *ban*, removing all rivals, and had indeed managed to achieve that goal by the end of the year.[32] In short, the Rauch regime, replete as it was with allegiances based on personal and political patronage, was not one that fostered unity. Disunity was constantly surfacing, not just undermining Rauch's position in both Vienna and Budapest (where the minister responsible for Croatian affairs, Emerik Josipović was a personal enemy), but also casting doubt on the regime's rhetoric that it deserved the trust of ordinary Croatians.[33]

---

[29] Kršnjavi, *Zapisci*, vol. 2, 513: Kršnjavi was sceptical about any special royal backing. Rauch took Franz Joseph's willingness to patronize a major art exhibition in Zagreb (sending Rauch six thousand crowns to buy up key works) as one example of tangible royal support. Rauch to Daruváry, letters of 30 April and 9 May 1908, Kabinettsarchiv, HHStA, Karton 26, Geheimakten. See also news reports on the imperial audiences: *Ustavnost*, 28 April 1908, 2; *Ustavnost*, 8 June 1908, 2–3; and *Ustavnost*, 13 June 1908, 1.

[30] "Čestitanje svietlom banu," *Ustavnost*, 1 July 1908, 1. The opposition naturally scoffed at this, claiming that Rauch's days were numbered, and that when the wielders of power sobered up they would see clearly that "an entire nation can neither be trampled upon nor exterminated": "Rauchov položaj," *Srbobran*, 30 June 1908, 1.

[31] "Bericht des Banus Baron Rauch."

[32] Nikola Czernkovich (1845–1917) remains an interesting figure for research: there is little written about him despite his notoriety in these years, and he hardly appears in Croatian encyclopaedias.

[33] For the disloyalty of Czernkovich and Josipović, see the gossip in Kršnjavi, *Zapisci*, vol. 2, 521, 528–30, 538, 540. Czernkovich's relations with Koloman Mixich, the minister for education and religion, were especially bad.

In relation to the latter concern, the regime made consistent efforts to cultivate and claim a healthy level of allegiance among the Croatian population. In July 1908, Rauch undertook an extensive motor tour through the western counties of Lika and Modrus-Rijeka, and even crossed the dualist border to visit the town of Knin in Austrian Dalmatia. His use of an automobile on this tour was designed to highlight his program of modernization and to cement his personal connection to the grassroots. Indeed, immediately upon assuming office, he had announced his plans to tour the country by car. This had aroused scorn from Coalition circles and inspired some puns to the effect that "the homeland will soon be covered with smoke [German: *Rauch*] and will start to stink strongly of it."[34] Not everything went smoothly on his July motor tour, not least in Serb-dominated Knin, where he was met by a small crowd of protesters, or on the Croatian coast at Novi Vindolski, near Rijeka, where wires were dangerously stretched across the road to sabotage his progress. Both incidents were interpreted as assassination attempts and attributed respectively to Serb "rabble-rousers" and to Coalition firebrand Frano Supilo (whose home town was Rijeka).[35]

Nevertheless, on the basis of the initial evidence, we should question the standard view that Rauch's "regime enjoyed absolutely no support in Croatia."[36] Indeed in many quarters, automatic respect was always shown before the *ban* as the leading Imperial official representing Croatia, and therefore as someone in a position to advance local needs in return for due allegiance. Even while Rauch prioritized vertical loyalty, pro-regime press reports also suggested a pattern of horizontal bonding at work as "the Croatian nation" came out to greet their *ban*. These rituals were observed on a brief car tour in May 1908 when, aside from the many who were attracted to events on the tour by the *ban*'s automobile or by the official ritual performed during such events, many others turned up to petition the *ban* to invest in local economic projects.[37] Similarly, when Rauch made a tour of Slavonia (eastern Croatia) a year later, he received a surprisingly warm welcome, with only minimal protests even from the Serb population. The *ban* himself emphasized that these receptions had not been artificially staged.[38] The problem for historians is how to interpret these public "performances"—this *façade* of loyalty—vis-à-vis the actual underlying mindset.

---

[34] "Kr. zemaljski automobile," *Pokret*, 15 May 1908, 1. See also an early cartoon where Rauch drives his car off a cliff: "Početak konca," *Koprive* no. 3, February 1908, 1.
[35] "Svietli ban u Lici," *Ustavnost*, 14 July 1908, 1; Veridicus, *Kroatien im Jahre 1907-1908*, 26-7.
[36] Miller, *Between Nation and State*, 115.
[37] "Kr. zemaljski automobile," *Pokret*, May 15, 1908, 1. In Lasinja, for example, fifty people petitioned for an iron bridge over the river Kupa. In July, Rauch was received with great festivity in the beflagged town of Brinje (by peasant and school delegations): "Putovanje svietlog bana po Lici," *Ustavnost*, 13 July 1908, 2.
[38] See "Svietli ban o svom putovanju," *Ustavnost* 22 June 1909, 3.

Neither can the alternative competing political discourses over "loyalty" be ignored. Loudest in the public domain were always those of the *pravaši* and the Croat-Serb Coalition, in both cases attacking Rauch and Hungary while also taking violent swipes at one other. The nationalist interpretation of Croatian loyalty promoted by the *pravaši* around Josip Frank seems the most clear-cut interpretation of the concept, defining it as being opposed to anything "un-Croatian." This meant excoriating anybody who offered homage to Hungary or who dared to betray Croatia's sacred "state right." Scorning Rauch's unionist agenda from the outset, the Frankist party's newspaper wrote: "It is not possible to serve both the Croatian and the Magyar nations [...] In the heart of everything Croatian there nestles a deep loathing towards everything Magyar."[39]

Even more despicable for the Frankists was the enemy within who sought to divert the nation from its true patriotic and nationalist course. Croat-Serb Coalition politicians, who had flirted with Budapest up until 1907, were always termed "young Magyarones" as a consequence by the Frank party. Here, as in so much of the discourse about political loyalty, stances were presented as clear-cut moral choices. Thus Frano Supilo, the Coalition leader, was portrayed as sly, malicious and unpatriotic—someone who could only atone for his sins against the nation by openly advising people to support Frankists.[40] Naturally, the characterization of Supilo and friends as national traitors was also justified on grounds of their firm alliance with the Serb Independent Party. The Frank party's own commitment to the "true Croatian nation" was regularly defined in ethnic terms, against the Magyars outside, and against the Serbs inside the Croatian national territory. As Izidor Kršnjavi, the party's leading ideologist, put it, "The Serbs are no less our opponents than the Magyars."[41] Most Frankists did not want any real dialogue with either group, except via hostile rhetoric—and indeed Serbs were disparagingly referred to as "Vlahs": i.e. as an alien, immigrant element within Croatia (and one that was in any case often allied to the Magyars).[42]

Yet during the Rauch era, this simple bundle of negative stereotypes obscured a much messier picture. As revealed in *Koprive*'s nativity cartoon of late 1907, and notwithstanding the Frankists' anti-Magyar rhetoric, Josip Frank himself had secretly talked to Wekerle on the birth of the Rauch regime, hoping to finally gain power for his own party under some new type of

---

[39] "Baron Pavao Rauch: ban," *Hrvatsko pravo*, 8 January 1908, 1; "Rauchov program i Magjari," *Hrvatsko pravo*, 18 January 1908, 1.

[40] "Sumnjivo preporučivanje," *Hrvatsko pravo*, 22 January 1908, 1.

[41] Izidor Kršnjavi to R.W. Seton-Watson, 29 September 1909, quoted in *R.W. Seton-Watson and the Yugoslavs: Correspondence 1906–1941*, ed. Hugh and Christopher Seton-Watson et al, vol. 1, *1906–1918* (London: British Academy, 1976), 48.

[42] "Dr Medaković: dvostruki denuncijant," *Hrvatsko pravo*, 13 February 1908, 1. Here Medaković is described as "one of the most loathsome of our Vlahs." Ibid.

authoritarian regime. One historian has even seen fit to consider these talks an important watershed, "a first stage in the intensification of a traitorous atmosphere" in Croatia.[43] Talks with the Magyars were certainly a dirty secret that slowly began to leak out, eventually leading to a major split in the Frank party in April 1908. Given that Frank's opportunistic tactics were prone to be labelled "Magyarone"—at odds with everything the *pravaši* stood for—he was unsurprisingly much more inclined to flirt openly in the direction of the Austrian Imperial authorities, as his overriding loyalty to the monarchy was unquestioned. Only looking in this direction could he expect support from military and other "Greater Austrian" circles who hoped to construct a loyal power base in Croatia. He also had a tendency to invoke or imagine the goodwill of Franz Joseph and his ministers in Vienna towards his program of a Greater Croatia, in return for his own allegiance to the dynasty.[44]

A good example of this illusion in action occurred in November 1908, in the heat of the Bosnian crisis. The reconstituted Frank party resolved to recruit a special Croatian voluntary unit which could be mobilized against Serbia, claiming that the idea had the support of the king and the Austrian ministry of defense. After the initiative had been launched with great fanfare in Zagreb on 5 November, it slowly became clear that Vienna—mindful of international tensions—had changed its mind, much to Frank's resentment. As a result of the episode, he was forced once more to put out feelers towards Hungary to prevent complete political isolation.[45] The story proves the point once more that, within the dualist power structure, all Croatian politicians felt bound at times to maneuver tactically between Vienna and Budapest in pursuit of their goals for the Croatian homeland. For Frank, this loyal vertical maneuvering naturally worked best if Vienna and Budapest were both inclined to reciprocate with policies attuned to his party's nationalist agenda. Thus, in 1908–9 the triangular relationship seemed to click into place, with all sides united in their commitment to an anti-Serb crusade.[46] Even if the Croatian voluntary unit had proven a step too far, the Frankists could at least applaud the regime for launching its treason trial against the Serb traitors within. The question of where precisely Frankist allegiances lay nevertheless re-

---

[43] Gross, "Hrvatska uoči aneksije," 164–6.
[44] Ibid., 157–62. For the Frank party splits: Ibid., 209–15; Gross, *Povijest pravaške ideologije*, 352–4. See also Kršnjavi, *Zapisci*, vol. 2, 518, 531. For Frank's strong interaction with military and diplomatic circles in Vienna, see Stjepan Matković and Marko Trogrlić, eds., *Iz korespondencije Josipa Franka s Bečom: 1907–1910* (Zagreb: Hrvatski institut za povijest, 2014).
[45] Kršnjavi, *Zapisci*, vol. 2, 546–8, 550–2, 554 (about Frank's article in the Budapest newspaper *Pester Lloyd*).
[46] A further example was the monarchy's annexation of Bosnia, which Frank naturally interpreted as a step towards creating a Greater Croatia. See his telegram of thanks to Franz Joseph on the same day that the voluntary unit was announced: Frank to Franz Joseph, 5 November 1908, Kabinettsarchiv, HHStA, Karton 26, Geheimakten.

mained a complicated issue. By 1909 Frank was unofficially backing Rauch, while at the same time taking care to preserve a certain distance in order to keep his Croat constituency on side.

If "treason" as the precise antithesis of "trust" became the watchword of the regime, it was the Croat-Serb Coalition who first ran with this terminology and fleshed it out with concrete criteria. When Rauch had termed the Coalition forces "anti-dynastic" and treasonable, the Coalition press had proceeded to satirize some novel interpretations of "anti-dynastic" behavior (Fig. 3).

Fig. 3: "Anti-Dynastic Scenes in Croatia under Baron Rauch's Government: 'In the Name of the Law – Traitor – I Arrest you!'" *Koprive* no. 3, February 1908, 4.

It then turned the argument on its head, attacking the *ban*'s misuse of his own position. One forum in which these onslaughts occurred (since the *Sabor* had been shut down) was the Hungarian parliament, which a delegation of Coalition deputies from the *Sabor* continued to attend and to use to its advantage. As the Serb lawyer Dušan Popović noted in a dramatic speech there in May 1908, Rauch was behaving arrogantly and unconstitutionally in identifying himself with the king as the true bearer of sovereignty. In other words he was the disloyal one, the real traitor to monarch and nation—especially since he was riding rough-shod over Croatia's own constitution by ignoring the *Sabor*.⁴⁷ Others in the Serb press put it more graphically: that Rauch had not hesitated every day "to rinse his filthy mouth with the royal personage."⁴⁸ They challenged him to present proof that they, and not Rauch, were the actual traitors. For, as the key Serb mouthpiece *Srbobran* argued, elsewhere across the Empire there flourished parties and peoples (Magyars, Poles, Italians) who acted in an anti-dynastic manner and yet suffered no harm. In Croatia, by contrast, Serbs and Croats were traditionally expected to endure any regime passively, obediently professing their absolute loyalty. It was now time to do something about their status as "helots."⁴⁹

It was partly out of this violent rhetoric that the idea of a treason trial emerged. Why exactly the Rauch regime proceeded in this direction from mid-1908 is usually ascribed by historians to Imperial anxieties about an external Serbian threat.⁵⁰ Baron Alois Lexa von Aehrenthal, foreign minister in Vienna, had received mounting intelligence since late 1907 of Greater Serbian propaganda being spread in the region, at a time when he was seriously planning to annex the provinces of Bosnia and Herzegovina to the Empire. Proof of a dangerous Serbian threat to the Empire would be a useful tool in justifying the annexation to international public opinion. In late March and early April 1908, Rauch was personally informed of these concerns by Aehrenthal. When Aehrenthal elaborated on the news reaching him from Belgrade of Serbian machinations, he was careful to recognize that he as foreign minister could not order the Croatian *ban* precisely what to do; therefore he counselled Rauch to gather evidence of Serbian interference in Croatia, perhaps with the help of the Frankists.⁵¹ The message was reinforced by Wekerle in Budapest. On the basis of the evidence set before him, Rauch felt able to conclude that there was indeed a treacherous link between the Serb Independent Party and Belgrade. He also knew he had full backing from his superiors to act cautiously but firmly with "extraordinary measures."⁵² *Ustavnost* even

---

⁴⁷ "Govor Dra Dušan Popovića," *Srbobran*, 14 May 1908; Veridicus, *Kroatien im Jahre 1907–1908*, 21. It is noteworthy that Frano Supilo himself recommended boycotting the Hungarian parliament, but he too felt bound at times to flirt with Budapest, and also Vienna. Gross, "Hrvatska uoči aneksije," 220–2. See for example the cartoon in *Koprive* where Supilo canoodles with his female lover Wekerle while the "wretched chauffeur" Rauch scowls in the corner: "Odpušteni chauffeur," *Koprive* no. 10, 6 June 1908, 1.

⁴⁸ "Antidinastičar na banskoj stolici," *Srbobran*, 19 May 1908, 1.

⁴⁹ "Zašto smo veleizdajnički," *Srbobran*, 1 May 1908, 1.

⁵⁰ See for instance Gross's overly determinist discussion in which she implies not only that Wekerle and Aehrenthal envisaged a trial of Serb traitors from the start, but that they created the Rauch regime precisely in order to further this agenda and justify an annexation of Bosnia: Gross, "Hrvatska uoči aneksije," 159, 190, 192ff.

⁵¹ Schuster, "Der Agramer Hochverratsprozeß," 16–8. Rauch himself told Aehrenthal that only the Frank party could provide a counter-weight to increased Serbianization in Croatia.

⁵² Ibid., 18; Rauch to Daruváry, 4 April 1908, Kabinettsarchiv, HHStA, Karton 26, Geheimakten.

announced that Aehrenthal, Wekerle and Rauch had taken decisions to "localize" the Greater Serbian propaganda, adding darkly that "When and what methods will be used to check this movement will depend on how the situation develops."[53]

Historians such as Mirjana Gross, in focusing squarely on the build-up to the Bosnian crisis and Aehrenthal's agenda, have played down the messy local dynamic that underlay the Zagreb treason trial. The trial in fact stemmed directly from Rauch's own predicament amidst intensifying Croatian political discourse about loyalty and treason. He was being consistently targeted as a "degenerate" in Croatia's Serb press, and in May 1908 finally felt forced to challenge Bogdan Medaković, the Serb leader, to a duel (though no duel ever took place, the rhetoric served to seriously polarize the two sides). He thereafter became ever more convinced that, in order to cure Croatia of its sickness, he needed to target the Serbs; he equated their tactics with "barbarous" Belgrade, whose program amounted to "centrifugal agitation threatening the security of the state."[54] His enemies might well complain that he himself was employing "non-European methods," but—in a telling comment on his view of Croatia—he questioned whether "the people here" were really Europeans anyway since it was said that the Balkans began at the Styrian border.[55] In May, some informed commentators continued to feel that Rauch had no coherent policy towards the Serbs apart from his zeal in abusing them as "traitors."[56] Yet from this period onwards, the outlines of the regime's own imaginings of the Croatian nation were becoming steadily sharper, in a process that received strong encouragement from Vienna and Budapest. Loyalty was defined morally in terms of Croatia's main "historic" allegiances—to Catholicism and to the dynasty—against an alien Serbian Orthodox threat.

By July 1908, prominent Serbs were being arrested all across Croatia.[57] By the summer, the regime felt it had ever clearer proof to substantiate its own accusations (though in fact that 'proof' amounted to forged documents from Belgrade). Rauch felt able to purr contentedly, "the devil that the Serb Independent Party had painted on the wall, has now appeared in its own person."[58] Writing deferentially to Aehrenthal in August, he summarized future prospects as follows:

---

[53] "Ministar Aehrenthal u Budimpešti," *Ustavnost*, 13 April 1908, 2.
[54] "Bericht des Banus Baron Rauch über seine Amtstätigkeit in 1908"; Veridicus, *Kroatien im Jahre 1907–1908*, 21–2. The notion of "barbarous" Belgrade was consistently employed with reference to the violent assassination of King Aleksandar Obrenović of Serbia in 1903.
[55] Rauch to Daruváry, 9 May 1908 (reproduced in Iveljić, *Anatomija*, 238). This letter referred in fact to abuse from the Croat paper *Pokret*, but it is clear that Rauch now saw Serbs as the key Achilles heel of the Coalition.
[56] Kršnjavi, *Zapisci*, vol. 2, 528.
[57] Schuster, "Der Agramer Hochverratsprozeß," 50–2.
[58] Veridicus, *Kroatien im Jahre 1907–1908*, 28.

I hope I can say with some confidence that the political situation will clear significantly in the next few months, for the court action against Serb propaganda is already proceeding. Through this, the objective facts of the case have already become very clear and fully coincide with the secret reports of your Excellency and the Hungarian government. We will now proceed further with the investigation. About twenty or twenty-five [Serbs] may be dealt with where the subjective case is more or less proven, so that their conviction for high treason can be confidently assured.[59]

Indeed, once the prosecution began matching the accumulated evidence against the relevant law, its criteria for determining loyalty or disloyalty became further crystallized. Paragraph fifty-eight of Austria's criminal code, which had force in Croatia, defined "high treason" as attempting either violently to change the government, or to dismember part of the state. These clauses suggested a clear-cut definition.[60] In fact, in Austria-Hungary—as in Russia and Germany—the law also included the crime of "preparation to commit treason" as well as actually carrying out such a treasonable act; so the criteria for defining treason could be almost as vague as those used to define the concept of loyalty.[61]

Rauch's regime always implied a clear understanding of what was treasonable, based on paragraph fifty-eight. But at the same time loyal newspapers hinted darkly and irresponsibly that "dishonest" citizens might not deserve a place in the Croatian nation. This sort of coverage opened the door to a veritable witch hunt against Serbs. Rauch might well have seen his priority as anaesthetizing Serb politics ("one cannot kill off 7,000 Serbs," he once privately remarked),[62] but he too sometimes let slip remarks that publicly stereotyped all Serbs as plotters against the regime.[63] In response to such rhetoric, the Coalition forces now took aim. They challenged how the law on treason was being abused, suggesting at the same time that such misuse was common

---

[59] Rauch now expected the Coalition to fall apart. Rauch to Aehrenthal, 9 August 1908, HHStA, PA XL/171 (Interna).

[60] Croatia's criminal code largely followed Austria's from 1852, with some adjustments made to suit the Croatian-Hungarian framework. See the standard Croatian text book on criminal law by Josip Šilović, especially the clauses on treason: Josip Šilović, *Kazneno pravo* (Zagreb: Narodne Novine, 1893), 298–302.

[61] See on this point the standard contemporary work: Fritz van Calker, "Hochverrat und Landesverrat. Majestätsbeleidigung," in *Vergleichende Darstellung des deutschen und ausländischen Strafrechts: Vorarbeiten zur deutschen Strafrechtsreform; Besonderer Teil*, ed. Karl Birkmeyer, Fritz van Calker, and Reinhard Frank, vol. 1, *Verbrechen und Vergehen gegen Staat und die Staatsgewalt* (Berlin: Otto Liebmann, 1906), 42–46.

[62] Kršnjavi, *Zapisci*, vol. 2, 537. This was in response to Kršnjavi telling Rauch: "Serbdom is a difficult question. We must make Serbs politically harmless but allow them to live." Ibid.

[63] See for example, Rauch's interview to the Hungarian newspaper *Pester Lloyd* in Budapest as reported in *Ustavnost*: "Ban u Budimpešti," *Ustavnost*, 23 October 1908, 2; "Šta je veleizdaja?" *Ustavnost*, 22 August 1908, 1. This article specifically compared evidence of "the plot" with the law on treason as explained in Josip Šilović's textbook.

practice in Austria-Hungary among zealous statesmen who wished to flaunt their own loyalty in the pursuit of personal advantage. The most withering criticism came from Alexander Badaj, a former civil servant in the Croatian ministry of justice. Publicly attacking the catch-all nature of paragraph fifty-eight, which criminalized "preparation to commit treason", he criticized the Rauch regime for exploiting the loophole: "The accusation of high treason is the severest weapon in the penal code. [...] One does not deal with sparrows using cannons. Hercules used his cudgel against the Hydra and not against mice."[64] For Rauch such criticism was simply proof of the Coalition's audacious disregard for the law and the power of the state: his enemies were now trying to make victims out of the criminals in order to deflect attention from their own treacherous agitation.[65]

* * *

Let us turn briefly to consider the high treason trial itself, for out of that event were to emerge new interpretations of 'loyalty'.[66] When the trial began in Zagreb in March 1909 (it was to drag on for seven months), issues connected to the loyalties of Rauch or of the Croat-Serb Coalition moved into the background. The focus was now on the allegiance of those Orthodox inhabitants of Croatia who called themselves Serbs, mainly living in the southwest and east of the country. In the decision to prosecute the case, as one defense lawyer exclaimed, "a tribunal has been set up to pass judgement over what is dynastic and what is anti-dynastic."[67] In other words, the public clash of opinions of 1908 was now being tested in law, but twisted in a way that suited the external struggle of the Empire against the kingdom of Serbia, as well as suiting "Croatian national interests" as interpreted by both Rauch and the Frank party. The regime was sure it could get a conviction for treason, and (dangerously) risked a very public display of its power. For the 'traitors' to normal society had to be exposed; the trial was therefore reported daily in the press in order to reach the public domain and set an example.

This power struggle produced some entertaining clashes in court on the subject of loyalty. The prosecution case was put by Milan Accurti, the state prosecutor. He was firmly backed by Josip Tarabochia, the presiding judge, who was quite prepared to tell one defendant "you will get what is coming to

[64] "Dr Badaj o 'veleizdajničkoj' aferi," *Pokret*, August 25, 1908, 1.
[65] Rauch to Daruváry, letters of 27 and 29 August 1908, Kabinettsarchiv, HHStA, Karton 26, Geheimakten.
[66] This discussion is truncated since I am writing a special journal article about the treason trial itself.
[67] Speech of Dušan Popović in: *Stenografski zapisnik, sastavljen kod kr. sudbenog stola u Zagrebu 3. ožujka 1909. i sliedećih dana o glavnoj raspravi povodom optužnice, koju je podnielo kr. državno odvjetničtvo u Zagrebu dne 12. siječnja 1908. broj I. 1263–08. protiv Adama Pribićevića i 52 druga radi zločinstvena veleizdaje* (Zagreb, 1909), 153.

you."⁶⁸ Since he also stressed that the court alone could interpret what was 'treason', the defense lawyers openly announced that it was a political trial.⁶⁹ Prosecutor Accurti went much further than simply accusing the Serb Independent Party of plotting a takeover of Croatia by neighboring Serbia. Serb leaders and officials were accused of fomenting "anti-dynasticism," simply by propagating the very notion of a Serb ethnicity on Croatian territory. The key hotbed of subversion was said to be the quiet village of Vrginmost on the border with Bosnia, where Accurti and his officials had tried to gather a mass of incriminating evidence. Hoisting Orthodox flags in the Serbian colors, possessing pictures of King Petar I of Serbia, even writing in the Cyrillic script (something that had been legalized in 1888), were all deemed evidence of treason, proof that certain Orthodox Christian subjects of the monarchy had been incited to form a dangerous allegiance outside the state borders. Making a swipe at the Croat-Serb Coalition, Accurti repeatedly disparaged the whole idea that there might be any such thing as a common Serb-Croat nation. Simply spreading any theory of "one nation with two names" constituted treason because of what it implied in relation to political unity between Croatia and the hostile state of Serbia. In short, the accused in violation of paragraph fifty-eight were plotting to detach territory from the Habsburg monarchy.⁷⁰

For the defense lawyers this last point was indeed problematic. For in the trial some of the accused openly declared that south Slav unity was a reality. Others like Adam Pribićević certainly had good political ties to Serbia. His diligent defense lawyer Hinko Hinković duly visited Belgrade during the trial in order to collect material for his case; Hinković directly challenged the state evidence and warned about another Dreyfus affair in the making.⁷¹ But the impressive defense team also attacked the prosecution's reductionist assumptions on how patriotism worked within the Empire in general, as well as in terms of Serb allegiances in particular. The Serbs of Croatia, they stressed, were indeed "genetically" the same as the Croats, but they were also of a separate ethnicity: their identity was not an artificial creation.⁷² They not only loved the Croatian fatherland (and therefore hated Croatia's real enemy, Hungary), but could also look back on a proven record of loyalty to the Habsburg dynasty since 1849.⁷³ And as for interpretations of their symbols or of the Cyrillic script as evidence of anti-dynastic sentiment, there were plenty of examples from elsewhere in the Empire that rendered such interpretations

---

68 Josip Tarabochia to Valerijan Pribićević: Ibid., 251.
69 Speech of Hinko Hinković: Ibid., 12.
70 Speech by Accurti: Ibid., 801.
71 Speech by Hinković: Ibid., 98. (Tarabochia cut Hinković off and forbade him to speak in this tone).
72 Speech by Dušan Popović in which the word *genetečki* (genetically) was used: Ibid., 231.
73 Speech of Miloš Borojević: Ibid., 489; Speech of Medaković: Ibid., 1314.

nonsensical. As the Serb lawyer Dušan Popović argued, "We must be very careful. If today we find an Italian who has sympathy for the Italian king or a Czech who has sympathy for the Russian Tsar, we might conclude that he too is an anti-dynastic person."[74] The comparison was dismissed by the prosecution, which claimed that the Serb Independent Party had a focused political agenda that gravitated outside the borders of Austria-Hungary and transgressed the acceptable bounds of allegiance.[75]

If we consider this long legal battle over the nature of treason and disloyalty in Croatia, it is clear that there were many irregularities in how the trial was conducted. The evidence was largely circumstantial, the hostile witnesses were probably bribed, the defendants had been held in prison for over six months before trial. Hinko Hinković even before the trial wrote that the Habsburg *Rechtsstaat* was being abused to an extent resembling prerevolutionary France; in his words, there existed a "Croatian Bastille."[76] The British historian R.W. Seton-Watson, who attended some sessions of the trial, went on to publicize it in the West and called it "one of the grossest travesties of justice in modern times," rivalling the Dreyfus affair, and earning "for Croatia an unenviable notoriety in Europe."[77] Yet the prosecution case was not totally full of holes. Many of the defendants had indeed been enthusiastically promoting Serb culture in Croatia; as one remarked, he had sucked his Serbdom from his mother's breasts.[78] Some had inclinations which were borderline 'treasonable', for example Rade Malobabić who would later be involved in the assassination of Archduke Franz Ferdinand.[79] The problem for the regime was in finding enough evidence to prove that these Serb activists were also 'traitors' under paragraph fifty-eight: in league with Serbia and working consciously against the Habsburg monarchy.

After a 150-day trial which continued until after the Bosnian crisis was over, much to the annoyance of Aehrenthal in Vienna, a verdict was announced in October 1909.[80] Thirty-one of the accused were convicted (including the Pribićević brothers, Adam and Valerijan who were both sen-

---

[74] Ibid., 153.
[75] See Accurti's intriguing comparison with the "single political nation" of Czechs and Germans living in Bohemia: Ibid., 801–2.
[76] Hinko Hinković, "Istražni zatvor veleizdajnika," *Pokret*, 23 September 1908, 1–2.
[77] Seton-Watson, *The Southern Slav Question*, 184, 208; idem, *Absolutism in Croatia* (London: Constable, 1912), 8.
[78] Speech of the Orthodox priest Nikola Ercegovac: Ibid., 558. Accurti asked in reply whether Ercegovac had also sucked "anti-dynasticism"; this caused uproar in the court and proceedings were temporarily suspended.
[79] Ibid, 431–47: Malobabić behaved particularly defiantly when interrogated by Accurti.
[80] Rauch had insisted to Franz Joseph in May 1909 that all of the accused should be prosecuted fully. However, Aehrenthal's desire to shorten the trial, not least because of its denunciation in the European press, led Rauch in June to urge Accurti to accelerate the process: Schuster, "Der Agramer Hochverratsprozeß," 118–19.

tenced to twelve years' imprisonment) and twenty-one were acquitted. Yet for both the Rauch regime and the convicts themselves, the dramatic result of the trial was to be short-lived. In late 1909, a libel trial conducted in Vienna against the famous Austrian historian Heinrich Friedjung uncovered the fact that the evidence used in Zagreb had been based on forged documents.[81] Accurti's entire prosecution case fell apart. The revelations resulted in the release of the "Zagreb traitors" (although they were never officially pardoned), leaving them with even greater moral authority. It also left Rauch's own position finally untenable, forcing his resignation in January 1910.

The trial debacle might otherwise have presaged calmer times for Croatia, but neither the violent rhetoric of the period nor the trial could be easily forgotten. Nikola Tomašić, Rauch's immediate successor as *ban*, found it impossible to reconcile the various mutually suspicious political groupings. And in the eyes of many, the *Rechtsstaat* was never fully restored. Most notably, the regime's arbitrary use of treason law in 1909 was not invalidated. When Hinković tried to secure a full pardon for the defendants and open recognition of the trial's illegality, he was himself put on trial for abusing the judicial system and in 1911 sentenced to six months in prison.[82] By 1912 Slavko Cuvaj, another new *ban*, proceeded on the advice of Budapest to revert fully to absolutist rule, assuming the title of "Imperial Commissar" and governing in blatant disregard for the constitution. As Seton-Watson noted at the time, "the dictatorship of Mr Cuvaj is unique in the annals of modern Europe."[83] Thanks to this trend towards further authoritarianism, the Croatian opposition (even the Frankists) began to take a more unified view of what Croatian national allegiance meant in reality. In sharp contrast, the Hungarian regime had learned little from the Rauch era on how to re-engage and cultivate Croatian allegiance on either the vertical or the horizontal plane.

* * *

This article has explored the various conflicting notions of Croatian loyalty during a time of heightened political tension. That the Rauch era saw a new layering of definitions of loyalty and treason was due to a power contest not just within Croatia, but also internationally in the Habsburg monarchy's deteriorating relationship with nationalist Serbia. The nature of the authoritarian political regime in Croatia framed the way in which such allegiances were actually performed (as opposed to just being spoken about). Thus, as we have seen, almost all the main political players of the period continued to feel

---

[81] Hodimir Sirotković, "Pravni i politički aspekti procesa 'Reichspost'-Friedjung," *Starine* 52 (Zagreb, 1962): 49–180.
[82] "Dr Hinković pred sudom," *Pokret*, 26 May 1911, 1–2; "Šest mjesici tamnice," *Pokret*, 30 May 1911, 1–2.
[83] Seton-Watson, *Absolutism in Croatia*, 51.

bound to follow paths of vertical loyalty towards Vienna and Budapest, playing within the rules of the dualist system in the hope of achieving benefits for their respective causes. At the same time, a burgeoning Croatian civil society in the years after 1903 ensured that more powerful horizontal loyalties were emerging that the educated elite could no longer ignore. Not least the colorful press of the period—which Rauch's regime was fatally unable to fully censor—tended to trumpet such partisan allegiances, claiming that their particular newspaper represented the true national voice. In practice, however, it was vertical loyalties that still mattered most in prewar Croatia, while horizontal conceptions of loyalty were to require a more democratic political system in which to flourish. The period was nevertheless a time when morphing processes in allegiances had begun to accelerate or, as one veteran observer noted in his diary in 1908, "Friendship in this land changes like a kaleidoscope."[84]

The mirror-image discourse about 'treason' presents us with a Hungarian or Habsburg regime in crisis in the years before the Great War. The regime showed itself to be particularly careless in arbitrarily branding political opponents as anti-dynastic and in equating this characterization with treason. The power struggle that followed involved the use of the ultimate legal weapon— an indictment for high treason[85]—but in this context, in contrast to the usual inevitable outcome of treason trials, the "traitors" emerged victorious. The impact was disastrous for the Rauch regime in the short term, but was also to prove calamitous in the long term for both the Hungarian government and indeed the Habsburg dynasty, whose legitimacy and credibility was severely weakened. It is true that by 1914, when Budapest reintroduced constitutional rule, the political atmosphere in Croatia seemed more tranquil. Yet as the First World War began, the discourse on loyalty and treachery was to resurface immediately, in the first instance targeting Serbs, but also challenging any tendency to insubordination on the part of Croats.[86] Not least, despite the pre-war debacle, the wielding of treason law continued in Austria and Croatia.[87] Croatian loyalties to Hungary and to the Habsburgs were thus to face their final test, and by 1918 many individuals had concluded that the Austro-Hungarian Empire no longer provided a secure framework capable of hosting the Croatian nation.

---

[84] Kršnjavi, *Zapisci*, vol. 2, 512.
[85] Otto Kirchheimer, *Political Justice: The Use of Legal Procedure for Political Ends* (Princeton: Princeton University Press, 1961), 76.
[86] This continuity in perceptions of southern Slav treachery, before and after 1914, has been well analysed in the case of Styria. See Martin Moll, *Kein Burgfrieden: Der deutsch-slowenische Nationalitätenkonflikt in der Steiermark 1900–1918* (Innsbruck: Studien, 2007).
[87] See Mark Cornwall, "Traitors and the Meaning of Treason in Austria-Hungary's Great War," *Transactions of the Royal Historical Society* 25 (2015): 113–134.

Viorica Angela Crăciun

THE DEMOCRATIC PARTY OF BUKOVINA AND ITS NATIONAL AND IMPERIAL LOYALTIES (1902–1918)

At the beginning of the twentieth century the set of issues that has come to be known as the "national problem" was becoming increasingly acute in most of the provinces under the rule of the House of Habsburg. Thus, the Duchy of Bukovina, the empire's easternmost and also one of its least developed provinces, found itself in an extremely complex situation as a result of issues of nationality. Home to no less than eleven officially recognized ethnic groups, the duchy was a veritable mosaic of nationalities, a sort of Austria-Hungary in miniature. From the second half of the nineteenth century on, from among all the nationalities living there, the region's Romanian population began seeking to establish their political preponderance in the province, arguing their case on the basis of historical right. Up until the first decade of the twentieth century, the region's Romanian political parties were primarily concerned with achieving a privileged position for the sections of the population they represented. Representatives of these parties constantly contested any social or political progress demanded by any of the other nationalities of the region, and especially by the province's Ruthenians. A major change of direction in the Romanian political discourse was produced by the appearance of Aurel Onciul on the political scene and his establishment of the Democratic Party. Onciul proposed a change of approach, away from confrontation and in the direction of a more collaborative posture, a stance that was not made any easier by the region's history and ethnic diversity.

The province had previously been part of the Voivodeship of Moldova, which from the second half of the fifteenth century on—with brief interludes—had been mostly under Ottoman suzerainty. However, this status had not produced any decisive change to the ethnic make-up of the voivodeship. Thus, at the time the province was eventually annexed by Austria in 1775, it was still generally considered to be "Moldavian" or even "Romanian" in terms of national character.[1]

---

*   This work was supported by the European Social Fund in Romania, under the responsibility of the Managing Authority for the Sectoral Operational Programme for Human Resources Development 2007–2013 (grant POSDRU/107/1.5/S/78342).

[1]   Romanian historiography, starting with the second half of the nineteenth century, stressed the purely Romanian character of the province at the time of its incorporation

From 1775 until the mid-nineteenth century, the new province, officially named *Bukowina*, experienced a constant influx of German and Jewish immigrants, who settled predominantly in the cities, but also the steady arrival of another notable group—Galician Ruthenians, who settled preponderantly in the northern, more rural areas of the province.[2] The first two ethnic groups had some effect on the ethnic character of the province, but they did not have the effect of decisively transforming it. In contrast, however, the number of Ruthenians living in the province progressively increased to the extent that by the beginning of the twentieth century their numbers had actually surpassed the Romanian population in imperial statistics, though not to the extent that they had become an absolute majority.[3]

The figures of the 1900 imperial census give an idea of the complex ethnic mix in Bukovina at the time. In 1900, out of a total of 730,195 inhabitants in the Duchy of Bukovina, 297,798 identified as Ruthenians while "only" 229,018 thought of themselves as ethnic Romanians.[4] This situation was largely unchanged in terms of percentages as reflected by what was to be the last census taken in the duchy, in 1910.[5] It was clear that none of the national-

by the empire, with the purpose of justifying claims of Romanian national and political supremacy in the province and, after 1918, to justify the annexation of the province by Romania on the basis of historical and national rights. See, among others, Nicolae Iorga, *Neamul românesc în Bucovina* (Bucharest: Minerva, 1905); Dimitrie Onciul, *Din istoria Bucovinei* (Chernivtsi: Universitas, 1992); Aurel Morariu, *Bucovina. Date din punctul de vedere: administrativ, politic, financiar, industrial, economic, agricol, școlastic, juridic, eclesiastic, etc., etc.* (Bucharest: Teodosiu Jonnițiu Fii, 1915); Ilie Grămadă, *"Bucovina și Basarabia"* (unpublished manuscript); Aurel Morariu, *Bucovina, 1774–1914* (Bucharest: Pavel Suru, s.a.); Ion Nistor, *Istoria Bucovinei* (Bucharest: Humanitas, 1991); and Ion Nistor, *Românii și rutenii în Bucovina. Studiu istoric și statistic* (Bucharest: Edițiunea Academiei Române, 1915).

2   Unlike most Romanian historians (Ion Nistor, Dimitrie Onciul, Teodor Balan, Mihai Iacobescu, etc.), who regarded Bukovina as a purely Moldovan-Romanian province from an ethnic point of view in 1775, I reckon that there already was a population of Ruthenians at least in the north of the territory, even before the arrival of emigrants from Galicia at the beginning of the nineteenth century. My view is lent plausibility by the fact that the area in question was a border region. However, I would not regard this group of "indigenous" Ruthenians as having been large enough in 1775 to essentially alter the province's ethnic character.

3   See Nistor, *Românii și rutenii în Bucovina*; Ilie E. Toroutiu, *Populația și clasele sociale din Bucovina* (Bucharest: Lupta, 1916) or *Comitetul Românilor din Bucovina pentru Expoziție, Românii din Bucovina-privire scurtă asupra desvoltării lor pe teren cultural și economic dela încorporarea Bucovinei în Monarhia Austro-Ungară până la 1906* (Chernivtsi, 1906).

4   Likewise, there were also 159,486 Jewish-Germans (i.e. people declaring themselves Germans of the Judaic religion), 96,150 Jews, 63,336 Germans, and 26,857 Poles. Others (including Armenians, Hungarians, Turks, Russians, etc.) made up a total of 10,112; see Nistor, *Românii și rutenii în Bucovina*, 156.

5   The final results of the census were also published in *Viața Românească*, February 1912, 279–83; see also Helmut Rumpler and Peter Urbanitsch, eds., *Die Habsburgermonarchie*

ities constituted an absolute majority and that the difference in size between Romanian and Ruthenian populations, though quite significant in absolute figures, did not automatically imply the political supremacy of the latter group. This state of affairs was further complicated by the empire's censitary voting system. In terms of national representation, the electoral system favored the great landowners in particular, the great majority of whom were Romanian, though Poles and Armenians were also represented in much smaller numbers, along with members of the German-Jewish bourgeoisie. At the same time, the electoral system clearly disadvantaged Ruthenians—an overwhelmingly peasant population almost completely unrepresented in the upper strata of society. From a look at the balance of parliamentary forces around 1900 in the imperial Chamber of Deputies and the Diet of Bukovina, it is clear that Romanians held the most privileged position of all the nationalities of Bukovina. Romanian representatives held five out of a total of eleven seats for the province in the Chamber of Deputies of the Imperial Council[6] and thirteen out of thirty-one in the Diet of Bukovina[7] while Ruthenians held only two and four seats respectively in these bodies. Although, as these figures clearly reflect, Romanians were politically privileged, the situation looks very different if one considers the social base upon which this political representation rested. For example, out of the thirteen seats in the Diet held by Romanians after the 1898 elections, six were taken from the constituency of the large landowners, one was reserved for the Greek Orthodox metropolitan bishop and of the remaining seats held by Romanians there were only two that neither formed part of nor had any connection with the great boyar families.[8]

However, this situation was about to change at the political level in Bukovina. In a development affecting the region's Romanian population in partic-

---

1848–1918, vol. 9/2, *Soziale Strukturen. Die Gesellschaft der Habsburgermonarchie im Kartenbild. Verwaltungs-, Sozial- und Infrastrukturen. Nach dem Zensus von 1910*, ed. Helmut Rumpler and Martin Seger (Vienna: Österreichische Akademie der Wissenschaften, 2010).

[6] Apart from these deputies there was also one Polish-Armenian as well as three German-Jewish representatives in the parliament ("German-Jewish" was the official designation since Jews were not recognized as a distinct national group as such—they were included on the electoral lists as Germans). For a detailed analysis of the electoral system and the election results of March 1897, see Mihai-Ștefan Ceaușu, *Parlamentarism, partide și elită politică în Bucovina habsburgică, 1848–1918. Contribuții la istoria parlamentarismului în spațiul central-est european* (Iași: Junimea, 2004), 198–201.

[7] Six Germans and four Polish-Armenians were also elected to the Diet in September 1898, while three deputies declared themselves independent but ultimately became members of either the Jewish or German group. See ibid., 336–40.

[8] For the final result as well as the unfolding of the electoral campaign, see Ioan Cocuz, *Partidele politice românești din Bucovina, 1862–1914* (Suceava: Cuvântul Nostru, 2003), 253–66; Teodor Bălan, *Lupta pentru tricolor. Un capitol din istoria politică a Bucovinei, 1898–1904* (Bucharest: Academia Română, 2008), 34–40.

ular, two major tendencies began to make themselves felt in the region, and indeed the empire as a whole, at the start of the twentieth century: the process of democratization and the intensification of national struggles.

Starting in 1897, the profile of the typical voter in the political life of Bukovina began to change. The first step in this process was the introduction of two electoral colleges in which universal suffrage applied to elections to the Imperial Council. This was followed by the achievement of a universal right to vote in 1907. This meant that the empire's political forces began having to address the masses and those masses in turn became increasingly aware of their individual national identities. Like other provinces within the Dual Monarchy, Bukovina too saw the emergence of new political organizations set up by "the youth" or "the nationals" as opposed to those representing "the old" or "the conservatives." Primarily founded by and composed of intellectuals who exhibited an unprecedented degree of intransigence in relation to national issues, these new and widely popular factions were mainly concerned with issues relating to the national question. But, as a consequence of the empire's censitary electoral system, this new movement had to arrive at a compromise in Bukovina: i.e. the young nationals were forced into an alliance with the faction representing the great boyars. Thus, a single party of the Romanians, which was to remain active on the political stage from 1892 to 1900, came into being. However, this unified front was to rupture in 1900 precisely as a result of disagreements between the "old" conservative aristocracy and the "young" nationalists.[9]

Competition between the two groups for the support of the electorate ensued with two opposing programs emerging. On one side, the nationalists advocated a dual strategy, involving both a struggle against other nationalities in the effort to secure economic and institutional advantages, combined with opposition to the Austrian authorities, whose attitudes were characterized as having an anti-Romanian bias. On the other side of the equation, conservatives not only hoped for restrictions to be imposed on the rights of other nationalities, but also for the preservation of their own social privileges, in return for which they were quite ready to collaborate with the authorities.[10] The demands made by both camps were claimed to be justified by the historical rights of Romanians in the province.

It was in this atmosphere that a new name emerged in 1902 into the political arena in which the Romanians of Bukovina acted. That name was Aurel

---

[9] The works of Marian Olaru are also illustrative of the period: "Aspecte ale vieții politice în Bucovina la sfârșitul secolului al XIX-lea (I)," *Analele Bucovine* 4, no. 2 (1997): 399–409; Marian Olaru, "Aspecte ale vieții politice în Bucovina la sfârșitul secolului al XIX-lea (II)," *Analele Bucovine* 5, no. 1 (1998): 123–34; and Marian Olaru, *Mișcarea națională a românilor din Bucovina la sfârșitul secolului al XIX-lea și începutul secolului al XX-lea* (Rădăuți: Septentrion, 2002).

[10] Cocuz, *Partidele politice românești*, 273–300.

Onciul. The son of a Romanian priest, a graduate of the University of Vienna[11] and a man who had worked within the imperial bureaucracy since his graduation,[12] Onciul initially sought to join the Romanian "youth" movement. However, disappointed by their refusal to guarantee him a place on their electoral lists, he then decided to establish his own political organization: the Democratic Party of the Romanians from Bukovina.[13] Though the party had among its members many prominent personalities, up until its dissolution in 1918 it depended heavily on the name and work of its founder and president, Aurel Onciul.

From the outset, Onciul's primary political objective was to pursue progress for Bukovina in the interests of its Romanian population, an aim that he believed implied the pursuit of progress for Austria as a whole as well, as only Austria could provide the necessary conditions for the general progress of the Romanian nation in Bukovina. But in order to achieve this end, any question of national struggle would have to be eliminated from the equation, and the resulting "reconciliation of the people would immediately end aristocratic rule," since "the caste interest of the aristocracy [...] constitutes the premise of

---

[11] Aurel Onciul (1864–1921) was schooled at the Theresianische Akademie in Vienna and was awarded a doctorate in law at the University of Vienna in 1886, cf. Juridische Facultät, Nationale, 1885, 48, Archiv der Universität Wien [Archive of the University of Vienna] (hereafter AUW).

[12] He performed junior functions in the Ministry of Education and Religious Affairs and afterwards in the Interior Ministry as well as serving as district commissioner in Moravia from 1896 to 1900. At the moment there is only one monography dedicated to Aurel Onciul, written by his grandson, Aurel Constantin Onciul, *Aurel Ritter von Onciul und der Nationale Ausgleich in der österreichischen Bukowina. Eine wissenschaftliche Dokumentation* (Nuremberg: ARVO, 1999), but it does not contain sufficient biographical data and is more than biased in its content.

[13] A relevant document regarding this is the letter addressed by Onciul to Romanian nationalist leader Iancu Flondor on 1 October 1901, cf. Aurel Onciul to Iancu Flondor, 1 October 1901, dosar 11, 1–3, Fond Iancu Flondor, Arhivele Naționale Istorice Centrale, Bucharest [Central National Historical Archives] (hereafter ANIC). Among other materials, the document contains Onciul's plea for a single unified Romanian party and expresses his relative optimism on a possible reconciliation between the various Romanian political factions, at the same time as stressing the necessity for concerted Romanian action if the national question in Bukovina was to be resolved to the satisfaction of Romanians. As Onciul wrote to Flondor, "It is an illusion to expect national achievements by the grace of a government which, as in the Austrian case, views its calling, from the point of view of maintaining the integrity of the state, precisely in countering national aspirations. In the other parts of the monarchy, roles are distributed in such a manner, that the government defends the state's interests, while the people's representatives [defend] their national interests; thus, through the simultaneous action of the two powers, a resolution is produced corresponding to some extent to both the state's exigencies and to those of national liberty."

people's discord, because it is only through this discord that it can maintain its privileged position."[14]

Onciul's main objectives, and therefore those of the Democratic Party, were thus the following: firstly, to turn the gaze of the Bukovina's Romanians away from Bucharest and towards Vienna and, secondly, to implement a series of reforms aimed at bringing about "the progress" of the region's Romanian population at a political, economic, cultural and social level. These two aims were of course opposed to the political programs of the other two Romanian parties on the scene at the time: the nationalists who sought a rapprochement with the Kingdom of Romania, and the conservatives—the established political leadership of the community—who advocated preservation of the *status quo*.

The most effective tool used to propagate "democratic" ideas was provided by the print media. Between 1902 and 1914, Onciul owned and managed four gazettes: *Privitorul* (1902–1903), *Voința Poporului* (1902–1908), *Foaia Poporului* (1910–1914) and *Die Wahrheit* (1908–1914). The front pages of all of them were almost exclusively taken up by leading articles under his byline. In most of these articles specific contemporary issues were dealt with in the context of the region's domestic political strife at the time. But Onciul did not simply consider himself just a Romanian figure from Bukovina, but also an active Austrian citizen, and he more often than not used the column inches reserved for him to explain his own policies and those of his party as part of a larger frame: the frame provided by the empire. Characterizing himself as "Austrian to the backbone,"[15] Onciul did not see this as in any way inconsistent with his Romanian nationality.

According to his vision, Bukovina at the time was currently living its "golden age." Austrian rule was the best of all the possible worlds for the province's inhabitants: Romanians had no reason to complain because "for a few years now, they have been left to themselves, have been governed in a European style and have been in a position to shape their own fate."[16] All this meant that they have faced no oppression and that no obstacle has been placed in the way of their national development. There was certainly room for improvement in the situation, but only within Austria, for "Romanian politics in order to be national can only be Austrian."[17]

Even before Onciul, the Romanian political class had also on numerous occasions stressed their own adherence to the dynastic succession and the attachment of Bukovina's Romanians to the emperor. Promoting and con-

---

[14] Aurel Onciul, "Problema Austriacă," *Privitorul*, 1 October 1902, 1–4, here 3.
[15] Aurel Onciul, "Raportul politic între România și Austria și împăcarea românomaghiară," *Foaia Poporului*, 22 February 1914, 2–3, here 3.
[16] Aurel Onciul, "Spre lămurire," *Foaia Poporului*, 19 March 1911, 4–5, here 4.
[17] Aurel Onciul, "Condițiunile existenței Românilor (I)," *Privitorul*, 1 May 1902, 1–3, here 2.

tributing to the cult of the emperor had been an impulse characteristic of Austrian Bukovina since the beginning of the nineteenth century, but the phenomenon increased in intensity during the reign of Franz Joseph I (1848–1916), generating an attachment on the part of the empire's subjects to the concept of Austria—a phenomenon referred to as Austriacism.[18]

Franz Joseph was portrayed both as a representative of God on Earth and also as a *pater patriae*. Every inhabitant of Bukovina was expected to put trust in the emperor's good judgment and in his desire to take care of every one of his subjects. They were expected not to doubt that in his wisdom His Majesty the emperor "on the strength of a level of experience that [only] few of God's chosen could have, the experience of a man's lifetime, the experience of good days and bad days, will find the suitable path to secure the good of the empire and his subjects."[19] The emperor was portrayed as constantly worried and anguished by

suffering which brings the monarch, seated at the helm, close to the humble working citizen whose concerns for tomorrow appear to be the same as His, from these reflections the cement of solidarity with the Crown flows out, an upspring of that sentiment which provides an ever more solid basis for patriotic sentiments.[20]

Thus for Onciul it was beyond doubt that "being a Bukovinian means loyalty to the empire."[21]

However, Aurel Onciul was able to transform this loyalty and patriotism of the Romanians into something with more focus, making it a central point of his political doctrine. He did not stop at merely establishing a state of affairs, but was determined to actually improve on it, and at the same time provide what he felt were extremely rational and pertinent reasons and explanations to support his viewpoint.

---

[18] Marian Olaru, "Ducatul Bucovinei și Imperiul Austro-Ungar. Dimensiuni politice ale raporturilor dintre provincie și centru la sfârșitul secolului al XIX-lea și începutul secolului al XX-lea," *Analele Bucovinei* 9, no. 1 (2002): 81–95, here 85. The Transylvanian scholar George Bogdan Duică portrayed the Bukovinian Romanians as "the most loyal Austrians" and pointed out that "it was not restraint, but their character that made them devoted to the dynasty," cf. Marian Olaru and Ștefan Purici, "Bucovinism și Homo Bucovinensis," *Analele Bucovinei* 3, no. 1 (1996): 5–11, here 6. Likewise, a memorandum of 19 September 1899 addressed to prime minister Count Franz Anton von Thun-Hohenstein, penned by the leaders of the Romanian political class in Bukovina, contained a reminder that "Bukovinian Romanians count among the most loyal and patriotic of the Austrian peoples," and that the love of this people for fatherland and emperor "cannot be doubted without calumny," cf. Marian Olaru, "Două memorii reprezentative pentru situația social-politică a românilor bucovineni la sfârșitul secolului al XIX-lea," *Analele Bucovinei* 2, no. 1 (1995): 179–205, here 200.
[19] "Zile grele," *Gazeta Mazililor și Răzeșilor Bucovineni*, 8 December 1912, 177–79, here 178.
[20] Ibid., 179.
[21] Olaru, "Aspecte ale vieții politice (II)," 129.

Declaring that "Bukovinian Romanians are Austrian and dynastic to the backbone" and that "in the eyes of the people of the countryside, the emperor is a kind of Providence – the personification of justice and grace," he proposed that the traditional tenet held by the Romanians—that "I am a good Austrian even though I am a Romanian"—be modified to read "I am a good Austrian precisely because I am a Romanian."[22]

After analyzing "the whole of Austrian history from the year 1867 up until the present," Onciul came to the conclusion that history represented nothing less than "a whole series of national frictions that paralyze the evolution of the state and consume its powers."[23] The correct means of achieving progress was as Onciul saw it, "strengthening democratic elements by restraining the privileges of the great landowners and broadening the electoral rights of the masses, perhaps even going as far as to introduce universal suffrage."[24] But this suffrage was to be accompanied by a delimitation of electoral districts on the basis of ethnicity. Onciul argued that "the only means of salvation is the autonomy of nationalities, namely national delimitation and the creation of national delegations."[25]

The problem could not be solved solely at a local level, but only for the empire as a whole. Onciul arrived at his own solutions to resolve "the national crisis" in which the monarchy was entangled. Of course, his ideas in terms of reorganizing the empire were not necessarily novel at the time.[26] Indeed his thoughts did not reach the sophistication and popularity of the model proposed by Transylvanian Aurel C. Popovici—author of the extremely pop-

[22] Aurel Onciul, "Condițiunile existenței Românilor (IV)," *Privitorul*, 15 June 1902, 1–4, here 1.
[23] Onciul, "Problema Austriacă," 3.
[24] Ibid.
[25] Ibid.
[26] There were many major Austrian figures who proposed reforms. See the work of Tyrolean Member of Parliament Viktor von Andrian-Werburg, *Oesterreich und dessen Zukunft* (1840); František Palacký, who proposed an exclusivist "Austro-Slavism"; the plans of Aurel C. Popovici; the works of socialists Karl Renner, *Grundlagen und Entwicklungsziele der österreichischen-ungarischen Monarchie, die Krise des Dualismus* (1904); and Otto Bauer, *Die Nationalitätenfrage und die Sozialdemokratie* (1906). None of these solutions, however, ever enjoyed widespread support from within the ruling circles until 1918. Moreover, the emperor himself, for whom the final decision was reserved, never approved of any of these proposals. Nevertheless, one should not underestimate the impact of the ideas that Onciul had discovered in the works of various authors, both preceding him and contemporary to him. Surely, such ideas and the potential for success of such plans were decisively influenced by the implementation of the "Moravian Compromise." In 1905, Moravia was divided into districts according to nationality. The language of administration within these districts became German or Czech, depending on the nationality dominant locally. At the same time, all minorities had the right to address provincial tribunals in their native language. In addition to this, one-man-one-vote was introduced. Thus, every citizen was sure to have his national identity respected, regardless of which group formed the ethnic majority in a district.

ular work *Vereinigte Staaten von Groß-Österreich* (The United States of Greater Austria), published at the beginning of the twentieth century.[27] However, Popovici acknowledged Onciul as the precursor from whom he obtained the idea of combining "numerous national states within the framework of a unitary Austrian federal state."[28]

Geographical determinism is one of the main elements in Onciul's thought on "the national question," while at the same time drawing on the premise that "in its efforts to be national, politics has to accommodate itself [...] to the circumstances, which in the case of a deeply rooted people will be identical with their geographical location"[29]: or, in other words, to what we now call geopolitics. Within the Danube watershed there are nations "too large to die out, but too small however to be capable of affirming themselves alone in the face of the great nations that surround them. For this reason, in order to reciprocally secure their continued existence, these nations are bound to combine their forces; to federalize."[30] And through this measure they can ensure that they are equipped to defend themselves in the face of their main danger threatening their survival: Russia.[31]

Austria, he argued, should organize itself into a confederation composed of all the nations of the Danube. Consequently, those which are not yet part of the confederation should join and those divided by borders should reunite, exclusively under the protection of the Viennese emperor. Onciul argued that "the transformation of Austria into a great Danubian confederation of nation states, [...] cannot be achieved, while the empire unites mere fragments of peoples and not whole nations,"[32] each of these fragments harboring the permanent aspiration to sooner or later become part of a whole. And the Romanian people, which Onciul (and not just Onciul) hoped to see united, represented a case in point. In his view, however, Romania could not flourish and grow in strength except under the protection of Austria-Hungary, its only friend in the face of Russia. In his view any independent Greater Romania would not stand a chance against her greedy eastern neighbor, Russia, and he thus pleaded for an alternative solution: "I hope Romanians will become closer to the monarchy. In my opinion, such a relationship would con-

---

[27] Aurel C. Popovici, *Die Vereinigten Staaten von Groß-Österreich. Politische Studien zur Lösung der nationalen Fragen und staatrechtlichen Krisen in Österreich-Ungarn* (Leipzig: Elischer, 1906).

[28] Aurel C. Popovici, *Stat și națiune. Statele Unite ale Austriei Mari. Studii politice în vederea rezolvării problemei naționale și a crizelor constituționale din Austro-Ungaria* (Bucharest: Albatros, 1997), 124.

[29] Onciul, "Condițiunile existenței (I)," 2.

[30] Ibid.

[31] Ibid.

[32] Ibid., 3.

stitute an ideal friendship, one which would illustrate our relations with Romania in the same way as those of Bavaria with Germany."[33]

In Onciul's opinion, there would be no danger of any loss of national identity within a strong Austria, for by the beginning of the twentieth century it had become impossible to denationalize an entire people and it was consequently no longer necessary to attach the empire's provinces inhabited by Romanians to the Kingdom of Romania, as the people of those provinces ran no risk of losing their identity.

Onciul continually contrasted the civilizing mission of Austria in Central Europe, against the image of a weak Romania, a place characterized by superficiality and wedded to the illusory: "Only a few people know that under this splendid appearance hides the old oriental misery, that the claims of Romanian civilization are but a gloss, that the thin fashionable and stylish higher layer conceals an immense mass of wretched and unhappy people."[34] He still observed the "burdensome legacy" left by Turkish rule and believed that "moral flaws as well rooted as those of the Phanariote[35] boyars cannot be eradicated in the span of merely a century."[36]

Onciul's articles portray him as a very loyal Austrian citizen. In his view, the empire's nationality problems could be solved without it having to be dissolved. He warned his fellow Austro-Hungarian Romanians that "speculating on catastrophes is incompatible with the loyalty to the fatherland."[37] Any Bukovinian adherent to Daco-Romanianism should be aware that their project of *Groß-Rumänien* (Greater Romania) contains within itself the seeds of its own apocalypse since "the re-annexation of Bukovina cannot come about but with Austria's ruin, and Austria's ruin is identical to the destruction of all Romanianism."[38] Aurel Onciul therefore advocates loyalty to the Habsburg Empire precisely in order to protect Romanian national identity and develops a whole cluster of ideas to support his view.

Widely portrayed in subsequent Romanian historiography as a traitor of the Romanian cause precisely because of his pro-Austrian and allegedly anti-Romanian position, Onciul was nonetheless by far the most successful Bukovinian politician during the period in which he was active. His party won the

---

[33] Onciul, "Raportul politic," 2.
[34] Aurel Onciul, *Reedificarea României. Un studiu al reformelor necesare* (Chernivtsi: Societatea tipografică bucovineană, 1918), 1.
[35] This is a reference to the upper-class Greeks originating from the Phanar district of Istanbul who were appointed Hospodars in Moldavia and Wallachia. The era of their dominance in these regions became known as the Phanariot age and was synonymous in the popular mind with corruption, malpractice, and waste.
[36] A. Vrânceanu, "Stările noastre," *Privitorul*, 15 March 1903, 4–6, here 5. Aurel Onciul signed parts of his articles in his *Privitorul* review using the pseudonym A. Vrânceanu.
[37] Aurel Onciul, "Condițiunile existenței Românilor (III)," *Privitorul*, 1 June 1902, 1–3, here 1.
[38] Onciul, "Condițiunile existenței (IV)," 1.

largest number of seats held by Romanian forces in all elections that took place during the relevant period. As an imperial deputy and member of the Diet from 1902 to 1918, he was the central political figure for the Bukovinian Romanians—their "golden calf and national idol."³⁹ All other democratic leaders were continuously in his shadow and only very few remained faithful to him throughout the period being studied. Onciul's strong personality allowed him to lead his party into successive alliances with other parties, both Romanian and of other nationalities, without suffering any loss in popularity as a result of his constant swinging back and forward. His most important achievement as a man of politics was his success in securing the passing of a number of laws in the Diet, and in subsequently obtaining the necessary imperial sanction for them, the most important of which being the electoral law of 1910 for the duchy, often referred to as the *Ausgleich*⁴⁰.

In the spring of 1914, when Onciul changed the name of his Democratic Party to the Romanian Peasants' Party (thus indicating a focus on one particular single social category as his preferred target audience), one correspondent of Bucharest-based newspaper *Universul* reported that this party was capable of producing "great changes in the political life of Bukovinian Romanians,"⁴¹ underlining once again the attachment of the peasantry to Onciul as a political leader.

The choice to address this social category in particular came naturally when one considers the new law on the election of deputies to the Diet and the introduction of universal suffrage for elections to the parliament. Also, it cannot be ignored that on the eve of World War I more than 80 percent of the Romanian inhabitants of Bukovina lived in rural areas and worked in agriculture, tending to properties of less than five hectares.⁴² For another thing, Onciul's party, which defended active loyalty to Austria, thus naturally leading it into disagreement with nationalist forces, scored notable successes from

---

39 From this ironic label, which appeared in *Viaţa Nouă* on 22 March 1913, the organ of a Romanian nationalist group with whom Onciul was in conflict at the time, one gets a flavor of the political reality of the epoch, as well as something of its style.
40 The model upon which this law was based was the "Moravian Compromise" (see note 26). Onciul, who lived in Brno until 1906, enthusiastically saw how the compromise had solved the national problem between Czechs and Germans in Moravia and considered that such a model would be ideally suited for the complex Bukovinian situation too. See for details regarding this 1910 law Gerald Stourzh, "Der nationale Ausgleich in der Bukowina 1909–1910," in *Die Bukowina. Vergangenheit und Gegenwart*, ed. Ilona Slawinski and Joseph P. Strelka (Bern: Lang, 1995), 35–52; Rudolf Wagner, *Der Parlamentarismus und nationale Ausgleich in der ehemals österreichischen Bukowina* (Munich: Südostdeutsche, 1984); and Mihai-Ştefan Ceauşu, *Parlamentarism*.
41 "Din Bucovina," *Universul*, 18 April 1914, 2.
42 See Emanuel Turczynski, *Geschichte der Bukowina in der Neuzeit. Zur Sozial- und Kulturgeschichte einer mitteleuropäisch geprägten Landschaft* (Wiesbaden: Harrassowitz, 1993); Filaret Doboş, "Zece ani de viaţă agricolă în Bucovina," in *Zece ani dela Unire (a Bucovinei)*, ed. Ion Nistor (Chernivtsi: Glasul Bucovinei, 1928), 151–178, here 156–157.

the very beginning. This fact illustrates the lack of impact that nationalists, who found their support from among the intelligentsia, could exert on the province's most populous social category, that of the peasantry.

Meetings of both the Romanian Peasants' Party and its forerunner, the Democratic Party, often opened and closed with great manifestations "of sympathy for the Emperor Franz Joseph, for whose quick recovery unanimous pleas have been made."[43] Such demonstrations were supposed to represent the real sentiments of the peasantry towards the House of Habsburg.[44]

From the start of World War I and until August 1916, Onciul publicly called for Romania to join up in the struggle alongside the Central Powers. The publication of an interview with him in the pro-German *Moldova* newspaper in which he discussed the subject generated strong reactions, especially among Romanian Ententists.

In the interview, which appeared under the heading "The Romanian stance as assessed by a leading Romanian of Bukovina" (Atitudinea României judecată de un eminent fruntaș român din Bucovina), Aurel Onciul stressed that "being realistic, the crucial factor in determining the external policy of a country is its geographical location,"[45] and Romania must take into account that it is located on the shores of the Black Sea, between Russia and the Dardanelle Straits, and that it was no secret anymore that, "forced by its vital interests" and "under the pressure felt by a natural power," Russia aimed to get to the Dardanelles by the shortest route: through Romania. This Russian need thus "makes the preservation of an independent Romania an impossibility," a fact that should in the normal course of events make Russia "the eternally natural enemy of Romania."[46]

Any potential Russian victory would threaten the existence of Romania to a much greater extent than an Austrian triumph, which would make Austria "the object of Russian hatred for the sole reason that it stands in the way of Russia on its path to Constantinople."[47] In the case of a Russian victory, however, there would be "no doubt that Romania would have to abandon any of its [post-]war calculations, and submit to being occupied by Russia."[48] This occupation would follow "either immediately or within a decade, after which Romania, as a reward for its act of suicide, would be enlarged for the sake of appearances to include Transylvania and Bukovina," thus making it into a second Poland. Likewise, he drew attention to the assertion that the country's "love for the French is a legacy of the Phanariotes" and claimed it to be a fact

---

[43] "Din Bucovina."
[44] Ibid.
[45] "Atitudinea României judecată de un eminent fruntaș român din Bucovina," *Moldova*, 20 September 1915, 1.
[46] Ibid.
[47] Ibid.
[48] Ibid.

that Romanians simply cannot see that "the French ever since Napoleon the Great were always ready to give up Romania to the Russians as booty."[49]

Upon the reopening of the Imperial Council on 30 May 1917,[50] the floor of the Chamber of Deputies provided a space in which representatives of the Romanians of Bukovina could constantly assure the House of Habsburg and the Austrian government of the loyalty of the section of the electorate that they represented. Indeed, this was the main goal of reopening the institution: to demonstrate the unity and loyalty of the empire's various nations. Of the six deputies of Romanian nationality,[51] the most vehement in proclaiming the loyalty of his Austrian compatriots was without a doubt Aurel Onciul.

During the meeting of 12 June 1917 he reiterated his commitment to what had been the main trope of his political discourse for more than fifteen years:

> We Romanians, have as our most ardent wish to be all united together, including Romanians of Bukovina, Hungary, Bessarabia and even of the Kingdom of Romania, under the same scepter, and happily agree to enter into a Greater Austria in order to enjoy a guarantee for our free development. Our aspirations are directed towards this single goal and we therefore have no reason whatsoever to object to any steps taken for the good of the state. We unconditionally submit to the monarchy. We wish to live within its borders and consenting to the historical mission of Austria, in total freedom and on the basis of our natural right of self-determination. For these reasons, we ask to be allowed to take our place under the sun of Austria-Hungary.[52]

Another speech given by Onciul on 9 November was identical in content.[53] Aside from reaffirming his adherence to Austria and to pursuing the idea of fulfillment of the Romanian national project under Habsburg rule,[54] Onciul argued that the victory of the Central Powers in the war was a necessity. Such

---

[49] Ibid.
[50] Even though the legislative period would normally have concluded in the fall of 1917, according to Imperial Decree no. 30 of 30 July 1917, the sitting was extended until 31 December 1918; cf. Oswald Knauer, *Das österreichische Parlament von 1848–1966* (Vienna: Bergland, 1969), 16.
[51] According to the election results of 2 April 1911 Bukovinian Romanians were represented in the Viennese parliament by forest inspector Gheorghe Sârbu, Alexandru baron of Hurmuzachi, judge Teofil Siminovici, professor Constantin Isopescu-Grecul and former district commissioner of Moravia Aurel Onciul. On top of this, the socialist delegate Gheorghe Grigorovici was elected for a German-Jewish district of the province. For more details regarding these elections see file 11137, f. 52–57, fond 3 K.k. Bukowiner Landes-Regierung, Arhivele Statului Regiunea Cernăuți [State Archives of Chernivtsi District] (hereafter ASRC).
[52] "Haus der Abgeordneten. 4. Sitzung der XXII. Session vom 12. Juni 1917," *Österreichische Nationalbibliothek. ALEX Historische Rechts- und Gesetzestexte Online*, accessed 8 April 2016, http://alex.onb.ac.at/cgi-content/alex?aid=spa&datum=0022&size=45&page=1112.
[53] Cf. "36. Sitzung der XXII. Session am 9. November 1917," *Österreichische Nationalbibliothek. ALEX Historische Rechts- und Gesetzestexte Online*, accessed 8 April 2016, http://alex.onb.ac.at/cgi-content/alex?aid=spa&datum=0022&page=2817&size=45.
[54] Ibid.

a victory would, of course, mean Romania's defeat, but in Onciul's view this was a necessary price to pay because, though he constantly stressed the need for Romanian unity, he could not see any other way of achieving this end other than by pursuing the approach that he had defended since the start of his political career.

As a result of his image as a denigrator of Romanians and of the Kingdom of Romania,[55] an image that could not simply and suddenly disappear after 1918, Onciul's political career was destined to end with the fall of the Habsburg Empire. In the post-war effort to forge not simply a single unitary administrative and political structure for all Romanians, but also a single, monolithic shared history, most of the controversial figures representing the *ancien régime* were either demonized or erased altogether from public discourse and history textbooks. Ignored by contemporaries after 1918, and even by subsequent historians, the historical figure of Onciul has only recently been brought back to the center of debate on Romanian historiography, and even then only to be denounced for his "anti-Romanian" approach to politics.[56]

Though Onciul's ideas and the manner in which he went about his politics are neither unique nor entirely original, we nevertheless regard his political

---

[55] In a letter written while under arrest by the Romanian authorities due to his protest against Romanian troops entering Bukovina, addressed to the new delegate minister of Bukovina, Iancu Flondor, on 9 December 1918, Onciul stressed "Austria is dead, and with it my politics died too. No revival is possible, and any transfiguration on my part is beyond my capacity", cf. Aurel Onciul to Iancu Flondor, 9 December 1918, dosar 11, f. 57, Fond Iancu Flondor, ANIC.

[56] The main critique leveled against Onciul is connected with his agreement with the Ruthenian community of Bukovina, concluded on 6 November 1918. Onciul, as the self-appointed "Commissioner for Upper Moldova" signed a document on that date ceding the northern administrative area of Bukovina to the Ruthenian representatives for the province. Moreover, on hearing that the Romanian army had crossed the border and entered Bukovina, Onciul appeared before the Romanian government in Iași to request that this agreement be respected and that the army should not cross the Siret Line—the boundary between the Romanian and Ruthenian parts of Bukovina as agreed on 6 November. An even more frequent accusation was that he had entered into less than beneficial alliances with Ruthenians and Jews during the early part of his political career. See Iorga, *Neamul românesc în Bucovina*; Nicolae Iorga, *Istoria poporului românesc*, vol. 4/2 (Bucharest: Editura Casei Şcoalelor, 1928); idem, *Supt trei regi. Istoria unei lupte pentru un ideal moral și național. România contemporană de la 1904 la 1930*, 2nd ed. (Vălenii de Munte: Datina Românească, 1932); Nistor, *Zece ani dela Unire*; Nistor, *Istoria Bucovinei*; Mihai Iacobescu, "Elita românilor bucovineni între anii 1862–1918", in *Procese politice, sociale, culturale și economice în Bucovina, 1861–1914. Aspecte edificatoare pentru o Europă Unită? Materialele Conferinței științifice internaționale, Rădăuți, 20–22 septembrie 2000*, ed. Ştefan Purici (Suceava: Editura Universității Suceava, 2000); Marian Olaru, "Aurel Onciul și revista 'Privitorul'," *Analele Bucovinei* 1, no. 2 (1994): 281–89; idem, "Activitatea politică a lui Aurel Onciul, 1904–1918," *Analele Bucovinei* 2, no. 2 (1995): 275–89; and Marian Olaru, "Despre crezul politic al lui Aurel Onciul," *Analele Bucovinei* 4, no. 1 (1997): 175–80.

biography and his successes as important from the perspective of Romanian adherence to what may be called the Greater Romania project. The union of 1918 was primarily the result of a combination of happy accident and quick-footed adaptation of the Romanian royalty, the kingdom's government and its political class to favorable post-war conditions. Romanian struggles for emancipation outside the borders of the Romanian Old Kingdom played a relatively minor role in the process. The union of Bukovina with Romania perfectly fitted the post-war scenario. There had existed a significant movement agitating for national emancipation within the Austrian province, but that movement only became politically dominant from the fall of 1918 on—up until that time most Bukovinian Romanians had remained loyal to Austria. Onciul was one of the most important architects of this consistent pattern of loyalty to the Crown. Nevertheless, the allegiance he defended was in no way self-destructive to the interests of Romanians. All through his political argumentation, Onciul consistently encouraged Bukovinian Romanians to adopt and cultivate their national identity, all the while stressing that their national (Romanian) and supranational (Austrian) identities were complementary. Onciul argued that only within Austria's boundaries, and under the protective shield of the Habsburgs, could the Romanian nation safely flourish. In return for the protection of Austria and for the provision by the empire of favorable conditions for Romanian national development, he urged Romanians to be faithful Austrian citizens.

Peter Bugge

LOYAL IN WORD AND DEED
The Czech National Movement and the Habsburg Monarchy
in the Long Nineteenth Century

A striking feature of the Czech national movement from its early beginnings in the late eighteenth century and almost until the demise of the Habsburg monarchy was its persistent support for the retention of the monarchy. This was expressed in numerous declarations of loyalty to the Habsburg monarchs and in the general behavior of the broad population in war and peace. Whether during the occupations of the Napoleonic Wars and the Austro-Prussian War of 1866 or at the outbreak of the Great War in 1914, the overwhelming majority of Czechs in Bohemia and Moravia remained loyal to their King and Emperor. Radical nationalist parties had only minimal following in the decades before 1914.[1]

This persistent imperial loyalty in word and deed represents a challenge to the more common theories of nationalism. If one were to follow Ernest Gellner's definition of the phenomenon as "primarily a political principle, which holds that the political and the national unit should be congruent,"[2] one would have to accept that the Czech national mobilization, like most of its kind in East Central Europe during the nineteenth century, largely occurred without the factor of nationalism: as a rule, as Miroslav Hroch has shown, the national movements within the Bohemian Lands aspired only to some kind of autonomy.[3] One might be tempted to explain this as merely a

---

[1] Unsurprisingly, this phenomenon of Czech dynastic loyalty was largely either neglected or disputed in both Czech interwar and communist historiography. Since 1989, however, there has been renewed interest in the subject, with historian Jiří Rak recently publishing a monograph that richly documents how "a loyal relationship to the Habsburg Monarchy and its rulers for long decades provided one of the constitutive elements of Czech thought." Jiří Rak, *Zachovej nám Hospodine: Češi v Rakouském císařství 1804–1918* (Prague: Havran, 2013), 11.

[2] Ernest Gellner, *Nations and Nationalism* (Oxford: Blackwell, 1983), 1. Eric Hobsbawm too uses this definition, adding that since the French Revolution, revolutionary democrats and nationalists had alike subscribed to the equation of state = nation = people. Eric J. Hobsbawm, *Nations and Nationalism since 1780: Programme, Myth, Reality* (Cambridge: Cambridge University Press, 1990), 9, 22–3.

[3] Miroslav Hroch, "Nationales Bewußtsein zwischen Nationalismustheorie und der Realität der nationalen Bewegungen", in *Formen des nationalen Bewußtseins im Lichte zeitgenössischer Nationalismustheorien: Vorträge der Tagung des Collegium Carolinum in*

pragmatic acceptance of autonomy as a logical precursor to national independence, but the fact that leading figures of the Czech national movement repeatedly declared their commitment to the Habsburg monarchy as a multinational state speaks against any such interpretation. The most famous expression of this view stems from the pen of František Palacký, for decades the undisputed leader of the Czech national movement, who as "a Czech of Slavonic blood" in a letter of 11 April 1848 to the revolutionary German Vorparlament in Frankfurt, refused to take part in any attempt to affiliate the Bohemian crownlands with Germany, declaring instead in the strongest possible terms his commitment to the Austrian "union of nations": "Assuredly, if the Austrian State had not existed for ages, it would have been a behest for us in the interests of Europe, and indeed of humanity, to endeavor to create it as soon as possible."⁴

In his critique of the "high-political school of nationalism," Alexander Maxwell has shown how the leaders of the Slovak national movement of the nineteenth century continually stressed not merely the possibility, but the naturalness of dual nationality—of being Slovak in cultural terms and Hungarian politically—and hence of having dual loyalties. Maxwell concludes: "If nationalism implies loyalty to a state, then the nineteenth century Slovak intelligentsia, including Kollár, Hojč, Štúr, Hurban, Daxner, Pauliny-Tóth, Hodža and Hlinka, consisted of *Hungarian* nationalists."⁵

According to Maxwell, Slovak political loyalty was unequivocally directed towards the Kingdom of Hungary, and not to the Habsburg monarchy as a whole. This made the Slovak situation far less complex than that of the Bohemian Lands, where political loyalty could be directed towards any of four supra-ethnic entities: to one's own crownland (Bohemia, Moravia, or Austrian Silesia), to the Bohemian crownlands as a whole, to the "Cisleithanian" part of the monarchy (after the 1867 *Ausgleich*), or to the greater Habsburg Empire. The choice of politico-territorial framework was closely connected to

---

Bad Wiessee vom 31. Oktober bis 3. November 1991, ed. Eva Schmidt-Hartmann (Munich: Oldenbourg, 1994), 39–52, here 45.

4   From the English translation of the German original. František Palacký, "Letter sent by František Palacký to Frankfurt," *The Slavonic and East European Review* 26, no. 67 (1948): 303–8, here 306.

5   Alexander Maxwell, *Choosing Slovakia: Slavic Hungary, the Czechoslovak Language and Accidental Nationalism* (London: Tauris Academic Studies, 2009), 66. Original emphasis. These examples illustrate the limitations of Anthony D. Smith's definition of nationalism, which—although it acknowledges that not every national movement has made it a priority to acquire a state for its nation—insists that it is a central proposition of the ideology of nationalism that "[t]he nation is the source of all political and social power, and loyalty to the nation overrides all other allegiances." Anthony D. Smith, *National Identity* (London: Penguin, 1991), 74.

the question of to whom or what the Czechs[6] should feel loyal, to the ruler or to his state. And this question could be bifurcated even further. The person of the monarch could be revered in his capacity as Emperor of all Austria or as King of Bohemia or Margrave of Moravia, whereas loyalty to the state might relate to some idea or other of its ideal shape or to a given constitutional order. Inevitably, actors both within and outside the Czech national community had strong opinions on the specific direction and precise shape taken by Czech loyalty to the Habsburg monarchy.

At a general level, non-national loyalties pose a permanent challenge to national movements. Whereas the rationale for non-national loyalties is complex and may have both highly emotional and purely pragmatic roots, the appeal to national allegiance is at core based on a claim of sameness, an invocation of the organic unity of the people and/or the nation. This principle of identification ideally allows absolute claims to be made on the individual: claims that each individual owes it to his or her nation to think, speak, buy, consume, act, love and if necessary also hate in the national spirit. But any calls for social action legitimized solely by references to national duty of this type cannot forever replace and surpass socially ingrained familial, professional, local, confessional and other loyalties.[7] Consequently, national identity should not be seen as a linear, almost teleological process of acquisition, but as a situational disposition, activated in moments described by Rogers Brubaker as "nationness as event."[8] With these observations in mind, we can now turn to a brief outline of how the Czech national movement sought to balance between supranational loyalty and national interest over the course of the long nineteenth century.

The profundity of Czech dynastic loyalty provided a leitmotif in a speech that has commonly been held to represent the first significant articulation of Czech national demands, Josef Dobrovský's September 1791 address to Emperor Leopold II in honor of his coronation as King of Bohemia. In his speech, "On the Devotion and Allegiance of the Slavic Peoples to the House of Austria," Dobrovský sought to convince the Emperor of the need to strengthen the position of the Czech language in education and the civic administration. He used mostly utilitarian arguments, but he bolstered his plea with an emotional appeal to the Emperor to remember and honor the "allegiance, obedience and loyalty" that the Czechs and other Austrian Slavs had

---

[6] Until late in the nineteenth century it would probably be more accurate to refer to Slavic-speaking Bohemians and Moravians. See Milan Řepa, *Moravané nebo Češi? Vývoj českého národního vědomí na Moravě v 19. století* (Brno: Doplněk, 2001).

[7] Martin Schulze Wessel, "'Loyalität' als geschichtlicher Grundbegriff und Forschungskonzept: Zur Einleitung," in *Loyalitäten in der Tschechoslowakischen Republik 1918–1938: Politische, nationale und kulturelle Zugehörigkeiten*, ed. Martin Schulze Wessel (Munich: Oldenbourg, 2004), 1–22.

[8] Rogers Brubaker, *Nationalism Reframed: Nationhood and the National Question in the New Europe* (Cambridge: Cambridge University Press, 1996), 16–21.

shown to the Habsburgs over the centuries. In this way, Dobrovský sought to counter any accusations that the estates that formed the early modern political nation of Bohemia—and by extension the Bohemian people and its Czech speaking element in particular—had a pre-disposition to disloyalty.[9]

There had been an uncomfortable episode in November 1741, when during the War of the Austrian Succession a Bavarian-French army had occupied Prague, and Charles Albert of Bavaria seized the opportunity to proclaim himself King of Bohemia. The great majority of the Bohemian estates swore an oath of fealty to him, and the young Empress Maria Theresa was only saved by the support of the Hungarian estates. Although their Bohemian counterparts were quick to change sides with the fortunes of war, swearing allegiance also to Maria Theresa at her coronation as Queen of Bohemia in May 1743 (and although Maria Theresa chose to scapegoat only the Bohemian Jews for the Kingdom's disloyalty), the suspicion that the Hungarians were warmer in their fealty to the Habsburgs was to linger on.[10] A second major issue was the stigma that had become attached to Bohemia and the Czechs as heretics and dethroners since June 1619, when the largely Protestant estates of the Bohemian crownlands had opted to depose Ferdinand II. During the Baroque period it became a major concern for Catholic Czech patriots to remove this stigma, and Dobrovský chose to address the issue head on, explaining the dethroning as a brief aberration caused by Czech naivety and a sincere belief in the very rules of religious tolerance that the Habsburgs had since come to embrace with Joseph II's 1781 Patent of Toleration.[11]

The next generation of Czech patriots showed even greater fervor in cultivating the motif of dynastic loyalty as an innate quality of the Czechs and the Slavs. Vladimír Macura tells us how its leading voice, Josef Jungmann, when translating the famous chapter on the Slavs from Johann Gottfried Herder's

---

[9] For an introduction to, and excerpts from the speech (containing a somewhat different translation of the original German title) see Balázs Trencsényi and Michal Kopeček, eds., *Discourses of Collective Identity in Central and Southeast Europe: Texts and Commentaries*, vol. 1, *Late Enlightenment: Emergence of the Modern 'National Idea'* (Budapest: Central European University Press, 2006), 97–103.

[10] On the events of the 1740s, see Marie Bláhová, Jan Frolík, and Naďa Profantová, *Velké dějiny zemí Koruny české*, vol. 10, *1740–1792*, ed. Pavel Bělina, Jiří Kaše, and Jan P. Kučera (Prague: Paseka, 2001), 20–31, 34–40. Dobrovský referred to the rivalry with Hungary only indirectly, by challenging "any other nation subject to the Imperial Austrian scepter" to name an instance where it had surpassed or even matched the Czechs in terms of loyalty. Trencsényi and Kopeček, eds., *Discourses of Collective Identity*, 1:100.

[11] Rejections of the stigma of disloyalty in Czech Baroque Catholic patriotism and its impact on Dobrovský is discussed in Josef Petráň and Lydia Petráňová, "The White Mountain as a Symbol in Modern Czech History," in *Bohemia in History*, ed. Mikuláš Teich (Cambridge: Cambridge University Press, 1998), 143–163, here 150. See also Jiří Rak, *Bývali Čechové: České historické mýty a stereotypy* (Jinočany: H & H, 1994), 51–2, 137.

"Ideas for a Philosophy of the History of Mankind,"[12] went so far as to simply omit a sentence where Herder had predicted that the Slavs would one day liberate themselves from their "slave chains." He did so in order to ensure that no one would use the prediction to question the loyalty of the Slavs.[13] Such frequent demonstrations of loyalty and allegiance were undoubtedly the product of the belief that without them any hope of monarchical sympathy for the aspirations of the Czech patriots would be in vain, but they also reflected the widespread paternalistic conservatism that characterized the Bohemian middle classes at that time, including the small section of that social class made up of nationally conscious Czechs.[14]

Conversely, Franz I and his cabinet never sought to build any popular pan-Austrian identity, remaining largely content with building their legitimacy on the principle of unconditional loyalty to the monarch.[15] An oft-quoted remark of Franz, "I hear he is a patriot for Austria. But the question is whether he is a patriot for me,"[16] is emblematic of this policy, a policy that has been described as reactive, deficient, and anachronistic.[17] But when Jan Křen argues that "Official Austria deliberately closed its mind to modern

---

[12] Johann Gottfried Herder, *Ideen zur Philosophie der Geschichte der Menschheit* (Riga, Leipzig: Hartknoch, 1785-1792).
[13] Vladimír Macura, *Znamení zrodu* (Jinočany: H & H, 1995), 67-8. Jungmann expressed his faith in the good will of Emperor Franz on numerous occasions, including his famous first "Conversation on the Czech language" (Rozmlouvání o jazyku českém) of 1806, where he finishes up by declaring that the "faithful father of the nations, Franz, will lend his ear to the wish of the faithful millions [...] and fully be the father of his Slavs." Rak, *Zachovej nám*, 30.
[14] Jiří Rak, "Dobrý císař František, jeho kancléř a jejich Češi," in *Biedermeier v českých zemích: sborník příspěvků z 23. ročníku sympozia k problematice 19. století; Plzeň, 6.-8. března 2003*, ed. Helena Lorenzová and Taťána Petrasová (Prague: Koniasch Latin Press, 2004), 19-23; Rak, *Zachovej nám*, 28-45.
[15] Anna M. Drabek, "Patriotismus und nationale Identität in Böhmen und Mähren," in *Patriotismus und Nationsbildung am Ende des Heiligen Römischen Reiches*, ed. Otto Dann, Miroslav Hroch, and Johannes Koll (Cologne: SH, 2003), 151-70, 156-60; Miroslav Hroch, *Na prahu národní existence: touha a skutečnost* (Prague: Mladá Fronta, 1999), 93-99; and Jiří Kořalka, *Tschechen im Habsburgerreich und in Europa 1815-1914: Sozialgeschichtliche Zusammenhänge der neuzeitlichen Nationsbildung und der Nationalitätenfrage in den böhmischen Ländern* (Munich: Oldenbourg, 1991), 27-32.
[16] Quoted from Alan Sked, *Metternich and Austria: An Evaluation* (New York: Palgrave Macmillan, 2008), 179.
[17] Veronika Sušová, "Integrační role rakouského císaře v rakouské státní propagandě 19. století", *Kuděj* 6, no. 1 (2004): 32-46, here 34-5; Steven Beller, "Kraus's Firework: State Consciousness Raising in the 1908 Jubilee Parade in Vienna and the Problem of Austrian Identity," in *Staging the Past: The Politics of Commemoration in Habsburg Central Europe, 1848 to the Present*, ed. Maria Bucur and Nancy M. Wingfield (West Lafayette, IN: Purdue University Press, 2001), 46-71, here 46.

forms of state integration, and above all to nationalism,"[18] he neglects to let us know what any Austrian nationalism might possibly have looked like in the year of 1820. More to the point, Miloš Havelka talks of a process in the first half of the nineteenth century in which the principle of identity and the idea of an ethnically defined nation asserted themselves vis-à-vis the principle of rationality and the idea of a political nation, while also discussing how far the concept of civic loyalty continued to mediate between state and nation, legality and legitimacy.[19]

Křen's claim that the Emperor's policy was deliberate is significant. Alan Sked agrees but, unlike Křen, he also holds the policy to be thoroughly rational. As an absolute ruler, Franz rejected the principle of popular sovereignty, and he was convinced that it would be both impossible and immoral to merge the many nationalities within the monarchy into a single national body. If Sked is correct, the policy of the Habsburgs should be seen not as deficient, but as a well-considered alternative to a potentially disruptive nationalism. This was also how Austrian officer and diplomat Joseph Christian Freiherr von Zedlitz described the attitude in 1838:

> Has one not had to recognize that one of the happiest fundamental ideas of the Austrian public administration has long ago declared itself: namely the complete respect for every nationality that forms an integral part of the Monarchy? This excellent and liberal view has splendidly fulfilled a difficult task: it has formed the heterogeneous elements into a whole, something that other states with their systems of centralization have not been able to achieve. The government lets Germans be Germans, Bohemians Bohemians, and Italians Italians [...] All it expects is that all these nationalities find a shared focal point in the love for the Austrian fatherland and the dynasty.[20]

Potentially, a conflict of loyalties could arise between love of the broader all-Austrian fatherland and love of one's own crownland, but in practice the government treated the two as harmoniously coexisting dimensions of the same noble feeling, and limited their demands for a coherent all-Austrian patriotism to state bureaucrats only. It was fully accepted that Czech patriots, like the population at large, primarily saw Bohemia as their fatherland and paid homage to the monarch in his capacity as King of Bohemia.[21]

---

[18] Jan Křen, *Konfliktní společenství: Češi a Němci 1780–1918* (Prague: Academia, 1990), 33. Křen adds: "Against all these [Italian, German, and Slavic] nationalisms, Austria was unable to build its own 'nationalism,' building only a state patriotism of a specific anational kind, in which loyalty to the Habsburg 'house' and traditional regionalism mixed with 'a German way of life' and a German cultural and linguistic hinterland." Ibid., 34.

[19] Miloš Havelka, "Úředník a občan, legitimita a loajalita," in *Opomíjení a neoblíbení v české kultuře 19. století: Úředník a podnikatel; Sborník příspěvků z 26. plzeňského sympozia k problematice 19. století, Plzeň, 23.–25. února 2006*, ed. Helena Lorenzová and Taťána Petrasová (Prague: Koniasch Latin Press, 2007), 19–29.

[20] Quoted from Kořalka, *Tschechen im Habsburgerreich*, 30.

[21] Jiří Rak, "Za vlast a národ proti světoborci," in *Mezi časy... Kultura a umění v českých zemích kolem roku 1800: sborník příspěvků z 19. ročníku Sympozií k Problematice*

This ambiguity was unproblematic under conditions of absolutism, but the issue of politico-territorial conflicts of loyalty was to emerge as soon as the revolution of 1848 led to calls for a new constitutional order. With Palacký, the Czech liberal elites also refused to join a German federation, remaining faithful to the Habsburg monarchy and to Austria. They enthusiastically welcomed the promise of a constitution and—agreeing with Karel Havlíček's exclamation on 16 March 1848, "Constitution! Liberty! [...] Blessed words that immediately unite the nation with its sovereign"—they understood their new constitutional freedoms as basically a gift from "our King Ferdinand, who is a kindhearted and honest man to us faithful inhabitants of the Bohemian Crown."[22] Accordingly, the Czech elites in Prague decided to put their case for full equality between the Czech and German languages and communities and for the autonomy for the Bohemian crownlands within a new constitutional order in the form of two petitions to Ferdinand dated 16 and 29 March 1848. The first petition in particular was heavily sprinkled with appeals to "the fatherly kindheartedness of our majestic King" and assurances that the only goal of his loyal subjects was "that we stand mightily and firmly under the imperial banner of Austria." The two texts frequently oscillated between "King" and "Emperor" making little differentiation between the two and, although the second petition was more assertive and precise in its demands for crownland unity and autonomy, and therefore appealed mostly to "Your Grace as Bohemian King," it never addressed any possible disjunction between the roles of King and Emperor: note in particular the frequent use of the formal address *Vaše cís. královská milost* (Your Imperial Royal Grace).[23]

Throughout the tumultuous events of 1848, despite German Liberal accusations of the opposite, Czech politicians remained faithful to the Habsburg monarchy and to their old paradigm of unconditional loyalty to the Emperor.[24] Only towards the very end of the constitutional experiment, when the new Emperor Franz Joseph ordered the dissolution of the Austrian *Reichstag* (Imperial Diet) in Kremsier/Kroměříž, did a few solitary voices flirt with

---

19. století, Plzeň, 4.– 6. března 1999, ed. Zdeněk Hojda and Roman Prahl (Prague: KLP, 2000), 147–53; Sušová, "Integrační role," 35–9.

[22] The two quotations are taken from newspaper articles by Karel Havlíček, published on 17th and 19th March 1848. Quoted from Karel Havlíček Borovský, *Dílo II: Pražské noviny, Národní noviny, Slovan* (Prague: Československý spisovatel, 1986), 140, 142–3.

[23] The two petitions are printed in Jan M. Černý, *Boj za právo: Část I; Až do rozpuštění sněmu Kroměřížského, 11. března 1848 – 7. března 1849* (Prague: Karolinum 2007), 34–38, 109–12.

[24] According to Macura, the widespread notion that dynastic loyalty was a Czech national virtue contributed to the negative Czech attitude to the revolutions in Vienna and Hungary in the fall of 1848 and to the active support of the Austrian government. Macura, *Znamení*, 68; Milan Otáhal, "Čeští liberálové v roce 1848," *Sborník historický* 37 (1990): 93–128, here 105–6.

more radical alternatives. Despite these voices, an attitude of resignation and subordination was the more frequent response to the dissolution, or at its most radical, a self-conscious declaration of disappointment, as expressed, for example, in Karel Havlíček's words of 14 April 1849:

> The nations are God's and not the Emperor's [...] We will always remain Czechs, like the Magyars and the Italians, and we will never become Austrians, but only citizens of the Austrian Empire [...] Everybody will be happy to call himself a citizen of the Austrian Empire when it becomes an honor, but thus far no-one has any reason whatsoever to be an Austrian patriot: thus far we see neither any benefits nor any glory for us to come from this Austrian union.[25]

The similarities with the argument of von Zedlitz are evident, but so are the new nuances in the discourse. Where von Zedlitz had spoken of "nationalities," Havlíček had *národy* (nations), and whereas the former stressed the legitimate expectations of a benevolent government—its subjects must show their love and loyalty to the Emperor and the Austrian fatherland—the latter introduces the concept of citizen, making the patriotism, and hence loyalty, of such citizens conditional on the performance of the government. Havlíček's deictic "we" may be taken to refer both to the Czech nation and to the transnational category of Austrian citizens. In any case, his call for reciprocity challenges the purely vertical understanding of loyalty of the absolutist era. In a constitutional monarchy, it is not just the citizens, but also the monarch who must loyally obey the established constitutional order.

The gradual return to absolutism after 1849 would later show just how alien this viewpoint was to the young Franz Joseph. From 1860 on, however, whether reluctantly or not, he was forced to accept the introduction of constitutional rule in Austria. The exact rules of this new dispensation—including the relationship between the representative assemblies of the Austrian State as a whole and the individual crownlands—were the subject of intense negotiations and strife throughout the 1860s. The Czech national movement was also among the groups seeking to get its way on the issues important to it, although it was to meet with little success. Its aim was to gain recognition of "Bohemian state rights"—the idea that despite all the political and administrative centralization that had happened in Austria since the eighteenth century, the lands of the Bohemian Crown still, from the point of view of constitutional law, formed an autonomous body within the Habsburg monarchy, and that the Bohemian (and Moravian) Diets should therefore have a broad range of powers conferred to them. This "state rights program" was directed against both the centralist model of a strong, all-Austrian parliament and Hungarian calls for a dualism that would grant the Hungarian Crown a special status within the Empire. Sections of the Bohemian nobility supported

---

[25] Borovský, *Dílo II*, 193.

this program, while the overwhelming majority of the German Bohemian political classes rejected it. In any case, it found little support in Vienna.[26]

The Czech national movement used two political instruments in its efforts to promote this program. First of all, a flurry of petitions appealed to the monarch as guarantor of the constitution and as the highest source of justice in the realm. At least twelve such memoranda or petitions were produced between 1865 and 1873, seven in the name of the Bohemian Diet, two in the name of the Moravian Diet and three signed by leading representatives of the national movement. On only one occasion were the wishes of this narrow circle of the politically privileged elite complemented by signatures from outside its ranks: the petition of opposition forces advocating state rights for Bohemia to the Emperor of 17 January 1873, had the signatures of 270,000 citizens of Bohemia appended to it.[27] Secondly, all these appeals went hand in hand with a boycott of what was considered by the Czech national movement to be the "illegal" and "illegitimate" *Reichsrat* (Imperial Council) in its various incarnations both before and after 1867. This form of "passive resistance" was thought to add moral weight to the Czech viewpoint.

Assurances of loyalty and fidelity play a significant role in all these documents. Obviously, phrases such as "the obediently loyal Diet of the Kingdom of Bohemia" (Address of the Bohemian Diet, 20 March 1866) form part of the conventional rhetorical repertoire of such petitions, but the claims and the conduct of the appellants were also explained as being the logical consequence of their loyalty to an inviolable triune: to their Emperor and King, to their own land and people, and to the Empire as a whole. In the words of the memorandum of 10 October 1871, on what was generally referred to as the Fundamental Articles:

> With proud appreciation we gratefully received the assurance that You kindly remember the irrefutable fidelity with which the inhabitants of the land of Bohemia have always supported the throne of its King—the same unalterable fidelity with which we have always considered the defense of the rights of the Bohemian Crown a sacred duty to our fatherland, to the Monarchy, and to our Monarch.[28]

---

[26] For standard surveys of Czech politics in the nineteenth century see Křen, *Konfliktní společenství*; Otto Urban, *Česká společnost 1848–1918*. Both books have been translated into German.

[27] The survey is based on a comprehensive collection of documents in Pavel Cibulka, ed., *Politické programy českých národních stran 1860–1890: Edice politických programů*, vol. 3, (Prague: Historický ústav, 2000). Undoubtedly, the list needs to be complemented with further petitions to the Emperor that were not of nationwide political significance.

[28] "Address of the Bohemian Diet to the Emperor and King," 10 October 1871, printed in Cibulka, *Politické programy*, 168–71, here 168. For the German version, see: "Úterý 10. října 1871", *Poslanecká sněmovna České Republiky: Digitální repozitář*, accessed 13 April 2016, http://www.psp.cz/eknih/1870skc/2/stenprot/004schuz/s004004.htm. The Fundamental Articles was a compromise that was to introduce a kind of subsidiary

This idea was expressed even more forcefully in the petition of 17 January 1873:

> In these sober times we therefore also feel bound by our unyielding loyalty to our Monarch and to our fatherland to raise our voice to that instance wherefrom the Austrian nations alone continue to expect salvation in their discord and conflicts. We turn directly to the sacred throne of Your Excellency, in order to put a stop to a course that will lead to the ruin of the Empire, and by which everything that is sacred and valid in the Bohemian Kingdom will be destroyed, so that it can be prevented that any steps be taken along a road on which one can never achieve the satisfaction of the nations united under Your scepter.[29]

For the national movement and its allies among the Bohemian nobility, the most important proof that Franz Joseph recognized this logic would be by the act of allowing himself to be crowned King of Bohemia. This act, a cornerstone in the fulfilment of the Bohemian state rights program, would provide a strong parallel to his Hungarian coronation of 1867. In the words of the Bohemian Diet of 26 September 1870:

> If with such an agreement [one that recognized the status of the Bohemian Crown] the inner harmony between ruler and nation is happily reached, then—and this is our urgent wish—may it also be bestowed through shining expression in the majestic deed of a coronation ceremony. Then the Bohemian nation will be in a position to greet with jubilation the sacred sign of the independence of state rights and the sovereignty of the Bohemian State on the anointed forehead of Your Majesty.[30]

In the eyes of Czech politicians, as among the broader population, the value of this act was so immense that the concrete shape of the future constitutional relationship between the kingdom of Bohemia and the Austrian state as a whole almost seemed to be of secondary importance.[31]

The Czechs' apparent firm belief in the efficacy of such declarations of loyalty and appeals to the monarch's sense of justice testifies to an enduring traditionalism in the Czech understanding of politics. As Jiří Rak has pointed out, the Czech political elites insisted that Franz Joseph act as an absolutist

---

dualism within Austria, giving increased autonomy to the Bohemian Lands. It was to fail under Austrian German and Hungarian resistance, and under the lukewarm reception with which it was greeted in Moravia and Silesia. See also the "Declaration of the Bohemian Diet responding to the Emperor's Rescript" of 26 September 1870: "We are however conscious that we are acting out of loyalty to our deepest conviction—a conviction which is a common attribute held by the overwhelming majority of the nation of Bohemia;—we are conscious that we fulfill our duty to the Land, just as we do also to the Empire and to the Dynasty," Cibulka, *Politické programy*, 163; the German version may be found at "Středa 5. října 1870," *Poslanecká sněmovna České Republiky: Digitální repozitář*, accessed 13 April 2016, http://www.psp.cz/eknih/1870skc/1/stenprot/008 schuz/s008001.htm.

[29] The petition is reprinted in Cibulka, *Politické programy*, 187–8, here 188.
[30] Ibid., 163.
[31] The "Address of the Bohemian Diet to the Emperor and King of 10 October 1871," speaks ecstatically about the almost magical significance of a coronation for national healing as the symbolic confirmation of the tie between nation and ruler. Ibid., 171.

ruler—with complete disregard for the constitutional assemblies and principles to which he had committed himself between 1860 and 1867. What is more, they had no "Plan B" when it turned out that the Emperor refused to do so. The enormous disappointment at the collapse of the Fundamental Articles and at what was perceived to be a broken promise to hold a coronation ceremony therefore led Czech politicians into an almost schizophrenic state in which they refused to comply with the Emperor's request to send representatives to the *Reichsrat* to negotiate a deal and at the same time claimed that this very disobedience constituted proof of their loyalty to their rightful king. Public protests were passionate but, as the Czech elites were unable to countenance any serious alternative to staying within the Habsburg Monarchy, they returned to their policy of loyal passive opposition and to an interpretative frame within which they beheld a benign ruler surrounded by evil advisors.[32]

As a side effect of these developments, the adjective *ústavověrný* or *verfassungstreu* ("constitutionally loyal") took on an invective significance in Czech political discourse. But whereas the Czechs professed their fidelity to a shadowy constitution without any legal force, their opponents among the German-Austrian liberals and the informally organized party called the "Union of Constitutionally Loyal Large Landowners" were (as the latter group's name suggests) loyal to a constitution that had actually been promulgated for the Austrian half of the Empire (informally referred to as "Cisleithania") by the Emperor in December 1867. And as this constitution guaranteed a number of liberal civil rights, the German-Austrian liberals had little problem in presenting the Czech boycott policy as a reactionary disregard of the obligations associated with these rights, thereby justifying the harsh sanctions that were imposed against the Czech protests at the time.[33]

Eventually, towards the end of the 1870s, the futility of passive resistance forced the Czech national movement to recognize *de facto* the new constitutional order as the platform upon which to continue its "fight for Austria," and in October 1879 the Czechs took their seats in the Cisleithanian parliament. Although in 1882 the German liberal Max Menger, in a heated debate with his Czech *Reichsrat* colleague Tomáš Garrigue Masaryk, declared that for him it was "high treason to speak of there being any Bohemian state in existence,"[34] accusations of Czech disloyalty to Austria could be justified neither by Masaryk's nor other Czech attempts to modernize the program for

---

[32] Rak, *Zachovej nám*, 162–74.
[33] Pieter M. Judson, *Exclusive Revolutionaries: Liberal Politics, Social Experience, and National Identity in the Austrian Empire, 1848–1914* (Ann Arbor: The University of Michigan Press, 1996); Křen, *Konfliktní společenství*, 194–203; and Rak, *Zachovej nám*, 173.
[34] Jonathan Kwan, "The Austrian State Idea and Bohemian State Rights: Contrasting Traditions in the Habsburg Monarchy, 1848–1914," in *Statehood Before and Beyond Ethnicity: Minor States in Northern and Eastern Europe, 1600–2000*, ed. Linas Eriksonas and Leos Müller (Brussels: Lang, 2005), 243–73, here 268.

state rights, nor the annual Czech declaration, ritually repeated at the opening of the *Reichsrat* since 1879, that they were participating under protest and had not abandoned their convictions on the continued validity of the state rights of Bohemia.

From the 1880s on, this Czech "petition fever" abated considerably, in part because it had become increasingly evident that the Emperor would continue to insist that the December Constitution formed the only basis for any further negotiations of national political issues, and in part because such direct appeals to the Monarch as sovereign had started to look archaic as the active work of the parliament became the standard mode of political discourse and as Czech society became increasingly bourgeois. Hugh LeCaine Agnew and Jan Havránek have argued that as it became evident that Franz Joseph had no intention causing himself to be crowned King of Bohemia, the Czechs began to honor the Bohemian Crown as a purely national symbol, independent of the monarch and the dynasty.[35] This view is surely correct, but it should not be read as an expression of any radical Czech alienation from their ruler. The overwhelming majority of the Czech population and their political representatives preserved a fundamental loyalty to Franz Joseph until his death on 21 November 1916.[36] In the final decades of his life, the Emperor was primarily revered as a supranational and nonpartisan mediator between his subject nations, a role he himself took very seriously.[37]

The court intensively cultivated this image of the Emperor as mediator and protector of the unity of the multifarious Empire. The Emperor's birth-

---

[35] Hugh LeCaine Agnew, "The Flyspecks on Palivec's Portrait: Francis Joseph, the Symbols of Monarchy, and Czech Popular Loyalty," in *The Limits of Loyalty: Imperial Symbolism, Popular Allegiances, and State Patriotism in the Late Habsburg Monarchy*, ed. Laurence Cole and Daniel L. Unowsky (New York: Berghahn Books, 2007), 86–112, here 99, 107; Jan Havránek, "Český historismus druhé poloviny 19. století mezi monarchismem a demokratismem," in *Historické vědomí v českém umění 19. století*, ed. Tomáš Vlček (Prague: Ústav teorie a dějin umění ČSAV, 1981), 27–36, here 32–5.

[36] On Czech reactions to the death of Franz Joseph see Rak, *Zachovej nám*, 401–9.

[37] Agnew, "Flyspecks," 102–5; Sušová, "Integrační role," 40–4; and Rak, *Zachovej nám*, 214. Jeremy King has argued that the Habsburg regime as a whole accepted this mediating role in a "triadic" relationship with the Czech and the German national movements. Jeremy King, "The Nationalization of East Central Europe: Ethnicism, Ethnicity, and Beyond," in *Staging the Past*, ed. Bucur and Wingfield, 112–52. The army remained one of the areas where Franz Joseph preserved and insisted on preserving his prerogatives as an absolutist ruler. Consequently, when entering into service soldiers swore an oath of allegiance to the Emperor personally, and not to the state that he represented, see Rak, *Zachovej nám*, 217. According to István Deák, this bond of personal fealty provided a strong incentive for the Austrian officer corps to act as an ethnically disinterested guardian of the monarchy. István Deák, *Beyond Nationalism: A Social and Political History of the Habsburg Officer Corps, 1848–1918* (Oxford: Oxford University Press, 1990), 4–9.

days and jubilees were carefully staged,[38] and every visit of the Emperor to the Bohemian Lands was prepared in great detail to illustrate this role. Since the 1860s the court strove meticulously to ensure that the Emperor included appearances at both Czech and German institutions when visiting Bohemia. As national antagonisms became increasingly territorialized, any stay at a "Czech" city, including Prague, had to be balanced by a visit to a "German" city such as Reichenberg/Liberec.[39] In ethnically mixed and predominantly Czech cities Franz Joseph carefully alternated between Czech and German in his utterances. On each visit, the Emperor expressed his gratitude for the loyalty shown by the inhabitants of the given locality in strictly ritualized phrases. And all this was no mere pretense; Franz Joseph remained—with his visit to Prague in June 1868 being the major exception—the object of much reverence and attention on the part of the local populace and notables.[40]

The cult of the Emperor as the incarnation of Austrian state patriotism was not the only means of promoting the idea that a multinational Austria could provide a meaningful home for all its citizens. Ernst Bruckmüller has studied how school books of the time sought to approach the issue in a differentiated way. Whereas history books for primary schools promoted identification with the linguistic and national community it was designed for, albeit linked with a narrative of that community's positive relationship to the Habsburg state and its dynasty, history text books for secondary schools—a key arena for the education of the monarchy's elites—put far more emphasis on the state as a whole and on a pan-Austrian patriotism. Here, "fatherland" always referred to the Empire as a whole in contrast to the individual "Crown Land" or *Heimat* (homeland). The radical nationalism that constituted a real presence among some groups of students should not, Bruckmüller holds, lead one to the conclusion that such efforts to promote Austrian loyalty through education were entirely futile.[41]

---

[38] Daniel L. Unowsky, *The Pomp and Politics of Patriotism: Imperial Celebrations in Habsburg Austria 1848–1916* (West Lafayette, IN: Purdue University Press, 2005); Cole and Unowsky, eds., *Limits of Loyalty*; and Peter Urbanitsch, "Pluralist Myth and Nationalist Realities: The Dynastic Myth of the Habsburg Monarchy; A Futile Exercise in the Creation of Identity?," *Austrian History Yearbook* 35 (2004): 101–41.

[39] This was the case in 1891, when the Emperor visited Prague as patron of the Provincial Jubilee Exhibition (Zemská jubilejní výstava) which in the event was boycotted by the Germans of Bohemia. Similarly, in 1901 the Emperor went to Aussig/Ústí nad Labem after having spent a week in Prague, and in 1906 a visit to Reichenberg/Liberec had to be followed by a stop in Kuttenberg/Kutná Hora. Agnew, "Flyspecks," 98–103; Jiří Pernes, *František Josef I.: Nikdy nekorunovaný český král* (Prague: Brána, 2005). Pernes carefully records every visit that Franz Joseph made to the Bohemian Lands.

[40] On the 1868 visit see Pernes, *František Josef I.*, 177–80; Rak, *Zachovej nám*, 158–61.

[41] Ernst Bruckmüller, "Patriotic and National Myths: National Consciousness and Elementary School Education in Imperial Austria," in Cole and Unowsky, eds., *Limits of Loyalty*, 11–30.

Still, the most potent instrument for securing loyalty on an everyday basis was probably the steadily broadening concrete, practical linking of Austrian citizens and their associations, including those defined on a national basis, into the state. Gary Cohen has described the trend in the decades before 1914 as follows:

> Rather than making any excessive claims for democratization as such, it seems better to speak of the increasing *penetration* of public interests into some areas of government decision making, their growing *implication* in the functioning of parts of the state administration, and perhaps an advancing *cohabitation* of public interest groups and political parties with the state bureaucracy.[42]

A consequence of this embedding and cohabitation was that nationalist politicians and organizations learned to operate within the structures of the state, and grew to appreciate its court system and public services. In the 1890s, leading Young Czech politician Josef Kaizl made it a major goal for the Czech national movement to penetrate the Austrian state apparatus and get their proportional share of administrative and government positions. Rather than seeking an unattractive "*Kleinstaatlichkeit* ("small-state condition") à la Serbia," which was what the state rights program was campaigning for, Kaizl argued, Czech society should capitalize on the many opportunities at hand within the larger Austrian state to achieve prosperity and obtain political influence.[43] This "long march" through the Austrian bureaucracy was of course unthinkable without full acceptance of the responsibilities associated with these offices. If Vienna was to welcome nationally conscious Czechs making their careers in the civil service, the Czech national movement conversely had to accept that an oath of allegiance to the Monarchy did not constitute an offense against the nation.[44]

Often, Czech national politicians and media were vocal in their criticism of "Vienna." This critique, however, did not necessarily imply abandonment of the earlier discourse that professed a deeply rooted loyalty among the Czechs towards the House of Habsburg. "The whole Czech people [*lid*, P.B.] still stand in a closer relation to their King and Emperor than the extent dictated by parliamentarianism," declared the moderate journal *Čas* (Time) in 1890.[45] While loyalty was presented as a Czech national virtue, the opposite

---

[42] Gary B. Cohen, "Nationalist Politics and the Dynamics of State and Civil Society in the Habsburg Monarchy, 1867–1914," *Central European History* 40, no. 2 (2007): 241–78, here 259. Original emphasis. Cf. Kwan, "Austrian State Idea," 257.

[43] Quoted from Křen, *Konfliktní společenství*, 253. On the new Czech strategy of *pénetration pacifique* see also ibid., 254–6.

[44] The relationship between Czech civil servants and the national movement has not been studied sufficiently. See however Aleš Vyskočil, *C. k. úředník ve zlatém věku jistoty* (Prague: Historický ústav, 2009); *Opomíjení a neoblíbení*, ed. Petrasová and Lorenzová.

[45] Quoted from Blanka Soukupová, *Česká společnost před sto lety: Identita, stereotyp, mýtus* (Prague: Pastelka, 2000), 48. Also, the Czech Social Democrats, whose discourse

was argued for Austrian Germans: as all too willing servants of Berlin, they were presented as never having much of a care for the good of the Monarchy as a whole, in an argument that suggested the pro-German and anti-Slavic policies of Vienna to be not merely unjust, but no less than ignorant and dangerous.[46] The social, economic, and political advances made by the Czechs towards the end of the nineteenth century were thus accompanied by a growing self-confidence, although the national movement (with only a few minor exceptions in radical circles) was not yet ready to specify the consequences of its loyalty to the Monarchy not being met with appropriate recognition and reward. "Austria has not understood its real task and benefit,"[47] Young Czech politician Eduard Grégr claimed in 1897, while Karel Kramář, also a Young Czech, had declared with great self-assurance in 1892:

> [...] nor do we wish to weaken the Empire through our becoming more independent; we will give to it what it needs to assert its authority, and we are also capable of appreciating the necessity of a big, united territory of the whole Empire for many economic tasks, and the happier we are, the more willing our sacrifices for the Empire will be.[48]

Sacrifice and loyalty to the national cause were also asked of the Czech national community but the national parties, which by the late 1890s had become very disparate in policy and style, found it difficult to agree on the specific characteristics of the cause and spent substantial energy in mutual infighting.[49] National associations devoted considerable resources to mobilizing and imposing discipline on large segments of the population who showed signs of national indifference on issues considered vital to the national interest—the way they spent their money, their choice of school for their children, etc. As Tara Zahra and Pieter Judson have shown, conduct indifferent to the national cause did not disappear with the advent of national mass politics, and policies designed to secure national loyalty from parents could have the effect of reinforcing what the nationalists despised as national "hermaphroditism," as families learned to maneuver between the offerings of the various competing national movements.[50] From the perspective of the individual, there was no strict disjunctive either/or between national indifference and

---

on loyalty differed significantly from that of the bourgeois national movement, remained politically loyal to Austria. Ibid., 73–100.

[46] Ibid., 10, 14, 24, 44–6 etc. Further examples of this line of reasoning can be found in Rudolf Jaworski, "Jungtschechische Karikaturen zum Nationalitätenstreit in Österreich-Ungarn. Die Prager 'Šípy' (1887–1907)," *Bohemia* 22, no. 2 (1981): 300–41, in particular 312, 323–4.

[47] Soukupová, *Česká společnost*, 24.

[48] Ibid., 46.

[49] Cohen, "Nationalist Politics," 267–8.

[50] Tara Zahra, *Kidnapped Souls: National Indifference and the Battle for Children in the Bohemian Lands, 1900–1948* (Ithaca: Cornell University Press, 2008), 32; Pieter M. Judson, *Guardians of the Nation: Activists on the Language Frontiers of Imperial Austria* (Cambridge, MA: Harvard University Press, 2006).

national identification, but instead a contextual choice that became concrete as calls upon one's national loyalty began to reach the limits of their perceived meaningfulness. Consequently, these calls did not merely have to overcome traditional loyalties, whether religious or parochial in social or geographical terms. The modernization of Austria and the enormous growth in secondary and tertiary education in the Empire produced new interest groups and communities with transnational feelings of solidarity and loyalty, which practiced a mostly inconspicuous internationalism in art, science, technology, and matters of economy.[51]

So, in the Austrian civil society that was evolving at the time "nationalist loyalties found expression alongside strong class and interest group allegiances as well as continuing loyalties to the state, its laws, and administration,"[52] and even among historians—practitioners of the most eminently national of all scholarly disciplines of the nineteenth century—the confines of the national environment could provoke strong feelings of claustrophobia. "Things will never be better here, until a draft opens here of foreign air, or foreign airs. That is alas heresy, but it is the way things are", Jaroslav Goll, professor of history at the Czech University of Prague, wrote to his protégé Josef Pekař in Berlin in 1894, while encouraging him to "breathe in the world spirit, so as not to choke later."[53]

This constant emphasis by Czech voices that loyalty and disloyalty were matters of national character was to turn against the national community itself with the outbreak of war in 1914. In German nationalist agitation the Czechs, as Slavs and hence consanguineous with the Serbian and Russian enemy, came under collective suspicion of disloyalty or even treason. Despite the unproblematic mobilization that was conducted within the Czech population, such a wary view was not without supporters within the Supreme Army Command (*Armeeoberkommando*) and in the Cabinet, which saw fit to introduce measures of collective repression against Czech national organiza-

---

[51] Gary B. Cohen, *Education and Middle-Class Society in Imperial Austria, 1848–1918* (West Lafayette, IN: Purdue University Press, 1996), 254; Peter M. Bograd, "Beyond Nation, Confession, and Party: The Politicization of Professional Identity in Late Imperial Austria," *Austrian History Yearbook* 27 (1996): 133–54, in particular 134–8, 146–7; Catherine Albrecht, "Chambers of Commerce and Czech-German Relations in the Late Nineteenth Century," *Bohemia* 38, no. 2 (1997): 298–310; Elisabeth van Meer, "'The Nation is Technological': Technical Expertise and National Competition in the Bohemian Lands, 1800–1914," in *Expert Cultures in Central Eastern Europe*, ed. Martin Kohlrausch, Katrin Steffen, and Stefan Wiederkehr (Osnabrück: Fibre, 2010), 85–104; Katherine David-Fox, "Prague-Vienna, Prague-Berlin: The Hidden Geography of Czech Modernism," *Slavic Review* 59, no. 4 (2000): 735–60; and Lucie Kostrbová, *Mezi Prahou a Vídní: Česká a vídeňská literární moderna na konci 19. století* (Prague: Academia, 2011).

[52] Cohen, "Nationalist Politics," 244, 276–7.

[53] Quoted from Kateřina Bláhová, *České dějepisectví v dialogu s Evropou, 1890–1914* (Prague: Academia, 2009), 9, 17.

tions. The authorities made themselves very clear on how the Czechs were expected to express their loyalty to the Habsburg state, making demands that put Czech politicians under enormous pressure from above and eventually even from below as the war made a rethink of the relationship between national and imperial loyalties increasingly urgent.54

With the suspension of parliamentary activity after the outbreak of war the official understanding of the implications of loyalty between ruler and subjects regressed drastically. In the constitutional era, Czech declarations of loyalty had gone hand in hand with appeals to the Emperor to reward loyalty shown with a corresponding benevolence towards their needs and wishes. Now, such calls for reciprocity were no longer tolerated. Instead, the government and a host of local and regional authorities insisted that all Czech political representatives (like those of every nationality within the Monarchy) declare their unconditional loyalty to the Emperor and his Empire. And they were not disappointed. Ivan Šedivý has estimated the number of such declarations at a thousand or more from Bohemia alone, about half of which came without any order having to be made from above, but at the initiative of the relevant Czech institutions themselves. The most ostentatious and sincere of such declarations tended to come from smaller town and rural district councils, schools, and Catholic organizations.55

Probably the most famous (or notorious) dictate from above was a letter dated 31 January 1917 from the Presidium of the Czech Union (*Předsednictvo Českého Svazu*), an association of Czech members of the *Reichsrat*, to the Emperor. The letter was written in response to the note by the Triple Entente powers to Woodrow Wilson of 10 January 1917, which had mentioned "the liberation of the Czechoslovaks from foreign rule"56 as one of the Entente's war aims. The Czech writers proved more than willing to counter the note with a declaration of loyalty, but their draft proposal, which included a range of modest political demands, was dismissed by Foreign Minister Ottokar Czernin. He simply dictated a new text in its place, stating in unconditional terms that "the Czech nation as always in the past, so also in the present and in the coming time sees its future and the conditions for its development only under the Habsburg scepter."57 The humiliation that this step represented dealt a serious blow to the loyalist position, and was eventually to mark a

---

54 Ivan Šedivý, *Češi, české země a Velká válka 1914–1918* (Prague: Nakladatelství Lidové Noviny, 2001).
55 Ibid., 202–13, 387, note 207; Ivan Šedivý, "České loajální projevy 1914–1918 (malá textová sonda)," *Český časopis historický* 97, no. 2 (1999): 293–310; and Rak, *Zachovej nám*, 390–401.
56 Quoted from Křen, *Konfliktní společenství*, 426.
57 Jan Galandauer, *Vznik Československé republiky 1918: Programy, projekty, předpoklady* (Prague: Svoboda, 1988), 59–61, 282 (full text of the document); Urban, *Česká společnost*, 605–6. Romanian, Croatian-Slovenian, and some Italian parliamentarians were also forced to issue such declarations of loyalty.

turning point in Czech attitudes. From late 1917 on, Czech loyalty to the House of Habsburg was clearly on the wane, although until almost the very end one can talk neither of any uniform Czech attitude to the Emperor and the Monarchy nor of any widespread disloyalty that could be suppressed only by force.

The collapse of Austria-Hungary in 1918 was to immediately wipe away from public memory any trace of Czech feelings of loyalty towards the Habsburgs and their monarchy.[58] Citizens and civil servants alike were now expected to show loyalty to a democratic, republican nation state founded in the name of a unitary Czechoslovak nation.[59] This change has been described as a transformation from a triadic relationship between the supranational Habsburg authorities and the two national movements in the Bohemian Lands to a dualism between a nationalized and nationalizing Czechoslovak state and its German minority.[60] While this theoretical framework makes perfect sense as an ideal type, the schema could, if applied too rigidly, lead one to exaggerate the radical nature of the rupture of 1918.

Before 1914, Czech and German national activists had indeed appealed to the Emperor and his state apparatus as neutral arbiters of the various interests within the Empire, and numerous civil servants had harbored a genuine identification with their supranational role, and acted accordingly. But neither the court in Vienna, nor the various echelons of the Habsburg bureaucracy were completely free of the influence of their own cultural and educational backgrounds, or by the contemporary public discourse, as the exaggerated restrictions imposed on Czech national organizations in the 1914-15 period showed.[61] Conversely, principles and traditions of civil rule of law and of constitutionalism lived on among the judges, civil servants and politicians of the first Czechoslovak republic, many of whom had served in similar func-

---

[58] For an astonishing example of rapid turncoating at a Prague school see Jiří Rak, "Staříčký mocnář a tatíček Masaryk," in *19. století v nás: Modely, instituce a reprezentace, které přetrvaly*, ed. Milan Řepa (Prague: Nakladatelství Historický Ústav, 2008), 267-73; Rak, *Zachovej nám*, 414-5.

[59] For detailed discussions of how various professional groups and religious and ethnic communities addressed this situation see the essays in Schulze Wessel, *Loyalitäten in der Tschechoslowakischen Republik*.

[60] As argued in Brubaker, *Nationalism Reframed*, the old triad was replaced by a new triadic framework of national minorities, the state undergoing the nationalization process in which they lived and the external national "homelands" that could make claims over them. For the Bohemian Lands see King, "Nationalization of East Central Europe," 140-1; Jeremy King, *Budweisers into Czechs and Germans: A Local History of Bohemian Politics, 1848-1948* (Princeton, NJ: Princeton University Press, 2002), 5-6; Zahra, *Kidnapped Souls*, 10-2, 107, 112; and Judson, *Guardians of the Nation*, 245-6.

[61] Despite the work's promising title, these issues are covered only sporadically in Peter Urbanitsch, "The High Civil Service Corps in the Last Period of the Multi-Ethnic Empire between National and Imperial Loyalties," *Historical Social Research* 33 (2008): 193-213.

tions before 1918. And at the other end of a scale that ranged from formal to charismatic authority and hence legitimacy, one may well see in the widespread and systematically promoted cult of Masaryk—a cult in which petitions to the President played a significant role—as a continuation of deeply rooted premodern models of expression of popular loyalty towards a just and benevolent patriarchal monarch.[62]

---

[62] Peter Heumos, "Die Arbeiterschaft in der Ersten Tschechoslowakischen Republik," *Bohemia* 29, no. 1 (1988): 50–72, here 69–71; Peter Bugge, "Czech Democracy 1918–1938: Paragon or Parody?," *Bohemia* 47, no. 1 (2006–7): 3–28, 22–3; Rak, "Staříčký mocnář a tatíček Masaryk," 269–72; and Matěj Kotalík, "Panovnický kult a kontinuita monarchismu v období první Československé republiky," in *19. století v nás*, ed. Řepa, 286–92.

Martina Niedhammer

LOYALTY AS A TOOL OF ANALYSIS FOR THE SELF-IMAGE OF MINORITIES
Prague's Jewish Upper Middle Class in the First Half of the Nineteenth Century

More than a Curiosity: Introduction

In the autumn of 1835, the Austrian Emperor Ferdinand I and Empress Maria Anna embarked on a trip to the Lands of the Bohemian Crown.[1] Their travels took them by way of Prague's capital, where an extensive schedule awaited them. Within just a few days, the royal guests had already attended numerous receptions and banquets as well as a festive illumination of Prague's city center at night, which had been especially organized in their honor.[2]

One of the social institutions to which the royal couple wished to pay a courtesy visit was the *Pomologischer Verein* (Pomological Association). Formed in 1819 as a section of the *k. k. patriotisch-ökonomische Gesellschaft in Böhmen* (Royal and Imperial Patriotic Economic Society in Bohemia),[3] it had made it its mission to maintain and improve yields in the Bohemian fruit and wine-growing industry. To this end, it ran its own horticultural center, which hosted several tree nurseries.[4] Its members, totaling 172 individuals in 1835,[5] came partially from the Bohemian nobility, and partially from the middle class, in which educated circles from within the bourgeoisie (clerics, professors and teachers) were proportionately over-represented. In addition

---

[1] Cf. general press coverage, particularly in "Bohemia" (numerous articles and poems marking the occasion of the imperial couple's visit in September and October 1835) as well as *Hlasy wlastenců při radostném wjtánj GG. Cjsařských Králowských Majestátů Ferdinanda I. a Marie Anny w Praze dne čtwrtého řjgna 1835* (Prague, 1835).
[2] This took place on the night of 5 October 1835, see Karl Preyßner, "Telegraph von Prag," *Bohemia. Ein Unterhaltungsblatt*, 9 October 1835, n.p.
[3] "Geschichte der k. k. patriotisch-ökonomischen Gesellschaft," *Monatsschrift der Gesellschaft des vaterländischen Museums in Böhmen* 1, no. 2 (1827): 44–50, 49.
[4] *Kurzer Beitrag zur Geschichte der k. k. patriotisch-ökonomischen Gesellschaft im Königreiche Böhmen mit Rückblick auf die Thätigkeit und den geistigen Fortschritt derselben während des letzten Decenniums* (Prague, 1862), 9.
[5] Cf. "Mitgliederverzeichnis des Pomologischen Vereins," in *Schematismus für das Königreich Böhmen auf das Schaltjahr 1836*, ed. Königliche böhmische Gesellschaft der Wissenschaften (Prague, 1836), 325–30.

to these groups, a large number of public officials also belonged to the association. Thus, government officials from the various Bohemian territories appeared as honorary members alongside members from the high nobility, whose participation was traditional whenever such associations were founded in the period up until the March Revolution.[6] Their participation, along with the active commitment of the educated bourgeoisie, allows us to draw some conclusions on the ideational positioning of the Pomological Association: it quite clearly regarded itself as patriotic towards its country and supportive of the state in the enlightenment tradition, and therefore strove to advance the progress of domestic agriculture, mainly in the interests of socio-economic development. However, the communication of popular scientific knowledge to a wide audience, by organizing garden shows, for example, was not a priority, in contrast to the later *Gartenbau-Gesellschaft* (Horticultural Society)[7], which was founded in Prague in 1843.

The association used the occasion of the imperial couple's visit to show off its latest success in the field of fruit breeding. However, as the reporter in attendance for the Prague newspaper *Bohemia* commented at the time, it was less the artistically arranged harvest products that attracted the attention of the visitors than eighteen little girls ranging from the age of eight to twelve years old in traditional dress.[8] They represented the sixteen districts of Bohemia, plus the Egerland area and the royal capital of Prague, and presented the royal guests baskets with fruit and flowers.[9]

It was indeed a setting altogether typical of the Biedermeier period, very much like other events that one so often encounters in the press of the time and in numerous commemorative books marking such occasions. Yet a quick glance behind the scenes is enough to deprive the picture of the coherence it seeks to project. Not only did most of the girls not come from the districts and regions which they were supposedly representing, as indeed any attentive observer could guess, but neither were the local origins of the participants of any particular significance on this symbolic occasion. In any case one particular remarkable fact was that one of the flower girls represented a district whose own administrative center would not have tolerated her presence in its midst. For Julie (von) Lämel (1825–1874), daughter of the banker and wholesale merchant Leopold (von) Lämel (1785–1869), in fact belonged to one of the most important Jewish families in Prague in the first half of the nineteenth century. She was hence precluded from staying for any extended pe-

[6] "Ehrenmitglieder in alphabetischer Ordnung," in ibid., 326–27.
[7] Cf. the short extract of the association's history in *Handbuch des Königreiches Böhmen für das Jahr 1846,* ed. Königliche böhmische Gesellschaft der Wissenschaften (Prague, 1846), 505.
[8] Karl Preyßner, "Der Besuch Sr. Majestät des Kaisers Ferdinand in der Obstausstellung des pomologischen Vereins für Böhmen. Am 11. Oktober 1835," *Bohemia. Ein Unterhaltungsblatt,* 25 October 1835, n. p.
[9] Ibid.

riod in Budweis, the center of the very district which she was representing in honor of the imperial visit.

As a glance at the list of names of the flower girls reveals, the then ten-year-old Julie Lämel was apparently the only Jewish girl who actively took part in the festivities.[10] The fact that it was precisely her who represented Budweis, a city proud of the royal privilege it had held since 1506, which denied Jews the right to settle in the town,[11] seems particularly mischievous when set against this background. We can only speculate as to why exactly Julie was chosen for this role—especially considering that her father was not a member of the Pomological Association. It is possible that Julie Lämel had her well documented friendship with Anna Bamberger[12] to thank for her role—Anna was the daughter of the association's managing director Jakob Bamberger.[13] A determining factor may also have been that Julie's father, Leopold Lämel, frequented circles whose normal self-image was similar in many ways to that of the Pomological Association.[14]

Nevertheless, Julie Lämel's participation in the festivities for the imperial couple is a reminder to historians of the fragility of such supposedly tangible personal categorizations as religious, ethnic or linguistic affiliations. Were either Julie Lämel herself or her parents aware of the double role that Julie as Jew and representative of the Prague middle class automatically took on for the reception in honor of the imperial couple? Or is it rather a case of retrospective attribution imposed *ex post* upon the protagonists of the time?

Minorities and Their Loyalty (or Loyalties)

Even if in the wake of various "cultural turns" nobody seriously questions anymore the instability of ethnic and cultural attributions, their analysis and

---

[10] Cf. ibid. Preyßner lists the names of all the flower girls participating in the reception. In most cases, their origins can be identified with the help of the *Schematismus für das Königreich Böhmen auf das Schaltjahr 1836*.

[11] Oskar K. Rabinowicz and Yeshayahu Jellinek, "Ceske Budejovice," in *Encyclopaedia Judaica*, ed. Michael Berenbaum and Fred Skolnik, 2nd ed., vol. 4 (Detroit: Macmillan Reference USA, 2007), 552. The prohibition of Jews taking up residence in Budweis was only revoked in the course of the Revolution of 1848.

[12] That is, at least, what is reported in the memoirs of Eduard Hanslick (1825–1904), who was born in Prague, a music critic and friend of the Lämel family: Eduard Hanslick, *Aus meinem Leben*, vol. 1 (Berlin, 1894), 220.

[13] Königliche böhmische Gesellschaft der Wissenschaften, ed., *Schematismus für das Königreich Böhmen auf das Schaltjahr 1836*, 325. Jakob Bamberger was at the time "freiherrlich Wimmerscher Wirthschaftssekretär" (the economic secretary of the barony of Wimmer). The daughter of his employer, Charlotte von Wimmer, was also one of the flower girls.

[14] Regarding the person Leopold Lämel, cf. generally Martina Niedhammer, *Nur eine "Geld-Emancipation"? Loyalitäten und Lebenswelten des Prager jüdischen Großbürgertums 1800–1867* (Göttingen: Vandenhoeck and Ruprecht, 2013).

verbalization still presents methodological difficulties. Although over the years countless tools have emerged dedicated precisely to this end—one need only think of the concept of "hybrid identity"[15] or of the idea of "situational ethnicity"[16]—such instruments are all too often pushed to their limits when one tries to use them to reveal the simultaneity (or otherwise) of individual self-definitions.

It goes without saying that this problem is particularly obvious in the case of minorities. Thus, for example, members of Prague's Jewish upper middle class played a significant role in economic, social and religious life in the Bohemian capital in the first half of the nineteenth century. Owing to the fact that they did not deny their Jewish origins by converting or by adopting an aggressive religious indifference, instead accepting the legal and social restrictions enforced on Jews in Austria at the time,[17] they cannot be considered in wider societal terms simply as an acculturated marginal group. However, neither can they be considered simply "normal" members of Prague's Jewish community—too great was their social pulling power to lump them in together with their fellow believers.[18]

For any closer investigation and presentation of the often complex self-image of this small group of people, some idea of which we can glean from the above-described scenario, the concept of "loyalty" would seem to be a particularly appropriate tool. Amongst the strengths of a model of exposition based on this concept is its associative potential—a property that should not, however, be taken as synonymous with any conceptual imprecision.[19] In particular, the voluntary willingness that is an essential characteristic of conferring loyalty, along with the (largely) unconditional commitment that is associated with it, reveal an emotional momentum that has the ability to explain

---

[15] For an example see Simone Lässig, *Jüdische Wege ins Bürgertum: Kulturelles Kapital und sozialer Aufstieg im 19. Jahrhundert* (Göttingen: Vandenhoeck and Ruprecht, 2004).

[16] Till van Rahden, *Juden und andere Breslauer: Die Beziehungen zwischen Juden, Protestanten und Katholiken in einer deutschen Großstadt von 1860 bis 1925* (Göttingen: Vandenhoeck and Ruprecht, 2000).

[17] These included special provisions relating to family, work and social life. Thus the notorious *Familiantengesetze* (Familiants Laws) limited the number of Jews living in the Bohemian Lands until 1848 by permitting residency in each land to only a certain number of families. In a similar vein, the practice of numerous professions and the freedom of movement were severely restricted.

[18] The social significance that Prague's Jewish upper middle class had in the first half of the nineteenth century for both Christian and Jewish circles can be assessed based on the frequency with which this small group of people is mentioned in the local non-Jewish press as well as in the Jewish regional press.

[19] For the relationship between loyalty as a tool of analysis and colloquial connotations of the term, cf. Martin Schulze Wessel, "'Loyalität' als geschichtlicher Grundbegriff und Forschungskonzept: Zur Einleitung," in *Loyalitäten in der Tschechoslowakischen Republik 1918-1938. Politische, nationale und kulturelle Zugehörigkeiten*, ed. Martin Schulze Wessel (Munich: Oldenbourg, 2004), 1-22, 1-2.

the apparently contradictory attitudes and actions betrayed by protagonists in particular situations. This is why loyalty cannot be prescribed, but must be based on a personal decision made in the face of a range of alternative actions. Furthermore, it becomes exceptionally effective in precisely those situations where one's expectations are either not met or only partially met by the opposite side.

Both of these facets were significant as far as Prague's upper middle class was concerned. On the one hand, they clung ostentatiously to their affiliation to Judaism even though the aforementioned choice between conversion and religious indifference would have provided a convenient escape from their legally and socially disadvantaged position. On the other hand, the expectations of members of the class were time and time again disappointed, particularly from the direction of the public authorities, from whom they hoped for an early improvement in the legal position of their fellow-believers. A typical illustration of this is a letter dated 9 November 1837 from Simon Lämel, grandfather of Julie the flower girl, to his French great-nephew, Gustave d'Eichthal, in which he laments the fact that the imperial house had been taking next to no notice of the numerous efforts made by individual Bohemian and Austrian Jews to achieve emancipation for the Jewish population: "We do not know to whom we should turn, whether it should be the Emperor, the Archduke Ludwig or Count Metternich to whom we should resort, since one always meets with a willing ear yet with little or no success."[20] Similar pronouncements were also conveyed by Simon's son Leopold, who nevertheless repeatedly showed his loyalty to the Austrian state, as demonstrated by his daughter Julie's participation in the reception for the imperial couple at the Pomological Association.

Loyalty versus Situational Ethnicity

Against this point, admittedly, one can make two objections: for one thing, there is an obvious proximity between the notion of loyalty and the concept of "situational ethnicity", and, for another, the inner attitude of the person conferring his or her loyalty can only be deduced with difficulty from the available written sources, which complicates any evaluation of that person's actual intentions. The concept of "situational ethnicity" postulates a consciousness of common ancestry and culture within a particular social group. However, this consciousness is only expressed on certain occasions (which is

---

[20] "Man weiß nicht, wohin, an wen man sich bei uns wenden soll, ob man zum Kaiser, zum Erzh. Ludwig oder zum Fürsten Metternich seine Zuflucht nehmen, da man zwar überall willig Gehör, aber wenig oder gar keinen Erfolg findet." Simon Lämel to Gustave d'Eichthal, Vienna, 9 November 1837, MS 13749/71, Lettres adressées pour la plupart à Gustave d'Eichthal, Manuscrits et correspondances relatifs aux Saint-Simoniens, Supplément 4, Manuscrits de la Bibliothèque de l'Arsenal, Bibliothèque nationale de France.

what makes it situational) and to varying degrees of intensity, which explains why it does not necessarily come into conflict with other feelings of belonging along the lines of class, gender or nation.[21] Against this, the acceptance of diverse—sometimes conflicting—loyalties means enjoying the advantage of not having to operate with barely measurable degrees of belonging, but rather being able to take advantage of a variety of overlapping bonds to show something that many protagonists openly strived for: an at least partial merging of individual loyalties that were central to their everyday needs, thereby surmounting their situational status. Nonetheless, this process was by no means always successful, as in the case of Julie Lämel, whose bond with Judaism had the (erroneous) identification with her Bohemian home place superimposed upon it. In other cases, however, it was entirely possible to achieve this trick: in 1847, for example, as represented by the publication of a *Gedenkblatt* (commemorative page) by Leopold Lämel to mark the abolition of Bohemia's special Jewish tax (Fig. 1).[22]

This lithograph can be read as an attempt to present the civic and religious loyalties of Prague's Jewish upper middle class as being compatible with each other, and to anchor the point visually. Precisely this relationship of loyalty was probably particularly in question due to the fact that the Christian population repeatedly construed the lowly legal status of the Jewish population as the result or consequence of Jewish "unreliability" and/or "disloyalty".

This traditional line, which has its origins in the old Christian accusation of "Jewish perfidy" and was manifested in particularly stark terms during Christian Good Friday Prayers of the Faithful "oremus et pro perfidis Judaeis,"[23] has endured into modern times in a modified form. Indeed the religiously motivated reservations as to the moral reliability of Jews remained virulent amongst non-Jews well into the nineteenth century—and it was not seldom that such reservations should find their way into the practice of law.

---

[21] Rahden, *Juden und andere Breslauer*, 20–1.

[22] Commonly referred to as the Bohemian Jewish tax, this was a special levy that the Bohemian Jewish population had to pay collectively since 1748. It was the result of lengthy negotiations between Maria Theresa, the Bohemian Jewish community and various regional authorities in relation to the return of the Jewish population, which had been expelled from Prague between 1745 and 1748. The tax, which was felt to be unfair and degrading by those affected by it, was abolished by Ferdinand I in 1846. See also Niedhammer, *Nur eine "Geld-Emancipation"?*, 154–75.

[23] For the Good Friday Prayer of the Faithful on Jews as well as the initiatives to modify them, cf. Hubert Wolf, "Liturgischer Antisemitismus? Die Karfreitagsfürbitte für die Juden und die Römische Kurie, 1928–1975," in *Judentum und Katholizismus: Gemeinsamkeiten und Verwerfungen vom 16. bis 20. Jahrhundert*, eds. Florian Schuller, Giuseppe Veltri, and Hubert Wolf (Regensburg: Pustet, 2005), 253–69. The accusation of perfidy was deleted in 1959–60; a complete revision of the deeply controversial prayer's text took place in the course of the Second Vatican Council and appeared in the new Roman Missal in 1970.

Loyalty as a Tool of Analysis for the Self-Image of Minorities 163

Fig. 1: Leopold Lämel, "Gedenkblatt," 1847, Děkový list za zrušení židovského daně (Commemorative page on the occasion of the abolition of the Jewish tax), sign. 49873, Fond Leopold Lämel, Archiv židovského muzea v Praze.

Thus until 1846, Austrian Jews had to swear a special oath whose purpose was not so much to accommodate the needs of the Jewish witnesses as to place the witnesses themselves under a general suspicion of perjury.[24] In a roundabout way, a genuine religious reservation had turned into a political argument that would clearly grow in significance with the advance of modern nationalism.

The *Gedenkblatt* confronted this prejudice with an ingenious collage of illustrations whose sometimes ambiguous elements reveal the overlap between the religious and civic bonds of Prague's upper middle class. That is why the two lions in the frieze can be read both as a symbol of Bohemia and as one of Judaism.[25] In a similar vein, one can make some interpretations of the architecture of the Gothic-style building whose design is modelled on a Torah shrine: just as a non-Jewish observer may have understood the Gothic element as the "epitome of Christian piety" or even read it using national interpretation as "German,"[26] so could a Prague Jew just as easily have seen it as reminiscent of the most significant religious building in his or her community, the city's Old-New Synagogue.

Furthermore, some parts of the lithograph are laid out so as to complement each other: the Hebrew and German citations from Psalm 45,[27] for example, as well as the Austrian emperor's anthem,[28] which are both incorporated into the frieze. They not only symbolize the two relevant strands of loyalty but also depict the two sides indispensable to the relation of loyalty: the

---

[24] For the form of the "more judaico" oath routinely used in Austria, see Israel Taglicht, "Nachlässe der Wiener Juden Teil II. 1786–1848," in *Nachträge zu den zehn bisher erschienen Bänden der Quellen und Forschungen zur Geschichte der Juden in Österreich*, ed. Arthur Goldmann, Israel Taglicht, and Bernhard Wachstein (Vienna: Historische Kommission der israelitischen Kultusgemeinde, 1936), 125–264, here 246.

[25] The lion (Hebrew: *arje*) is regarded as the symbol of Judaism because in the Bible it is equated with the tribe of Judah. (Gen. 49:9). This is also shown in the frequent use of male first names with the meaning "lion," such as Arje Lejb, Jehuda Lejb, or names that derive from it, such as Leopold. Jehuda Feliks, S. David Sperling, and Louis Isaac Rabinowitz, "Lion," in *Encyclopaedia Judaica*, ed. Michael Berenbaum and Fred Skolnik, 2nd ed., vol. 13 (Detroit: Macmillan Reference USA, 2007), 61–63.

[26] Hubertus Günther, "Die Gotik als der europäische Baustil," in *Europäische Erinnerungsorte*, vol. 2, *Das Haus Europa*, ed. Pim den Boer et al. (Munich: Oldenbourg, 2012), 137–50, 147 and 145–46.

[27] On the left-hand side, Psalm 45:7: "Thy throne, O God, is forever and ever. The sceptre of your kingdom is a right sceptre!," and on the right-hand side, Psalm 45:18 [it is incorrectly given as 45:8 on the *Gedenkblatt*]: "I will make thy name to be remembered in all generations: therefore shall the people praise thee for ever and ever."

[28] The opening lines of the emperor's anthem "*Gott erhalte unsern Kaiser! Unsern Kaiser Ferdinand!*" (God Save Our Emperor! Our Emperor Ferdinand!), left and right above the pediment together with a blessing held by an eagle over the middle pediment. "*Heil, Segen und Dank dem Herrscherstamme Österreichs*" (Hail, Blessings and Thanks to the Ruling Dynasty of Austria); these texts are not quoted verbatim, but instead are roughly summarized in the Hebraic inscription above the Thora curtain.

interplay of the person giving his or her loyalty—in this case, Prague's Jewish upper middle class—with the party to whom that loyalty is given—the Austrian imperial house. The translation of the text of Jewish provenance from the original Hebrew into German, the language understood by its intended readers, thus emphasizes the seriousness of the party expressing his loyalty, showing how he wants to make his declaration of attachment to the imperial house intelligible to everyone. At the same time, the citations give the viewer a clear visual image of the close ties of the originator with his Jewish origins. This occurs optically through the presence of Hebraic letters on the *Gedenkblatt* as well as through the use of a decidedly Jewish (and not at all Christian) version of the Psalm. The two verses date back to 1783, when Moses Mendelssohn (1729–1786)[29]—who was considered an icon of German-speaking Judaism by Orthodox Jews and supporters of the Reform Temple alike—published his celebrated translation of the Book of Psalms.

It is precisely this complementary representation of the two separate strands of loyalty, which makes it clear one can reject definitively any purported restriction on the concept of loyalty by virtue of any discrepancy between the declaration of the person conferring his loyalty and his inner attitude. Loyalty represents a phenomenon of long-term commitment, geared towards the future and there would therefore be a wish that the opposite party should acknowledge it accordingly.[30] Far more important than the always controversial question of the authenticity of sources, and particularly of personal testimonies, is a sensitive, combinative reading of them that reflects on the fact that loyalties, unlike situational ethnicity, can indeed be declared separately, but that they do not have to be. An exemplary proof of this fact is a comparative reading of the reception by flower girls of the imperial couple discussed above with the *Gedenkblatt* on the occasion of the abolition of the Bohemian Jewish tax.

Translated by Jaime Hyland.

---

[29] Moses Mendelssohn, trans., *Die Psalmen* (Berlin, 1783).
[30] Schulze Wessel, "'Loyalität' als geschichtlicher Grundbegriff," 2.

Doris Danzer

COMMUNIST INTELLECTUALS IN THE GERMAN DEMOCRATIC REPUBLIC EXPERIENCING CONFLICTS OF LOYALTY

Introduction

We often use the word "friend" as a form of address. It usually sounds intimate, as a term that inspires trust, but often also feels like a cookie cutter. I will never, dear Willi, address you as "dear friend" or begin a letter with the same words—in spite of the fact that we truly are friends. I have no intention of philosophizing, but it will be understood when I say that in a relationship between two comrades who are immutably bound to one another for our whole lives by the Party and by our shared struggle, a strong community in shared struggle develops that can never be tarnished [...]. One always has the unconditional certainty about one another that we will always be true to our class and true to our Party, and will give our all and risk all wherever we are stationed for our great cause. When one knows that about one another, then it is more than friendship that binds us together [...].[1]

This quote is taken from a letter received by Communist author Willi Bredel (1901–1964) from his comrade in the *Sozialistische Einheitspartei Deutschlands* (Socialist Unity Party of Germany, SED), Erich Glückauf (1903–1977), to mark his sixtieth birthday. It was reproduced in a memorial booklet published on the occasion of Bredel's birthday in 1961 by East Berlin publisher, *Aufbau*. In the book we can find further personal dedications to the man in which the various authors—Party officials and fellow writers—congratulated him in a similar manner and at the same time used the opportunity to express their commitment to the Communist Party.

Such declarations of loyalty were part of the repertoire of Communist intellectuals of Willi Bredel's generation, who are considered by historical researchers amongst the founding fathers and mothers of the *Deutsche Demokratische Republik* (German Democratic Republic, GDR).[2] "Friendship," "comradeship," "solidarity," "faith" and "loyalty" were among the terms that frequently came up in such declarations. As is clear from this example, they show not just the especially close emotional relationship between two persons, but also—and indeed more prominently—their connection to the Party.

---

[1] Erich Glückauf, "Brief aus Berlin," in *Willi Bredel: Dokumente seines Lebens*, ed. Willi Bredel (Berlin: Aufbau, 1961), 239–40, here 239.

[2] Annette Leo, "Die Falle der Loyalität: Wolfgang Steinitz und die Generation der DDR-Gründerväter und -mütter," in „*Auch in Deutschland waren wir nicht wirklich zu Hause*": *Jüdische Remigration nach 1945*, ed. Irmela von der Lühe, Axel Schildt, and Stefanie Schüler-Springorium (Göttingen: Wallstein, 2008), 299–312, here 304.

Belonging to the Party is not merely equated to friendship, but superordinated to it.

In these sources, personal friendship is closely connected with the Party. But when one considers the contradictory, sometimes counter-productive processes of development that the *Kommunistische Partei Deutschlands* (Communist Party of Germany, KPD) underwent in the course of its history from its foundation in 1918 to its transformation into the state party, the SED, in 1946 and afterwards, the question needs to be asked how these attitudes affected the intellectual cadres of the Party and the friendships between its members. How did Communist intellectuals bring their social relationships into tune with the changing ideological and practical demands of the Party? When they came up against restrictions, what conflicts were produced and how were they resolved?

These questions can be dealt with in this contribution only rudimentarily through highlighting selected biographical episodes in the lives of individual Communist intellectuals. For this purpose, we have selected in Willi Bredel, publisher Wieland Herzfelde (1896–1988) and author Anna Seghers (1900–1983), three of the founding fathers and mothers of the GDR, all of whom were born around 1900, and all of whose life courses and careers were closely associated with the KPD/SED. Their example can provide a basic stencil to trace out the loyalties maintained by Communist intellectuals of their generation to the Party and the State.

The concept of loyalty can serve as a useful category in analyzing this relationship. It is particularly well adapted to the purposes of this field of research as an analytical category, as it indicates an attitude that lies behind the many-faceted relationships of trust that people voluntarily enter into in the course of their lives in society: for such abstract collectives as nations, ethnic groups or generations as much as for concrete organizations and institutions such as political parties, and for their representatives. In addition to this, the concept of loyalty can be bundled together with what is characterized in the sources in the case concerning us with such politically or morally and emotionally loaded terms as "friendship," "comradeship" or "solidarity." Beyond this, as an analytical category, loyalty also allows one the opportunity to make judgements on the self-image of individuals, to fathom how they gave their loyalty or withheld it at particular moments in their lives.[3]

---

[3] In this regard, compare the following studies on loyalty as a research concept from the field of Eastern European studies: Otto Luchterhandt, *Nationale Minderheiten und Loyalität* (Cologne: Wissenschaft und Politik, 1997), 17–21; Martin Schulze Wessel, "Einleitung: Loyalität als geschichtlicher Grundbegriff und Forschungskonzept," in *Loyalitäten in der Tschechoslowakischen Republik 1918–1938: Politische, nationale und kulturelle Zugehörigkeiten*, ed. Martin Schulze Wessel (Munich: Oldenbourg, 2004), 1–22; and Volker Zimmermann, Peter Haslinger, and Tomáš Nigrin, eds., *Loyalitäten im Staatssozialismus: DDR, Tschechoslowakei, Polen* (Marburg: Verlag Herder-Institut, 2010).

Precisely for research into relationship of intellectuals with communism,[4] which has been a hotly debated topic for almost one hundred years, this approach has proved profitable over the last fifteen years in historical studies on human mental dispositions as illuminated by individual or collective biographies.[5] The authors of such work—who mainly studied Communists of Jewish background who had been politicized and socialized in the Communist movement during the Weimar Republic, had been victims of German fascism, survived exile in the West under difficult conditions and had finally returned to Germany in the second half of the 1940s—revealed in their studies not simply those aspects of loyalty that had a restricting effect on their individuality, but also the side of that concept that tended to reinforce their identity, and were thus able to offer an insight into the motivations of the collective that they were studying. Thus they could plausibly explain why it was that despite the authoritarian style of leadership of the SED government in the late 1940s and 1950s, such people chose to settle in the Eastern part of the country or in Berlin and could not be turned away from their collectively nourished dream of a Socialist German society: This was less because they aspired to power and influence, were ideologically blind[6] or were successfully kept in line by the Party,[7] and more because of the political loyalty and emotional connection they nurtured with their comrades of the same generation in the Party. The quotation given at the opening of this article bears impressive witness of this point.

According to such studies, loyalty had already turned out to be "a trap" by the end of 1956 at the latest, as it became clear that, despite the first official denunciation of the crimes of Stalin at the XX Congress of the *Kommunisticheskaia partiia Sovetskogo Soiuza* (Communist Party of the Soviet Union, KPSS) in February and the reform movements that emerged in Poland and Hungary in the summer, the SED regime would not be pursuing a liberalizing political course.[8] For loyalty's sake, despite their disappointment, the intellectual founding mothers and fathers of the GDR simply accepted uncritically

---

[4] See, for example: Julien Benda, *La trahison des clercs* (Paris: Grasset, 1927); François Furet, *Das Ende der Illusion: Der Kommunismus im 20. Jahrhundert* (Munich: Piper, 1996); and Jens-Fietje Dwars, "Der Intellektuelle verrät sich allemal: Anmerkungen zu einem Kampfbegriff," in *Verrat: Die Arbeiterbewegung zwischen Trauma und Trauer*, ed. Simone Barck and Ulla Plener (Berlin: Dietz, 2009), 317–21.

[5] Leo, "Die Falle der Loyalität," along with Karin Hartewig, *Zurückgekehrt: Die Geschichte der jüdischen Kommunisten in der DDR* (Cologne: Böhlau, 2000), as well as Braun's chapter in support of Leo: Matthias Braun, "Die Loyalitätsfalle der Remigranten," in Braun, *Kulturinsel und Machtinstrument: Die Akademie der Künste, die Partei und die Staatssicherheit* (Göttingen: Vandenhoeck und Ruprecht, 2007), 39–47.

[6] Furet, *Das Ende der Illusion*.

[7] Dieter Schiller, *Disziplinierung der Intelligenz: Die Kulturkonferenz der SED vom Oktober 1957* (Berlin: Gesellschaftswissenschaftliches Forum, 1997).

[8] Hartewig, *Geschichte der jüdischen Kommunisten*, 336, 413, 613; Leo, "Die Falle der Loyalität," 310; and Braun, *Kulturinsel und Machtinstrument*, 39–47.

the fact that the regime was now acting even more severely against all opposition movements and yet further curtailing their own artistic freedom.

However, the fact that this renunciation of intellectual independence first emerges at the end of an individually experienced, sometimes protracted and painful process of recognition that played itself out in the first decade after the foundation of the GDR in my opinion has still not yet received enough emphasis. As individual biographical examples show, intellectuals made multiple attempts in the first decade after the foundation of the GDR to distance themselves from the influence of the Party—even at the level of personal relationships, in the process repeatedly encountering conflicts of loyalty. Their failures in these attempts were accompanied by a gradual process of alienation from the Party. The more the Party curtailed the autonomy of the intellectuals, the more their loyalty to it faded. Subsequently, some moved over into a sort of blind obedience, while others began to search out new loyalties that they could make compatible with their Communist convictions.

The present contribution occupies itself with the latter phenomenon. In this effort we will investigate the relationship of intellectuals with the Party and the State at two levels: at the semantic level, in other words at the level of expressed declarations of loyalty, and at the level of behavior, where we make a differentiation between vertical loyalty (to the Party and the State) and horizontal loyalty (to friends and family). At both of these levels, a contradiction that characterized the relationship of intellectuals to party discipline will become clear.

The Semantic Level

"In the case that a war against the Soviet Union should break out, it is the duty of all honest people to place themselves clearly and decidedly on the side of the Soviet Union, and to defend her with every effort."[9] It was thus that Anna Seghers responded in a questionnaire posed by the International Bureau of Revolutionary Literature (IBRL) to Communist-oriented writers in 1930 to the hypothetical question as to how she would respond to a declaration of war by the so-called imperial powers against the Soviet Union. The survey was carried out in the lead up to the Second International Conference of Proletarian and Revolutionary Writers, which took place in the Soviet town of Kharkov in November of the same year, and to which Seghers had been invited. For a young writer like her, who had only become well known two years previously for her prize-winning stories "Aufstand der Fischer von St. Barbara" (Revolt of the Fishermen of Santa Barbara) and "Grubetsch" and had only then become a member of the KPD, the invitation was an important accolade.

---

[9] *Internationale Presse-Korrespondenz* 10 (1930), cited from Anna Seghers, *Über Kunstwerk und* Wirklichkeit, vol. 3, *Für den Frieden der Welt*, ed. Sigrid Bock (Berlin: Akademie, 1971), 11, 275.

Young intellectuals of her generation who sympathized with the KPD competed keenly for such signals of recognition from the Party. They did so not just with statements in which they expressed their approval of the political course currently followed by the KPD or by taking a clear stance in defense of Soviet interests, but also by attempting to adjust their literary output to the sometimes contradictory requirements of proletarian and revolutionary literature or by reporting favorably on their first travels through the Soviet Union.[10] Through such stances they qualified themselves for prominent roles within the Party, which required in return credible public avowals of loyalty to win attention and votes for themselves. Thus, in the early years of the Party, proofs of loyalty were useful to both sides of the equation, both to the intellectuals and to the Party.

This was to change in the 1930s, as systematic control of members began to be enforced within the KPSS and the KPD in exile in the Soviet Union. The background for these measures was a partially well-grounded and partially vague fear principally felt by the leadership of the KPSS of internal threats, of war and of espionage. Every individual party member was ascribed personal responsibility for success or failure in defending against enemies and exposing traitors. The focus of the activities of party control commissions and the Soviet secret service was concentrated particularly on those people who occupied prominent positions in the Party or in society and who were generally considered particularly loyal. As well as such figures, foreigners—including German officials and intellectuals who had found shelter from the persecution of the *Geheime Staatspolizei* (Secret State Police, Gestapo) in the Soviet Union—were particularly affected by the "Stalinist purges."[11] Intellectuals were now expected to declare their loyalty to both the German and the Soviet Communist Parties and to their leaderships in the course of an already well-established ritual of "self-criticism," in order to exculpate themselves of any suspicion of disloyalty and, more concretely, of espionage in the service of the Gestapo. These declarations were bound to be excessive, since in the context of the time any withdrawal of trust by the Party would mean several years of imprisonment in the GULAG (Glavnoe upravlenie lagerei, Main Camp Administration) or even death to the unfortunate party member. Thus at the time every Communist intellectual was literally risking his or her neck with every word he or she said. In such processes "the ability to withdraw one's

---

[10] For an example of this, see Franz C. Weiskopf, *Umsteigen ins 21. Jahrhundert: Episoden von einer Reise durch die Sowjetunion* (Berlin: Malik, 1927); Egon Erwin Kisch, *Zaren, Popen, Bolschewiken* (Berlin: Reiss, 1927); and compare Eva Oberloskamp, "Geschichtsbild und Identität: Die historische Einordnung der Sowjetunion durch deutsche und französische Linksintellektuelle (1917–1939)," in *Identitäten in Europa: Europäische Identität*, ed. Markus Krienke (Wiesbaden: Deutscher Universitäts-Verlag, 2007), 209–30.

[11] See Karl Schlögel, *Terror und Traum: Moskau 1937* (Bonn: Bundeszentrale für Politische Bildung, 2008), 517.

attention from the personal, and in case of dire need to abandon colleagues and friends to their fate [...] was considered a positive thing for a Comintern [Communist International, D.D.] official."[12]

Under these extreme circumstances, a session of "self-criticism"—in other words, a declaration by a party member on the current political situation and on party discipline before a commission especially convoked for the purpose—set in train a process of alienation from one's own identity and from one's social surroundings, one which left marks on the Communist intellectuals of the GDR from Bredel's generation well into the 1950s and 1960s. They built up a distance from one another, from their social relationships, from their identity as writers and as party members, all of which they later had great difficulty in overcoming. This was also ensured by the checks on SED members that were carried out following a Stalinist model from 1949 on, and by the bullying practiced by party representatives in state institutions in the GDR in the 1950s, which victimized especially party members from intellectual circles who had been in exile outside the Soviet Union, especially in the western hemisphere. If a party member failed this type of loyalty test, he or she was stripped of all political posts and functions in a process that also implied the threat of social isolation and penury. If, however, after a time on probation, purged members would be rewarded for their obedience—as expressed by repeated services to the Party—and be accepted back into its ranks. In such cases of rehabilitation, their loyalty could be corroborated through some sort of symbolic act: for example, in the form of an avowal of loyalty by an accredited member. Thus, Alexander Abusch, journalist and party official—who had lost all his political posts in 1950 as a result of the internal party inquiry in the wake of the Noel Field espionage affair and had offered himself to the *Staatssicherheitsdienst* (State Security, Stasi) as a "secret informant" and in the same year was allowed to return to his cultural and political activities—was once more referred as a "friend" by Johannes R. Becher, a member of the Party's executive committee in the context of a birthday greeting published in the press.[13]

At the same time, the process of alienation produced an inflationary spiral of declarations of loyalty, which breathlessly expressed ecstatic obeisance to Stalin and senior officials close to him, and to the leaders of Eastern European Communist parties. And intellectuals in the GDR played their part in

[12] Alexander Vatlin, "Der Einfluss des Grossen Terrors auf die Mentalität der Komintern-Kader: Erfahrungen und Verhaltensmuster," in *Stalinistische Subjekte: Individuum und System in der Sowjetunion und der Komintern, 1929-1953*, ed. Brigitte Studer and Heiko Haumann (Zurich: Chronos, 2006), 217–32, here 228.

[13] Johannes Becher, "Bildnis eines Freundes: Alexander Abusch zum fünfzigsten Geburtstag," *Aufbau* 2 (1952): 138–44; cf. Hartewig, *Geschichte der jüdischen Kommunisten*, 164. The Party's proceedings against Abusch were discontinued in 1951 and he resumed his cultural and political work. In the same year he committed himself to work as an *Inoffizieller Mitarbeiter* (informal collaborator, IM) for the Stasi.

this. An example of this could be found in a 1963 work of the *Aufbau* publishing house, in which writers, artists, scientists and pedagogues congratulated Walter Ulbricht on his seventieth birthday. It includes an article by Wieland Herzfelde in which he praises Ulbricht's supposed flair for language and literature.[14] Herzfelde's friend, Oskar Maria Graf, however, saw this as "cynical soft-soaping"[15] and considered it grounds for him to end their friendship.[16]

But even party intellectuals saw in this practice of excessive expressions of loyalty the danger that such terms as "friendship," "comradeship" and "loyalty" could lose their plausibility and authenticity. This worry is suggested by the author of this article's opening quotation, and points to the problem of semantics brought on by the amalgamation of private and political friendship in the context of Socialism. It is not just that the term of address "friend" is used with multiple meanings in the rhetoric of parties of the workers' movement and instrumentalized for political purposes, but is being altogether emptied of meaning.[17] It was on this basis that Erich Glückauf came to the conclusion that he should avoid using the expression "friend" when personally addressing his "real" friends.

At the Practical Level

How the loyal attitudes of intellectuals towards the Communist Party or their refusal to give that loyalty was expressed in everyday dealings is sketched out in the section to follow. To do this we bring into focus party intellectuals' social relationships—family relations, friendships and romantic connections, all of which such intellectuals maintained both before and after their entry into the KPD in the 1920s and all through the membership checks made on them by the SED in the 1950s—and examine such ties in the context of their relations with the Party. Because it was at precisely these two points in history

---

[14] Wieland Herzfelde, "In Prag," in *Walter Ulbricht: Schriftsteller, Künstler, Wissenschaftler und Pädagogen zu seinem siebzigsten Geburtstag*, ed. Alexander Abusch and Willi Bredel (Berlin: Aufbau, 1963), 111–12.

[15] "Brief, Oskar Maria Graf an Wieland Herzfelde, 19. Oktober 1963," in *Oskar Maria Graf in seinen Briefen*, ed. Gerhard Bauer and Helmut F. Pfanner (Munich: Süddeutscher Verlag, 1984), 318–19.

[16] Cf. Doris Danzer, "Eine (un-)mögliche Freundschaft," in *Jahrbuch 2011 der Oskar Maria Graf-Gesellschaft*, ed. Ulrich Dittmann and Hans Dollinger (Munich: Allitera, 2011), 105–25.

[17] This harks back to the postulates of fraternity and equality of the French Revolution. It was the general term of address used by like-minded comrades during the process of communitarization that occurred as the workers' movement of the nineteenth century took shape, and had served well under conditions of political repression and exile, and during the splintering off of radicals from the moderate Socialist parties in the twentieth century, as a means of differentiation from political opponents.

where we can most clearly appreciate dislocations between vertical and horizontal loyalties.

When one considers the direct consequences that becoming a member of the KPD had for Anna Seghers, Willi Bredel or Wieland Herzfelde in the 1920s, one can see no radical break with the life habits maintained by any of them up until then, nor with their social relationships at the time. More likely their joining the Party forms part of a process of politicization and socialization in Communist ideas and the Communist environment that had already begun, which was to continue afterwards all the more forcefully. In the process, existing social relationships, or horizontal loyalties, were progressively equated with or subordinated to vertical loyalties, or loyalties to the Party. How this process occurred was still at that time to a large extent dictated by the Communist intellectuals themselves.

Thus Wieland Herzfelde interpreted his work in the Malik publishing house as work for the Party. He had clearly dedicated himself to communism in terms of a range of publications produced by the publisher, which was exclusively made up of progressive, socially critical avant-garde literature. In addition to this, his staff was overwhelmingly made up of members of the KPD, who had either already belonged to the Party before they began working with the publisher or became members in the course of their recruitment to Malik. The decisive influence of Herzfelde on this state of affairs is witnessed not only by some of his colleagues, but also by his friends, family members and the two wives he had been married to during the period.[18] They also belonged to the KPD and were active in the publishing company.[19] In the case of Wieland Herzfelde, social relationships in his professional and private life where thus closely connected with those of the Party.

Something similar can be said of Anna Seghers: she also became a member of the Communist Party after meeting and getting married to László Radványi, the Hungarian Communist revolutionary and academic, in 1924. However, Seghers formally became a member only in 1928, four years after her wedding, in the same year in which she became well known as a writer. Her membership of the Communist Party could be interpreted as a break with her social origins, as Seghers alias Netty Reiling was the daughter of bourgeois Jewish parents from Mainz. But Seghers herself saw no contradiction between her commitment to communism and her bourgeois origins.

---

[18] Doris Danzer, *Zwischen Vertrauen und Verrat: Deutschsprachige kommunistische Intellektuelle und ihre sozialen Beziehungen, 1918–1960* (Göttingen: V&R unipress, 2012), 141–45.

[19] The same applies to Willi Bredel's two wives: His first wife, Lisa, was a member of the Sozialdemokratische Partei Deutschlands (Social Democratic Party of Germany, SPD), but switched to the KPD during the course of her partnership with Willi Bredel. Maj-Ingrid Bredel, his second wife, was already a committed communist and member of the Sveriges Kommunistiska Parti (Communist Party of Sweden, SKP) before she met Willi in the early 1940s in Moscow.

Even after she became a KPD member she maintained her connection with her parents and pursued what could be characterized as bourgeois lifestyle, in which—like many of her Communist comrades—she lived in the more bourgeois neighborhoods in southwest Berlin and employed both household servants and a nanny in order to be able to write literary texts and to engage in party work.[20] She thus attempted to retain her horizontal loyalty to friends and family and her vertical loyalty to the Party after joining up at an equal status in parallel with one another. This is also shown a few years later, when she referred to her "family" in reference not just to her husband and children, but also to the group she belonged to of party writers in exile.[21]

While in the 1920s, at the moment of their first entry into the Party and in the first few years of in it, Herzfelde and Seghers could individually and independently reconcile their existing social and emotional relationships into their membership without breaking with their existing loyalties, by the time of the GDR this was no longer possible. In the SED-run state loyalty to the Party had pre-eminence over everything else, and Party discipline was valued over any individual, personal friendship—a circumstance which intellectuals were hesitant to recognize, thus giving rise to numerous conflicts.

For example, Anna Seghers was able to convince Herta Geffke, chairperson of the special commission charged with investigating the Noel Field affair, in her declarations before the *Zentrale Parteikontrollkommission* (Central Party Control Commission of the Communist Party, ZPKK) on 13 September 1950.[22] Her declaration on the already sentenced officials, Paul Merker and Alexander Abusch squared with the view of the SED. According to this view, Merker and Abusch had, as leaders of the KPD group in exile in Mexico in the 1940s, broken away from the official party line and acted without official authority. For this reason, Seghers had come into conflict in Mexico, especially with Merker. When questioned on her acquaintance with Noel Field, the alleged spy, she told the committee that it had been limited to two encounters in Prague in the years 1947 and 1948 and said nothing at all about the fact that good friends of hers—namely the couple Egon Erwin und Gisela Kisch—not only knew Field very well, but had also introduced him to her. Seghers' tactic of merely confirming what the party leadership already knew or what it wanted to hear, and to remain silent on anything that might be damaging to herself or her friends, turned out to be a clever one: in the years to follow, she was to receive only excellent reports in political evaluations of

---

[20] Christiane Zehl Romero, *Anna Seghers: Eine Biographie 1900–1947* (Berlin: Aufbau, 2000), 194–96.
[21] Danzer, *Zwischen Vertrauen und Verrat*, 259.
[22] See the minutes of the interrogations by the ZPKK on Noel H. Field: "Aktennotiz, Herta Geffke, Berlin, 13. September 1950," 59, Sign. DY 30/IV 2/4/112, France-Mexico, L-Z, Stiftung Archiv der Parteien und Massenorganisationen der DDR im Bundesarchiv (hereafter SAPMO-BArch).

her,[23] which was to allow her to make her way to the very heights in the world of literature in the GDR.[24]

However, both her own experience as a witness before the ZPKK and her ring-seat view of how colleagues and comrades lost their political position in the course of internal Party checks and had to fear for their very existence left a substantial mark on the way she conducted herself. Thus Seghers remained silent on her Jewish heritage in the SED questionnaires she responded to in the early 1950s on her personal history, at a time when contemporary processes against alleged Zionist conspiracies were being conducted in the Soviet Union and other countries of Eastern Europe. In the fall of 1950, she fended of the repeated demands of the Party to move from West to East Berlin and to renounce her Mexican citizenship in favor of citizenship of the GDR.[25] She was later to write *Der Mann und sein Name* (The Man and His Name), her 1952 novel in which she dealt with the Noel Field affair and its consequences for trust among comrades, whose first edition was dedicated to Stalin-loyalist Mátyás Rákosi. Anna Seghers was intimidated by the internal party checks and had made the decision to submit to the SED's demands, and her subsequent attempts to free herself from them were to prove unsuccessful.

Willi Bredel followed a similar strategy in the face of the process against publisher Walter Janka of the *Aufbau* publishing house, with whom he felt a bond through their shared experiences in the Spanish Civil War. After the arrest of the latter at the end of 1956, Bredel intervened personally with Walter Ulbricht on his behalf.[26] For this reason in early 1957 the *Ministerium für Staatssicherheit* (Ministry for State Security, MfS) began monitoring not only his telephone conversations with Janka's wife Charlotte, but also his reactions as he sat on the witness bench beside Anna Seghers, Bodo Uhse and Helene Weigel during the process against Janka before the *Oberstes Gericht der DDR* (Supreme Court of the GDR, OG) in summer of the same year.[27] But, like all the other intellectuals of his generation, Bredel remained silent during the trial. In addition, during the thirty-third session of the Central Committee of the SED in October 1957 as part of an act of "self-criticism", he was forced to recognize being disappointed in his friend Janka.[28] That Bredel was acting against his will, however, in order to demonstrate his loyalty to the Party in

---

[23] See cadre files on Anna Seghers: "Beurteilung, Joachim Mückenberger, Berlin", 11 March 1954, 43 Sign. DY 30/IV 2/11/ v. 3154, SAPMO-BArch.

[24] In 1951 she was awarded the Stalin Peace Prize, and in 1952 she was appointed president of Deutscher Schriftstellerverband (Writers' Association of the GDR, DSV).

[25] See cadre files on Anna Seghers, 14, 20, Sign. DY 30/IV 2/11/ v. 3154, SAPMO-BArch; cf. Zehl Romero, *Anna Seghers*, 96–97.

[26] Rolf Richter, *Willi Bredel: Ein deutscher Weg im 20. Jahrhundert* (Rostock: Neuer Hochschul-Schriften-Verlag, 1998), 110.

[27] Walter Janka, *Die Unterwerfung: Eine Kriminalgeschichte aus der Nachkriegszeit*, ed. Günter Kunert and Günter Netzeband (Munich: Hanser, 1994), 121, 137.

[28] Richter, *Willi Bredel*, 110.

public is demonstrated by his conduct after Janka's release in December 1960. Though Janka had then not yet been rehabilitated, Bredel did not distance himself from him as was usual in such cases, but invited him and his wife to have dinner at his house.[29]

As will be clear from this example, intellectuals of the generation of Bredel and Seghers were forced into a balancing act in the early years of the GDR in order to be true both to their promises of loyalty to the Party and to their friends. This can be seen in their ambivalent, sometimes contradictory conduct. However, they were ultimately to fail in their efforts and were forced to submit to the Party's diktat if they wished to remain members and did not want to dispense with the ideal and material privileges that they, as members of the cultural elite of the GDR, were granted by the SED leadership.

In Place of a Summary: An Outlook

Something that remains as yet missing from this contribution to the topic of the relations of loyalty of Communist intellectuals and which unfortunately cannot be provided within its remit is a treatment of the topic on a geographical plane; that is to say on the plane of the nation state and international and transnational relationships. In particular for the social circle selected for this work such a perspective could yield useful insights, since intellectuals of the generation of Bredel, Herzfelde and Seghers had operated in an international context since the period in exile forced on them by National Socialist persecution from 1933 on. Although most of them remained rooted in the world of the German language due to their chosen professions, and though their political work was almost entirely directed towards the question of how Germany should be shaped after the war, they had inevitably distanced themselves from German reality in the course of their exile in Europe and elsewhere. But that they could no longer gauge precisely the real living conditions and mentalities of the German population was to become clear to most of them only when they finally returned to a Germany physically and morally destroyed by the twelve years of Nazi dictatorship. Especially intellectuals of Jewish heritage like Anna Seghers feared and felt the continuing anti-Semitism in the country and regarded the German people with suspicion, maintaining a critical distance from them.

Among the Communist intellectuals of their generation, a process of alienation affected them not only at a political level but also in terms of national identity, particularly for returnees from the Western Hemisphere—from Great Britain, Sweden, the USA or Mexico. Their return to Germany and to the Soviet Occupation Zone was approved too late for them to be in a position to take up leadership positions in the state and party apparatus. Such

---

[29] Walter Janka, *Spuren eines Lebens* (Reinbek bei Hamburg: Rowohlt, 1992), 446.

posts had already been taken up by comrades who had spent their exile in the Soviet Union. Added to this were the internal party checks of the SED, along with the reprimands and expulsions that they brought with them, as well as the continuing bullying and disciplinary measures taken routinely by party representatives. And finally, the worldly sophistication of that emigrant generation in the GDR of the 1950s was stigmatized as "cosmopolitanism" and marginalized from the foundational narrative of the GDR.[30] Thus, the long-cherished hopes of this collective during their exile to be able to participate in the development of socialism in Germany were bitterly disappointed.

These experiences provided the background for Herzfelde, Seghers and their contemporaries to begin to tie together their experiences and contacts in European and non-European exile and to turn them to use in the creation of a network of Communist intellectuals, particularly in the Socialist countries of Eastern Europe. Thus it can be seen that Anna Seghers attempted to respond to the feeling of "coldness" and rootlessness that she felt on her return to Berlin in 1947 with continued travel—whether to family members and friends or to congresses of Socialist writers or to the world peace movement. She celebrated her fiftieth birthday, for example, at the Second World Peace Congress in Warsaw.[31]

Similar examples can be effortlessly listed out for Seghers' fellow intellectuals. Any profound analysis of the international context within which the intellectuals of the GDR moved would seem potentially profitable in particular in response to the question of what loyalties they felt themselves bound to in this regard. Did they develop new, transnational loyalties through their activities in both informal and institutional networks in and around such organizations as the World Peace Council, the International Center of Poets, Essayists and Novelists (PEN) or the Socialist Writers' Congresses? And what happened to those loyalties when the system of what became known as the Eastern Block began to disintegrate? Precisely this dimension of loyalty deserves to be given further attention in the context of the study of Communist intellectuals.

Translated by Jaime Hyland.

---

[30] Leo, "Die Falle der Loyalität," 306.
[31] Zehl Romero, *Anna Seghers*, 109.

Heléna Tóth

FROM CONTENT TO RITUAL
Name-Giving Practices and Political Loyalty in Hungary (1880–1989)

Political loyalties tend to be generated and cultivated in times of peace as much as in times of crisis. Rites of passage occupy a special position in the processes involved. Although political loyalties usually become most apparent during times of upheaval, and although they are often produced by events involving sacrifice and through situations in which people are forced to make choices between competing loyalties (between family and political party, for example), actors and political systems manifest and cultivate emotional connections between the individual and the wider political community in times of relative stability too.

Rites of passage appear at the intersection between the public and the private spheres. Baptisms, weddings and funerals are private matters endowed with social significance, a fact which loads them with political potential. In addition to their place of mediation between individuals and various layers of social organization, rites of passage have another feature that makes them a potential political resource: they are events in which emotional ties between individuals and the community (the family, religious and political groups and, ultimately, society at large) are both manifested and shaped. Broadly speaking therefore, rites of passage are relevant to the generation and expression of political loyalty in two ways. Firstly, to build on the argument of Theodore Kemper, one might suggest that every rite of passage must constitute an imprint of broader power relations if it is to be effective as a ritual.[1] Secondly, following James Connor, one might argue that the feeling of loyalty is an emotion produced by and existing in interaction with other emotions.[2]

The political relevance of rites of passage is perhaps most immediately obvious in widely publicized, large-scale, symbolic events such as state-sponsored funerals for example, in which the political community is staged as a "ritual community."[3] However, this paper takes a different perspective, focusing rather on the rites of passage celebrated in the course of the bio-

---

[1] Theodore D. Kemper, *Status, Power and Ritual Interaction: A Relational Reading of Durkheim, Goffman and Collins* (Farnham: Ashgate, 2011), 2–4.
[2] James Connor, *The Sociology of Loyalty* (New York: Springer, 2007), 41–5.
[3] Katherine Verdery, *The Political Lives of Dead Bodies: Reburial and Postsocialist Change* (New York: Columbia University Press, 1999).

graphies of ordinary people. Through an analysis of name changes, baptism and of socialist name-giving ceremonies in Hungary from the end of the nineteenth century right through to the 1980s, the paper shows that naming practices during the period played an instrumental role in relation to the creation and cultivation of political loyalty in *three different ways*.

First, names and name-giving practices were used as a vehicle by ordinary people to express their belonging to the political community. The particular way in which this occurred depended on contemporary definitions of the body politic and changed over time. Up until the end of the Second World War markers of national and (by association) ethnic belonging played a central role in drawing out the boundaries of political communities, and hence the form and content of naming choices played a key role as visible markers of ethnic origins, and of the political loyalties implied by those origins. The establishment of the communist regime in Hungary changed the criteria for membership of the political community: class origins and the commitment to the communist ideology became the markers of (assumed) political reliability. As we shall see, during the communist era ordinary people demonstrated their loyalty to the regime not through their choice of names but through the rituals they used in name-giving.

Second, names and name-giving practices were an arena in which conflicting loyalties were manifested and could often be reconciled. This role became particularly important after the Second World War, when the relationship between state and church was completely severed. The changing relationship between the coalition government and the churches between 1945 and 1949, and between the communist regime and the churches after the founding of the Magyar Népköztársaság (People's Republic of Hungary) in 1949 reveals the extent to which the state considered participation in church rites (including baptism) as a sign of political unreliability. The introduction of a range of specifically socialist rites of passage from 1958 on brought a new dynamic into this state of affairs—a dynamic that was to have unintended consequences. In discussions on the choice between various rites, the everyday lives of ordinary people gave concrete shape to what contemporaries often referred to as the competition between world views.

Although the concrete forms in which names and name-giving practices were endowed with political relevance changed radically from the last couple of decades of the dual monarchy to the 1980s in Hungary, those forms had a common denominator throughout the period: i.e. that governments treated statistics on name changes, baptisms and, later, socialist name-giving ceremonies as indicators of the strength of political loyalties among the population in general. Thus the Hungarian government considered the large number of name changes that occurred at the end of the nineteenth century (during which time citizens in the Hungarian half of the dual monarchy frequently changed their "foreign sounding" family names to more Hungarian ones) as proof that efforts to shape the public sphere of this multiethnic state into a specifically Hungarian national project were bearing fruit. Similarly, propagandists for the Magyar Szocialista Munkáspárt (Hungarian Socialist Workers' Party, MSzMP) much later read with consternation the statistics on low rates of participation in Socialist name-giving ceremonies in the 1960s as an indicator for a low level of support among the population for the Socialist way of life.[4] In other words, various political regimes believed that statistics on name-giving and naming practices provided a quantitative measure of the willingness of the population to commit to specific albeit very different political agendas, whether defined in national terms or based on Socialist humanism. It should be said that the correlation between names and actual political loyalties was significantly more complicated than the statistics could suggest. Nonetheless, the fact that the statistics were in fact read in this way could be considered the third way in which names and name-giving practices of ordinary people had direct relevance to the ways in which political loyalty was manifested and understood.

These three connections between practices of name-giving and political loyalties provide the basis for the two main arguments of the paper. First, that as the criteria for assessing political loyalties shifted over time from an ethnic-national understanding of the political community to one based on class (and on personal world view), the ritual form of name-giving practices gradually became more important than the actual content and form of the name as a marker of political loyalty. Second, that in the competition between world views, the introduction of specifically Socialist rites of passage inadvertently left behind liabilities. The introduction of Socialist name-giving ceremonies provided a specific measurable marker of the popular appeal of the Socialist way of life, showing up its popular weaknesses against what might be called the "religious world view," but also against those who remained indifferent to either stance.

From Assimilationism to Ritual Structures: Names and Name-Giving as Expressions of Political Loyalty in Hungary from the 1880s to the End of the Second World War

Nomen atque omen wrote Plautus in *The Persians* in the second century BC, meaning that one's name determined one's fate. At the end of the nineteenth century, while family names did not perhaps define one's entire fate in the

---

[4] Members of the *Állami Egyházügyi Hivatal* (State Office of Church Affairs understood Socialist rites of passage as a key weapon in the struggle against the "religious ideology," a struggle they considered "objectively necessary in a Socialist society." ("Szakmai továbbképzés az Állami Egyházügyi Hivatal dolgozói részére") [Program for the Advanced Training of the Members of the State Office of Church Affairs], 1974, XIX A. 21 e.t-00010-1/c-1974, Magyar Országos Levéltár [Hungarian State Archives] (hereafter MOL).

Hungarian half of the Austro-Hungarian Empire, they did definitively demarcate one's career chances in the Kingdom of Hungary. Hungary was a multiethnic state in which 46.6 % of the population reported Hungarian as their mother tongue in the 1886 census. Although mother tongue does not always equate to ethnicity, it was used by bureaucrats as an indicator to measure the relative size of ethnic groups. Besides Hungarians, the Kingdom's larger ethnic groups included Rumanians, Germans, Slovaks and a sizeable Jewish community. According to the 1868 Hungarian law on nationalities, all these groups together politically constituted "a single nation, the indivisible, unitary Hungarian nation."[5] The public sphere, including the bureaucracy and educational institutions, reflected this concept of the indivisibility of the nation in a way that occluded the multiethnic reality of the body politic, however: full effective membership in the Hungarian nation ultimately meant adopting the Hungarian language, and very often a Hungarian family name along with it.

As Viktor Karády and István Kozma argue in *Név és Nemzet* (Name and Nation), the so-called Magyarization of foreign sounding family names took place mostly without any direct pressure having to be exerted.[6] It resulted either from the self-definition of applicants as "Hungarian" regardless of their ethnic origins or out of hopes of social mobility that applicants intended to secure by fitting in with the dominant grouping within the political culture.[7] Name changes were primarily an urban phenomenon and were closely associated with industrialization and the level of education. Most ethnic groups living in the Kingdom were represented among applicants for changes of name, but members of the Jewish community accounted for the overwhelming majority. For the "Magyars of the Mosaic persuasion" changing the family name was part of an unofficial "contract of assimilation," that had existed between the liberal nobility and reform Judaism since the beginning of the nineteenth century, and that promised Jews political membership in the nation in exchange for religious reforms and their adoption of the Hungarian language.[8] Whether the motivations behind name changes were primarily to express belonging to the Hungarian nation or to further career chances in the Hungarian-dominated public sphere, the act of changing one's name was an investment into the political *status quo*.

---

[5] László Péter, *Hungary's Long Nineteenth Century: Constitutional and Democratic Traditions in a European Perspective; Collected Studies* (Leiden: Brill, 2012), 344–74.

[6] Viktor Karády and István Kozma, *Név és nemzet: családnév-változtatás, névpolitika és nemzetiségi erőviszonyok Magyarországon a feudalizmustól a kommunizmusig* (Budapest: Osiris, 2002).

[7] Ibid., 50. This fascinating and meticulously researched study is a seminal work on this topic and this following section, in particular the statistical data, heavily relies on the work of Karády and Kozma.

[8] Ibid., 52.

Although applications for change of name that were made throughout the nineteenth century were generally granted, it was only in the 1880s that the government began to actively make a systematic effort to encourage the phenomenon. Preparations for the celebration of the millennium of the foundation of the Hungarian state in 1896, along with efforts to speed up ethnic acculturation within the Kingdom of Hungary, created an atmosphere in which name changing enjoyed broad political support. From this point on the "Magyarization" of family names began to be imbued "clearly and consciously with political intentions to accentuate the image of the Hungarian nation state, and to strengthen the Hungarian character of society."[9] Name changing became cheaper and easier; a number of organizations were founded to promote name changing, and pressure to change one's family name increased on groups that the government could influence directly—most prominently people in the civil service.[10] As a result of these concentrated efforts, the number of name changes rose rapidly in the 1880s, slowing down thereafter—but nonetheless remaining a substantial phenomenon until the First World War.

In the aftermath of the First World War, the basic background conditions in which people changed their family names were transformed radically. New reasons emerged to exchange foreign sounding family names for Hungarian ones. On top of this, the state created a new set of incentives to encourage such choices. With the dissolution of the Austro-Hungarian Empire, the Kingdom of Hungary lost significant parts of its territory. In the newly-created Hungarian state, 89.6 % of the population identified Hungarian as their mother tongue in 1920 and over 70 % of those whose primary language was different were also able to speak Hungarian.[11] Campaigns in the 1930s in favor of the Magyarization of family names therefore took what was then seen as a discrepancy as their starting point: although the language of the country was now predominantly Hungarian, many family names still reflected the multi-ethnic history of the state. The government tried to remedy this situation by committing to a campaign to encourage citizens of the Hungarian state to shed foreign sounding family names. This campaign differed from earlier initiatives in one significant point. While in the nineteenth century it was often debated whether Jews should be allowed the opportunity to gain full membership in the Hungarian political nation through assimilation, the policy in relation to name changing remained liberal. This was not the case from the 1930s onwards. Although the main goal of the government was generally to eradicate the traces of the country's multiethnic historical past, racial laws made changing the "Jewish-sounding" names of converted Jews more difficult. Beginning in 1938 it was outright prohibited for Jews who had

[9] Ibid., 50.
[10] Ibid., 65.
[11] Ibid., 115–6.

not already converted to Christianity at the time of application to change their names.¹²

With the collapse of the fascist regime in Hungary and the end of the Second World War, the prohibition on Jews changing their names ended. Many of the Jews who had survived deportation and other forms of persecution during the Second World War took the opportunity to change their family names, in part out of fear of further persecution and also as a "reaction to the trauma of persecution."¹³ Many Jews who could imagine living in Hungary even after the traumatic experiences of the 1930s and 1940s wanted to erase one of the markers that had made them recognizable as Jews and thus vulnerable. Aside from the Jews, the second large group among the applicants for a Hungarian sounding family name after the Second World War also saw their future to lie in Hungary and changed their names to remove a vulnerability, but for a different reason. This group was made up of ethnic Germans who considered themselves Hungarian and were trying to avoid forced relocation to Germany. All in all, the numbers seeking to change their surnames in the period after 1945 quickly reached the sort of figures they had seen before the First World War.¹⁴

Political loyalty played a central role in applications for name changes in the immediate postwar years. In 1945–6 more than half of the applicants gave "national sentiment" as a reason for their wish to change their family name. In the year 1945, 53.2 % of petitioners identified their motivation as including the desire to explicitly state their belonging to the Hungarian nation.¹⁵ Another rationale frequently given for name change included "family reasons" (27.2 %) and "repudiation of the ethnic implications expressed by the name" (27.2 %). Family reasons was a very broad category: it could express, amongst many other things, a desire to dissociate oneself from a politically compromised family member or to make one's name match that of another family member who had already Magyarized his or her name in the past. The "repudiation of the ethnic implications" of an existing name could stand for a similarly broad category of motivations, including the desire not to be attached to names consisting of the word for a particular ethnic group, such as *zsidó* (Jew) or which evoked associations with a particular ethnic group. The exact contours of the emerging political landscape had yet to form in 1945 but those who changed their family names were making a commitment to a future in the state of Hungary, a country in which they believed that the topic of nationality would continue to play an important role.

---

¹² Ibid., 146.
¹³ Ibid., 275.
¹⁴ Ibid., 269.
¹⁵ The petitioners were allowed to give more than one reason in their applications. Ibid., 290.

From Content to Ritual 185

While the motivational category "national sentiment" could also mean very different things for different applicants, the otherwise malleable concept was endowed by the authorities with specific content during the evaluation of applications. Since the nineteenth century the name changing process was ultimately a bureaucratic affair involving no separate parallel ritual: applications and their assessment were tasks assigned to the Belügyminisztérium (Ministry of Internal Affairs). For members of the Jewish community, changing the family name was often just one assimilation strategy among many, including conversion to Christianity. However, even for them, the name change itself was essentially a bureaucratic act carried out by state authorities. In the aftermath of the Second World War, however, this bureaucratic aspect of each application was endowed with a direct connection to systems of loyalty. Several new elements were added to the application process. Not only was the applicant required to get a certificate of good conduct from the police to show that they (1) did not have a criminal record and (2) had not been significantly involved in the Hungarian fascist movement. They also had to be able to present a personal recommendation from one of the parties of the postwar government to certify their political reliability and loyalty.[16] What this meant was that the suitability of the applicant had to be vouched for by one of the political parties of the coalition government, which consisted of the Magyar Kommunista Párt (Hungarian Communist Party, MKP), the Szociáldemokrata Párt (Social Democratic Party, SZDP), the Nemzeti Parasztpárt (National Peasant Party, NPP), the Polgári Demokrata Párt (Civic Democratic Party, PDP), the Független Kisgazdapárt (Independent Smallholders' Party, FKgP), or the Magyar Radikális Párt (Hungarian Radical Party, MRP—which, despite its name, was effectively a liberal conservative party). The political programs defended by these parties covered a broad spectrum. The Hungary of the future as imagined by a member of the Independent Smallholders' Party was likely to differ significantly from anyone whose credibility as an applicant for name change was certified by the Hungarian Communist Party. This meant two things: First, when applicants identified "national sentiment" as the main reason for their change of name, the *aggregate* of their applications mirrored the broad political make-up of the postwar government, but also limited possible interpretations of the concept of loyalty to the spectrum of political positions that were consensually accepted as legitimate from 1945 on. Second, at the same time, *individually,* each application was embedded into systems of loyalty to a specific party and could therefore be linked to a specific political agenda. Overall, the previously purely bureaucratic process of changing one's surname had thus become politicized in a new way, as the process was now effectively connected with an extensive investigation into each applicant's past and present. The name change was now

---

[16] Ibid., 280, 284.

not only the promise of loyalty it had always been, but was also the product of already existing loyalties.

The spectrum of acceptable political positions quickly became more restricted in postwar Hungary. By 1947 the Independent Smallholders' Party (the strongest of the postwar parties) was broken up and significantly weakened. Then, in the summer of 1948, the Hungarian Communist Party eliminated the Social Democratic Party through creating an alliance with them, forming the Magyar Dolgozók Pártja (Hungarian Workers' Party, MDP) and in August 1949, the newly formed party presided over the birth of the People's Republic of Hungary. While the practice of changing foreign sounding family names to Hungarian ones continued in this new political atmosphere, it did so at a significantly lower intensity and under an entirely different rationale. Thus, in the period between 1951 and 1956 the three most common reasons given for a name change were "family reasons" (41.4 %), "clarifying the legal status of a name one already has" (30.7 %), and "aesthetic considerations" (25.1 %). An explicit reference to "national sentiment" occurred in a mere 12.5 % of the petitions, and showed a declining trend (1951: 19.8 %, 1954: 10.9 %, 1956: 10.9 %).[17] The reason for this was that in the newly emerging political structure, the markers of loyalty had changed. As Karády and Kozma argue, the definition of political loyalty after 1948 was no longer primarily based on the traditional appeal to nationalism/nationality. Considerations of class and signposts signaling adherence to the correct "world view" now had at least as much weight in assessments of political reliability than considerations of ethnicity or variety of nationalism based on ethnicity. In the 1950s, "the act of changing of one's family name became an increasingly private affair. Although the act continued to be regulated by the state, which registered such name changes in the civil registry, the state's only involvement was as the regulating and registering body."[18]

As we shall see in the section to follow, even in the immediate aftermath of the Second World War, the ritual side of name-giving was already gradually becoming a more important signifier of political loyalty than the form or the content of an individual's name. Before looking at this shift in detail, we need to add a qualification to this argument. First, the stronger emphasis now put on the ritual side of name-giving as an expression of political identity did not mean that the "content" of names had lost their significance altogether. Unfortunately, there has as yet been no study written on the distribution of *forenames* after the Second World War, but there is plenty of anecdotal evidence for their continued symbolic importance. Mátyás Rákosi, the first secretary of the Hungarian Communist Party and later general secretary of the Hungarian Workers' Party, recalled in his memoirs that on his tours across Hungary in the late 1940s he was often asked to meet children who were

[17] Ibid., 342.
[18] Ibid., 353.

called Mátyás, his hosts implying that there was somehow a special connection between him and the population at large through these namesakes. As Rákosi writes in his memoirs about one such visit to the countryside:

[It was] as if I had been attending a happy village fair. There was no end to toasts, I had to taste the various hams and sausages, I received hundreds of invitations and I had to pet at least 10 little children called Mátyás on the head, who were christened after me [sic! "akiket rólam kereszteltek el"] and [whose parents] now seized the chance to show them to me.[19]

The significance of this small, symbolic act is not diminished by the fact that it would be difficult to extrapolate anything more generally from the meaning of the name Mátyás in Hungary of the 1940s and 1950s. Unlike the cases where work brigades asked Rákosi, "our wise leader," for official permission to bear his full name "Brigade Mátyás Rákosi," the decision to call a child Mátyás might have any of a great many different motivations, including but not limited to referencing Matthias Corvinus, a popular Hungarian king from the fifteenth century, stories about whom had become part of Hungarian folklore. In addition to direct references to Rákosi himself, there is anecdotal evidence to suggest that members of the Hungarian Communist Party were thinking more broadly about naming practices as the expression of a particular social order. For example, when the son of the minister of foreign affairs of the Hungarian People's Republic, László Rajk, was born in 1949, Rajk discussed long the name of the child with his wife. In the end, they settled for László, although Rajk had misgivings about giving his son the same name as his own, as he considered the practice feudal.[20]

Connecting the Leader to the Family: Mátyás Rákosi, the Godfather Who Receded out of Reach

After the end of the Second World War, the rituals surrounding name-giving gradually became more important markers of political loyalty than the content and the form of the names given during such rituals. The history of rites of passage as *loci* for the expression of political loyalty can be divided into two phases for the period from 1945 to 1989, with the introduction of a specifically Socialist rites of passage in 1958–9 serving as the *caesura* between the two phases. The first phase can be further subdivided into two halves: the time before and after the establishment of the one-party system. The relationship between political loyalty and rites of passage had its own specific dynamic in each of these phases.

---

[19] Mátyás Rákosi, *Visszaemlékezések, 1945-1956* (Budapest: Napvilág, 1997), vol. 2, 736. Rákosi also points out that, initially, these children received a present from him but that this practice was soon ended.
[20] Andrea Pető, *Rajk Júlia* (Budapest: Balassi, 2001), 79.

In the aftermath of the Second World War, rites of passage almost automatically became politicized. In the newly-established Republic of Hungary, the public presence of religion and of the institutional churches was severely restricted. Churches lost their land holdings during the land reform of 1945, losing other properties, including schools, hospitals and charitable establishments, quickly afterwards. Although the first postwar government in Hungary was based on a coalition of parties not all of which were directly hostile to the churches or religion in general, the Hungarian Communist Party was in a powerful enough position to put most of its radical propositions through. This resulted from the fact that although the Hungarian Communist Party received a mere 17 % of the votes in the first postwar elections, it had received key positions in the new government, including the Ministry of Interior, as a result of pressure from the Soviet Union.

Communist ideology had a clearly formulated position towards religion. According to Marxist theory, religion was seen as a system which would eventually disappear, though at the time the Hungarian Communist Party considered it a dangerous enemy on two counts: both as an institution and also as a way of viewing the world. Baptism therefore almost automatically became a political matter as the Hungarian Communist Party began to accumulate political influence. Whether or not one baptized a child became a political statement. Prior to the introduction of a specifically socialist rites of passage, citizens of the new Hungarian Republic could indicate political leanings by baptizing their children (or choosing not to do so). When one considers that in the immediate aftermath of the Second World War over 90 % of the population was baptized, the symbolic gesture of choosing not to baptize a child carried weight, even if the gesture constituted merely the absence of a ritual rather than any positive affirmative act.[21]

The second way ordinary people could demonstrate political loyalty to the Hungarian Communist Party was to invite leading members of the party to stand as godparents for their children, thus adding a new layer of meaning to the religious rite of passage. Such practices were not new. Even before the Second World War there was an established tradition of endowing the baptism ritual with political content. Miklós Horthy, regent of the Kingdom of Hungary in the interwar period, or Ferenc Szálasi, head of the Nyilaskeresztes Párt (Arrow Cross Party) in the 1940s, were often invited to become godfathers for the children of ordinary citizens. In some rare cases, a number of these historical figures stood as godfathers for consecutive children within the same family, establishing an immediate connection between various layers of Hungarian history and the history of the relevant family.[22] A broad range of motivations might have been behind inviting a politically prominent

---

[21] Ignác Romsics, *Magyarország története a XX. században* (Budapest: Osiris, 2001), 318.
[22] András Kő and Lambert J. Nagy, eds., *Levelek Rákosihoz* (Budapest: Maecenas, 2002), 19–20.

figure to become godfather to a child aside from any actual expression of political loyalty, including pure opportunism (in the expectation of receiving a valuable gift for the child). This long-established practice continued after the Second World War, but the fact that the new pool of desirable godfathers included the top echelons of the Hungarian Communist Party indicated a fundamental change in the dynamics of such politicized baptisms.

In the immediate postwar years, the Hungarian Communist Party invested its energies primarily in fighting the church as an institution and less directly on attacking the idea of religion in itself. When it came to making a public presence at religious rites of passage, initially at least, Mátyás Rákosi showed a degree of flexibility. Like a number of other prominent political figures, Rákosi accepted several invitations to stand as godfather for children and also attended a number of politically important religious funerals between 1945 and 1949 (this was the period during which Rákosi was starting to build his public persona but before the official establishment of the Hungarian People's Republic). The flexibility he showed in this regard was a relatively small compromise he was willing to make for as long as the Hungarian Communist Party was forced to share power with other parties after the war. It is certainly no coincidence that the only photograph taken of Rákosi by the Magyar Távirati Iroda (Hungarian Press Agency, MTI) showing him in his capacity as godfather dates from 1945.

Fig. 1: "Budapest September 1945. Mátyás Rákosi (third from the left), the first secretary of the Hungarian Communist Party (MKP) as godfather with his godchild (third [child] from the left), among women and children." (Foto: © Magyar Távirati Iroda, MTI). Interestingly, the man on the right, presumably one of the husbands, was not included in the title.

It is difficult to tell exactly what ordinary people expected from this relationship. The motivations behind such hybridized rituals ran a wide gamut. It is probably safe to say that no Hungarian family that invited Rákosi to be the godfather of their children actually expected him to join the family circle regularly for Sunday lunch. They did, however, generally expect to receive a gift of one sort or another, and they were usually right. In addition, and perhaps even more importantly, when Rákosi accepted such an invitation, it created an illusion of some sort of reciprocity. In the years after the baptism ceremony, the families of his godchildren wrote to him frequently on various grievances (mostly to do with difficulties at work or with financial problems) and always began their letters with a reference to the family bond. Historian Balázs Apor argues convincingly that the dissemination of Rákosi's biographical details played a key role in the establishment of a communist cult of personality in Hungary.[23] When families invited Rákosi to stand as godfather to their children, what they intended by the act was to link their own biographies with that of someone who embodied the political power of the state. The invitation was a symbolic gesture, as was the act of accepting that invitation. In some cases, no doubt, rites thus hybridized served as a way to reconcile conflicting loyalties. Although the Hungarian Communist Party was in general extremely uncomfortable with some of its members being religious, the fact remains that some of them indeed were. "To be honest, it is a very difficult thought that the child will not be baptized," a devoted communist woman wrote to Rákosi, asking "to what extent would I be sinning against the party and democracy if I had the child baptized despite disapproval?"[24] The act of inviting Rákosi to participate in the ritual solved this problem at least to some degree from the point of view of the parents of the child.

From the point of view of the church, however, this was anything but a satisfactory solution to such conflicts of loyalties. The political use of godparenthood was not a new phenomenon in Hungary, but the long-established practice took on an entirely new dynamic when Mátyás Rákosi was the figure being invited to participate in a baptism. Such political leaders of the past as Miklós Horthy and Ferenc Szálasi were also absent political participants in baptisms, but the latter two figures were either closely linked or at least not in direct opposition to a Christian understanding of the body politic. Such figures were therefore, from the point of view of the ritual itself, acceptable participants in a baptism. In contrast, not only was Mátyás Rákosi not a Christian (he came from a Jewish family), he also represented an ideology which was clearly, openly and militantly atheistic. Therefore, every baptism actually performed in which Rákosi stood as godfather could be considered to be a

---

[23] Balázs Apor, "Leader in the Making: The Role of Biographies in Constructing the Cult of Rákosi," in *The Leader Cult in Communist Dictatorships: Stalin and the Eastern Bloc*, ed. Balázs Apor (Basingstoke: Palgrave Macmillan, 2004), 63–82.
[24] Letter with no date, printed in Kő and Nagy, eds., *Levelek Rákosihoz*, 23.

reflection of the peculiar power relations between the churches and the state after the war. It was clearly not a relationship between equals.

The full extent of the implicit political pressure on priests to perform such rituals expressed itself visibly when a priest refused to do so. One such example can be found in Gergely Cserháti, a Catholic priest from the small municipality Bácsbokod. In the summer of 1947 Cserháti refused the request of a local family to baptize their eleventh child with Mátyás Rákosi standing as godfather. Rákosi, however, had already agreed to be the godfather and was due to be represented by the local party secretary at the ceremony. Cserháti refused to cooperate. When the Györe family appealed to him with the argument that they were simply following an established tradition, as Miklós Horthy had also stood as godfather in the olden days, the priest replied that "perhaps Protestants [Horthy was Protestant, H.T.] or other religious communities did so, but not the Catholics—and anyway what sort of fascist example are you following?"[25] As a compromise, the priest suggested that maybe the local party secretary could become the godfather, as he was at least baptized a Catholic, but that Rákosi remained out of the question as a candidate for the role. During a trial to which he was subjected later, Cserháti emphasized that he had never claimed that Rákosi's political program kept him from participating in the baptism. The person of Rákosi and the political agenda he represented were, however, inextricably linked in postwar Hungary. Those priests who carried out such political baptisms understood this and acted accordingly, recognizing and acknowledging the contemporary power relations. In August 1949, when Cserháti was officially charged with "antidemocratic activities and agitation," an explicit reference was made to his refusal to carry out the baptism for the Györe family and he was condemned to three years in prison and the confiscation of half of his wealth. The date of his arrest and imprisonment is telling: by the fall of 1949 the communist take-over in Hungary was complete. The state had become a People's Republic, ruled by the Hungarian Workers' Party.

The establishment of the one-party system had consequences for the trajectory of politicized baptisms. The communist cult of personality involved the creation (and cultivation) of a particular persona for the political leader.[26] The boundaries that defined the "persona" of Rákosi shifted after 1949, destabilizing the old profile and creating a new one at the same time. Even the real-life Rákosi himself was not entirely sure about the Rákosi "persona" when it came to accepting invitations to stand as a godfather to newborn citizens of the People's Republic after 1949. When the parents of quadruplets

---

[25] Károly Hetényi Varga, *Papi sorsok a horogkereszt és a vörös csillag árnyékában*, vol. 2, *A Kalocsa-bácsi, csanádi, erdélyi, nagyváradi egyházmegyék üldözött papjai* (Abaliget: Lámpás, 1994), 34.
[26] E. Afron Rees, "Leader Cults: Varieties, Preconditions and Functions," in *Leader Cult in Communist Dictatorships*, ed. Apor 4.

born in May 1952 asked him to be the godfather of the firstborn of their four babies, Rákosi wrote a somewhat confused note to his secretary on the margin of their letter: "Do we still accept invitations to be a godfather? As far as I know, we do not. We should send a present though."[27] His secretary marked on the letter: "Gift sent, June 16."[28] Rákosi refused the invitation to stand as godfather for the firstborn of the quadruplets despite the fact that the social background of the family (the father was a forester) theoretically made them a good subject for communist propaganda, and even despite the fact that the birth of the four babies had put a potentially valuable journalistic spotlight on the Csordás family. There were various reasons why Rákosi declined to take the role. One of them was probably that the Csordás family was ultimately too poor for propaganda purposes. It would have been difficult to demonstrate the success of socialism by holding up a family that was after all unable to support their four newborn children on its own. In the event, the children were taken into a foster home where they spent the first few years of their lives.[29] The second, more important, reason for Rákosi to decline the invitation was that—although Rákosi's political "persona" followed the Stalinist model, that portrayed him as a father figure after the establishment of the one-party system—the actual, real-life Mátyás Rákosi began to recede out of reach. Rákosi was no longer available to act as a relative, to stand as a godfather, even when it was clear that the symbolic family bond created by the role was of limited practical significance.

This produced a paradox: once the People's Republic had become established, the spectrum of means that communists had available to them to demonstrate their loyalties to the Party through rites of passage actually became more limited than they had been previously. Rákosi was no longer willing to make the sorts of small compromises he had used to make in the late 1940s, and politicized baptisms became a thing of the past. As the public sphere gradually became dominated by the Hungarian Communist Party through the 1950s, and as ordinary people were expected to express their loyalty to the regime repeatedly in frequent political parades, as well as through "voluntary" participation in collectivized agriculture and in the ruthless spurring on of industrialization, the realm of rites of passage was left entirely to

---

[27] Letters with no date, printed in Kő and Nagy, eds. *Levelek Rákosihoz,* 20–1.
[28] Ibid.
[29] The fates of these children occupied the media for several years. They were featured in a group picture on the title page of the Christmas issue of the popular illustrated magazine *Képes Újság* (Illustrated Newspaper) in 1963, they were featured several times in the news: "The Csordás brothers" in *Magyar Filmhíradó* (Hungarian Filmnews) August, 1955: 1955/30; "The Csordás Quadruplets are five years old" in *Magyar Filmhíradó* November 1957: 1957/46; "The Csordás Quadruplets are eleven years old" in *Magyar Filmhíradó* July 1963: 1963/23; "The Csordás Quartett" in *Magyar Filmhíradó* October 1970: 1970/44. Even the Hungarian People's Army tried to capitalize on the fame of the quadruplets and made a short movie of their experiences as army recruits.

the church. Thus the only way for devoted communists to show their loyalty in this particular aspect of everyday life was to forego the rite altogether. This situation was to change in 1958.

The Introduction of Socialist Rites of Passage: A Caesura with Unintended Consequences

In the fall of 1958 the Central Committee of the Hungarian Socialist Workers' Party identified the sphere of culture as the main battleground in the struggle against the religious world view.[30] In many ways the emphasis on building socialist culture was a logical outcome of the long-term policy of the Hungarian Communist Party, but in this respect the context was new. With Stalin's death, Mátyás Rákosi's political position in Hungary was significantly weakened. The de-Stalinization process that took place everywhere in the Soviet sphere of influence from 1953 on was in the end also destined to claim Rákosi as one of its victims. The process triggered several reform processes all across Eastern Europe. The Poznań protests in Poland in June 1956 and the Hungarian Uprising in October 1956, for example, showed both the extent of discontent with communist rule and the extent to which the Soviet Union was prepared to go to keep its satellites in line. One of the sacrifices made by the communists during the revolution of 1956 in Hungary was the very Hungarian Workers' Party (or MDP, established in 1948) itself. In the hope that the creation of a new party would conjure up at least the illusion of legitimacy for the government that was established under Soviet control, the Hungarian Socialist Workers' Party (MSzMP) was born under the leadership of János Kádár.

In the two years between the end of the street fighting in Budapest and the emergence of new guidelines in the struggle against the religious world view, the topic of rites of passage had been on the minds of the leaders of the new party. For instance: how and where should the victims and "perpetrators" of the "counter-revolution" be buried?[31] Such practical questions gave the subject of rites of passage immediate and tangible relevance to the country's rulers. While the Hungarian Communist Party had initially targeted the church as an institution (concentrating on its land holdings, infrastructure and organization), now it focused its efforts on fighting the church on its "home ground": in the field of rites of passage. In response to the party's directive on the struggle against the religious world view, the Népművelési Intézet (Institute for People's Education) was commissioned to draw up scripts for Socialist alternatives to religious rites of passage. Barely a couple of

---

[30] István Mészáros, *Kimaradt tananyag*, vol. 2, *A diktatúra és egyház, 1957–1975* (Budapest: Márton Áron, 1994), 47–53.
[31] István Rév, *Retroactive Justice: Pre-History of Post-Communism* (Stanford, CA: Stanford University Press, 2005), 26–30.

months later, members of the institute submitted its initial position papers to the agitation and propaganda section of the party, including suggestions for a full set of rites of passage, including wedding, funeral and—most relevant to this paper—baptism-like ceremonies.[32]

The first hastily-written position papers on the topic of Socialist rites of passage were quickly put into practice, though the models presented to the public remained works in progress. By October 1959, barely a year after the party directive, the weekly news showed footage of an early Socialist naming ceremony.[33] The parents of two babies were celebrating their children's name-giving in what seemed to be the apartment of an affluent family. The babies—one boy and one girl—were not related: they were probably chosen to demonstrate that the name-giving ceremony was designed for all children, regardless of their gender. The furniture and the decoration of the apartment were intended to signal the financial security and high living standards that socialist families were supposed to be enjoying. The newsreel showed the person officiating at the ceremony (a justice of the peace or registrar), a small group of select guests and finally the gifts that the babies had received. Limited footage from the newsreel was later used in further propaganda material. Two years later, in 1961, the Institute for People's Education published a series of slides on Socialist rites of passage in which they used a shot from the 1959 newsreel, portraying the printed invitations to the name-giving ceremony to provide a sample event.[34] The rest of the slides showed large-scale ceremonies at a house of culture and at a factory, in which a number of children underwent a collective name-giving ceremony. The two chosen locations underscored the close connection between the values of Socialist society and the name-giving ceremony. The houses of culture were founded in order to build (and disseminate) Socialist culture, while the factories were consid-

---

[32] The initial task of the institute was to work out a socialist form of funeral, but even its earliest position papers covered a whole range of rites of passage. No author, but probably produced by the Népművelési Intézet (Institute for Public Education), "Vázlat a szocialista családi ünnepsegekkel kapcsolatos témajelentéshez" [Outline for the report on socialist family celebrations], [n.d.], 2, document 28, box 7, XIX A 21 c 000.2.1, MOL. For the example of the position paper dated Budapest, 22 December, 1958, Népművelési Intézet, Népművelési adattár [Database of the Institute for Public Education], 807, today in the Library of the Magyar Művelődési Intézet (Hungarian Institute for Culture). The former archival material of the Institute of Public Education was broken up: some material was transferred to the MOL, another part remained at its original location. The latter is still identified by the original institutional cataloguing data, hence the single archival number, 830.

[33] *Magyar Filmhíradó* October 1959: 1959/41.

[34] Series of slides were often sent out to houses of culture. They provided an effective medium for visual propaganda, as most houses of culture had a slide projector. Slide collection (*diafilm*), 1961, Népművelési Intézet, *Társadalmi ünnepek* (The direct translation of the title is "Social celebrations" which sounds slightly misleading. The term referred, of course, to "socialist society".)

ered more than merely a workplace: the context of the factory was expected to structure various aspects of the personal lives of its workers as well as their working lives and careers. Work brigades were intended both as a unit of production and as a social unit. The choice of locations suggests that the authors of the new rite wanted to make it look accessible and attractive all across the social scale. Whether it was held in the homes of the Socialist elite or in the factories, the name-giving ceremony was intended to contain a strong collective element.

The content and form of the name-giving ceremony were works in progress. The point of the ceremony was to welcome newborn children into Socialist society. Speeches were usually short, combining quotations from literary works containing texts on the importance of children as the "builders of our Socialist future."[35] Besides the speech-making, the ceremony usually also included a musical section and, both in factories and houses of culture, the local pioneer youth organizations took part in the celebration, singing songs and reciting poems. It brought together various generations of Socialist society, from infants through the children at school to adults. Besides the aspect of the ceremony that celebrated Socialist society in general, the name-giving ceremony also created its own specific social bonds: by the mid-1960s, babies were also being provided with Socialist "godparents" just as in the church ceremony.[36] Authors of handbooks on name-giving repeatedly drew attention to the importance of creating a dignified atmosphere for the ceremony by paying particular attention to the decoration of the room. Besides the Hungarian national flag and its coat of arms, the use of simple works of modern art was encouraged. The organizers often implemented this instruction by procuring a wall tapestry depicting a mother and child. As the author of one particular pamphlet on name-giving ceremonies complained in 1975, such tapestries—colloquially referred to as the "Socialist Holy Mary"—were tasteless, but "their owners cling to them for some mysterious reason."[37]

The introduction of the Socialist rites of passage created ways of demonstrating political loyalty in an affirmative manner within the private sphere. The timing of the ceremony's introduction is intriguing. The new rite was introduced precisely at the same time when the Socialist regime was reevaluating how public indifference to it should be treated: whether that indifference should be considered a legitimate political position in socialist Hungary.

---

[35] Sound extract from the animated movie *Habfürdő* (Bubble Bath) from 1979, directed by György Kovásznai, at min. 73–74. Kovásznai recorded a real-life name-giving ceremony and used the sound unaltered in his movie.

[36] Introducing the institution of a socialist godparenthood was designed to make the name-giving ceremony more appealing to the population. "Névadó, polgári házasság, temetés" [Name giving, civil wedding, funeral], Szombathely, 15 July 1965, 1, document 26, box 7, XIX A 21 c 0002 002 1, MOL.

[37] Endre Udvardi Lakos, *Módszertani útmutató névadó ünnepségek rendezéséhez* (Budapest: Népművelései Propaganda Iroda, 1975), 10.

Unlike during the Rákosi era, when the relationship between state and citizens could be summarized according to the tenet "whoever's not with us, is against us," János Kádár turned the dictum on its head, now evaluating silent indifference as a signal of political support. Accordingly, while in the early 1950s citizens of the newly-founded Socialist state were expected to participate in large-scale, collective events to demonstrate their enthusiasm for the construction of socialism, during the Kádár era, such expectations were lower. One could argue that, paradoxically, demonstrations of loyalty only became genuinely possible after the generalized coercive pressure on ordinary people to publically declare their loyalty to the regime had abated. These lower expectations opened up a space for voluntary, affirmative demonstrations of political support on a personal level, and the new rites of passage became a means of making such demonstrations. This perspective should not be taken to mean that none of the participants in the political parades of the early 1950s genuinely believed in the communist regime, that all letters of devotion sent to Rákosi were farces or that everyone who invited Rákosi to be the godfather of their child was acting merely opportunistically. What could be said, rather, is that as pressure lessened on the citizens of the Hungarian People's Republic to provide public support for the regime, any gesture that did so had a stronger effect.

There is evidence to suggest that the authors of Socialist rites of passage—and a small group around the figure of Zoltán Rácz in particular—were genuinely committed to creating a vehicle to strengthen the emotional bond between citizens and the Socialist system but they were very aware that this was a risky project. They argued that Socialist rites of passage were an important vehicle for demonstrating the viability of a Socialist culture in society. Rácz pointed out that if the party was unable to create rites of passage to mark the important turning points in an individual's biography with dignity, it would reflect badly upon the entire project of building socialism. "Dignity" was a term that came up regularly in internal correspondence on Socialist rites of passage. Rácz and his colleagues were aware that they were not on firm ground: what they were doing, after all, was attempting to create a brand new, Socialist tradition. In this effort, they were moving into an area where the churches had incomparably more expertise.[38] In the late 1940s, the celebration of politicized baptisms reflected the degree of coercion that the state was exercising over the churches at the time. But in the 1950s and 1960s, Socialist culture and religion were pitted directly against each other. Baptism occupied one column in the statistics on rites of passage, while the Socialist name-giving ceremony had another. This presentation amounted to a visual representation of the way in which the two rites functioned: not as the hybridized

---

[38] Debate at the meeting of the Fővárosi Tanács Végrehajtó Bizottsága (Executive Committee of the Council of Budapest), 28 December 1962, 120, microfilm reel 10946, XXIII 102.a, Budapest Főváros Levéltára [Budapest City Archives] (hereafter BFL).

ceremonies of the 1940s, in which two unlikely partners were united through coercion, but as two separate, independent choices.

This does not mean that the competition between Socialist rites of passage and religious rites after 1958 was a competition on a level playing field, in which each side was given an equal chance. Party members, especially the higher echelons, were put under pressure to choose the Socialist ceremonies rather than the church rites, and there were repercussions if they refused to do so. In practice, this resulted in cases where people chose both rituals: a family's dead might be buried with the presence of socialist funerary orator but with the priest taking over in the evening to give the graveside blessing, while new-born babies could well have both a naming ceremony and a religious baptism. However, direct pressure was not exercised on the population at large to choose Socialist rites over religious ones. Moreover, although the restrictions on party members' church attendance persisted, the general relationship between the church and the state was slowly settling down into a sort of equilibrium. By 1958, Kádár had already announced that although there was a need to fight against the religious world view, "the relationship between the state and the church is currently a loyal [lojális, H.T.] one."[39] This "loyalty" was actually the result of a successful campaign of intimidation that had brought the two main Protestant denominations more or less in line with the Socialist project by the early 1950s, and was also making inroads into the Catholic church.[40] The pontificate of Paul VI—and especially the aftermath of the Second Vatican Council—began a new chapter in the relationship between the Vatican and the Socialist bloc. In addition, the removal of Cardinal József Mindszenty, with the consent and the assistance of the Vatican, by putting him into permanent exile in 1971 was an important milestone towards the stabilization of state-church relations at the diplomatic level. It is safe to say that by the 1960s the mere fact of being religious did not automatically put one's loyalty towards the socialist project into question.

The new rites of passage, and the name-giving ceremony in particular, were met with a wide range of reactions among the population. Some mocked the new ritual openly. For example, Irén Psota, a popular actress, participated in a name-giving ceremony for nine dogs. The event was televised and caused an uproar in the higher party circles.[41] Local party officials

---

[39] János Kádár, "Beszéd az angyalföldi választási nagygyűlésen, 1958 október 15", in *A szocializmus teljes győzelméért* (Budapest: Kossuth, 1962), 11.
[40] For cooperation and conflicts between the Protestant church and the Socialist regime, see for example Lajos Ordass, *Önéletrajzi írások*, vol. 1, ed. István Szépfalusi (Bern: Európai Protestáns Szabadegyetem, 1985). Also, for a general overview of the churches under Communism see: Jason Wittenberg, *Crucibles of Political Loyalty: Church Institutions and Electoral Continuity in Hungary* (Cambridge: Cambridge University Press, 2006).
[41] Minutes of the meeting of the Executive Committee of the Council of Budapest, 20 November 1968, microfilm reel 10959, XXIII 102 a, 130, BFL.

and the directors of factories, on the other hand, believed that it was their obligation to ensure that as large a number of workers as possible took part in the ceremony. Internal reports on the new rites of passage describe several cases where rewards (in the form of cash or gifts) were given to people who brought their children to name-giving ceremonies as well as instances in which workers were intimidated into participating in such ceremonies together with their families.[42] Members of the Institute for People's Education considered all such responses to be corrosive to the wider project of creating a Socialist culture. As the exasperated anonymous author of one particular report wrote in relation to critical and ironic reportage on Socialist rites of passage: "Certain circles within the church are referring to this matter too, asserting that even the communists themselves have ... [such a poor] opinion [of socialist rites, H.T.], that they wonder how it's imaginable we should bury our dead in this manner?"[43] Also, as Zoltán Rácz pointed out, if people had to be either cajoled or coerced into taking part in name-giving ceremonies (or any other socialist rite of passage) then such rituals would never acquire any ability to convince people in and of themselves.[44]

As time went on, the Socialist name-giving ceremony matured into an established part of everyday Socialist life, though not in exactly the form or to exactly the same extent as its creators had initially intended. The form of the rite that proved to be most sustainable was neither the small-scale elite ceremony (as presented in the 1959 newsreel), nor the large-scale factory event (as presented on the 1961 series of slides). The most standard form of the rite was a collective ceremony in which a number of babies were given their naming ceremony simultaneously at the local civil registry office. The lines that defined the social collective in each such a shared ceremony were not, however, defined by the factory. It could be said that the establishment of the name-giving ceremony met with some limited success. It certainly became more popular than the secular funeral ceremony, achieving something of the popularity of the Socialist wedding, though never quite reaching the same peak of influence. In its peak years during the early 1980s, over 30 % of newborn babies in any given year received a name-giving ceremony. By way of comparison: the rate for secular funerals stabilized at around 16 %, while over 70 % of weddings were secular.[45] With its 30 % share, the name-giving ceremony had yielded solid though not overwhelming results. Besides, the name-giving ceremony suffered from the same problem faced by all Socialist rites of

---

[42] "Vázlat a szocialista családi ünnepségekkel kapcsolatos jelentéshez", 5.
[43] "Észrevételek a 'Jelentés a szocialista társadalmi szertartások helyzetéről és feladatairól' c. anyagról" [Remarks on the material titled "Report on the state of socialist rites of passage and tasks in this field"], 6, document 30, box 7, XIX-A-21-c 000.2 1, MOL.
[44] "Vázlat a szocialista családi ünnepségekkel kapcsolatos jelentéshez," 5.
[45] Edit Köpeczi Bócz, *Az Állami Egyházügyi Hivatal Tevékenysége* (Budapest: Akadémiai, 2004), 126–9.

passage: once a set of Socialist rites of passage was introduced it was now possible for the first time to see and measure the size of the section of population indifferent to it.

The group of those who might be characterized as *demonstratively* indifferent dwindled as time went on. While in the 1960s an average of around 10 % of babies were given neither a naming ceremony nor a baptism, this number sank to around 1.5 % in the first half of the 1980s.[46] In other words, by the middle of the 1980s the overwhelming majority of the population were opting for either baptism or the Socialist name-giving ceremony—or in some cases both. So, what exactly did this mean in terms of political loyalty? None of the Socialist rites of passage should be read as a simple marker for political loyalty during the Kádár era. Not all parents who celebrated a name-giving ceremony for their child were wholehearted supporters of the Socialist regime and of course not all parents who did not do so were automatically enemies of the state. A name-giving ceremony was often a handy solution for parents in religiously mixed marriages who wanted to celebrate the birth of their child but found the baptism option difficult. For others, choosing the name-giving ceremony was the product of peer pressure (typically in the 1960s), while it seems pretty certain that political opportunism also sometimes played a role in choosing the rite. It is safe to say, however, that people who decided to celebrate the Socialist rite of passage were thus deciding to *adopt affirmatively at least one particular aspect of Socialist culture*. Thus, even if participation in name-giving ceremony cannot be translated directly into an indicator of strong political loyalty, it can certainly be read as a marker of a general willingness to participate in a secular political culture. As Zoltán Rácz put it: the Socialist rites "give a chance for participants in it to express their willingness to *take on* the Socialist type of community."[47] Rácz's choice of word is telling: he used the verb "*vállalni*," which I translate here as "to take something on," but it also contains the meaning of "to pledge something." In other words, the introduction of this rite enabled participants to make a public statement of their support for the Socialist way of life and in that capacity the rite constituted quite as strong (or as weak) a statement as celebrating its church-held counterpart.

The introduction of Socialist rites of passage brought with it several unintended consequences. It was a risky enterprise. Although the state supported the new rites through a variety of channels (propaganda, infrastructural support and atheist-oriented education at schools, for example), this did not change the fact that the introduction of Socialist rites put the party in a vulnerable position. The blunders of funerary orators, name-giving ceremonies that showed poor taste and any possible hollowness in the entire ritual would

---

[46] The last statistical data comes from 1985.
[47] Zoltán Rácz, *Családi események, társadalmi szertartások* (Budapest: Kossuth, 1981), 8. Emphasis added.

reflect negatively on the overall project of building a Socialist culture. Moreover, even if those involved in the creation of a Socialist culture knew that the battle against the religious world view would take a long time, the struggle appears to have reached an impasse by the middle of the 1980s. After more than twenty years of commitment to the name-giving ceremony, over 60 % of the population still continued to have their children baptized, a figure that began to rise again in the second half of the 1980s. After a period of vigorous growth in the 1970s, the number of name-giving ceremonies appeared to stagnate and even decline in the decade that followed. While it would be an exaggeration to suggest that these numbers foreshadowed the fall of the communist regime in 1989, the name-giving ceremony as a way to generate (and to express) an emotional bond with the broader political community had reached a plateau by the mid-1980s—and not a very high plateau at that. Once Socialist rites of passage had been introduced, the competition between the competing world views in relation to religion became both visible and concretely measurable through statistics on participation in name-giving ceremonies, weddings and funerals, and ultimately it was not at all clear that Socialism was winning the competition between the two forms of ritual.

Conclusion

A key component of the phenomenon of political loyalty is a person's willingness to express a commitment to the political community. By the end of the nineteenth century at least, naming practices in Hungary could be considered an expression of such commitment. My formulation here is very careful and deliberate. There might be many possible motivations that could result in a decision to change one's foreign-sounding family name to a Hungarian one or to organize a Socialist name-giving ceremony for one's child. In all cases, however—regardless of the intentions of the actors—governments in regimes of all stripes would inevitably interpret name changes and choices made between the various available rites of passage as a sign of general support for their current political agendas. Whether the signal provided was in the content and form of the name (as it tended to be up until the end of the Second World War) or the ritual used in giving a child his or her name (after the establishment of the communist rule), both actors and state considered the topic of names and naming to be important areas in which emotional bonds between the individual and the body politic could be generated and demonstrated.

To some degree one might consider it an artificial enterprise to examine a single rite of passage in such a study as this. After all, rites of passage were only one area of everyday life among many in which regimes looked for indicators to measure the extent of the political support they enjoyed among the population. That said, of all rites of passage, name-giving ceremonies offered the broadest spectrum of possible interactions between ordinary people and consecutive political regimes, ranging from the act of choosing the right form of a name through creating a direct link between the family and the political leadership to expressing acceptance of a particular world view. As the criteria used to define membership of political projects changed with the passage of time, so did the particular way in which this aspect of everyday life took on some level of political meaning. Focusing on practices of name-giving has allowed us to identify a broad range of the dynamics that gave shape to this connection.

Todd H. Weir

SPURIOUS LOYALTY IN THE SOVIET BLOC
Four Perspectives

Public declarations of loyalty to the state and its communist leadership were a prominent feature of the Soviet Union and its cold-war client states. They took many guises. Affirmations of loyalty formed part of the backdrop to everyday life, appearing, for example, on billboards printed with slogans such as "learning from the Soviet Union means learning to win" and hung on factory and school walls in the German Democratic Republic. By contrast, affirmations of loyalty sometimes took center stage in the drama of party life, such as when members were called up on to perform "self-criticism." During the László Rajk conspiracy trial of 1949, for example, one of the accused expressed the wish for just punishment for having "severely injured the interests of the Hungarian People's Republic [...] my own people and [...] the whole international working-class movement."[1] Between these extremes, state employees, intellectuals, and organizations were called upon to participate in minor rituals of loyalty. Some had a local character, such as the sending of telegrams of enthusiastic approval immediately after speeches by Nicolae Ceaușescu at communist party congresses, in which the sender often quoted the Romanian president's own words.[2] Other rituals were universal, such as the academic practice of inserting a Lenin citation or a reference to the October Revolution in the preface of a book, even on subjects with no relation to twentieth century history.[3] These acts of loyalty appear staged, sometimes even awkwardly so. They were part and parcel of the fabricated self-presentation of state socialism that exerted and continues to exert a parti-

---

[1] Lazar Brankov was a Yugoslav communist, accused by the Hungarian court of spying on behalf of Tito. For his testimony, see *Lazslo Rajk and his Accomplices before the People's Court* (Budapest: Budapest Printing Press, 1949), 292.
[2] Liviu Papadima, "Sprache und Diktatur," in *Lexikon der Romanistischen Linguistik*, vol. 1, no. 2 (Tübingen: De Gruyter, 2001), 512–525, here 519.
[3] In her memoirs, Rita Kuczynski recounted how she learned to make the "formal declarations of faith to Marxism-Leninism" required by philosophers in the GDR. She eventually hit upon the "optimal ratio for the citations, after that I did not hear any more complaints: for every five Marx citations, one from Lenin." The point was to prove that "the prophets Marx, Engels, and Lenin understood Hegel better than Hegel himself did." Rita Kuczynski, *Wall Flower: A Life on the German Border*, transl. Anthony Steinhoff (Toronto: University of Toronto Press, 2015), 70.

cularly strong fascination on foreign observers.⁴ Already in the 1920s, Western critics began to accuse the government of masking reality behind a screen of propaganda images and model factories. They spoke of latter-day "Potemkin villages" with reference to the eighteenth-century Prince Potemkin, who had reportedly erected facades along the Dnieper River to impress Tsarina Catherine and a visiting delegation of European diplomats. At night, Potemkin supposedly had these mobile villages moved downstream and reconstructed at the next stop on the itinerary of the entourage.⁵

Whether painted on facades or rehearsed to be spoken in public assemblies, contrived expressions of loyalty appear to have been a hallmark of the Soviet system. Their spuriousness begs for diachronic and synchronic comparison utilizing the growing literature on loyalty in modern states. Because this literature did not develop around the Western encounter with the Soviet Union, loyalty appears to offer a neutral category that might overcome some of the drawbacks of other analytical categories commonly applied to communist regimes, such as dictatorship or totalitarianism. As such, comparisons based on loyalty could help normalize the Soviet system as an object of historical analysis.⁶ Yet, some caution is advised. Historians have demonstrated that the story of the Potemkin villages was a legend with a tenuous relationship to historical reality. Initially developed by Prince Potemkin's detractors, the story was subsequently picked up by opponents of Russia, particularly those in the West.⁷ In a similar fashion, there is a danger involved in taking models of loyalty largely developed in the West and applying them to communist regimes. Like the legend of the Potemkin village, such models may serve to demonstrate Soviet exceptionalism. To avoid this pitfall, the forced expressions of loyalty in the Soviet system are best approached from several perspectives. As an experimental effort in this direction, the following essay sketches out four such perspectives. It begins with two generic understandings of loyalty that have been used to place the Soviet case in a comparison with the West. For balance, it then proposes two system-specific explanations of why it came to the mass production of statements of loyalty in the Soviet Bloc. The first centers on the political culture of the communist par-

---

4   This fascination extends to the keen interest Western observers take in late-Soviet dissident art: Boris Groys, "The Other Gaze: Russian Unofficial Art's View of the Soviet World," in *Postmodernism and the Postsocialist Condition: Politicized Art under Late Socialism*, ed. Boris Groys and Ales Erjavec (Berkeley: University of California Press, 2003), 55–89.
5   Simon Sebag Montefiore, *Prince of Princes: The Life of Potemkin* (London: Orion, 2000), 379–83.
6   Volker Zimmermann and Peter Haslinger, "Loyalitäten im Staatssozialismus. Leitfragen und Forschungsperspektiven," in *Loyalitäten im Staatssozialismus: DDR, Tschechoslowakei, Polen*, ed. Volker Zimmermann, Peter Haslinger, and Tomáš Nigrin (Marburg: Verlag Herder-Institut, 2010), 3–23, here 5–7.
7   Michael David-Fox, *Showcasing the Great Experiment: Cultural Diplomacy and Western Visitors to the Soviet Union, 1921–1941* (New York: Oxford UP, 2011), 101–141.

ties, while the second identifies demands for statements of loyalty arising from within the mechanism of state planning.

Divided Loyalty

The starting point of most generic theories of loyalty is the positive attachment felt by the individual towards a group.[8] Loyalty only becomes a political issue when it is divided and the individual's simultaneous connection to two groups becomes a source of potential conflict. There is a clear utility to employing loyalty as an analytical category for studying the history of that half of Europe that eventually came under Soviet rule. Prior to 1917, the Ottoman, Austro-Hungarian, and Russian empires ruled over highly heterogeneous populations, in which different religious, ethnic and social groups lived cheek by jowl in a patchwork of administrative units, making for an endless assortment of potentially divided loyalties.[9] The problem was not solved, but in many ways exacerbated by the collapse of empires and the emergence of new nations in Eastern and Central Europe following the First World War.[10] Democracy and nationalism only heightened expectations that each citizen could and should be loyal to only one state and one people. The result was that minorities became more suspect.[11]

A first explanatory model for the high levels of spurious loyalty in the Soviet Bloc would thus center on inherited and new problems of divided loyalty. The manner in which the Soviet Union sought to coordinate multiple, potentially competing sovereignties in an imperial context has been discussed, in exemplary fashion, for the case of the military alliance of the so-called Warsaw Pact countries.[12] Militaries are particularly well suited for such an analysis, because of their need to ensure loyalty in the face of the existential threat

---

[8] Indicative of the personal starting point of most theories of loyalty, political theorist Simon Keller asks whether it is "a behavior, an emotion, a cognition, a contractual arrangement or a metaphor for interconnectedness?" Simon Keller, *The Limits of Loyalty* (Cambridge, UK: Cambridge UP, 2007), 10; James Connor, *The Sociology of Loyalty* (New York: Springer, 2007).

[9] Laurence Cole, *The Limits of Loyalty: Imperial Symbolism, Popular Allegiances, and State Patriotism in the Late Habsburg Monarchy* (New York: Berghahn, 2007).

[10] Pieter Judson refers to these successor states as "new empires." Pieter Judson, *The Habsburg Empire: A New History* (Cambridge, Mass.: Harvard UP, 2016), 442–452.

[11] Martin Schulze Wessel, ed., *Loyalitäten in der Tschechoslowakischen Republik 1918–1938: Politische, nationale und kulturelle Zugehörigkeiten* (Munich: Oldenbourg, 2004); Alois Mosser, ed., *Politische Kultur in Südosteuropa: Identitäten, Loyalitäten, Solidaritäten* (Frankfurt am Main: Peter Lang, 2006); Peter Haslinger and Joachim von Puttkamer, eds., *Staat, Loyalität und Minderheiten in Ostmittel- und Südosteuropa 1918–1941* (Munich: Oldenbourg, 2007).

[12] See Jens Boysen, "In the Service of 'the People' and of the 'Socialist Community': The Loyalties of Military Elites in the Polish People's Republic and the GDR (1970–1990)" in this volume.

posed by mortal combat. They use ritual verbalizations of loyalty, such as oaths, to inculcate willingness to fight and prevent soldiers from shifting allegiances according to the tides of war.[13] Oaths also form the basis of court martial and are hence a means of coercion. In the case of the Warsaw Pact, the armies of the "people's republics" employed a discourse of loyalty that carefully harmonized and calibrated three "objects" of sovereignty: the working class represented by the communist party, their respective peoples and their national histories, and the international revolution guaranteed by the Soviet Union. Yet, although military discourse affirmed that the armies of the Warsaw pact member states were a "brotherhood of arms," military leaders essentially prohibited their soldiers from interacting with members of other nations during joint military exercises out of fear that such fraternization might lead to undesirable alliances.[14]

Loyalty and Hegemony

A second explanation of the prominence of rituals of loyalty in the Soviet Bloc is that they were a compensation for a lack of legitimacy. Whereas democracies have the advantage of being able to produce legitimacy through the mechanisms of elections and equal treatment under the law, communist dictatorships, like other authoritarian states, had to employ other means. Historians have argued that modern dictatorships relied on pseudo-democratic means, such as plebiscites and block voting, to enhance their legitimacy.[15] In addition, they sought to buy popular support or at least popular acceptance through social policies, such as land reform, democratization of education, and provision of consumer goods.[16] Historian Konrad Jarausch names the purchase of such "reluctant loyalty" the essence of the state socialist model of "welfare dictatorship."[17]

Despite the relative stability of this model of rule, when comparing the Soviet and American zones of influence in Europe, historians and political scientists (especially from the United States) have commonly concluded that American hegemony was more secure because it received largely uncoerced

---

[13] Nikolaus Buschmann and Karl Murr, eds., *Treue: Politische Loyalität und militärische Gefolgschaft in der Moderne* (Göttingen: Vandenhoeck & Ruprecht, 2008).
[14] Boysen, "In the Service of 'the People' and of the 'Socialist Community'."
[15] Ralph Jessen and Hedwig Richter, eds., *Voting for Hitler and Stalin: Elections under Twentieth Century Dictatorships* (Frankfurt am Main: Campus, 2011).
[16] See the essays by Peter Hübner and Christoph Boyer in: *Loyalitäten im Staatssozialismus,* ed. Zimmermann, Haslinger, and Nigrin.
[17] Konrad Jarausch, "Care and Coercion: The GDR as Welfare Dictatorship," in *Dictatorship as Experience: Towards a Socio-cultural History of the GDR,* ed. Konrad Jarausch (New York: Berghahn, 1999), 47–72, here 62.

support from the Western European governments and populations.[18] As the uprisings in 1953, 1956, and 1968 made clear, Soviet military force was required to maintain communist rule in East Central Europe. If, following Antonio Gramsci and Niccolò Machiavelli, hegemony is defined as a form of domination in which consent outweighs coercion,[19] then the need for avowals of loyalty would appear in inverse proportion to actual hegemony. In other words, statements of loyalty stood in for actual consent.

We may, however, take the theory of hegemony in another direction and explain staged statements of loyalty not as evidence of a deficit of legitimacy, but rather as an enabling element in the Soviet system of rule. Here we might benefit from a brief comparison with British rule in India, which historian Ranajit Guha characterized as "dominance without hegemony."[20] In order to achieve hegemony, Guha argues, the colonial state would have had to homogenize Indian society and incorporate it into the liberal order, a feat accomplished in Britain itself. In India the British state was not only unable, but unwilling to follow this course and relied instead on its military superiority, i.e. on coercion. This reliance on coercion was not so much a failing, as a precondition for the exploitation of the colony. Nonetheless, in an age of liberalism, it was imperative that the British state "disguise" its use of coercion by creating a host of historical myths that justified its rule. This Guha called a "spurious hegemony."[21]

The question then arises: for whom was the spurious hegemony performed? Or, if transposed to our case: who were the audiences and what were the functions of the staged rituals of spurious loyalty in the Soviet Bloc? In the Potemkin legend, the village spectacles on the river banks of recently conquered territories in South Russia were staged for outsiders, i.e. for Catherine's traveling entourage of European monarchs and diplomats. Similarly, the assumption of those who alluded to "Potemkin villages" in the early Soviet Union was that the communist state was creating fictive sites for the eyes of Western tourists. Yet, according to historian Michael David-Fox, this misses the mark. The state created and filmed showcase sites of industrial deve-

---

[18] John Lewis Gaddis, *We Now Know: Rethinking Cold War History* (New York: Oxford University Press, 1997). For two contrasting views on the effectiveness of American cultural and economic expansion into Europe after the war, see Reinhold Wagenleitner, *Coca-Colonization and the Cold War: The Cultural Mission of the United States in Austria After the Second World War* (Chapel Hill, N.C.: University of North Carolina Press, 1994) and Tony Judt, *Postwar: A History of Europe since 1945* (New York: Penguin, 2005), 221.

[19] Political theorist Partha Chatterjee has applied this definition of hegemony to various aspects of Indian history, including recently, Partha Chatterjee, "Five Hundred Years of Fear and Love," in idem, *Lineages of Political Society: Studies in Postcolonial Democracy* (New York: Columbia University Press, 2011), 33–52.

[20] Ranajit Guha, *Dominance without Hegemony: History and Power in Colonial India* (Cambridge, Mass.: Harvard Univ. Press, 1997), 72–79.

[21] Ibid., 72–73.

lopment, from collective farms to new factories, to serve as didactic models to teach foreigners and Soviet citizens alike. Sheila Fitzpatrick goes so far as to claim that during collectivization peasants were called upon to play roles in a "Potemkin world." She calls the specifically Soviet model of social transformation "Potemkinism": a "Stalinist discourse in which the defects and contradictions of the present were overlooked and the world was described not as it was but what it was becoming, as Soviet Marxists believed it necessarily would be in the future."[22]

Loyalty Needs Arising from Stalinist Party Culture and Worldview

"Potemkinism" is not yet an adequate explanation for the phenomenon of spurious loyalty, but it does call into question explanations that rest solely on the notion of divided loyalty or on a supposed deficit of legitimacy of the Soviet states as compared to the liberal Western democratic norm. It brings up the need to ask about the internal structures of loyalty specific to the communist system. To explore this, I want to open up two further perspectives on spurious loyalty, the first centering on the culture of the communist movement, the second on the needs of the state.

Historians are increasingly investigating Stalinism, not as a system of rule, but as a culture.[23] Examinations of personal relations among communist revolutionaries have revealed that the party culture was totalizing to the extent that friendship and even marriage were understood to be just one aspect of the collective of the party. Doris Danzer has shown that communist intellectuals in East Germany often mixed expressions of loyalty to friends with public affirmations of loyalty to this collective.[24] Jochen Hellbeck has investigated how the dialectical interaction between the party and the individual erased the distinction between the public and the private and contributed

---

[22] David-Fox, *Showcasing*, 114–121; Sheila Fitzpatrick, *Stalin's Peasants: Resistance and Survival in the Russian Village after Collectivization* (New York: Oxford UP, 1994), 16; Malte Rolf, "A Hall of Mirrors: Sovietizing Culture under Stalinism," *Slavic Review* 68, no. 3 (2009): 601–630.

[23] Katerina Clark, *Moscow, the Fourth Rome: Stalinism, Cosmopolitanism, and the Evolution of Soviet Culture, 1931–1941* (Cambridge, Mass.: Harvard UP, 2011); Sheila Fitzpatrick, *Stalinism: New Directions* (London: Routledge, 2000); Stefan Plaggenborg, ed., *Stalinismus. Neue Forschungen und Konzepte* (Berlin: Berliner Wissenschafts-Verlag, 1998); Eric Naiman, *Sex in Public: The Incarnation of Early Soviet Ideology* (Princeton, N.J.: Princeton University Press, 1997); Stephen Kotkin, *Magnetic Mountain: Stalinism as a Civilization* (Berkeley: University of California Press, 1995).

[24] Doris Danzer, *Zwischen Vertrauen und Verrat: Deutschsprachige kommunistische Intellektuelle und ihre sozialen Beziehungen, 1918–1960* (Göttingen: Vandenhoek & Ruprecht, 2012). See also the prosopographical studies of communist families and networks: Katy Turton, *Forgotten Lives: The Role of Lenin's Sisters in the Russian Revolution, 1864–1937* (London: Palgrave, 2007); Brigitte Studer, *The Transnational World of Cominternians* (London: Palgrave, 2015).

to Stalinist subject formation. Using diaries of young people from the 1920s and 1930s, Hellbeck shows how state demands for loyalty were internalized and affirmed as proof of personal purity and conviction.[25] The emotional ties forged between party and individual were essential to the functioning of party discipline mechanisms. The revolutionary's faith in the party's historical mission and the sacrifices made during struggle caused him or her to be anxious about the possibility of exclusion from the party collective. This emotional vulnerability drove members to participate in the ritual of "criticism and self-criticism," which was used to eliminate party pluralism and affix blame for structural problems to individual scapegoats.[26]

With the gradual elimination of genuine opposition within the Russian Communist Party by the late 1920s, the affirmation of loyalty was not enough to ensure safety within Stalin's faction. Sandra Dahlke has detailed how one of the leading ideologues of the early Stalinist period, Emelian Yaroslavskij, developed the figure of the double dealer (*dvurushnik*), who behind the mask of loyalty plotted the downfall of the party leadership. This turned dissimulation and feigned loyalty into a chief trait of supposed opposition. At this time the language of class war was transferred from the collectivization campaign into party disputes, and evidence of past deviations or alien class origin was used to "unmask" potential dissenters as "enemies of the people." In her prosopography of German communist leaders, Catherine Epstein showed how this practice was continued in the GDR, where party control commissions sifted questionnaires and cadre files for evidence of past disloyalty.[27]

Worldview is another element of party culture that led to high demands for loyalty. This is revealed in Heléna Tóth's investigation of the development of a communist alternative to Christian baptism in Hungary.[28] The state's decision to challenge the churches' monopoly over this ritual certainly was an outgrowth of the deep historical antagonism between the Christian churches and the socialist movement. However, it was also a manifestation of the fact that the communist party assigned to itself a larger realm of action than did the liberal state. This realm included aspects generally understood as religious. Communists interpreted their conflicts with the churches as part of the "struggle between materialist and religious worldviews," and structured their

---

[25] Jochen Hellbeck, *Revolution on My Mind: Writing a Diary under Stalin* (Cambridge, Mass.: Harvard Univ. Press, 2006).

[26] Lorenz Erren, *"Selbstkritik" und Schuldbekenntnis: Kommunikation und Herrschaft unter Stalin (1917–1953)* (Munich: Oldenbourg, 2008); Oleg Kharkhordin, *The Individual and the Collective in Russia: A Study of Practices* (Berkeley: University of California Press, 1999).

[27] Sandra Dahlke, *Individuum und Herrschaft im Stalinismus: Emel'jan Jaroslavskij (1878–1943)* (Munich: Oldenbourg, 2010); Catherine Epstein, *The Last Revolutionaries: German Communists and Their Century* (Cambridge, Mass.: Harvard University Press, 2003); Erren, *"Selbstkritik."*

[28] See Heléna Tóth, "From Content to Ritual. Name-Giving Practices and Political Loyalty in Hungary from 1880 to 1989" in this volume.

secular rituals around the former. This form of socialist secularism does not fit the process of modernization posited by sociologists, whereby functionally differentiated social spheres, including religion and politics, become increasingly autonomous.[29] In fact, the Stalinist brand of secularism appears to have worked in the opposite direction. It sought to erase rather than strengthen the boundary between the religious and the political, and the secular and the sacred. Hence these regimes sought expressions of loyalty in secular versions of religious rituals, not out of cynicism, but out of the demands of their totalizing communist worldview.[30] A similar moment of de-differentiation has been noted by Jens Boysen in the relationship between military and party. Rather than functioning as essentially non-political professional organizations tasked with national defense, the armies of the "people's republics" were called upon to act as extensions of the parties and thus vehicles for historical progress.[31] Demands for military loyalty in battle blurred with demands for political loyalty to the aims of revolutionary transformation.

It is now time to revise the first two explanatory models that I offered for the high demands for loyalty in state socialism, i.e. divided loyalty and lack of legitimacy. The old problem of divided loyalty was reframed by the socialist states. Given their totalizing worldviews, they necessarily perceived all institutions within civil society as potential competitors. The second model correlated the rise of manufactured expressions of loyalty to state coercion. One can begin a revision of this explanation with the observation that expressions of loyalty were not merely a mask of consent meant to cover a lack of hegemony. Avowals of loyalty were integral to the functioning of the bureaucratized and centrally planned communist state. Unlike real loyalty, spurious loyalty could be and was produced more or less according to plan.

Loyalty and Planning

The role of planning in socialist political economy brings me to the final perspective on loyalty in the Soviet Bloc, one offered by systems theory. Sociologist Niklas Luhmann argued that planning is impossible without a degree of

---

[29] On Soviet secularism, see Sonja Luehrmann, *Secularism Soviet Style: Teaching Atheism and Religion in a Volga Republic* (Bloomington: Indiana University Press, 2011); Catherine Wanner, ed., *State Secularism and Lived Religion in Soviet Russia and Ukraine* (Oxford: Oxford UP, 2012); Tam Ngo and Justine B. Quijada, eds., *Atheist Secularism and its Discontents* (London: Palgrave Macmillan, 2015); Victoria Smolkin, *A Sacred Space: How Soviet Atheism Was Born, Lived, and Died* (Princeton, NJ: 2017 forthcoming).

[30] For a discussion of the erasure of boundaries between science and religion in naturalistic worldviews, see Todd H. Weir, "The Riddles of Monism: An Introductory Essay," in *Monism: Science, Philosophy, Religion and the History of a Worldview*, ed. Todd H. Weir (New York: Palgrave Macmillan, 2012), 1–44.

[31] Boysen, "In the Service of 'the People' and of the 'Socialist Community.'"

trust. The complexity of the constituent parts of a system exceeds the capacity of the planner to know them. Unable to obtain the information needed to guarantee success, "the actor willingly disregards the missing information" and substitutes in its place trust. For this reason, Luhmann concluded, "trust rests on deception." This self-deception reduces complexity and allows for action.[32] Trust, in other words, is a currency that allows a system to function with imperfect information. The alternative, i.e. lack of trust, requires a greater investment in information gathering and, as the example of the bloated apparatus of East German *Staatssicherheit* (secret service, Stasi) shows, this can be very expensive for the operation of a system.

I would like to modify Luhmann's insight and propose the following thesis: where trust is not a given, declarations of loyalty may stand in as a further (counterfeit) currency that allows a system to continue to function. In other words, in a planned economy, spurious loyalty may be produced and reincorporated in the functioning of the system. To conclude this essay, I would like to apply this thesis to two phases of Soviet history roughly divided by Stalin's death in 1953.

The production of loyalty was particularly important in the process of "building socialism" in the Soviet Union after 1928 and again in the eastern half of Europe two decades later. Driven by the conjuncture of planning bureaucracy and the tradition of revolutionary voluntarism, the state carried out social transformation as a staged class struggle that was both carefully orchestrated and highly dynamic.[33] Collectivization, the most sweeping and violent campaign, depended on a feedback mechanism, whereby evidence of peasant resistance was needed to justify and unleash further state intervention. Rituals of loyalty were often staged precisely at the time and location at which the state separated peasants from their property, i.e. either upon the "voluntary" joining of the collective farm or at the show trials of recalcitrant "kulaks." These stagings were not merely didactic exercises for the public or cynical demonstrations of power, as historians writing in the 1990s often assumed.[34] They also produced the information in the form of reports and newspaper stories that was a necessary input in the feedback loop of expro-

---

[32] Niklas Luhmann, *Vertrauen: Ein Mechanismus der Reduktion sozialer Komplexität* (Stuttgart: Enke, 1968), 30.

[33] On staging in the Soviet system, see Keith Michael Baker, *Scripting Revolution: A Historical Approach to the Comparative Study of Revolutions* (Palo Alto: Stanford Univ. Press, 2015).

[34] Two historians who have viewed the role of ideology in collectivization in purely instrumental terms are: Lynne Viola, *Peasant Rebels under Stalin: Collectivization and the Culture of Peasant Resistance* (Oxford: Oxford Univ. Press, 1996); Wolfgang Bell, *Enteignungen in der Landwirtschaft der DDR nach 1949 und deren politische Hintergründe: Analyse und Dokumentation* (Münster-Hiltrup: Landwirtschaftsverlag, 1992).

priation and resistance.³⁵ The General Secretary of the East German communist party (Socialist Unity Party or SED) Walter Ulbricht exposed this feedback loop in a speech of June 1952, in which he laid out how he wanted to initiate the campaign for collectivization planned for the following month. He instructed the regional party secretaries to select farmers from an outlying region of the GDR, who would demand the formation of agricultural collectives from the government:

> We don't make any sort of statement. When comrades come and ask: So, what is your position on that? [...] Then we will say: Dear comrade! As you have seen in the press, the Second Party Conference of the SED is being convened. There we will certainly be able to give an answer to these questions."³⁶

What began as a carefully planned process of generating spurious information in the summer of 1952 gave way over the following months to partially uncontrolled production of information in the countryside, as real acts of resistance by farmers were coded as acts of "class struggle." Statements of loyalty to the revolution by the local agents of the state and the collective farms were important, not just because they justified the acts of state violence undertaken against such resistance, but because they enabled a ratcheting up of that violence. The state did not, and to an extent could not differentiate between real and staged information. The surprise came in the popular uprising of June 1953, when the forces of coercion appeared momentarily weak and the system, based on false information (also regarding the loyalty of the population), collapsed like a house of cards.

The near revolution in the GDR in June 1953 marked a turning point in the history of the communist system prompted by Stalin's death in March of that year. Despite the transition to a less violent mode of social transformation under Nikita Khrushchev and eventually to the relative stasis of "really existing socialism" in the Brezhnev era, the post-Stalinist cadre party continued to depend on the steady circulation of symbolic information. Even in post 1956 Hungary, which according to Tóth no longer demanded positive confession but simply passivity from its citizens according to the motto "who is not against us, is for us," the state still required larger and smaller acts of loyalty in order to persist.³⁷

---

35 Todd H. Weir, "Der Rausch im Plan: Ursachen und Folgen der Inszenierung von 'Klassenkampf' in der Kollektivierung der DDR-Landwirtschaft 1952–1953," *Deutschland Archiv* 2 (2004): 253–63.
36 Quoted in Jens Schöne, "'Wir sind dafür, dass über diese Fragen keine Berichterstattung erfolgt.' Die Kollektivierung der Landwirtschaft in der DDR 1952/53," in *Der Aufbau der "Grundlagen des Sozialismus" in der DDR 1952/53*, ed. Falco Werkentin (Berlin: Der Berliner Landesbeauftragte für die Unterlagen des Staatssicherheitsdienstes der Ehemaligen DDR, 2002), 71–94, here 78–79.
37 Tóth, op cit. Michael Brie refers to this strategy of one of trying to gain "acquiescence" (Hinnahme): Dieter Segert, "Loyalitäten im späten Staatssozialismus und ihr Wandel

A typical statement of loyalty from the Brezhnev era can be taken from the front page of *Trybuna Ludu* (People's Tribune), the organ of the Polish communist party (United Polish Workers' Party or PZPR) in 1976:

> The rhythm of daily work in our country is strong and even. Particularly now, when the people have affirmed their will to achieve the program of building socialism formulated at the VI and VII Congresses of the PZPR, the workers of all branches of industry strive through good work, understood as the fundamental obligation of each and every citizen and patriot, to lend their decisive support to party and government.[38]

The language used here to declare loyalty to several authorities mirrors that of the phase of building socialism, but its function appears quite different. Rather than producing emotions of fear, adoration, or identification that might have pertained to the "Potemkinism" of the early Soviet Union, the intention of this "wooden language" appears to have been the filling up of discursive space of the public sphere to prevent rather than provoke change. According to Romanian literary scholar Liviu Papadima the official discourse elaborated during the "offensive" or educational phase of communist information policy, i.e. as practiced during "building socialism," was repurposed to suit the needs of the subsequent "defensive" phase. Information became increasingly separated from its ostensible meaning and instead came to serve the "unitary functioning of the entire communication apparatus." Thus, he concludes, "a newspaper is only secondarily written for its readers, primarily, however, for those who oversee and censor the newspaper."[39] The same function may be claimed for spurious expressions of loyalty in late socialism, they served the self-organization and self-representation of the communist system.

Conclusion

Ernest Renan called the modern nation a "daily plebiscite," i.e. a self-reproducing community constituted by the continual affirmation of loyalty to shared ideals. Yet, rather like the idea of the social contract, this is more a myth of state formation than a quotidian event. The practices of loyalty in the Soviet states came much closer to constituting a daily plebiscite, albeit a manufactured one. Whereas Stalinist era leaders had wanted full-throated enactments of this plebiscite by the population, their late socialist counterparts were often

---

am Beispiel der intellektuellen Dienstklasse der DDR," in *Loyalitäten im Staatssozialismus*, ed. Zimmermann, Haslinger, and Nigrin, 205–221.

[38] Quoted in Patryk Wasiak, "Loyalität und Kinematografie in der Volksrepublik Polen: Der Fall des 'Mannes aus Marmor' von Andrzej Wajda," in ibid., 249–261.

[39] Papadima, "Sprache und Diktatur," 517. A personal anecdote may corroborate Papadima's point here. As an American exchange student in the GDR in 1988, my interest was drawn to the bold propaganda slogans on billboards that dominated public spaces. When I asked an East German companion what one of them meant, he looked up briefly and answered disinterestedly, "no idea."

happy enough to have statements of loyalty performed in a routinized form in the media.

What accounts for the high level of production and circulation of spurious loyalty in the Soviet Bloc? In this essay I have tested four answers. First, the Soviet empire inherited from its predecessor states and empires the problem of divided loyalties. Public statements of loyalty to state and party created an illusion of uniformity and delivered a warning to potential deviants. Second, as the communist state found itself forced to use violence to achieve its revolutionary ends and maintain its dominance, specious affirmations of loyalty loaned legitimacy to acts of coercion. These explanations are compatible with the wider literature on loyalty in comparative political history. In the second half of the essay, I instead asked after the qualities specific to the Soviet system that propelled the production of loyalty. I proposed, as a third answer to my leading question, that the culture and worldview of the communist parties created expectations for participation that far exceeded those common to liberal states. Finally, in a fourth answer, I took a systems-theoretical approach and proposed that declarations of loyalty be treated as items of information that were produced and circulated according to plan, because this iteration of affirmation was required for the reproduction of state and party. The spuriousness of this information became more obvious in late socialism, as professions of loyalty increasingly became an act that the state undertook on behalf of those from whom it desired support.

Jens Boysen

IN THE SERVICE OF "THE PEOPLE" AND OF THE "SOCIALIST COMMUNITY"
The Loyalties of Military Elites in the Polish People's Republic and the German Democratic Republic (1970–1990)

General Preliminary Remarks on Military Loyalty

The development of loyalty among the elite military functionaries of the Warsaw Pact states was governed by factors that could to some extent be seen as applying generally to all armies, and by some others that might be considered specific to the "real socialist" states. Aside from these factors, there were also country-specific factors that betray a more complex picture than that of a single, homogenous "bloc".

This essay contributes to the discussion on the extent to which, despite the deconstructed image of the "Eastern Bloc", structural elements can be identified that managed to hold the "socialist camp" together for more than four decades.[1] Negative factors, including Soviet hegemony and the various instruments of repression available to the Communist regimes, cannot on their own provide a sufficient explanation of that unity. In fact, in every country in the bloc there was a body of home-grown elite functionaries who contributed to the character of "real socialism" and whose members had intentionally decided on their career paths for the widest possible variety of motives.[2] The military constituted one particularly important functional elite among such groups. It did more than simply outwardly embody the feeling of solidarity between the socialist states among military personnel, endowing the alliance with its favoured specific values and ideas of order and hyperbolically characterising it as a "brotherhood in arms". Indeed, these military institutions, together with the "armed bodies" that operated in the interior of the socialist states (especially the state security and secret police service and the "normal"

---

[1] On this discussion, see Bogdan C. Iacob, "Is It Transnational? A New Perspective in the Study of Communism," *East Central Europe* 40, no. 1–2 (2013): 114–139; Justine Faure and Sandrine Kott, eds., "Le Bloc de l'Est en question." Special issue, *Vingtième Siècle. Revue d'histoire* 109 (2011).

[2] See, for example, on the Council for the Mutual Economic Assistance (Comecon) between eastern bloc countries the conference of the GWZO Leipzig "Economic Entanglements in East-Central Europe and the Comecon's Position in the Global Economy (1949–1991)," Leipzig, 14–16 November 2012.

police and/or militia cadres), formed part of a complex system for protecting the power of the dominant party.[3]

This contribution takes its starting point from a definition of the expression "loyalty" as an agreement among individuals or social groups to hold fast to a particular political line or regime, accompanied by the associated constructive behaviour. The term applies in general to all subjects of a state, although no more than formal compliance with the law is usually expected of "normal" citizens. However, a special additional quality of loyalty is expected from functionaries and authorities of the state, along with a higher level of commitment to the state (expected to be effectively lifelong in the case of civil servants).[4] In this context, in addition to pursuing economic motives (connected to their career paths), state functionaries also accept a special level of inner commitment. This extra commitment is expressed positively in the form of the special relationship of mutual trust that exists between the political leadership and functionaries, and negatively in the special punishments in store for any failure to show the loyalty expected of this privileged circle of people (which would be considered treachery by the political leadership).

In the case of *soldiers* this positioning took on additional weight through the fact that soldiery is the only professional group (with the possible exception of the police, the fire brigade, the paramedical professions and a few others) in which individuals are expected to put their very lives on the line for a defined common cause.[5] In this arrangement, the understanding of the nation *generally* adopted within the relevant (civil) society is an essential element in the ideational and emotional embedding of the military as a professional group within that society. For the more positively this embedding takes its shape, the more a person who has chosen the profession of soldier is likely to expect that his activities will receive the moral and material support of the society in whose name he acts.[6]

---

[3] *Im Dienste der Partei: Handbuch der bewaffneten Organe der DDR*, ed. Torsten Diedrich, Hans Ehlert, and Rüdiger Wenzke (Berlin: Links, 1998), 1–13.

[4] Jana Osterkamp, "Loyalität als Rechtspflicht: Verfassungsrechtliche Grundpflichten im Staatssozialismus," in *Loyalitäten im Staatssozialismus: DDR, Tschechoslowakei, Polen*, ed. Volker Zimmermann, Peter Haslinger, and Tomáš Nigrin (Marburg: Verlag Herder-Institut, 2010), 25–43, here 27.

[5] After a long period during which especially (western) German historical research has largely neglected the military dimension of the mechanisms of political domination, in a number of innovative research projects dealing with elites in the "real socialist" countries towards the end of the 1990s, military elites were gradually brought into the discussion. However, it is instructive that up to now this topic has been overwhelmingly dealt with by military historians. See Rüdiger Wenzke, "'Bei uns können Sie General werden...': Zur Herausbildung und Entwicklung eines 'sozialistischen' Offizierskorps im DDR-Militär," in *Eliten im Sozialismus: Beiträge zur Sozialgeschichte der DDR*, ed. Peter Hübner (Cologne: Böhlau, 1999), 167–200.

[6] Currently, this problem is seen for example in the situation of soldiers who had recently returned home from Afghanistan, and who very often did not receive the welfare sup-

In the Warsaw Pact,[7] which we represent here through the examples of the German Democratic Republic (GDR) and the Polish People's Republic, the grounds for and efforts to safeguard loyalty among soldiers were procured in the light of a range of specific factors:

- As a consequence of the ideological foundation of the political and social orders of members of the alliance, no moral or political objection could be allowed to arise against the expectation of military loyalty.
- The highest ranking officers in the military were mostly members of the Central Committee or Politburo of the ruling party, and thus also enjoyed membership of the *political* elite. In the GDR they were subordinated as a *nomenclature* body under the National Defence Council (*Nationaler Verteidigungsrat der DDR*, NVR). The Polish equivalent of the NVR, The Committee for National Defence (*Komitet Obrony Kraju*, KOK), had more of the character of a government authority though it was *de facto* ultimately subordinate to the Politburo of the Polish United Workers' Party (*Polska Zjednoczona Partia Robotnicza*, PZPR).[8]
- The weakness or complete absence of any separation of powers, the deliberate refusal to make any distinction between domestic and international security, and the claim to total leadership on the part of the regime together provided the grounding for a duty to obey among soldiers that went beyond the narrower military sphere and made their deployment for domestic purposes at least thinkable in principle.[9] In the case of Poland, such deployments became a reality in 1956, 1970 and 1981–83.
- Finally, the theory of proletarian internationalism combined with the political integration of the Warsaw Pact was to further complicate this ar-

---

port they needed from civil society (or from the state). See Andreas Timmermann-Levanas and Andrea Richter, *Die reden, Wir sterben: Wie unsere Soldaten zu Opfern der deutschen Politik werden* (Bonn: Bundeszentrale für politische Bildung, 2010).

[7] I use this generally accepted informal name instead of its official title—the "Warsaw Treaty Organisation."

[8] For the GDR, see: Matthias Wagner, "Gerüst der Macht: Das Kadernomenklatursystem als Ausdruck der führenden Rolle der SED," in *Gesellschaft ohne Eliten? Führungsgruppen in der DDR*, ed. Arnd Bauerkämper et al. (Berlin: Metropol, 1997), 87–108, here 91–92; for Poland, see: Andrzej Paczkowski, "Das Komitee für Landesverteidigung (Komitet Obrony Kraju) in den Jahren 1959–1991," *Projektgruppe Protokolle des Nationalen Verteidigungsrates der DDR: Verteidigungsräte im Warschauer Pakt*, accessed 28 October 2016, http://www.nationaler-verteidigungsrat.de/de/verteidigungsraete_im_warschauer_pakt/polen.

[9] Even if such a use of the military was ruled out in theory, as it was in the GDR in 1962, see: Rüdiger Wenzke, "Die Nationale Volksarmee, 1956–1990," in *Im Dienste der Partei*, eds. Diedrich, Ehlert, and Wenzke, 423–535, here 432. For a more detailed treatment of the subject, see: Joachim Hohwieler, "NVA und innere Sicherheit: Der Einsatz der Armee im eigenen Land," in *Nationale Volksarmee: Armee für den Frieden; Beiträge zu Selbstverständnis und Geschichte des deutschen Militärs, 1945–1990*, ed. Detlef Bald, Reinhard Brühl, and Andreas Prüfert (Baden-Baden: Nomos, 1995), 75–90.

rangement of loyalties as these factors now added supranational elements to the mix, with the result that "objects" of loyalty could now also be found outside the framework of the nation state.

This raises on the one hand the question as to what it was that professional soldiers—and especially the higher officer corps—felt to be the effective object(s) of their final loyalty; notably whether it was to be found on a national and/or supranational level. Fundamental to this question is the particular concept of "the people" or of "the nation" specific to the relevant country, as this concept formed an important element in the ideational foundation of the armies. On the other hand, it also needs to be asked if and to what extent the military elites of the Warsaw Pact states could be said to form an *epistemic community* (a community containing shared educational and technical orientation).

The GDR and the Polish People's Republic as Political and Military Members of the "Socialist Camp"

The text to follow takes the armies of the GDR and the Polish People's Republic in order to provide examples of the military loyalty under "real socialism" in the 1970s and 1980s. The restriction in time is defensible mainly due to the fact that one can truly speak of a substantial military integration of the Warsaw Pact only since the end of the 1960s.[10] The GDR's National People's Army (*Nationale Volksarmee*, NVA) in particular, which was eventually admitted as a "straggler"[11] into the alliance, was only to achieve the technical and political status of a full partner around 1970. This was symbolically expressed in that year in the form of a large-scale military manoeuvre in which NVA units, the Soviet Army, the Czechoslovakian People's Army and the Polish Army all took part for the first time on the territory of the GDR, under the title "Brotherhood in Arms" (*Waffenbrüderschaft*).[12] The establishment of the Warsaw Pact as a multilateral military alliance was of particular importance to the NVA, as it was only with the development of the GDR into a front-line state within the Soviet Bloc that the country began to enjoy

---

[10] Marco Metzler, *Nationale Volksarmee: Militärpolitik und politisches Militär in sozialistischer Verteidigungskoalition 1955/56 bis 1989/90* (Baden-Baden: Nomos, 2012), 122–24.
[11] While the GDR was one of the founder members of the Warsaw Pact in 1955, the NVA was founded as late as 1956 and was thereafter integrated into the structures of the alliance only very slowly. Ibid., 335–62.
[12] The great political significance that these military exercises had for the GDR is expressed in, among other places, NVA documents on the preparation for the event; see "Braterstwo Broni 1970," stock number 561/76/77 [File No. 13/20], Military Archives in Nowy Dwór Mazowiecki [Archiwum Wojskowe w Nowym Dworze Mazowieckim].

(largely) equal status with the other members of the alliance for the first time.[13]

One result of the multilateral integration of the Warsaw Pact armies was their severely restricted role in the alliance's structures, which were always dominated by Soviet staff officers. This situation provided a repeated cause of umbrage among the other members of the alliance, who would all have dearly liked their own officers to be appointed to the command bodies of the organization.[14] In any case, it was precisely such connections within the officer corps through the professionalization of military career paths—in addition to the contacts between top party bodies—that provided one of the most important mechanisms by which Soviet influence in Central Europe was secured. On the topic of the structural interdependence of the armies of the alliance, one should note that the NVA displayed a particularly high degree of integration, as almost all its units were subject to the command structures of the Warsaw Pact even in times of peace. The country's mobile land forces, in combination with the Group of Soviet Forces in Germany (GSFG), represented the 1st front of the Warsaw Pact at the forward line of confrontation with NATO, the airborne forces were integrated into the on-call system (*Diensthabendes System*)—i.e. the Soviet-led collective air defence system—and the People's Navy of the GDR, along with the Soviet Baltic fleet and the Polish Navy, together constituted the *United Baltic Fleet*.[15]

In Poland at the same time, in contrast, aside from those regular forces that were also largely integrated into alliance structures—and as a sort of compensation for the partial loss of sovereignty that this integration implied—[16] there was also a territorial defence structure (*Obrona Terytorialna Kraju*, OTK) that was referred to as an "interior system" (*układ wewnętrzny*), fully under the control of a national military command structure, which was primarily responsible for tactical and support roles as well as being expected to take on the role of providing interior security in time of war.[17]

---

[13] Metzler, *Nationale Volksarmee*, 337.
[14] Frank Umbach, *Das rote Bündnis: Entwicklung und Zerfall des Warschauer Paktes 1955 bis 1991* (Berlin: Links, 2005), 184–89.
[15] Gunter Holzweißig, *Militärwesen in der DDR* (Berlin: Holzapfel, 1985), 34–35.
[16] Dietrich Beyrau, "Dem sowjetischen Brutkasten entwachsen: Sowjetische Hegemonie und sozialistische Staatlichkeit in Ostmitteleuropa," in *Sozialistische Staatlichkeit: Vorträge der Tagung des Collegium Carolinum in Bad Wiessee vom 5. bis 8. November 2009*, ed. Jana Osterkamp and Joachim von Puttkamer (Munich: Oldenbourg, 2012), 19–44, here 31–32.
[17] Michael Checinski, "Polnische Armee und Offiziere in der Organisation des Warschauer Pakts: Militärpolitische Aspekte der Zeit seit 1957," pt. 2, *Osteuropa* 30, no. 12 (1980): 1303–15, here 1307–09. Interestingly, at the time of writing, the incumbent right-wing Polish government has announced plans, in the face of a perceived Russian threat, to reintroduce a similar system after the former one was abolished after 1990.

The Military and its Relationship with the "People" in the GDR and in the Polish People's Republic

The GDR, which had held fast to the vision of German unity all through the 1950s, began to make increasing efforts to define itself as an independent "socialist nation" in the years following the erection of the Berlin Wall in 1961. The revised 1974 constitution would be defined as being in the name of the "People of the German Democratic Republic".[18] The integration of the GDR into the "community of socialist states" was emphasised right from the outset. This orientation was not simply considered a consequence of the powerful presence of the Soviet Union, but would also have appeared to the leadership of the ruling Socialist Unity Party of Germany (*Sozialistische Einheitspartei Deutschlands*, SED) as the only viable way of justifying the GDR's existence as a state and of predicating that state with a rudimentary "national" identity and a sovereign capacity for independent action.

In addition, in both of the German states in the 1960s the concept of "post-nationalism"[19] had become *mutatis mutandis* a formative part of the society's mind set. This stance on the one hand rejected conventional German nationalism and a concept of geo-politics now considered inappropriate due to its instrumentalisation by National Socialism.[20] On the other hand, this post-nationalism turned both states enthusiastically towards the transnational and supranational ideas of the time, as represented in the west by ideas of European integration and in the East by the—much vaguer—vision of a "community of socialist nations".

Just as the Federal Republic accordingly became one of the most "integration-friendly" members of the European Economic Community (EEC) and later of the European Union (EU), the SED developed the idea of a "community of socialist states" as a supranational political structure more fully than any other governing party in the Eastern Bloc. Its "proletarian" manifestation of negative nationalism was even more radical than the "bourgeois" variant displayed by the Federal Republic in that the SED began to see both history and the present as something to be interpreted "in class terms— and to do so with more consistency than the other Soviet satellites.[21]

---

[18] See Hans Boldt, *Deutsche Verfassungsgeschichte: Politische Strukturen und ihr Wandel*, vol. 2, *Von 1806 bis zur Gegenwart* (Munich: Deutscher Taschenbuch-Verlag, 1990), 300–8.

[19] On this complex, see Jürgen Habermas, *Die postnationale Konstellation: Politische Essays* (Frankfurt am Main: Suhrkamp, 1998).

[20] As an introduction to this often rather shallowly discussed topic, see: Jan Wiktor Tkaczyński, *Die Geopolitik: Eine Studie über geographische Determinanten und politisches Wunschdenken am Beispiel Deutschlands und Polens* (Munich: Tuduv, 1993).

[21] On this general topic, see: Peter Joachim Lapp, *Traditionspflege in der DDR* (Berlin: Holzapfel, 1988).

In this process, the SED converted what had begun as a rather escapist "post-national" idea into a positive vision for the future: The era of the nation state was considered a thing of the past, to be replaced by a global order in which the GDR, notwithstanding its limited size, would be in a position to play an important role.

A rivalry began to develop between the GDR and Poland on the economic and military[22] levels as to who would take the second place beside the Soviet Union in the bloc.[23] Apart from the effect that this competition had on resources and geo-political interests, it also impacted on one particular aspect of nation building: in both countries, in spite of Soviet domination, "the people" as a body was formally defined as sovereign; and it was in the name of the people that the governing party made its decisions. A substantial difference lay in the fact that the Polish communist leadership, in contrast to the GDR, omitted to override the national roots of its own political thinking and activity through the discipline of placing it "in a class context". On the contrary, it actually founded its vision of "Polish socialism" on the basis of a partly public and partly unuttered "national" consensus.

During the intensifying economic and political crisis in Poland from 1976 on, this fact tended to favour the development of an opposition whose supporting arguments were founded both on human rights and on "national" arguments, which latter the regime, appealing for its part to the concept of "patriotism", would find difficult to counter.

A report by the intelligence body of the NVA, i.e. by its military defence unit, on the Polish Army issued on 22 November 1980 noted that rank-and-file soldiers and non-commissioned officers in particular showed open sympathy for the *Solidarność* (Solidarity) trade union and that the force's officers were perplexed and powerless as to what to do in the face of such attitudes. The report characterized the reason for the problem as follows:

due to the exaggerated patriotic instruction and patriotic work of the PA [Polish Army], built over the years upon a long tradition of victories and successes in the task of developing socialism, the mass of military personnel (soldiers and non-commissioned officers – but officers as well) are in a position neither to recognise the danger posed by the counter-revolutionary groups and their activities within the 'new' trade unions, nor to lead the ideological confrontation with these phenomena. [...] On the basis of this current state of awareness [it would appear that] any deployment of army units of the PA in the interior is fairly unlikely. [In addition,] due to events in the Polish People's Republic, the stability of the

---

[22] The claim of the Polish Army to its second-place position after the Soviet Army is made explicit, for example, in: Adam Marcinkowski, "Polen und seine Streitkräfte im Verteidigungssystem der Teilnehmerstaaten des Warschauer Vertrages," *Militärgeschichte* 26, no. 5 (1987): 423–30, here 428–29.

[23] On the early phases of this rivalry, see Sheldon R. Anderson, *A Cold War in the Soviet Bloc: Polish-East German Relations, 1945–1962* (Boulder, CO: Westview Press, 2001). For the 1980s, see: Burkhard Olschowsky, *Einvernehmen und Konflikt: Das Verhältnis zwischen der DDR und der Volksrepublik Polen, 1980–1989* (Osnabrück: Fibre, 2005).

morale and fortitude of the soldiers in the Polish Army in the fulfilment of their internationalist duties within the Warsaw Pact on the territories of other countries is no longer as strong as it was in the past.[24]

Such evaluations would later become less strident in the light of the efforts of the Polish leadership to improve political discipline in the army, but this distrust on the part of the NVA (and of the GDR's state security apparatus) was to remain.

There were constant demands upon the functionary elites of the GDR connected with the SED, including the (higher) officer corps of the NVA, to prove their inner loyalty to Marxist doctrine, by means of which the national (or post-national) future would be steered. In the education system sponsored by the army, too, the GDR was declared to be a new "Socialist Fatherland", whose people it was the army's role to defend militarily.[25]

Nonetheless, the very "people of the GDR", in whose name the SED claimed to act, remained an uncertain eminence, particularly since its relationship with the West German population could not be restricted, as the regime clearly would have liked, to one of normal "interstate relations" or even of "friendly co-existence." Significantly, contacts with West Germans were strictly forbidden among the professional soldiers of the NVA, and such soldiers were explicitly admonished to look upon members of the *Bundeswehr* (Armed forces of the Federal Republic of Germany) as class enemies, against whom they would be expected to fight.[26]

Another factor that should not be ignored was that other member nations of the Warsaw Pact never ceased to think in national(ist) terms, and thus to see citizens of the GDR primarily as Germans. This applied not least to Poland, whose national thinking had been further reinforced by the experience of the war. An antagonistic rejection of the Germans was the lowest common denominator of the new order that emerged after 1944 under the leadership of the communists. The latter had therefore made great efforts in

---

[24] "Information über die Lage in Polen Nr. 17/80," 22 November 1980, sheets 76–81, here sheet 79–80, Intelligence unit of the NVA, No. 32674c: "Informationen über die Lageentwicklung in der VR Polen 1980/81," DVW 1– GDR; Ministry for National Defence, Military Archive of the Federal Archives Freiburg [Bundesarchiv, Abteilung Militärarchiv, hereafter BArch-MA].

[25] For an introduction to this range of topics, see Matthias Rogg, *Armee des Volkes? Militär und Gesellschaft in der DDR* (Berlin: Links, 2008), 169–208; Michael Koch, *Der Wehrunterricht in den Ländern des Warschauer Paktes: Eine Untersuchung im historischen und schulpolitischen Kontext unter besonderer Berücksichtigung der UdSSR und der DDR* (Jena: Edition Paideia, 2006).

[26] Beate Ihme-Tuchel, "Armee des Volkes? Anmerkungen zur wechselseitigen Reflexion von Militär und Gesellschaft in der DDR," in *Militär, Staat und Gesellschaft in der DDR: Forschungsfelder, Ergebnisse, Perspektiven*, ed. Hans Ehlert and Matthias Rogg (Berlin: Links, 2004), 359–75; Günther Glaser, "Spezielle Feindbildproblematik von Armeeangehörigen der DDR im Spiegel militärsoziologischer und anderer Untersuchungen," in *Militär, Staat und Gesellschaft*, ed. Ehlert and Rogg, 459–87.

the early years to convince their people that the GDR was a different, "better" Germany.

The strategic ties of Poland towards the Soviet Union were similar in strength to that of the GDR. The difference was that in their relationship with the Soviets, the Poles neither had any moral dilemma to struggle with nor needed to dedicate any serious effort to theorising about the national character of their state. The "ethnic cleansing" of the country, partially carried out by themselves, but also conducted earlier by the Third Reich and the Soviet Union, had left them with an almost mono-ethnic Polish state. This fact allowed the development of an ethno-nationalist view of history.[27] The non-Polish portion of the population (i.e. the Germans, Ukrainians, Belarusians, etc.) were not only physically evacuated or resettled through the systematic action of the Polish Army, but were also excluded from the country's historical consciousness.

If one makes a comparison of the declarations contained in the constitution of the Polish People's Republic with that of the GDR, one sees that the former contained a legitimation of state power of a different type to the one expressed in the latter. It was unequivocally oriented towards the interests of the "Polish People" (a category always expressed in writing with capital initial letters in the original Polish text)—although this "People" was strictly speaking defined in the preamble and in several of its articles as the "working people of the cities and countryside" (*lud pracujący miast i wsi*). While the country's foreign policy was firmly embedded in the socialist camp by the provisions of the constitution, those provisions were clearly legally subordinate to the provisions that provided the country's national legitimation. Most importantly of all, the bond with Moscow—in contrast to the terms of the GDR's constitution—was not characterized either as "irreversible" or as "unbreakable".

Even more surprising was the fact that the Polish constitution did not have a single word to say either about the Warsaw Pact or about any "brotherhood in arms". Yet, despite all such contrasts with the text of the GDR's constitution, the political realities of the two countries appeared similar. Though Poland—in contrast to the GDR—had continuously enjoyed the status of Soviet ally from 1943/44 on, and was never nominally an occupied country, its political and geographical bonds to the alliance were nevertheless no less comprehensive than those of the GDR.

Within the "inner core" of the army constitution—namely in the oath of allegiance of the Polish Army, which every soldier (including all conscripts) had to swear—the text contained a substantially stronger commitment to the leading role of the PZPR and to the alliance. In the version used between 1952 and 1988, it contained the following formulae, among other elements:

---

[27] Marcin Zaremba, *Im nationalen Gewande: Strategien kommunistischer Herrschaftslegitimation in Polen 1944–1980* (Osnabrück: Fibre, 2011).

I swear to serve the Fatherland with all my power, to defend staunchly the rights of the working people as set out in the constitution, *to defend unbendingly the power of the people* and to be true to the Government of the Polish People's Republic. [...]
I swear to protect staunchly the freedom, independence and the borders of the Polish People's Republic in the face of the provocations of imperialism, to keep guard unbendingly *in a fraternal bond with the Soviet Army and the armies of the alliance* and, where necessary, to struggle bravely without sparing either blood or life in the defence of the Fatherland, for the holy cause of the independence, freedom and happiness of the People.[28]

This oath was very similar to the one introduced ten years later for the NVA. The inconsistency between the national and supranational references in the Polish People's Republic's foundational civil documents on the one hand and their military equivalents on the other, reflects the ambivalence of the Polish communists to the concepts of state and nation, and thus closely connected to their ideas on the "meaning" of history.

In July 1944, the communist armed forces under the Moscow-allied *Polish Committee of National Liberation* (*Polski Komitet Wyzwolenia Narodowego*, also known as the Lublin Committee) dropped the official name of *Polish People's Army* (*Ludowe Wojsko Polskie*, LWP) and re-named themselves simply the *Polish Army* (*Wojsko Polskie*, WP), adopting a name identical to that used by the Army of the pre-war Polish state.[29] They did so in order to be in a position to compete with the Polish *Home Army* (*Armia Krajowa*, AK), as part of a strategy that involved adopting a good deal of the nationalist patterns of thought practised by their political opponents.[30] The central referential object for their loyalty was the supposedly timeless concept of the "Polish People". Their view of history emphasised actual or supposed military accomplishments by that people, without making any further normative differentiation between such actions. At the very centre of a civic education merely superficially dressed up in Marxist terms was an aspiration to achieve the greatest possible level of geopolitical power for Poland; a claim grounded not

---

[28] In the Polish original: "Przysięgam służyć ze wszystkich sił Ojczyźnie, bronić niezłomnie praw ludu pracującego, zawarowanych w Konstytucji, stać nieugięcie na straży władzy ludowej, dochować wierności Rządowi Polskiej Rzeczypospolitej Ludowej. [...] Przysięgam strzec niezłomnie wolności, niepodległości i granic Polskiej Rzeczypospolitej Ludowej przed zakusami imperializmu, stać nieugięcie na straży pokoju w braterskim przymierzu z Armią Radziecką i innymi sojuszniczymi armiami i w razie potrzeby nie szczędząc krwi ani życia mężnie walczyć w obronie Ojczyzny, o świętą sprawę niepodległości, wolności i szczęścia ludu." Text according to the Law of 22 November 1952 concerning the oath of allegiance of the army, which can be seen at *Internetowy System Aktów Prawnych*, accessed 28 October 2016, http://isap.sejm.gov.pl/DetailsServlet?id=WDU19520460310. All emphases in the translation are the author's.

[29] Both in internal documents and in general conversation, however, the body continued to be referred to as the "People's Army," an expression in which the adjective *ludowe* was intended to express the connection with the "working people" and the party as the (supposed) champion of that collective.

[30] Zaremba, *Im nationalen Gewande*, especially 145–84.

least on the many victims that the country had counted during the recently concluded Second World War.

However, officially the intensive military preparation of the army and people was always justified on the basis of the alleged threat of a revisionist (West) Germany. It was on this basis that the unpopular alliance with the Soviet Union, and indeed the "socialist" regime itself, was justified. Thus, in contrast to the case of the GDR, Marxism-Leninism did not provide the primary basis for the legitimation of the regime. For this reason, in Poland tokens of loyalty of the party-ideological type by functional elites, such as army officers, were shown but less important; the officers' willingness to recognise the leadership of the PZPR in the *national* interest was the necessary and sufficient prerequisite for their positions. The result of this was that, while the degree of social militarization in Poland was maintained at a similar level to that of the GDR, it was held more in national than in international colours.

The Military as a Factor Shaping the Historical Consciousness in "Real Socialist" Societies: National and Transnational Traditions in the GDR and Poland

Differences between the two neighbours were also revealed in the ways in which they shaped their respective military traditions. In the GDR—as a result of its view of history as being marked by class struggle, the separation from the Federal Republic and its alliance with former enemies Poland and the Soviet Union—German military traditions were initially almost entirely abnegated, as not just National Socialism, but all earlier regimes in Germany were considered to have been reactionary and militaristic. As a countertradition, one harked back on the one hand to historical social conflicts open to being interpreted as class struggles, for example, the Peasants' Wars of the sixteenth century. On the other, there was also a tendency to appropriate the military traditions of Soviet history, and of the international workers' movement (such as the International Brigades in Spain).[31] However, some parts of German, and particularly Prussian, military tradition were adapted for use in the GDR—in particular the heritage of the post-1807 military reforms led by a group of officers around Gerhard von Scharnhorst—with the precondition that such reforms could be presented as "objectively progressive" according

---

[31] On the ideological grounding for these attitudes, see: Edgar Doehler and Rudolf Falkenberg, *Militärische Traditionen der DDR und der NVA* (Berlin: Militärverlag der DDR, 1979), 14–31; for a view from the Western perspective, see: Jörg Lolland, "DDR," in *Nationale Tradition in sozialistischen Armeen*, ed. Brenko P. Ahnsteiner (Bonn: Hohwacht, 1974), 37–70.

to the doctrine of historical materialism.³² Another compatible tradition was that surrounding the Prussian-Russian alliance during the war of liberation fought against Napoleon from 1813 to 1815. This older "brotherhood in arms" became the object of regular celebration from 1953 on, with the Monument to the Battle of Nations near Leipzig playing a particularly prominent role in commemorations. The development of this location as a "socialist-national" memorial reflected some of the contradictions in the historical vision of the SED regime.³³ In this vein, six units of the NVA were named after leading Prussian reformers and heroes of the Wars of Liberation, including Theodor Körner and Ferdinand von Schill, in the period between 1964 and 1987. While this was not a prodigious number compared against the many communist patrons chosen for NVA bodies, it did reflect that a certain amount of national culture of memory was "permitted" in an army otherwise assimilated to the ideology of internationalism.

The situation was substantially different in Poland: though even here central elements of the Soviet military culture of memory were adopted into the "revolutionary-internationalist" military tradition, this occurred in combination with elements of older, Polish national traditions. These included the rebellions of the nineteenth century, the border conflicts after the First World War and the participation of Polish troops in the Second World War. As early as 1956 on, these elements had already become predominant, so that in the army, as in many other areas of life, the Marxist view of things was severely circumscribed.³⁴

---

32 See Lolland, "DDR," 50–55, and the key word "Traditionspflege in der NVA," in *NVA in Stichworten*, ed. Ullrich Rühmland, 6th ed. (Bonn: Bonner Druck- und Verlagsgesellschaft, 1983), 211–214.
33 For the following see the outline by Steffen Poser, "Zur Rezeptionsgeschichte des Völkerschlachtdenkmals zwischen 1914 und 1989," in *Vom Kult zur Kulisse: Das Völkerschlachtdenkmal als Gegenstand der Geschichtskultur*, ed. Katrin Keller and Hans-Dieter Schmid (Leipzig: Leipziger Universitätsverlag, 1995), 78–104, here 93–100.
34 On the development of military traditions in Poland, see: Johann Black, "Polen," in *Nationale Traditionen*, ed. Ahnsteiner, 71–98; Jerzy J. Wiatr, *The Soldier and the Nation: The Role of the Military in Polish Politics, 1918–1985* (Boulder, CO: Westview Press, 1988), 131–42. On changes in the relative valuation of various locations of military historical remembrance by the Polish people, see: Klaus Bachmann, "Militär und militärische Traditionen in Polen im Spiegel unveröffentlichter Meinungsumfragen 1959 bis 1989," in *Der Warschauer Pakt: Von der Gründung bis zum Zusammenbruch, 1955–1991*, ed. Torsten Diedrich, Winfried Heinemann, and Christian F. Ostermann (Berlin: Links, 2008), 149–74.

"Brotherhood in Arms" as an Assumed Basis for Cooperation within the Alliance

The term "brotherhood in arms" was used to describe the basis upon which the allied armies cooperated within the Warsaw Pact. It suggested a long-term "standing fighting community" based on the similarity in the ideologies and social organisation of the countries involved, on the soldiers' (supposed) proletarian descent, on the various countries' similarly oriented military policies as well as of the shared leadership structures and command language in all the armies involved in the alliance.[35] This concept implied a closer relationship than that ordinarily required by a "conventional" alliance, and appealed in the last resort to an emotional bond. All this was referred to the romantic aspects of that "internationalist revolutionary" tradition, to which soldiers (and the wider public) should get acquainted as a shared heritage of all the socialist allies. In order to ensure the transnational coherence of this narrative, the communist parties instructed their armies on "solid political, economic, ideological and military strategic principles".[36]

For the NVA this initially posed the substantial problem that the Polish Army and other members of the alliance could trace back their "brotherhood in arms" with the Soviet Army to the Second World War (though at quite different points in time).[37] The NVA needed to find another foundation stone for the new alliance, yet one that was compatible with the World-War legend of their partners in the alliance. The way out was found in the doctrine of historical materialism, according to which the secular struggle between socialism on the one hand and capitalism and imperialism on the other had been fought on the international stage since 1945 (or even since 1917). It was through this vision that the political and ideological dependence of the NVA on the SED consisted, a dependence whose depth arguably had no parallel in the entire "Eastern Bloc". The self-confident SED leadership tended as a consequence to hold a sense of mission as an "avant-gardist force in world history", so that its action was moulded within the supranational frame provided by the "socialist camp".

Within this framework the GDR's leadership made serious efforts to popularise the idea of a "socialist" military alliance. "Days" and "weeks of brotherhood in arms" were organised for this purpose, events that gave ordinary citizens the opportunity to meet Soviet soldiers personally. The success of these efforts was, however, somewhat circumscribed by the Soviet side of the

---

[35] Rüdiger Wenzke, "'Sozialistische Waffenbrüder?' Über die Beziehungen der Nationalen Volksarmee der DDR zu anderen Warschauer-Pakt-Armeen," in *Der Warschauer Pakt*, ed. Diedrich, Heinemann, and Ostermann, 85–118, here 85–86.

[36] Petr P. Skorodenko, "Die Rolle der kommunistischen Parteien bei der Festigung der Waffenbrüderschaft zwischen den Armeen des Warschauer Bündnisses," *Militärgeschichte* 4 (1984): 291–96, here 291.

[37] On this topic see, for example: Marcinkowski, "Polen und seine Streitkräfte," 424.

equation, whose behaviour tended to be characterised by distance, distrust and sometimes even condescension. And on top of that difficulty, there was in any case an effective prohibition in place on fraternisation, not merely with civilians, but even including fellow "brothers in arms".[38] Polish officers reported that during joint manoeuvres in the 1970s and 80s not only were rank-and-file soldiers and non-commissioned officers forbidden from meeting up with their comrades in other armies after finishing their daily duties, but that the prohibition applied also to officers under staff officer rank.[39] These accounts confirm the presumption that the element of supra- and transnational cohesion within the Warsaw Pact was restricted to the highest military ranks.

In Poland, the strong emphasis on the nation and the palpably instrumentalist understanding of the alliance made the contradictions within the concept of "brotherhood in arms" easier to get over. The presence of Soviet troops in Poland was far less massive than in the GDR, so that they did not play all that great a role in the everyday lives of most Polish citizens (it did, though, in the towns with Soviet garrisons[40]). Likewise, the expressions of gratitude to the Soviet Union offered on the days upon which the "liberation of the country from fascism" was remembered were soberer in Poland than in the GDR.[41]

In the 1980s, the Polish political leadership—which one should remember was made up mostly of military officers from 1981 on—made an effort to bind up the above-discussed national emphases more tightly into the Marxist elements of their legitimizations of their rule.[42] This effort was primarily directed towards countering the anti-Soviet propaganda of *Solidarność*. Of particular importance was the impregnation of ideology into the Army, an institution seen in the period around 1980 to be the only reliable force for order that remained available to the authorities in Poland. So, on 4 November 1981, about five weeks before the declaration of martial law, through an order of the minister for national defence Wojciech Jaruzelski, the government or-

---

[38] Wenzke, "Sozialistische Waffenbrüder?," 95–100.
[39] An example is provided by a conversation with retired Polish lieutenant colonel Jan Bańbor in May 2012 (as the conversation was not recorded in writing, it is impossible to date it precisely).
[40] On the legacy of those garrisons, see Marcin Tujdowski, "Regained Cities: The Renewal of Postgarrison Towns in Poland," in *Declining Cities/Developing Cities: Polish and German Perspectives*, ed. Marek Nowak and Michał Nowosielski (Poznań, 2008), 129–53.
[41] Jan C. Behrends, *Die erfundene Freundschaft: Propaganda für die Sowjetunion in Polen und in der DDR* (Cologne: Böhlau, 2006), 364–65.
[42] Krzysztof Tyszka, *Nacjonalizm w komunizmie: Ideologia narodowa w Związku Radzieckim i Polsce Ludowej* (Warsaw: Instytut Filozofii i Socjologii Polskiej Akademii Nauk, 2004), 167–70.

dered that political education in the army in 1982 should include, among other things, the following content:

[...] to deepen the feeling of patriotism and internationalism among the soldiers, [...] to strengthen their feeling of brotherhood in arms with the Soviet Army and the other armies of the alliance and to enrich that feeling by means of new content and forms, [...] *to sharpen political awareness and to determinedly counteract outside influences in the defence of socialism [as well as to] further inspire among soldiers the ideational motivation and unbendable will to partake in the struggle against anti-socialist and counterrevolutionary elements.*[43]

The background to this was a realisation that during the 1970s ideological training had been neglected in favour of practical technical professionalization. This omission was acknowledged at the beginning of 1981 by the chief of staff of the Polish Army and deputy defence minister Florian Siwicki in an astoundingly forthright manner to the GDR minister for national defence, Heinz Hoffmann, who had been expressing withering criticisms of the situation in Poland. Siwicki admitted that "severe mistakes have been made, in particular over the last ten years (i.e. since 1970)—errors whose effects are now becoming obvious."[44]

Behind this rueful position one may however suspect opportunistic motives, as Siwicki often expressed the above-discussed "national" point of view on the past and present of Poland. This latter factor is betrayed by comparing the words of greeting exchanged by Siwicki and Hoffmann in 1985 on the occasion of the thirtieth anniversary of the signing of the Warsaw Pact for the bulletin of the Unified Supreme Command. Hoffmann, a convinced communist all his life, considered the most important aspect of his retrospective, that the NVA since 1956 "together with the Soviet Army, shoulder-to-shoulder with the Polish Army and the Czechoslovak Army in the centre of Europe, should fulfil its class role for society in protecting socialism and

---

[43] In the Polish original: "Wzbogacać u żołnierzy poczucie patriotyzmu i internacjonalizmu. [...] Umacniać i wzbogacać o nowe treści i formy braterstwo broni z Armią Radziecką i innymi sojuszniczymi armiami. Zaostrzyć czujność polityczną oraz zdecydowanie przeciwdziałać obcym socjalizmowi wpływom. Kształtować u żołnierzy ideowe motywacje i nieugiętą wolę walki z elementami antysocjalistycznymi i kontrrewolucyjnymi." Rozkaz Ministra Obrony Narodowej do szkolenia Sił Zbrojnych PRL w roku 1982, sign. IPN BU 1408/42, f. 6–22, here f. 13–14, Archive of the Institute of National Remembrance, Warsaw [Archiwum Instytutu Pamięci Narodowej, hereafter IPN]; emphasis in the original.

[44] Report of informal cooperator "Birnbaum" [i.e. the head of the main staff of the NVA, Lieutenant General Fritz Streletz] on the meeting of the members of the Central Committee of Polish United Workers' Party and deputy minister for national defence and chief of the General Staff of the Polish Army, Field General [Florian] Siwicki, on 27 January 1981, sheets 74–78, here sheets 74–75, vol. 2, part II, AIM 17164/81, Zentralarchiv Behörde des Bundesbeauftragten für die Stasi-Unterlagen (hereafter ZA, BStU). See the collections of "Parallel History Project on cooperative Security," accessed 8 December 2013, http://www.php.isn.ethz.ch/lory1.ethz.ch/collections/colltopic9f5a.html?lng=en&id=44998&navinfo=44755.

peace" and described in detail the structure and full integration of the NVA into the alliance with its "brother parties and armies."[45] For his part, Siwicki began his presentation with a reminder of the inter-war and war-time periods, drew parallels between "Hitler's fascism and Japanese militarism" on the one hand, and the current "imperialist aggressors" on the other. He stressed Poland's central role in the "heroic resistance" to "German fascism" and the "important contribution" of the Polish army to the allied victory, not least during the Battle for Berlin in 1945 "shoulder to shoulder with the soldiers of the Soviet Army". Since 1945 the "progressive forces of society" had built upon the legacy of this national resistance. The aim of membership of the Warsaw Pact, from a Polish perspective, was "as much to protect socialism as the independence of Poland."[46]

An Epistemic Community? The Higher Officers' Corps of the GDR and the Polish People's Republic as Component Parts of a Supranational Elite within the Warsaw Pact

The concept of an *epistemic community* describes a transnationally networked group of people connected together by specialist expertise and, by virtue of that expertise, often also by a common function. As a prerequisite for entry into the community, they will have often gone through a shared, or at least similar, education or training. There is a view that such a relationship has the properties of a kind of horizontal loyalty and that it complements the "traditional" national or territorial loyalty of the citizen.[47]

The extent to which the Warsaw Pact could be discussed in this connection is not easy to answer, since several variables must be considered:
- The strategic goals of the leadership: did it aspire to make the Warsaw Pact the core of a future global socialist state, or did it see the satellites rather mainly as a buffer zone enforced by the needs of security policy?
- The political goals of the various allies: did they have any interest in such an amalgamation?
- The behaviour of the officers in particular: did they see themselves primarily as being in the direct service of the alliance—i.e. effectively in the

---

[45] Kh. Gofman [Heinz Hoffmann], "Natsional'naia Narodnaia Armiia GDR," in *Informatsionnyi Sbornik Shtaba Ob"edinennykh Sil gosudarstv-uchastnikov Varshavskogo Dogovora* no. 29: 30 let OBG, Moscow 1985, sign. IPN BU 1413/20, Bl. 51–62, IPN Archive.

[46] Florian Sivitskii [Siwicki], „Narodnoe Voisko Polskoe," ibid., sheets 63–75.

[47] See Peter M. Haas' classic definition: Peter M. Haas, "Introduction: Epistemic Communities and International Policy Coordination," *International Organization* 46, no. 1 (Winter 1992), 1–35. For a more recent contribution on this concept, compare Patricia Clavin, "Defining Transnationalism," *Contemporary European History* 14, no. 4 (November 2005): 421–39.

service of the hegemon, or was that feeling outweighed by the wish to serve their own country through the alliance?

In the 1980s, sections of the western research community believed that they were observing the emergence of a *Greater Socialist Army*.[48] They based this judgement on a similar process of integration characterised the among the Warsaw Pact armies as the "convergence and amalgamation" (*zblizhenie i sliianie*) that was going on within the multinational Soviet armies and was being propagated more generally by the Communist Party of the Soviet Union (CPSU) as a pathway towards the creation of a "Soviet people". Apart from the fact that this internal Soviet process could not be considered a genuine process of integration, but rather as a form of Russification,[49] the idea went without any doubt much too far in its aspirations to achieve integration within this alliance.

It is, however, clear that both the GDR and Poland had a vital interest in the Warsaw Pact as a protective shield and strategic hinterland. In addition to this security-policy-based motivation, the regimes in East Berlin and Warsaw also sought to use the alliance to promote their own foreign policy interests. Both endeavoured to play their own independent role, at least occasionally, as a member of the pact on such international stages as the United Nations and the Commission on Security and Cooperation in Europe (CSCE). Their intention in doing so was by no means to weaken the alliance, but rather to increase their own international visibility.[50]

The increasing military integration of the Pact from the late 1960s on brought a number of both benefits and drawbacks to the member states. Its effect on standardising armament and equipment in the integration of Soviet planning and leadership structures facilitated cooperation and coordination between the armies. However, these integration measures also involved an asymmetrical structuring of the armaments industry in favour of the Soviet Union, whose attitude of suspicion and whose need for control prevented any

---

[48] Peer Lange, "Militärische Macht als Herrschaftsinstrument in Osteuropa," in *Die Sowjetunion als Militärmacht*, ed. Hannes Adomeit, Hans-Herrmann Höhmann, and Günther Wagenlehner (Stuttgart: Kohlhammer, 1987), 236–51, here 244.

[49] Zaur T. Gasimov, "Zum Phänomen der Russifizierungen: Einige Überlegungen," in *Kampf um Wort und Schrift: Russifizierung in Osteuropa im 19.–20. Jahrhundert*, ed. Zaur T. Gasimov (Göttingen: Vandenhoeck and Ruprecht, 2012), 9–25.

[50] For the GDR, see: Anja Hanisch, *Die DDR im KSZE-Prozess 1972–1985: Zwischen Ostabhängigkeit, Westabgrenzung und Ausreisebewegung* (Munich: Oldenbourg, 2012); for Poland: Wanda Jarząbek, *Hope and Reality: Poland and the Conference on Security and Cooperation in Europe, 1964–1989* (Washington, DC: Woodrow Wilson Center Press, 2008).

technological departure from being pursued by the other members. Added to this was the Soviet Union's nuclear monopoly.[51]

Neither was the extreme predominance of the Soviet Union ever overcome in the alliance's military structures. The Supreme Command and General Staff of the Unified Armed Forces of the Warsaw Pact were *de facto* subordinated to the Soviet General Staff. In the event of war, the allies' troops were to be integrated into the Soviet armies ("fronts") and all the important positions were occupied by Soviet officers, even within the formal structures of the Pact. Only a few positions in less sensitive areas remained vacant for the other allies.[52] This fact may appear somewhat peculiar, as a large proportion of Eastern European staff officers were trained at Soviet military academies from the 1960s on, especially at the Voroshilov Academy of the General Staff. Undergoing such training in the Soviet Union became a prerequisite for taking up posts at the rank of general back home.[53] Even within this narrow circle, however, the Soviet Union permitted only auxiliary functions to other alliance members. A 1992 study by the then Social Science Institute of the Federal Forces (*Sozialwissenschaftliches Institut der Bundeswehr*, SOWI), based on interviews with former NVA officers, provided information on the subjective perceptions of members of this group. According to the study, only especially ambitious officers applied to attend Soviet military academies. The reasons for the lack of enthusiasm could be found in the arduous conditions of life and study in the Soviet Union, and in long periods of separation of the family which such courses of studies often required. The experiences that students gained from such stays, while they did produce some disillusionment with the supposition of Soviet superiority, at the same time also inspired increased appreciation for the civilian population of the Soviet Union among students.[54]

Polish officers had participated in this form of training already since 1943, but the numbers of participants from that country too had grown considerably since the 1960s. Although precise totals are still unavailable, given the relative size of the Polish Army as compared to the NVA, one can presume that at least twice as many Poles were to graduate from such courses, so a to-

---

[51] On the basic outlines of Soviet policy in relation to the alliance, see: A. Ross Johnson, Robert W. Dean, and Alexander Alexiev, *Die Streitkräfte des Warschauer Pakts in Mitteleuropa: DDR, Polen und CSSR* (Stuttgart: Seewald, 1982), 26–38.

[52] This problem was negotiated at least subliminally between officers' committees of the Warsaw Pact in the 1970s, but the Soviet side had made at best only placatory, insubstantial concessions to such concerns; see: Checinski, "Polnische Armee," 1315, and Klaus Froh and Rüdiger Wenzke, *Die Generale und Admirale der NVA: Ein biographisches Handbuch* (Berlin: Links, 2000), 28.

[53] Froh and Wenzke, *Generale und Admirale*, 18–20.

[54] Sabine Collmer, Georg-Maria Meyer, and Hanne Isabell Schaffer, *"Begegnungen:" Deutsch-sowjetische Beziehungen im Spiegel der Wahrnehmungen von Offizieren der ehemaligen NVA* (Munich: Sozialwissenschaftliches Institut der Bundeswehr, 1992).

tal of at least ten thousand officers might be estimated up until the year 1990. On top of all this, from the 1970s on, the three neighbouring states of the GDR, Poland and ČSSR also provided places for each other's officer candidates in their respective military academies.[55] According to the General Staff of the NVA, fifty-seven Polish "military cadres" completed their studies at the "Friedrich Engels" military academy in Dresden between 1974 and 1986. In the opposite direction, however, the NVA sent only eleven officers to the "Jarosław Dąbrowski" Military Academy of the Polish Army in Warsaw between 1976 and 1986, though they had plans to increase that number in subsequent years.[56] Another fifteen NVA officers were trained in 1984 at the ČSSR military academy in Prague.[57] This sort of "horizontal" co-operation represented a—partial—departure from the 'radial' approach generally enforced by the Soviet leadership and may be interpreted as an indication of a certain decentralization in intra-pact relations.

The "Polish crisis" of 1980/81 represented a test of the "supranational" nature of the alliance. From a communist perspective, the Brezhnev doctrine, which—as much during this period as in 1968—formed the basis upon which decisions were made on possible interventions, was nothing more than the logical consequence of its "internationalist" understanding of the Pact. The dominant political perspective of the Polish leadership tended to look in a similar direction. In fact, the steps taken in preparation for an intervention by the Warsaw Pact countries in Poland were decided upon in close consultation with the leadership of the Polish state and of its army. Despite the massive pressure exerted by the Soviets at the time, any interpretation that tries to paint the turn of events as being imposed by external force only, would be mistaken.[58] On the contrary, the introduction of martial law on 13 December 1981 was agreed in parallel both by the Polish national leadership and by an alliance. It suited the interests of the Polish regime just as it responded to the wishes of Moscow and East Berlin.

---

[55] Jerzy Będźmirowski, *Współpraca Marynarki Wojennej PRL z flotami wojennymi Związku Radzieckiego i Niemieckiej Republiki Demokratycznej w zakresie kształcenia kadr* (Toruń: Adam Marszałek, 2007), 181.

[56] Section on the representative of the minister and head of the Main Staff, AZN 8641: Cooperation of the NVA/GDR with the defence forces of the Polish People's Republic 1981–1989, f. 121, BArch-MA.

[57] Numerical summary of NVA personnel who, as of 1 September 1984, are currently engaged as *Offiziershörer, Aspirant* or *Offiziersschüler* in the educational facilities in academic courses and vocational instruction of the Soviet defence forces and in the academy for Social Sciences at the Central Committee of the CPSU, f. 9, No. 14449, HA I, BStU.

[58] On this subject, see the interview with a spy within the Polish General Staff who worked for the USA until November 1981: Colonel Ryszard Kukliński, "Wojna z narodem widziana od środka: Rozmowa z byłym płk. dypl. Ryszardem J. Kuklińskim przeprowadzona w piątą rocznicę wprowadzenia w Polsce stanu wojennego," *Kultura* no. 4 (April 1987): 3–57.

The End or a New Beginning? National Responses to the Gorbachev Policy in the 1980s

Mikhail Gorbachev's assumption of office in 1985 brought the end of this at least lukewarm co-operation between Poland and East Germany. As the SED regime became increasingly isolated, the Polish government under Wojciech Jaruzelski began working closely with the new Moscow leadership. Nevertheless, the military cooperation between the GDR and the Polish People's Republic continued until the very end without encountering any significant problems. The East German and Polish army leaderships made renewed attempts even as late as 1989 to position more officers within the Warsaw Pact's leadership structures[59]—an indication that the army top brass in both countries were not expecting any quick end to the alliance.

After the post-communist transition and reunification in 1990, the hopes of the officer corps of the NVA to be accepted into the *Bundeswehr* were doomed to failure both in the face of planning relating to military strength and due to ideological reservations. Accordingly, as of 3 October 1990, most NVA officers not only became pensioners, but also became carriers of an alienated memory. Since the culture of memory of the post-socialist states has been largely renationalized since the transition, there is now effectively no transnational community of memory shared by former members of the old state-aligned elites in the affected countries. The effect of this is that veterans of the NVA have become isolated in terms of culture of memory.[60] In the Polish case, however, this re-nationalization was achieved mainly through the removal of Marxist slogans from everyday military life combined with a (renewed) pointed emphasis on the military achievements of the Polish people. The result of this process was that there is no recognizable interest now detectable in Poland in the maintenance of any transnational military memory relating to the Warsaw Pact and the uneasy allies of more than 40 years.

Translated by Jaime Hyland.

---

[59] See, for example, a recommendation of the Polish Marine Command of 17 February 1989, drawn up on the instructions of the General Staff of the Polish Army, to increase the participation of Polish officers in the structures of the Warsaw Pact's forces, f. 2–6, sign. IPN BU 1420/134, IPN Archive.

[60] Nina Leonhard, "The National People's Army as an Object of (Non) Remembrance: The Place of East Germany's Military Heritage in Unified Germany," *German Politics and Society* 26, no. 4 (2008): 150–63.

LIST OF ABBREVIATIONS

AK	Armia Krajowa (Home Army)
ANIC	Arhivele Naționale Istorice Centrale (Central National Historical Archives)
ASRC	Arhivele Statului Regiunea Cernăuți (State Archives of Chernivtsi District)
AVPRI	Arkhiv Vneshnei Politiki Rossiiskoi Imperii (Archive of Foreign Policy of the Russian Empire)
BArch-MA	Bundesarchiv, Abteilung Militärarchiv (Federal Archives, Department Military Archive)
BFL	Budapest Főváros Levéltára (Budapest City Archives)
Comintern	Communist International
CPSU	Communist Party of the Soviet Union
CSCE	Commission on Security and Cooperation in Europe
ČSAV	Československá Akademie věd (Czechoslovak Academy of Sciences)
ČSSR	Československá socialistická republika (Czechoslovak Socialist Republic)
DDR	Deutsche Demokratische Republik (German Democratic Republic)
DSV	Deutscher Schriftstellerverband (Writers' Association of the GDR)
EEC	European Economic Community
EU	European Union
FKgP	Független Kisgazdapárt (Independent Smallholders' Party)
GARF	Gosudarstvennyi Arkhiv Rossiiskoi Federatsii (State Archives of the Russian Federation)
GDR	German Democratic Republic
Gestapo	Geheime Staatspolizei (Secret State Police)
GSFG	Group of Soviet Forces in Germany
GULAG	Glavnoe upravlenie lagerei (Main Camp Administration)
GWZO	Leibniz-Institut für Geschichte und Kultur des östlichen Europa (Leibniz Institute for the History and Culture of Eastern Europe)

List of Abbreviations

HHStA	Haus-, Hof- und Staatsarchiv
HPNS	Hrvatska pučka napredna stranka (Croatian People's Progressive Party)
HSK	Hrvatsko-srpska koalicija (Croat-Serb Coalition)
IBRL	International Bureau of Revolutionary Literature
IM	Inoffizieller Mitarbeiter (Informal collaborator)
IPN	Archiwum Instytutu Pamięci Narodowej (Archives of the Institute of National Remembrance)
k. k.	kaiserlich-königlich (Imperial-Royal)
KKRN	Kievskii klub russkikh natsionalistov (Kiev Club of Russian Nationalists)
KOK	Komitet Obrony Kraju (Committee for National Defence)
KPD	Kommunistische Partei Deutschlands (Communist Party of Germany)
KPSS	Kommunisticheskaia partiia Sovetskogo Soiuza (Communist Party of the Soviet Union)
LVIA	Lietuvos valstybės istorijos archyvas (Lithuanian State Historical Archives)
LWP	Ludowe Wojsko Polskie (Polish People's Army)
MDP	Magyar Dolgozók Pártja (Hungarian Workers' Party)
MfS	Ministerium für Staatssicherheit (Ministry for State Security)
MKP	Magyar Kommunista Párt (Hungarian Communist Party)
MOL	Magyar Országos Levéltár (Hungarian State Archives)
MRP	Magyar Radikális Párt (Hungarian Radical Party)
MSzMP	Magyar Szocialista Munkáspárt (Hungarian Socialist Workers' Party)
MTI	Magyar Távirati Iroda (Hungarian Press Agency)
NPP	Nemzeti Parasztpárt (National Peasant Party)
NVA	Nationale Volksarmee (National People's Army)
NVR	Nationaler Verteidigungsrat der DDR (National Defence Council of the GDR)
OG	Oberstes Gericht der DDR (Supreme Court of the GDR)
OPI GIM	Otdel pis'mennykh istochnikov Gosudarstvennogo Istoricheskogo Muzeiia (Department of written sources of the State Historical Museum)
OTK	Obrona Terytorialna Kraju (Territorial Defence Forces)
PA	Polish Army

PDP	Polgári Demokrata Párt (Civic Democratic Party)
POW	Prisoner of war
PZPR	Polska Zjednoczona Partia Robotnicza (Polish United Workers' Party)
RGASPI	Rossiiskii gosudarstvennyi arkhiv sotsial'no-politicheskoi' istorii (Russian State Archive of Social and Political History)
RGVIA	Rossiiskii gosudarstvennyi voenno-istoricheskii arkhiv (Russian State Military History Archive)
SAPMO-BArch	Stiftung Archiv der Parteien und Massenorganisationen der DDR im Bundesarchiv (Foundation Archive of Parties and Mass Organisations of the GDR in the Federal Archives)
SED	Sozialistische Einheitspartei Deutschlands (Socialist Unity Party of Germany)
SKP	Sveriges Kommunistiska Parti (Communist Party of Sweden)
SNRS	Srpska narodna radikalna stranka (Serbian National Radical Party)
SOWI	Sozialwissenschaftliches Institut der Bundeswehr (Social Science Institute of the Bundeswehr)
SSS	Srpska samostalna stranka (Serb Independent Party)
SZDP	Szociáldemokrata Párt (Social Democratic Party)
TUP	Tovarystvo ukrainskykh postupovtsiv (Society of Ukrainian Progressives)
WP	Wojsko Polskie (Polish Army)
ZPKK	Zentrale Parteikontrollkommission (Central Party Control Commission)

CONTRIBUTORS

Dr. Jens Boysen, Institute of European History, Technical University of Chemnitz (Germany)

Prof. Peter Bugge, PhD., Associate Professor, School of Culture and Society – Eastern European Studies, Aarhus University (Denmark)

Prof. Mark Cornwall, PhD., Professor of Modern European History, Faculty of Humanities, University of Southampton (UK)

Viorica Angela Crăciun PhD., Independent Researcher, Iași (Romania)

Dr. Doris Danzer, Independent Researcher, Tiefenbach (Germany)

Dr. Franziska Davies, Assistant Professor, Chair of East and Southeast European History, History Department, Ludwig-Maximilians-Universität Munich (Germany)

Prof. Dr. Mikhail Dolbilov, Associate Professor, Department of History, University of Maryland (USA)

Tatiana Khripachenko PhD., Independent Scholar, St. Petersburg (Russia)

Prof. Alexei Il'ich Miller, Professor, Department of History, European University at St. Petersburg (Russia)

Dr. Martina Niedhammer, Researcher and Library Administrator, Collegium Carolinum, Research Institute for the History of the Czech Lands and Slovakia, Munich (Germany)

Prof. Dr. Jana Osterkamp, Visiting Professor, Chair of East and Southeast European History, History Department, Ludwig-Maximilians-Universität Munich; Researcher at Collegium Carolinum, Research Institute for the History of the Czech Lands and Slovakia, Munich (Germany)

Prof. Dr. Martin Schulze Wessel, Professor, Chair of East and Southeast European History, History Department, Ludwig-Maximilians-Universität Munich; Graduate School for East and Southeast European Studies, LMU; Director of Collegium Carolinum, Research Institute for the History of the Czech Lands and Slovakia, Munich (Germany)

Dr. Heléna Tóth, Assistant Professor, Department of Contemporary and Regional History, Institute for History and European Ethnology, Otto-Friedrich-Universität Bamberg (Germany)

Todd H. Weir, PhD., Associate Professor, Department of Christianity and the History of Ideas, Faculty of Theology and Religious Studies, University of Groningen (Netherlands)

Partisanenbewegungen: das slowakische Beispiel im europäischen Kontext

Martin Zückert / Jürgen Zarusky / Volker Zimmermann (Hg.)
Partisanen im Zweiten Weltkrieg
Der Slowakische Nationalaufstand im Kontext der europäischen Widerstandsbewegungen

Bad Wiesseer Tagungen des Collegium Carolinum, Band 37

2017. 328 Seiten, gebunden
€ 50,– D
ISBN 978-3-525-37315-6

Ausgehend vom Beispiel des Slowakischen Nationalaufstandes von 1944 fragen die Autoren des Bandes nach Entstehungsbedingungen und Organisationsformen slowakischer und anderer europäischer Partisanenbewegungen.

Die Partisanenbewegungen des Zweiten Weltkrieges sind ein wenig erforschtes Phänomen der europäischen Zeitgeschichte. Es mangelt an Studien, die Motivation und politische Orientierung der Partisanen sowie ihre gesellschaftlichen Kontexte beleuchten. Der Band befasst sich mit Entstehungsbedingungen und Organisationsformen slowakischer und weiterer europäischer Bewegungen. Die Autoren analysieren ihre politischen und gesellschaftlichen Hintergründe, präsentieren Beispiele für einzelne Gruppen und schildern Fälle des erinnerungspolitischen Umgangs mit Partisanen nach 1945.

Verlagsgruppe Vandenhoeck & Ruprecht | V&R unipress

www.v-r.de

Migration und Landschaftswandel im östlichen Europa

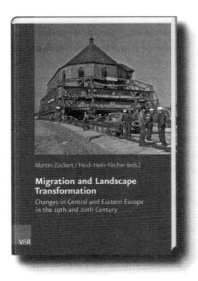

Martin Zückert / Heidi Hein-Kircher (Hg.)
Migration and Landscape Transformation
Changes in Central and Eastern Europe in the 19th and 20th Century

Veröffentlichungen des Collegium Carolinum, Band 134

2016. 205 Seiten, gebunden
€ 50,– D
ISBN 978-3-525-37313-2

Der Band untersucht den Zusammenhang von Migration und Landschaftswandel im östlichen Europa.

Viele Landschaften Ostmittel- und Osteuropas wurden durch die Folgen von Migrationen, insbesondere der Zwangsmigrationen während des Zweiten Weltkrieges und unmittelbar danach, nachhaltig verändert. Die Autorinnen und Autoren des Bandes untersuchen unter anderem an tschechischen, polnischen, ungarischen und russischen Beispielen, in welcher Weise dies geschah. Im Zentrum stehen staatliche Landschaftsplanungen im Kontext gesteuerter Migrationen sowie die Migranten selbst und ihr Umgang mit Landschaft. Analysiert werden zudem Interpretationen und Darstellungsformen von Landschaftswandel in Schulbüchern und auf Lehrpfaden.

Verlagsgruppe Vandenhoeck & Ruprecht | V&R **unipress**

www.v-r.de